RIGHT WHERE I
WANT YOU

JESSICA HAWKINS

A dragon disguised as a businesswoman breathed down my neck.

I'd been in that position more times than I could count—a desperate grab at coffee before work, applying mascara in line, praying sidewalk congestion wouldn't make me late. But on this particular day, it was the woman behind me breathing fire as she muttered, "It's not like I have *the most important meeting of my life* in five minutes."

I was actually early in hopes of making a good impression on my first day at a new assignment. Behind the café's register, my best friend, Luciano, scribbled on a paper cup while arching a manicured eyebrow at me. He shook his head—a warning to stay put—and tapped on the name he'd written.

GEORGE.

Message received, loud and clear. But Luciano hadn't been the one standing there for three minutes, withering under the wrath behind me.

Although it was a big day for me, I really *wasn't* in a

hurry, because I'd planned ahead. The night before, I'd lain out a respectable white blouse and navy skirt suit to lead a meeting dominated by men before mapping out all possible routes from Brooklyn Heights to Midtown. I didn't typically choose my outfits the night before like a grade schooler. The norm for me was hitting snooze too many times and leaving my fate in the hands of the public transportation gods.

But this assignment was different. I'd be working with men, and not *just* men, but so-called "bad boys." And I'd been given less than a week to prepare—not only my notes, but my mindset too. *Modern Man*, a men's interest monthly magazine, had already been losing market share before its creative director had been called out in a scathing exposé about sexism in the workplace. That was the environment I was walking into.

The woman exhaled another furious sigh against my hair. I turned and smiled at the brunette in a patterned blouse who tapped out something on her phone.

"You can go ahead of me," I said.

She took a moment to finish what she was typing before looking up. "What?"

"It sounds like you have somewhere to be. I'm early, so go ahead."

"Great." She stepped in front of me.

The man behind her moved up in line, passing me. "I'm late for work too," he said, turning away and effectively moving me to the back of the line.

My cheeks warmed. So he'd just assumed I'd let him go ahead too? That I wouldn't speak up? Giving up my spot in line was a good deed—I didn't have to do that. Well, maybe karma would handle this.

"Karma? That bitch was squashed by the M-fourteen bus while trying to catch up with my ex," Luciano had told me once.

I didn't agree. Karma may not have been swift, but it always got you.

I raised my hand to tap the man's shoulder, then hesitated. Hadn't he said he was also late to work? And I *was* early for once. The commute to my new job was thirty minutes, so I'd factored in possible A-train delays, traffic if I had to take a cab, or even the possibility of jumping on the ferry. I'd left myself enough time that, should disaster strike, I'd still be able to get my daily mocha latte—because not having one was on par with said disaster.

Of course, the subway had been smooth sailing and the commute a breeze.

So, I wasn't just early to work. I had another forty minutes before I needed to walk off the elevator and into *Modern Man* magazine's offices on the thirty-fifth floor of Dixon Media Tower.

I lowered my hand but stared daggers at the man's bald spot. *Do your worst, Karma.*

I could practically hear Luciano's thoughts as he stared at me and pumped dark roast into a cup. This was the sort of thing—getting pushed to the back of the line—that I was supposed to be working on. I wasn't doing such a great job of morphing from Georgina into George, the side of me that could stride into a new workplace and take over without batting an eyelash. As Georgina, though? I did things like pay full price at the Brooklyn Flea so I wouldn't have to haggle and apologize for slipping in an unidentified puddle and knocking over a candy display at Duane Reade.

I now had a half hour to get it together so I could confidently walk into the lion's den. And I *would*—just after I'd gotten my latte.

Luciano and I air-kissed when I reached the counter,

but he said, "It's not even nine in the morning, and you've already let *at least* two people wipe their feet on you."

"I'm early for work," I said, handing him exact change. "It was the nice thing to do."

"*Too* nice." He tapped the screen of an iPad to enter my order. "You're too nice."

"So, what's wrong with that?"

Luciano responded the way he always did. "Nothing, if you want to remain a spinster. Men love bitches, and bitches get what they want—like swift coffee or dates."

"Dates?"

"Yeah, you know, when two people decide they want to get to know each other better over dinner or drinks . . ."

I rolled my eyes as I zipped up my wallet. "Men might *think* they love bitches, but eventually that wears off. It did for Neal."

"You're wrong, and I would know—I am one, and I date them exclusively."

"A man or a bitch?"

"Both," he said. "And Neal might've left you for one, but seeing as he came crawling back to you soon after, he obviously couldn't keep up with her."

That was all I needed right now, to be reminded of my final conversation with my ex. I kept the memory at bay as I said, "I think you just proved my point."

He sighed. "I'm just saying, before Neal, you made your presence known. Now, it's like you feel guilty taking up space. I don't get how you can be so fierce at work and the opposite in your personal life."

Was it that bad? I was a gainfully employed dog mom, a Celtophile easily regaled with tales of Ireland over card games with my grandad, and a thirty-year-old spinster in training who'd been on exactly zero dates in six months . . .

I could almost get away with telling Luciano I was

happy to grow old with just my work and my dog, but he knew me inside out. We'd bonded over juice boxes and a mutual hate for our given names—school was that much more laborious writing *Georgina* or *Luciano* in cursive on every single paper or correcting the pronunciation of class-mates and teachers alike.

"Now get out of the way," Luciano said, brushing a lock of black hair from his forehead. "I have customers to serve."

"Oh, sorry," I said, hurrying over to the pick-up counter.

I took out some index cards and reviewed my upcoming presentation, quizzing myself on statistics as people filtered in and out of the café. My boss had taught me to practice public speaking surrounded by distractions. That way, nothing could take me out of the zone come game time. I'd pulled together this morning's presentation in only five days, yet I had the numbers down to an art. In a way, it *was* an art, compiling data in a digestible way that wouldn't make enemies out of the team I was about to join —or invade, depending on how they looked at it.

"Mocha latte," Luciano's coworker called out and set my drink on the bar.

I tucked the notecards under my arm and went to take the drink just as the woman next to me picked it up.

"Oh, I think that's mine," I said as she started to turn away.

"Mocha latte?" She looked over her shoulder at the barista, who nodded. "That's what I ordered."

"Me too," I said.

She checked the cup. "This says George."

"Yes, that's me," I said.

"George is a man's name. There are no men on this side of the counter."

"I know, but . . ." I sighed with frustration. "You were actually behind me in line."

"Impossible," she said, finally turning to me. "I didn't even wait in line. I walked right up to the counter."

I looked to Luciano, five feet away, for help. With one word, he could fix this for me, but instead he hummed Britney Spears' "Stronger" to himself and pretended not to hear us. "I mean that you came in after me," I clarified. "I saw you."

"You saw me come in?"

"Yes." At least, I was fairly certain I had. I'd looked up from my notes, silently quizzing myself when she'd walked in. Unless it'd been another blonde woman tall enough to wear flats with a power suit. "I think—"

"I don't have time for this. My name's Joan, that's close to George, so it must be mine," she said in one long breath and walked away with my drink.

But my name was closer. *Make my presence known.* I knew what Luciano was thinking. Now, *three* people had cut me in line before nine in the morning, and that was especially bad today of all days when I needed to be on point.

As she exited the café, Luciano placed a new drink on the counter. "Skinny mocha latte."

"*Skinny?* Are you kidding?" I made a face. "Does it at least have two-percent milk?"

"Non-fat."

I groaned. "Whipped cream?"

"Nope. And the mocha sauce is sugar-free."

"Lu," I whined. "I can't drink this garbage."

Luciano took a cup from the register and started the next order. "Well, I made a regular one and even added extra whipped cream for your big day, but you let someone else take it." He shrugged. "Should've spoken up."

He was punishing me, but it wasn't as if I hadn't tried

to convince her it was mine. "She didn't give me a chance. Why didn't *you* say anything?"

"Because she was right. There was no George around." He stopped and looked at me. "If a colleague of yours waltzed in right now and demanded she give your presentation today, would you roll over and let her?" With a sigh to let me know I'd disappointed him, he leaned over the counter and took the skinny drink back. "I'll remake this," he said, disappearing behind an espresso machine.

"I just don't want to start my day with confrontation," I called after him. "*Especially* today."

"Nobody does," he yelled back. "But if Georgina doesn't respect herself, why should anyone else?"

Respect wasn't an issue—at *work*. I was a fixer, and a damn good one. When I walked into a failing media company, I joined the team and guided them toward solutions. Yet when my ex had been struggling to finish school with a full-time job, *Georgina* had been persuaded to shoulder the burden. How could I argue that saving to take my family pub-hopping in Dublin for the holidays was more important than Neal's education? And could I really expect him to help with the crippling vet bills for a dog he hadn't even wanted? He'd told me he was quitting his job in insurance sales, and I'd accepted it without a fight. I'd do Ireland another time, I'd reasoned, so I could cover rent, bills, and healthcare while Neal earned his Master's. And he had. Right before he'd left me for a classmate.

The door jingled behind me, and a man's voice filled the space. "No, I'm at a coffee shop downstairs," he said. "Can't believe I'm starting my morning without Dunkin', but this sludge will have to do. It's for a good cause."

For anyone to suggest that Dunkin' Donuts was better than this place, which carried specialty, single-origin organic coffee, was absurd. I turned. The man on his cell was at least a head taller than anyone else. With boyishly brown hair, a square, tailored suit, and an even sharper jawline, he looked as if he'd walked right out of a magazine. Considering all the media companies on this block, it was entirely possible that he had come from a photoshoot.

"Hang on," he said into his cell as he approached the counter. He lowered the phone to his side and read Luciano's nametag. "Morning, Luciano. Can I get three coffees, two black and one iced with extra cream and sugar?"

"Name?"

He hesitated. "Can you write 'number one boss' on the iced coffee?"

Luciano nodded. "Coming right up."

"Thanks, man. Appreciate it." The man passed over his credit card before stuffing a five-dollar bill in the tip jar.

A generous tip *and* a sincere thank you? What planet had he come from? Not only was it out of character for a New Yorker, but it was even less so for such a beautiful specimen. Good god, he was something to look at with thick hair the color of my beloved morning mocha and broad shoulders that tapered to a lean waist. Tall and imposing, he seemed vaguely familiar, like an actor who'd suddenly started popping up in every hit movie, or the treadmill hunk who kept all the girls—and some guys—motivated at the gym. Except I had no doubt I would've remembered seeing him at my gym.

If I'd belonged to a gym.

He definitely did, if the bulges under his sleeves were any indication. Luciano loved men's pecs. My boss worshipped at the altar of ass and thigh. But I was all about the face. I loved jaws and noses as strong and distinguished as British royalty, features passed through generations. He had parentheses for laugh lines, and when he half-smiled, a semi-colon formed in one cheek—one perfunctory, deep dimple just slightly above a curved one at the edge of his mouth. I read him like a book that made you forget how—right to left, top to bottom, backward and forward.

He cleared his throat.

To cover up the fact that I'd been staring, I glanced away and continued rehearsing. Was there any greater distraction than a gorgeous man who smelled as if he'd spent the morning foraging for wood—or at least in the men's product aisle at Target? Fresh Blast, Classic Old Spice, Cool Rush—he was one of those, probably whichever smelled best. If I could remember my presentation in his presence, then I'd nail it later on.

He was at the pick-up counter now, closer than he had been moments ago. Without warning, he squatted at my feet. My breath caught as he reached past my ankle and under the counter. His forearm grazed my calf and I shuddered, goosebumps spreading like wildfire up my bare leg.

He stood and held out one of my notecards. "I think you dropped this."

I just stared at it, willing my hand to take it, but my body wasn't done being stunned by his nearness. I hadn't had a man between my legs in months. And he was still here, inches away, standing closer than a stranger would. As if we'd come here together. As if we were *leaving* together . . .

"By the way, the iced coffee isn't for me," he said gently, as if sensing my discomfort.

I took the index card, shoved it in my bag with the others, and met his eyes—the perfect summer green of the grass in Sheep Meadow where I'd sunbathed just last month. "I'm sorry?"

"I didn't just pull a Michael Scott and proclaim myself

number one boss. I'm actually buttering up *my* boss." He shrugged. "And I'm not above excessive flattery or caffeine."

I glanced around to make sure he wasn't talking to someone else, but we were alone. He was *flirting* with me— a man this attractive who was also well-versed in *The Office*. As soon as the thought hit me, my barely working brain short-circuited. With a chiseled jaw and smooth, styled brown hair, he was a marble statue away from Greek god status. My throat had gone bone-dry. Seconds ticked by, and I still hadn't answered.

"Hopefully this place does the trick," he continued with a smile. "I've never had the coffee here."

Slowly, I nodded, grasping at words. "It's not sludge."

He chuckled, a deep, sexy sound that made me wish I was funnier so he'd do it again. "You heard that, huh?"

"He's a master. At the coffee-making." Sweat formed along my hairline. "Er, he's a great barista—Luciano, I mean."

The man wasn't just intimidatingly large with equally impressive posture. Every piece of his look was perfectly in place, from a shiny gold tie that cut straight down the center of a crisp, white dress shirt to mahogany-colored wingtip brogues so polished I could probably see my own reflection in them. Heat crept up my chest and neck.

"So, is he a friend of yours, Luciano?" he asked. "Or . . ."

It would almost make more sense that a man this handsome and well-dressed would be talking to me to get to Luciano. Except, having grown up with a gay best friend, my radar for these things was usually pretty accurate, and I wasn't getting that vibe at all. "Just a friend," I said and tested the waters with, "He's available."

He smiled. "I wasn't asking for——" A small, high-pitched voice cut into our moment, and it took me a second to realize it was coming from the man's cell. He put it to his ear. "Justin," he said into the phone. "Forgot you were there." He hesitated, then gave me an apologetic look as he stepped away and asked, "What's this news that can't wait?"

Luciano handed my new drink over the counter. "Who's the sexy suit?"

"Not sure," I said, "but he's straight."

"As an arrow," Luciano agreed.

"If I had time, I'd stay to find out more, but I want to get upstairs a little early." I blew him a kiss as I turned to leave. "See you later."

I was about to exit the café when the door flew open, forcing me to jump back. Joan, the woman who'd taken my drink earlier, blew by me, stomping to the front. "This isn't skinny," she said to the barista.

Lu's coworker looked up slowly, his eyebrows cinched. "Sorry . . . ?"

"You made my drink wrong." She showed him where whole milk was marked on the cup. "It was supposed to be non-fat, sugar-free, without whip."

Luciano came out of the back with a tray of three drinks. "Number one boss," he called out.

I glanced over at the man in the suit, who was now pacing the far side of the café. He rubbed his temples with one large hand as he spoke into the phone. "*Now?*" he asked, sounding angry. "As in, this morning? When was that decided?"

"I didn't make your drink, ma'am," the barista said, calling my attention back.

"It doesn't matter who made it," Joan replied. "It's wrong."

"*I* made it." Luciano ignored her glare as he capped a drink and added, "Is there a problem?"

"It's not skinny. I want a new drink and *obviously* a refund for having to walk all the way back."

If she'd taken the correct drink in the first place, this wouldn't have happened. Luciano was likely thinking the same thing, because he looked right at me. He wasn't able to put her in her place without risking his job. The thought of doing it for him made me panic even though standing up for my best friend should've been a reflex.

"Well?" the woman asked Luciano. "Are you just going to stand there?"

"You actually picked up the wrong drink," he responded, finally facing her.

"So this is my fault?" Her neck reddened. "You should've written the correct name on it. Or don't they teach you that in barista school?"

"We'll be happy to remake it," Luciano said evenly, but I could tell he was trying not to snap.

"I'll take a refund too," she said, "and I'd like to see your manager."

The man in the gold tie walked back across the café. "A simple 'thank you' would do," he said to her as he tucked his cell in his breast pocket and turned his back to me. "Luciano just generously offered to remake a drink *you* mistakenly took. Why do you think it's okay to speak to him that way?"

I looked around him. Her expression fell as she took him in. "This isn't really your business," she said with less conviction.

"You're being unnecessarily rude, and as a human being, that's my business." He checked a heavy-looking chrome watch and picked up his drink tray. "He deserves an apology, and I hope you'll rethink what you tell his manager."

Watching the heroic way he put her in her place made my heart pound, both with adrenaline and a tinge of fear. I couldn't keep backing down to people like Joan, who had no consideration for others. Or Neal, who'd picked us an apartment closest to *his* subway line, had us visiting *his* family for holidays, and had me cook meals catered to *his* tastes.

Neal's parting words, said after makeup sex I'd regret until the day I died, had weighed on me ever since. *"Never should've left someone like you for a stronger woman, Georgina. They're way too much work."*

In other words, *someone like me* was easy. Weak. In the next breath, he'd asked me to skip my monthly visit with my grandad so we could stay in and catch up on *Altered Carbon*. Apparently, his 'stronger woman' didn't have Netflix.

For years, I'd done nothing but doubt myself in Neal's presence. That, and concede, yield, and compromise. Now, I used his words to incite myself. To fight back. To stop the cycle of putting others' feelings before my own.

Emboldened, I charged back to the counter. My adrenaline kicked in, and fleetingly, I even wondered if I'd have the courage to ask out mister gold-tie, green-eyes after this. But just as I approached, he swiveled on his heel, and we collided with only the drink tray between us.

"God*damn* it," he said, jumping back as iced coffee exploded on my blouse.

My mouth hung open as I raised my arms. *Goddamn it* was right. I hadn't accounted for accidents this late in the game. I definitely didn't have time to go home and change, but I'd have a hard enough time getting a roomful of men to take me seriously *without* a wet blouse.

Balancing the tray of surviving drinks in one hand, he tossed the fallen one with his other and grabbed a handful of napkins. "Today of all days," he muttered. "And the only drink I actually needed."

"I'm sorry," I said, and offered, "I'll replace it."

"It's fine." He dabbed at coffee splatter on his shirt then squatted to clean up the spill. "Just watch where you're going. Someone like you will get run over in this city."

I paled, only mildly aware the coffee shop had gone quiet. I didn't have to ask what he meant by *someone like me*. I wasn't big enough, not just in stature but in presence, to command consideration. The man didn't seem to care that *my* blouse was drenched in cold, sticky liquid.

It wasn't even that he'd said it in front of everyone, including Luciano, but that he'd so easily narrowed in on the insecurities Neal had left me with. A lump formed in my throat as people stared at us, but he didn't notice as he struggled to mop up every drop with the napkins.

In a fitted pencil skirt, I couldn't even bend down to help. "Luciano," I said, hating how my voice cracked. "There's a spill over here."

"He shouldn't have to clean up your mess," the man said.

My mess. Run over. Someone like me. What had happened in the last five minutes to turn "number one boss" into such a jerk? I'd spent half a year trying to move on from an ex who'd made me feel as small as this man was trying to. I was insignificant. In the way. Inconvenient.

Tears heated the backs of my eyes, but I swallowed through them.

I hadn't recognized Neal's behavior for what it was back then, but I was stronger now. This man didn't get to speak down to me just because he was bigger, more articulate, and more charming than most. Maybe nobody had ever stood up to him out of fear, but I forced myself to channel my inner George—or in Lu's words, "the bitch within."

"This isn't *my* mess," I said. "It's as much your fault as mine, and at least I owned up to it." My voice firmed, and I straightened my back. "*You* pretend to be a nice guy to get what you want, and then you dump all over the rest of us because you think you're better." A man bold enough to wear a gold tie surely assumed his devastating smile could get him out of anything. Not anymore. I'd never gotten the chance to tell Neal off the way he deserved, so for my former self, I continued, "Well, guess what? You're *not* better. You're worse. You told that woman to apologize, but you should take your own advice, you entitled *asshole*."

He froze in the middle of sopping up the drink and raised his beautiful green eyes to mine. "You'll call a stranger an asshole, but you can't even stand up for your supposed friend?"

As triumph coursed through me, shame followed. I remembered now why I hated confrontation. I wasn't good at it. I always folded. And more often than not, panic stole my words, leaving me without a defense. What could I even say? The man was right. I'd left a lifelong friend high and dry. As much as I wanted to think standing up for myself meant my confidence had finally returned, it was still hanging by a tenuous thread.

A few hot, frustrated tears slid over my cheeks. I quickly turned my face away, horrified that I'd given him the satisfaction of seeing me cry. Without looking back, I turned on my heel and bolted out of the café.

2

With handfuls of soggy napkins and coffee splatter on my freshly pressed Tom Ford shirt, I stared out the door after a woman who'd just called me an *entitled asshole* in front of a café full of people.

Life was really testing me this morning. It was one of the first days of fall, the crisp, colorful kind that would've normally made for a great start to the week—but not this one. Not even a beautiful woman or a grenade of an insult could make me forget the date.

As I'd hung up with Justin moments ago, my first instinct had been to call my mom and ask for advice. It didn't seem fair that I couldn't.

Not that anything about her death had seemed fair.

Could it really be possible that as of today, she'd been gone one whole year?

Each time that reality came crashing down, it was no less crushing, but this morning, I needed her more than ever. As if I wasn't already navigating an emotional mine-field of memories, I'd just found out my job was under threat too. The universe had pretty much dumped an ice-cold, extra-cream-and-sugar coffee on my Monday—and all over an auburn-haired beauty whose freckles disappeared when her face reddened.

A fact I only knew because I'd upset her. I'd made her cry. *Me.*

What would Mom have said to the way I'd spoken to her? Without a doubt, there would've been a verbal ass-whooping. The hole in my soul deepened a little with the knowledge that my mother would never put me in my place again—then hug me and tell me how to fix it.

A mop appeared in my line of sight. Luciano, the barista.

I stood to take it from him, but he held it back. "I've got this," he said. "There's a new iced coffee on the counter. You can take it and go."

I reached for my wallet. "How much do I owe you?"

He sighed and passed me the drink with a short, "We're square."

The redhead, who'd gone from shy to merciless in a moment, was a friend of his. It made my gut smart that I'd offended him. It was hardly the first time I'd stepped in to diffuse a confrontation like that, and in this city, it definitely wouldn't be the last. I just couldn't remember a time where I'd ended up the bad guy.

That seemed to be a theme with me lately, falling off a pedestal into a pile of *bad.*

I took the coffees and headed to work at a quick clip, hoping I could still salvage the last few minutes I had to save my team—and my own ass—from the mistake my boss was about to make.

I tried not to think about the fact that I'd overreacted. I had enough on my plate today, and I didn't have the time or attention to devote to a woman I'd never see again. Yet, during the short walk, she remained on my mind. It didn't help that she'd been enticing enough to get me flirting before caffeine.

Or that if Justin hadn't called, I would've kept up the conversation—if not because she was cute, then to find out why she was in the habit of befriending baristas, or why she'd had a back issue of *Modern Man* magazine sticking out of her bag.

Or that even the aroma of iced coffee couldn't mask her scent, something fresh and sweet, as if she'd frolicked in daisy fields and fallen asleep atop rainbows.

That was good, the rainbow thing. I'd have to keep that in my back pocket for a future piece.

I'd mistaken her silence for timidity, something the girls I normally dated didn't possess. I needed that—a clean break from my normal type, but was this woman more like them then I'd initially thought? She'd seemed nervous by our interaction, shivering as my sleeve had brushed her leg —but after our collision, she'd really let it rip. Perhaps my interest in her should've fizzled because of what she'd said to me, but then there'd been that slight tremor in her voice. Something about her personality didn't click into place, which left me wondering why . . .

"Pardon me," I said, pushing through a group of camera-toting tourists disembarking a huge red bus— because that was what good people did, even New Yorkers. We said *excuse me, thank you*, and *you're welcome*. New Yorkers had a reputation, but the world had it wrong. Were we direct and concise? Yes. Did we have somewhere to be five minutes ago? Yes. Was it likely we'd give directions every single time we were stopped? No. But we weren't rude about it. Despite being born and bred in Boston, I figured I'd earned the New Yorker title over a ten-year history that had spanned six apartments, three boroughs, twelve roommates, a summer internship, and four different positions at *Modern Man*. But the city drew all kinds of people, and *some* people, like the blonde woman who'd gone ape-shit over a stupid drink order, were just fucking rude.

And I had little patience for those who didn't stand up to rudeness, especially when it was directed at a friend. I'd gone too far if I'd made the mocha latte girl cry, but there was no excuse for staying quiet.

I'd needed that ass-kissing coffee as much as I'd needed the extra few minutes. It was a good thing I hadn't hung up on Justin as I'd been tempted to since Vance had gone from *number one boss* to traitor and changed the entire course of my morning—and my career. Now, instead of the charming plea I'd been practicing all weekend to get him to rethink his strategy, I'd be heading into a shit storm without an umbrella.

I gripped the coffee tray in my hands a little too tightly and strode on. People were relying on me to keep the integrity of the magazine intact. Not just my team, but our readership too.

Justin and I hit the lobby of Dixon Media Tower at the same time and made our way toward the turnstiles. "You shouldn't have," he said, attempting to pluck the iced coffee from the tray right before I pulled it back.

"That isn't for you, asshole."

"Aha. Then it must be a last-ditch attempt to change Vance's mind."

I punched the elevator call button. "How do you know I'm not waving the white flag?"

"Because ten minutes ago, you were bitching to me about the 'hack' he hired. By the way, who were you talking to that made you forget I was on the phone?"

"A woman, of course."

We boarded the elevator. "Was she hot?" Justin asked over everyone's heads.

"She called me an asshole."

"So you asked her out?"

"Why would I?"

"Hot *and* scary?" Justin blew out a breath. "It's a well-documented fact that Sebastian Quinn dates assholes—pardon my French, ladies."

A woman I recognized from the building rolled her eyes as if even *she* knew the type of women I went for.

My gut twisted as the elevator's digital numbers rose. Justin wasn't wrong—I'd made some questionable choices throughout my life where women were involved. That was in the past, though. One of the reasons I'd been drawn to the stunning redhead was that at first glance, she'd seemed the opposite of that. I'd caught her staring at me by the pick-up counter, but instead of fluttering her lashes, she'd shyly lowered her eyes and resumed studying, looking so damn *cute* murmuring to herself. Was she a student, newly arrived in the big city? I hadn't meant to insult her by suggesting she might get run over but *warn* her. This place wasn't for everyone.

Then again, it seemed she could handle herself just fine.

Shy? Cute? Polite? Maybe. I wasn't sure I'd call her *scary*, but my judgment was clearly off this morning.

"The only asshole on this elevator is the one with verbal diarrhea," I shot back.

"Oh, if you want to go poop jokes, let's do this thing," Justin said. "Conference room, one hour. Bring your shittiest material."

The woman grimaced, and the elevator eased to a stop, allowing her and most of the riders to exit. I wondered if it was actually their floor, or if they just wanted to get out of Justin's presence.

"So, did you?" Justin asked.

"Did I what?"

"Ask her out?"

I frowned. It wasn't that I'd sought out stuck-up women in the past, but they seemed to find me. Either that, or they were the only fish in the sea of Manhattan. Maybe work events and photoshoots weren't the best places to meet women, but apparently, neither was a coffee shop. Where else did that leave? The Internet? I shuddered. Justin had once written a harrowing first-hand account on the perils of dating apps that had nearly turned me celibate.

"Are you thinking about online dating again?" Justin asked.

I glanced at him. "How'd you know?"

"You always get a certain look when it comes up. I told you, ending up front row at a One Direction concert wasn't as bad as I made it sound."

"She had no right to trick you into that." The blind date had taken a turn for the worst when Justin had admitted to having a man crush on Justin Timberlake. Although we all idolized Timberlake, that didn't mean we were fans of boy bands, which was what his date had assumed.

"It's almost as bad as—" I cringed. "I can't even say it."

"Merkin?"

A man on the elevator glanced up from his phone.

"A vagina wig," Justin explained.

"Ah." The man nodded and returned to browsing Reddit.

Now, I wouldn't be able to get that image out of my

head all day. "I've already told you not to talk to me about that."

"I'll let you off the hook, only because of today's date." He nodded once at me. "How are you holding up?"

This day clocked in as one of my worse ones. I'd made a woman cry within minutes of finding out my job was in jeopardy a year *to the day* that I'd held my mom's warm hand for the last time as she'd succumbed to cancer. Somehow, my first fall without a mother was already upon us. Not that I was going to say all that to an elevator of strangers, or even to Justin. If I so much as tried, I'd never make it through the day. "I'm fine," I said and checked my watch for the umpteenth time since getting Justin's call. "I just can't believe Vance hired this guy without my input. You're sure it's a done deal?"

"Derek texted me because the guy has some kind of presentation, so he needed the projector set up. Want me to head to IT and grill Derek?"

"There's no more time." I switched the tray to my other hand and adjusted my tie in the reflection of the doors. "Meeting starts in fifteen."

Justin exited on thirty-five, but I rode the elevator up a few more floors. I walked through the executive level of Dixon Media Group to my editor-in-chief's office, game face on, even though the girl in the coffee shop had threatened my focus with her tears.

Vance's secretary was on the phone. I set one of the black coffees on her desk, and she smiled as she waved me through. I knocked once and entered. Reclined in a leather chair with a phone to his ear, my boss motioned for me to enter. I sat across the desk from him and set down the tray.

"Let me call you back," Vance said, eyeing the iced coffee. "I have a meeting downstairs."

As he hung up, I pulled out the drink and passed it over. "Extra cream and sugar."

"Sorry to break it to you," Vance said, accepting the cup, "but I already have an assistant, and she's not going anywhere. You're underqualified anyway."

"What's so hard about the position? Sucking dick or kissing ass—either way, I'm still on my knees."

"Jesus Christ, Quinn." Vance threw a palm in the air, shaking his head. "Don't even joke about that. HR has ears everywhere." He glanced around the room and said clearly, "There is no dick sucking happening in this office." He turned back to me. "And when have you ever kissed my ass —until now?"

"Vance, don't do this. Call off today's meeting and tell this guy to return to the bridge he crawled out from under."

"Can't." Vance stood and raised his cup to me. "But thanks for the coffee."

"I have to say my piece one last time."

"You've said it, I've heard it, and I've made my decision. Cream and sugar won't change my mind. I'm sorry."

"You could've given me some notice," I said. "You went and hired him without my input or approval."

"Bad PR waits for no man. The media is already having a field day with the exposé. They're throwing around phrases like *sexually charged workplace*, *chauvinism*, and *toxic masculinity*, whatever the fuck that means."

The words came at me like poison darts, and I had to stand there and take it. Because I'd done this to myself. I envisioned my mother making the sign of the cross after reading those things about her only son. It wasn't as if she hadn't known what people thought of me, but even if she knew those things weren't true, that didn't make it hurt any less.

"You promoted me years ago to turn this magazine around," I said, "and that's what I did, even though it cost me. You didn't have a problem with hypermasculinity or objectification of women when it was making the company money."

"Well, it's not anymore."

"But we can't ignore that it got us here. That's what has grown our readership. We're a men's lifestyle magazine that mainly covers beautiful women, some other stuff, and how not to fuck up with beautiful women. We've crafted an image of what goes on behind the scenes, and yes, it's exaggerated, but it sells our brand."

"Well, that 'brand' has come back to bite us in the ass. What was once an asset is now a liability. Not only has it garnered us national attention, but it's also the final feather in the cap of a shitty year for *Modern Man*."

As if I wasn't aware. My magazine had already been suffering before the exposé had gone and thrown punches at our content and my character. We had our moments like any group of men expected to report on our favorite topics, but we weren't bad guys. "If you hire someone to come in and soften our image, we can kiss the magazine goodbye." Along with my job and all the hard work I'd invested into it.

"I don't have to tell you subscription rates have not only stalled but have started to decline." Vance blew out a breath. "Look, I know it's been a tough year for you, but my hands are tied. You've had nearly four quarters to shift tactics, but after last week's PR debacle, advertisers have lost their patience."

What he wasn't saying was that *I'd* gotten us into this mess, but I knew better than to use my personal life as an excuse. Here, the bottom line ruled, and it'd been falling out from under us for a while. Being named in the exposé had only hurt our stock more. "Then give me an alternative, Vance, but don't bring in some bullshit consultant who's going to strip away everything that makes *Modern Man* what it is."

"There's only one alternative, and it's that I replace you, Sebastian. I don't want to do that, but something has to give."

"*Replace* me?" I sat back in my seat and gaped at him. This job was my *life*. I'd spent high school working my ass off for a scholarship to a top-tier university, and then my college years hustling to make every connection I could just for the chance at a summer internship in journalism. *Modern Man*, a struggling publication with small-time circulation, hadn't been my first choice, but I'd been grateful for a job in research and fact-checking. And the magazine had been on the brink of failure until I'd worked my way to the top and turned it around. This wasn't just my job—it was my blood, sweat, and tears. "We might not be standing here having this conversation if not for me. What about the past ten years?"

"As our creative director, you made this magazine what it is," he agreed, "but at the end of the day, it doesn't belong to you. It belongs to the advertisers and the board, and they're spooked. Dos Equis has already halved their budget, and Breitling is threatening the same if we don't turn things around now. Accepting help won't shrivel your balls, I promise."

"It's not a matter of pride," I said. Did I believe that? Not really. But I'd always been good at making my case. "It's that I know our reader inside out. You're bringing a man onto my team that you didn't even know we needed a week ago."

Vance leaned on the desk with steepled fingers. "Let me be clear, Quinn. I'm not bringing anyone onto *your* team. You'll be running things *together*. That's how co-management works. And you better make it work, because if it doesn't, you won't survive the next restructure. Consider this an unofficial warning."

My heart pounded. *Restructure? Co-management?* It made no sense. So the last year had been a bit stagnant. That was the economy. Subscription rates had to slow at some point—anyone in the industry knew that. And maybe it was true that since Mom's death, I'd been struggling to find meaning in what we did, but I shouldn't have to lose my job over it.

I took an absentminded sip of my coffee and cringed. I'd only strayed from my beloved Dunkin' Donuts for Vance. It was just another hit to my day, paying twice as much for a shittier cup of coffee before meeting my new babysitter. "If this goes south, it's on your shoulders," I said.

"I'm the editor-in-chief," Vance said, "there's so much shit on my shoulders, I might as well live in a toilet."

"Hey, that's good," I said wryly, standing. "You should submit it to the jokes department."

I took my crappy coffee back to my office. There was no getting out of this. My team and I had been strategizing ways to reach more potential subscribers since numbers had begun to fall off last year, but so far nothing had stuck. As creative director, it'd taken years, but I'd perfected my team. I knew all of their strengths and weaknesses—knew that Garth worked best with a deadline, and Albert without one, and that Boris's excitement waned unless I showed equal enthusiasm for his work. When they needed fresh ideas, I employed my dogs-and-dicks strategy. We ordered hotdogs and left our brains at the door as we sealed ourselves in my office to *dick*storm. No idea was too crude, macho, or gross. Poop jokes, double entendres, food fights, pranks. Once, a soul-baring discussion about how our moms had packed our lunch boxes had devolved into ranking hockey goalies by the sexiness of their wives. Maybe it wasn't politically correct, but by the end, we generally had three or four useable topics for that month's issue.

Story impregnation by idea ejaculation.

But would my co-manager see the brilliance of it? Was he too refined for dogs and dicks? Would he run crying to HR at the first sign of a crass joke? Break bro code and risk the safety we'd cultivated after years in a vault?

After I'd trashed the coffee and sent an intern on an emergency run to reliable old Dunkin' Donuts, my hometown staple, I went to my office to find Justin horizontal on my couch. "Don't you have your own kingdom to lord over?" I asked him.

"Yeah, but I already took my morning shit," Justin said.

"I'm talking about your cubicle, not the bathroom. Why are you always in here?"

"Booze. Couch. Privacy." He sighed. "I never understood why you get a corner office to yourself, and I have to share a box with Girly Garth."

"Exhibit A—we've only been at work fifteen minutes and you're already napping. You're a shitty employee."

Justin sat up on his elbow with a pout. "You don't mean that."

"You're lucky you're good at what you do, or you'd have been out on your ass a long time ago."

"Aw. I choose to see that as a compliment, so, thanks, honey."

Vance leaned into the office and nodded at me. "It's time. Better take your PMS medicine, or it could get ugly."

"Fuck off, both of you," I said as they laughed.

"Oh, stop sulking, Quinn," Vance said. "Do what she says, and things'll be back to normal in no time."

She? I started to ask who he meant, but a voice from the hallway spoke first. "That's great advice in most situations," a woman said. "You must be married."

Vance turned around. "Miss Keller. I'm sorry—you snuck up on me."

I raised my eyebrows. Keller? I'd heard the name before but hadn't been aware of any recent hires. I tried to see through the doorway.

"I'm sorry we didn't get to debrief upstairs," she said. "I meant to arrive a few minutes earlier but ran into an issue on the way here."

"No problem at all," Vance said. "Come and meet some of your team before the meeting starts."

I blinked. *Team?* Vance turned sideways for a pretty, petite, freckle-nosed woman with a mocha latte in one hand and a back issue of *Modern Man* sticking out of her bag. When our gazes met, her perfect posture faltered as she stopped short, and a wave of silky auburn hair fell over one eye. We each inhaled a sharp breath.

I stood face to face with the coffee shop sniper.

I'd been a bit harsh on her, yes—but not enough to warrant her taking it this far. "Did you follow me here?" I asked.

She pushed her hair out of her face. "Did *you* follow *me* here?"

"You two know each other?" Vance cut in.

Locked in a staredown with her, I didn't dare flinch. Or notice that her eyes were distractingly pale green. Or that her plump lips glistened with a fresh coat of gloss. Or that her coffee-stained, stuffy button-down had somehow morphed into a low-cut top that displayed cleavage she was trying—and failing—to cover with her blazer.

Fuck. There was a reason I'd chatted her up at the pick-up counter—she was hot, sizzling even, her hair a rich burgundy in the sunlight coming through my office windows.

I really needed my dick to stay out of this, at least until I'd gotten my bearings.

"We met downstairs," she said, not looking away from me. She tilted her head. "In fact, we practically shared a coffee."

"Great," Vance said. "Sebastian, meet George Keller. She'll be working alongside you the next eight weeks."

George Keller. It'd sounded familiar because it was a name Vance had thrown out last week along with the possibility of hiring a consultant. I slowly shifted my gaze from George to Vance, who had this thumbnail between his teeth. "You left out an important piece of information about George Keller," I said.

"Well—"

George looked at Vance as well. "You didn't tell him I was a woman?"

I snorted. "With a name like George, *he's* hardly to blame."

"It's *Georgina*," she snapped, then smoothed her hands over her skirt and shook her head. "I mean, in my personal life," she added coolly. "At the office, George is fine. Or Miss Keller will do."

"I'm not calling you Miss Keller like you're my grade-school teacher." I turned to Vance. "Why didn't you tell me?"

"There, uh, hasn't been a good time."

"Bullshit."

"Just the *idea* of bringing someone in made you cranky. I knew you wouldn't understand why I chose her until you saw Georgina's track record."

I took a lungful of air and looked back at George. Georgina. Miss Keller. Whatever-the-fuck. "I can't do this with her."

She frowned. God help me if she broke into tears again. But instead, she raised her chin and leveled me with a cool, "You can't do it without me."

Justin rubbed his hands together, excitement radiating off him. "Well, this is a very interesting turn of events indeed."

3

I hated being caught off guard in professional situations. Work was the one area I had it together thanks to a take-no-shit boss who'd gotten where she was by shattering glass ceilings for fun. But she was also a nurturing and supportive mentor to those she considered worth her time. She'd taught me how to girl-boss. How to take care of myself. And that I should never feel guilty about wanting more out of my career. She was why I could become someone else, someone like her, in order to walk into a crisis with my head on straight.

And she was why I stood here now, in front of my new co-manager. My new, *disarmingly handsome* co-manager—and the glue that held together the team I was about to join. A commanding, charming man who'd needed to believe I was also a man just to accept the *idea* of me. And a man who'd seen me cry.

Sebastian Quinn.

I hoped he didn't notice the slight tremble of my hands. He'd already witnessed perhaps the one thing a businesswoman couldn't come back from—showing emotion. How the hell did I expect him to take me seriously if he thought I might burst into tears at any moment?

From my hurried research on *Modern Man*, I'd red-flagged the magazine's creative director as one of the staff's biggest liabilities. I hadn't realized that man was Sebastian. And now it occurred to me why he'd looked so familiar at the café—I'd seen his image on the *Modern Man* website, had glanced over it in the exposé while in deep research mode, and had spotted him in social sections of magazines that'd covered *Modern Man*'s events but had assumed he was an editorial model.

I quickly filtered through what I'd learned in the short amount of time I'd had to look into him: owner of a high-end Fifth Avenue apartment, involved in an accident that ended with a totaled foreign sports car, considered a "bad boy" of publishing for the unapologetically masculine magazine he'd built, and a notorious playboy who couldn't be tied down and had left heartbroken actresses, socialites, and models in his wake.

Unfortunately, as I'd already proven, I belonged to the part of the female population that went wobbly-legged and tongue-tied around men like him. George didn't, though. As long as I could stay in character and see Sebastian for what he was—a colleague—I could do this. I had to, because I was a professional, and work came first.

"Let's introduce you to the rest of the staff," Vance said, interrupting the uncomfortable silence that had permeated Sebastian's corner office. "Come with me, Miss Keller."

Vance led us down a long hallway, past some conference rooms. From behind, Sebastian lowered his voice and said, "Is that a *tank top*?"

"At least it's dry." I tugged up the neckline. At a souvenir shop between the café and office, I'd swapped my crisp button-down for a ribbed Yankees jersey that'd only been available in extra-small.

"I'm not saying I don't like it," he continued. "But it's a good thing you weren't wearing it when I met you. I might've forgotten all about my morning meeting."

The back of my neck warmed. If there'd been any question that he'd been flirting earlier, here was my proof. He walked close behind me to keep our conversation private, and it reminded me of how he'd kneeled at my feet before we'd ever even made eye contact. Neal would've said my tank was too revealing for the office. Toward the end of our relationship, only an arched eyebrow over his coffee mug would've been enough to send me back into our bedroom to change.

My ex was the last person I needed to be thinking about in that moment, yet less than an hour in Sebastian's presence and I was second-guessing my outfit. And myself. I had to be careful. Dionne had sent me here for a reason. *Modern Man* needed a female touch. My past assignments had mainly consisted of publications for women by women, and Sebastian's staff had gone unchecked too long.

I had to play the game their way. If I came off as too assertive, I'd become the enemy and find myself ostracized from the group. In order for this to work, I had to truly be *in* the circle of trust, not at the fringes, and definitely not outside of it.

I couldn't let Sebastian undermine me. I dug into my purse, unzipped a side pouch, and pulled out an emergency mini bottle of Aleve. Turning my head over my shoulder, I tossed it back, and Sebastian caught it with a look of surprise. "For the PMS," I said with a wink to make absolute sure he knew I'd heard their earlier conversation.

I took the next moment for myself, though I could've used a whole *weekend* with Halo Top and *The New Yorker* to agonize over my morning—oh, who was I kidding? I wallowed by eating Häagen Dazs Mocha Chocolate Cookie straight from the carton while binge-watching every available episode of HGTV set in Dublin or any movie featuring Saoirse Ronan.

Vance had promised me full rein over *Modern Man*, but I could see now that there'd be no such opportunity while Sebastian was there. Even if the way we'd met couldn't have gone worse, I had to get it together. I hadn't come this far in my career by backing down when intimidated.

I double-checked that my blazer was buttoned, fixed my neckline again, and entered the conference room. Barely legible chicken scratch covered the whiteboard at the head of the room. Miniature football goal posts sat at opposite ends of the conference table, and in the middle, a battalion of G.I. Joe action figures held up a Dunkin' Donuts box. I followed a trail of rainbow sprinkles leading to the other man I'd seen but hadn't met in Sebastian's office. With unruly blond hair that perfectly offset his blue eyes, he smiled a mouthful of donut. Ah, the class clown. And a potential *in* if I played my cards right.

I set up my laptop at the head of the table and fiddled with the projector.

"Derek from IT should be here any minute," Vance said as more people filed in.

"I've got it." Imagine that—I'd done this probably thirty times before, and all without the help of a *boy*.

As I stood and surveyed the room, Sebastian entered, the last to arrive, as if he'd been loitering outside. A young man gave up his seat to Sebastian, joining a group gathered at the back. Sebastian was important around here, but was he more than a boss to these guys?

"Morning, everyone," Vance said, and the room quieted. "Please give a warm welcome to George Keller, who'll be joining our team as a publishing consultant and PR specialist for the next eight weeks."

I laced my fingers in front of myself and smiled, ignoring the rumble of whispers through the crowd.

"George comes to us with many successful years in media consulting and PR crises," Vance continued. "Remember how the features editor of *Moms and Babes* spent a month in rehab for opioids?"

The men mumbled. "I never heard that," one said.

"Exactly," Vance said, rocking on his heels and smiling as if he'd pulled off the feat of hiding her overdose from the press himself.

"I stopped the story before it leaked," I said, "then, with the help of her staff, we put out one of the magazine's best-selling issues to this day." I scratched under my nose. "Although, I *did* sign an NDA about the opioid thing, so if we could keep that in the room . . ."

Everyone laughed. Well, almost everyone. Sebastian just tapped his pen on his notepad.

"George has helped turn around several media-based companies, which resulted in over a million dollars cumulatively earned."

I nodded at Vance as he took the seat next to me. "Thank you for that generous introduction, but you're giving me too much credit. The real magic happens because of the team."

A mustached man to my left put up his hand. "What exactly is a publishing consultant and . . ."

"PR specialist," I finished.

"As you all know, *Modern Man* has experienced a few down quarters and more recently, it's been in hot water with the press." Vance spoke cautiously about what I could only assume was a sore subject. "George is here to get us out of it."

"How?" the man asked.

"Good question," I said. "You are?"

"Boris," he supplied.

"First, we're going to tackle the PR side of things, Boris. *MM*'s brand, messaging, and image needs work, and this is the perfect time to fine-tune it considering the magazine is under attack."

Someone from Sebastian's section of the conference table muttered under his breath, but I did my best to ignore it.

"Once I perform a little emergency PR magic," I continued, "then comes the part I love most about my job—getting to the bottom of why things have stalled when you should be thriving. I'll sit down with each of you to see how you feel the publication is doing and what improvements can be made. Entirely confidential, of course. We'll collaborate to refine *Modern Man*'s image and identify and remove the reasons we're losing our readership. But change begins with all of you."

Justin grimaced. "Change?"

"Justin doesn't do well with change," Boris said. "He likes the status quo."

"I'm the same," I said. That was more or less true—no human being really *loved* change, especially in the workplace—but in past assignments, I'd made the most headway commiserating with the team's resistance rather than fighting it. "It doesn't have to be extreme. We'll review and tweak, review and tweak, rinse and repeat. Baby steps to figure out why you've lost ground to your largest competitor—and how to regain it."

Sebastian stuck the capped end of his pen in his mouth. It was a small tell, but perhaps a clue as to what he was thinking. How did he feel that his ship had begun to sink under his command?

"You can also think of me as a job therapist," I said. "Feel free to come to me with anything. I'm here to uncover your untapped potential and exploit your strengths —*and* weaknesses—to the magazine's benefit as I whip you into shape."

"Uncover, exploit, whip," Sebastian listed as he made notes. "Maybe this won't be so bad after all. It'll be nice to be on the receiving end for once."

Some men chuckled. I sought out the only other woman in the room, who rolled her eyes with a shrug. *Typical.* If Sebastian thought this was a joke, he was about to learn a hard lesson.

"Don't let them get to you," Vance murmured.

I had no intention of that, but Vance's under-the-breath comments wouldn't do anything except undermine me. "It's okay," I whispered loud enough for Sebastian to hear. "A sense of humor will help ease the sting."

He narrowed his eyes at me, but that earned me a smile from the woman.

"Miss Keller has my complete support," Vance said. "For now, I request that everything go through George first, whether it's story ideas, advice, events, web, or print—"

"It's a shame we don't already have someone for that," Sebastian said. "Say, a creative director."

"This applies to you too, Quinn," Vance said. "Georgina lays eyes on everything."

"You promoted me years ago to take this magazine to the next level, and that's what I did. Now all of a sudden I have to run my ideas by someone else?" He glared. "I'm not doing that."

"You will. I don't care if Miss Keller wants to know the color and consistency of your morning dump."

"That . . . won't be necessary," I said.

With a light knock on the door, a pretty blonde girl who couldn't be more than twenty-one or twenty-two entered. She crouched in a way that the neckline of her billowy blouse exposed a nude bra. The room quieted as she rounded the table and smiled at Sebastian, but she whispered as she set a giant coffee cup in front of him. "Dunkin' delivery."

He smiled back at her. "Thanks, June. You saved me today."

She winked and slunk back out of the room as the guys watched. Maybe it was the cynic Neal had awoken in me, but I couldn't help wondering if Sebastian had slept with her or was working on it. Was anyone immune to his charms? Was I? Based on the way jealousy sparked in me —I wasn't. He'd captured my attention this morning with practically no effort on his part.

My cheeks warmed when I noticed only Sebastian had turned forward again, and he was scanning my face. As if reading my every thought, he raised a dark, knowing eyebrow, then reassumed his perma-scowl.

I cleared my throat, calling their attention back once June had closed the door behind her. "May I continue?"

A man signaled that he had a question. "Are we in trouble?"

Vance opened his mouth, but I spoke first. "No," I said, "but you're headed for it."

"Are you like Anthony Pellicano?" Justin asked. "You inflict pain and make things . . . go away?"

Sebastian sat back in his seat and spoke around the end of his pen. "She doesn't know who that is."

"You can think of me as Pellicano if that helps, minus

the dead fish and prison sentence," I said. Something like approval passed over Sebastian's face, but he quickly schooled it. "But when I say 'ease the sting,' I mean there'll be growing pains. Maybe an example will help. You're all aware *Modern Man* is one of the country's top ten men's interest publications, but do you have any idea how it tests with women?"

"Doesn't matter," Sebastian said. "Women aren't our demographic."

"That's where you're wrong," I said, then turned to Vance. "And therein lies one of your biggest problems. While I admit your publication has made great strides in the diversity arena, that only pertains to men. By ignoring the female demographic, you're automatically excluding fifty percent of the world's population."

"That's ridiculous," Sebastian said.

"Is it? Take a look at this pie chart." I picked up the remote and flipped the slide. "Women influence over eighty percent of consumer spending in the U.S. That's trillions of dollars you're leaving on the table by ignoring them. Of primary shoppers in a household, over fifty percent are women. Tell me, Mr. Quinn, who does the grocery shopping in your household—you or your wife?"

Sebastian flexed his right hand as his eyes flicked to my chest. I wasn't sure how, but I instinctively knew he was thinking about our pre-collision flirtation that morning. "That's sexist," he answered.

"I see. So, you do the majority of shopping for you and your wife?"

"I'm single." He smirked. "And I test great with women."

"So I've heard." I gave him my most sugary smile. "Unfortunately, I'm looking for someone who can score more than one night."

"My wife does the shopping," a man volunteered, and everyone turned to him. "I haven't stepped into a supermarket since I got married, and I'm fine with that."

"What's your name?" I asked.

"Garth."

"Thank you, Garth. That's precisely my point. Do you know the average wait time in a grocery store checkout line? Up to five minutes." I moved to the next slide without bothering to turn and check it. They could read. "What do grocery stores sell in the checkout aisles? Impulse buys." I hit the button again. "Do you know how much more likely women are to impulse buy than men?" I looked out at a sea of blank faces. Only the woman nodded. "Exactly my point," I said. "You don't know, because you don't know women. I do. And this is just a preview of the kind of research my agency has compiled."

Sebastian turned to Vance. "Are you hearing this? She's talking about single-copy sales in the grocery store aisle, a space everyone knows is dead."

"True, consumers are no longer bored at checkout," I said. "They have their phones, and the team back at my office is analyzing your online presence as we speak, but don't discount print yet. It supports digital, enhances branding, and draws in lifestyle readers with more disposable income."

"Anyone can Google statistics," Sebastian said. "How do you suggest we implement all that without alienating our male readers?"

"My agency actually conducted much of this research," I said, reaching under the table for my purse, "so, no, it's not available to anyone with a Wi-Fi connection. Part of what you're paying for is my data." I pulled an August 2017 issue of *Modern Man* from my bag and flipped to a Post-it near the middle. "Here we have a 'dating hacks for geeks' article authored by Garth Hurley and presumably edited by Sebastian."

Sebastian slid his tie through his hand. Its gold color only enhanced the idyllic green of his eyes, but he must've known that when he'd purchased it. He nodded me on.

"Your advice is that they use their brain power for 'something useful' such as memorizing *Modern Man*-approved pick-up lines or choosing books from the 'panty-dropper library' on the website."

"That page gets a lot of hits," pointed out a man I assumed worked in web.

"Then, you suggest they swap their glasses for contacts—which is *archaically* stereotypical—and their Star Wars t-shirts for a tailored outfit from Saks for the first date."

Garth pointed at Sebastian. "May the Fifth Avenue department stores be with you."

"Lastly, Garth, you've prepared talking points for these guys limited to the day's headlines, exotic travel, and healthy food and habits."

Garth shrugged. "Women love to talk about wellness and shit."

"You tell them never to bring up video games, math, or even books or movies unless they've familiarized themselves with something *Modern Man* deems 'sexy.' Basically, you tell them how to be someone else."

"I don't see the problem," Garth said, cinching his eyebrows. "They're geeks."

Was short and squat Garth with his mid-forties receding hairline and custard on his tie being deliberately obtuse? Or was it that hard for him to grasp that a relationship built on lies was doomed to fail? I set the magazine on the table. "The term *geek* has been rehabbed. Look at contemporary film and TV—geek is the new chic. Some women want a more sensitive, adept man. *Some* women find geeks incredibly sexy."

"Yeah," Justin agreed. "They're called geek-ettes."

I sighed, trying to decide where to start. "There's a difference between bettering yourself to meet a partner and flat-out deceit. What happens once he's used up his one outfit? Or when his date wants to cook him the broccoli rabe he claimed to love?"

"He'll eat the damn broccoli rabe whether he likes it or not," Sebastian said. "Everyone pretends to be someone else when dating. Have you ever been on Tinder?"

"Aside from making broad, false generalizations, you're shaming these guys for being themselves," I said. "And you're setting them up for failure."

"Albert here." A hand shot up in greeting, then gestured down the conference table at a heavy-set, bespectacled man with floppy, brown hair. "If you know of a better way to get Derek in IT a date, we're all ears."

Derek—I presumed—threw a balled-up napkin at Albert. "I have a girlfriend, you tool."

I rubbed my eyebrow, thinking. "Take my cousin Cyndi for instance. She's blonde with blue eyes, five-foot-eight, and does commercial modeling on the side. Her real job is a data scientist for the FBI, but nights and weekends, she's hooked on *Red Dead Redemption*. I'll bet she'd love to talk tech with you, Derek."

"She wouldn't give him the time of day," Sebastian said.

"And why not?"

"Because she sounds like the perfect woman."

The comment shouldn't have stung, but at five-foot-two with reddish hair that needed taming each morning, and coordination that had even failed me at *Mario Kart*, I was nothing like Cyndi. If Cyndi existed outside my imagination, that was. But was she the kind of girl who made Sebastian forget his morning meetings? And why did it matter to me? It didn't. It *shouldn't*.

"My point is," I said, powering through my self-doubt, "this 'how-to' doesn't take the woman into account at all. You need to identify interests for finding common ground. A woman—feel free to take notes—is much more likely than a man to fall in love based on proximity and personality rather than looks."

"That explains why Sebastian's perpetually single," Justin said.

"So you think I'm good-looking?" Sebastian asked him.

"I've heard that from women."

"Then at least I've got that going for me," Sebastian said. "You're just ugly and boring."

"A great sense of humor trumps all," I interjected. "With that, a man can win over almost any woman. So once our 'geek' has this information, he'll enter the interaction with a lot more confidence no matter how he looks. Even if he plays *Battlefront II*."

Some of the men laughed. "He just has to find his *Battlefront* princess," Albert said.

"Exactly. Common interest." I was still fuzzy on the details, but my research had shown that the recent release in the *Star Wars* franchise had been boycotted by true gamers. I'd spent part of last week brushing up on my references so I could at least pretend to be in the know. "Then we slap on a headline like, 'How to Meet Your Princess Leia.'"

"'How to Get Leia-d,'" Albert suggested.

Justin perked up. "How about 'Your Guide to Meeting a Geek Goddess'?"

I laughed. "Even better. I'm not here to brainstorm cover lines. I'll leave that stuff to you."

"So we have full creative control over headlines?" Sebastian asked.

I smiled. "Of course not. The cover is the face of *Modern Man*. I'm here to make sure people are not only picking up those issues but becoming repeat customers—and telling their friends about it."

"You're implying our current covers don't do that," he said.

"Right now, you're using women to show sex and say sex."

"Sex sells," Boris said so seriously, I couldn't help but sigh.

"There's nothing sexy about hitting people over the head with it," I explained. "I want you to show sex and say *class*. Say *smart*. Say *style*. Sell sex, not a back-alley screw."

Justin widened his eyes. "That paints a picture."

I shrugged. Men were visual creatures, right? "There's a female demographic—and male—that craves a men's magazine but is put off by most of our material. I can make this happen, provided you're willing to work with me, not against me."

"I think you'll be surprised to see how many female readers we have," Sebastian said.

"I *was* surprised when I got the numbers," I said, glancing at the upcoming deck of slides on my computer. I'd decided to play the next part by ear. I wasn't sure I should get into the exposé yet since it warranted a meeting of its own, and so I wouldn't potentially embarrass Sebastian within an hour of meeting him. That didn't worry me anymore. "Females make up a little under sixteen percent of your reader demographic."

"It's closer to eighteen," Sebastian said.

"It *was*. You've lost two percent this year, and we haven't even seen the results of the exposé yet. That's cause for concern, especially considering the industry standard is over twenty percent and women typically show higher brand loyalty than men." From the ensuing silence, I could tell nobody but Vance and I were aware of that. "Do I need to cover male readership too?"

"No," Sebastian said, shifting in his seat. "We're up to date."

I didn't like calling him out. I understood he fought this because he cared, and he deserved recognition—the magazine's readership had skyrocketed the year Sebastian had taken over. But it'd gone stagnant the last several quarters. That wasn't abnormal for a publication that'd grown at an exponential rate like *Modern Man*, but numbers had started to slide backward. I couldn't help wondering if something specific was affecting Sebastian's work performance.

I flipped to the next slide, page one of a ten-page spread with a bolded headline across the top: "The Bad Boys of Publishing." Sebastian flicked his thumbnail under the plastic lid of his coffee but kept his eyes on the screen behind me. "I know you've all seen this," I said. "Regardless of what's true or false, it has hurt us."

Sebastian shifted his gaze to me and stopped fidgeting with his drink. "You don't think it's all true?"

For the first time since I'd walked in, his bravado faltered. I hoped the exposé, at least, wasn't a joke to him. "It's definitely sensationalized to get eyeballs," I said, noting the way he nodded, "but there are some valid points at the core of it. *Modern Man* has been stuck in the same narrative that popularized it years ago and has since been recycling material. Now it needs to mature. The article paints us and some of our peers, including *Poised*, in a negative light."

"*Poised* is a woman's mag," he said. "It's basically the

female version of us. Why aren't you over there right now?"

"I'm in touch with them, but because I've consulted there before, they have the tools to survive this. Women's magazines have faced challenges like this since their inception. When a men's magazine and its leaders are accused of sexism, the implications are much different and the response requires a more strategic approach."

"We're not sexists," Justin said. "We do all this *because* we worship women."

I moved on to a photocopy of the magazine's advice column, *Badvice*, with a small round picture of Sebastian next to his byline. "In just this edition," I said, pointing behind me, "you recommend dating several coworkers at once, going Dutch with girls you don't want to see again, and that short men should wear lifts because, and I quote, 'the more height you have on her, the more she'll respect you.'"

Sebastian sat forward. "The column—"

"I know," I said. "It's *Badvice*—fake, terrible advice that the exposé definitely misled readers into believing was true. That's how I know the columnist was looking for a certain reaction. But the reason I agreed to take on this assignment is because I know you guys can do better than this."

Sebastian sat back again and picked up his coffee. I expected him to retort, but instead, he seemed to be listening. Maybe I was getting through to him. Or maybe the exposé already had. His demeanor had softened since I'd brought it up. Was he actually ashamed of the things they'd printed? And just how much of it was true?

Albert grimaced. "*Badvice* doesn't really work if it's not, um, a little . . . polarizing."

"Polarizing is okay," I said. "But I'd still like to phase it out."

Sebastian's mask slipped back into place. "You're missing the point of it—and *Modern Man*—completely."

"I promise I'm not here to turn you all politically correct," I said. "That's not what this pub is. Instead, we're going to elevate it. I want to immediately disassociate you guys with the sexist label. For the long-term, I want to make you a better magazine. When it comes to women, be deliberate, not callous." I flipped to the profile of Sebastian, one of the seven men in publishing that'd been targeted. It was accompanied by an image of him at an event in a tuxedo, grinning off to the side with a girl on each arm. I'd seen it more than once over the past week, but with only days to prepare, I'd been much more focused on the article's content.

I cleared my throat and read a paragraph off the screen.

"'Hemingway and Bukowski were maligned for their machismo, but at least they contributed significantly to American literature. Quinn and his team of equally objectionable men make no apology for their juvenile humor and misogyny. One source who prefers to remain anonymous claims Quinn told her 'the magazine is full of shit, but would you flush a golden turd?' Golden, because it has been said that *Modern Man* is one of the fastest growing publications of the decade. *We* say there's nothing modern about sexist rhetoric that pushes an old-school agenda to value women based on how they can serve men. *Modern Man* treats all women as sex objects.'"

I glanced at Sebastian, whose jawline had sharpened. Though I didn't wish this kind of character assassination on anyone, I was glad to see the words on the screen were getting to him. It would be easier to get him to let me help navigate him through these next couple months.

I skipped to the next passage I'd highlighted. "'The

creative director is no better. A love-'em-and-leave-'em lothario, he and his sidekicks treat the city like their playground, attending each party, restaurant, and club with a new 'delicacy' on their arms (a term that comes directly from Quinn's write-in *BadVice* column, in which he frequently associates women with food). Quinn's affinity for damaging beautiful women and flashy cars has landed his name on Page Six more than a few times. It's time for him to go. The good news? If he keeps it up, the magazine will soon be as obsolete as his caveman ways.'"

The room remained quiet. Sebastian had stopped clenching his teeth, but he tapped the end of his pen on his notepad in a slow, steady rhythm. I couldn't tell if he was more pissed or pensive, but I'd ripped off the Band-Aid and now the healing could begin.

Justin broke the silence. "A lot of that is overblown," he said. "There was *one* accident several years ago, and it wasn't even—"

"I never said that thing about the turd," Sebastian said. "At least not like that. I was trying to be clever, and she twisted my words."

"You know the source?" I asked.

"She's a woman I . . ." He glanced at Justin for help.

"I see." Considering I'd been aware of Sebastian's playboy reputation, it came as no surprise that he'd scorned some women along the way. I'd seen firsthand how easy it would be to fall under his spell. I wanted Sebastian to know I wasn't there to tiptoe around his bad rap. "You fucked her, so she fucked you back."

A few of the guys, including Sebastian, widened their eyes. "Jesus, no," he insisted. "After the conversation she was referring to, she assumed she was leaving the party with me and wouldn't take no for an answer. I had to be blunt with her, and she didn't take it well."

I wasn't sure what to make of that. Did Sebastian see himself as such a catch that he was turning away women left and right? And could I really challenge that, considering his magnetism had left me nearly speechless earlier? I wouldn't blame Sebastian for fibbing to cover his ass, but that wouldn't get us anywhere. "Much like a lawyer," I said gently, "I need honesty so I can anticipate any incoming problems."

"What I just told you is the truth," he said.

"Well, to the public, truth doesn't matter," I said. "I'll also need to be made aware of any interoffice, ah, relations." It wasn't the first time I'd made that request of clients, so why was I fighting off the blush creeping up my neck? Because it was the first time my personal interest overcame my professional one. I'd soon know whether Sebastian and June were more than coffee buddies.

"There are no relations," Justin said with a sigh. "Believe me, I'd know. The gossip around here is slower than Garth's comprehension on a good day."

"He's right," Vance said. "Fraternization has been strictly forbidden since Dixon Media had some problems at another publication." Vance quickly added, "But never this one."

"So I was right," Sebastian said. "You're more or less here to babysit us."

"Don't be babies, and I won't have to," I replied.

Vance applauded. He'd heard some of this over the phone already, at least what I'd been able to pull together in such a short amount of time, but he still seemed impressed. A few joined in, and others looked to Sebastian for direction. He was definitely more than a boss to these guys. It irked me that he scowled. My presentation had been short, sweet, and backed by numbers—men appreciated that. There was no denying I'd made my point. Why wasn't he applauding? Because he didn't, others refrained as well.

"We'll do whatever we can to accommodate you, Miss Keller," Vance said.

I smiled out at the men, and a few smiled back. Progress. "Call me George," I said, addressing them all. "Except for you," I said to Sebastian when I caught him looking at my chest. I adjusted my neckline. "While I'm brandishing the whip, Miss Keller will be fine."

More laughing, and this time, Boris slapped Sebastian on the back. "Lighten up, Q."

Vance stood. "Thanks, George—"

"What's with the tank top?" Sebastian asked, shrugging Boris off. A smirk touched his face as he added, "Not exactly appropriate office attire." He settled back and stuck an ankle over one knee.

Even though I'd questioned my outfit earlier, the fact that Sebastian thought he had me made me want to do the opposite of shy away. So I went with it and addressed the room. "Someone spilled coffee on me this morning."

"No way," Garth said. "Are you all right?"

"Fortunately, it was iced." I caught the end of Justin's glance across the table. "The nearest store with clothing only had souvenirs," I continued, "so I was forced to improvise. But that's okay, because instead of telling you this next very important detail about myself, I can just show you."

A few men shifted in their seats as I slowly unbuttoned my blazer. Sebastian wore an unreadable expression but watched me, twisting his pen cap between his fingertips. I opened my jacket and stuck my hands on my waist to show off the logo printed across the front of the top. "I don't want there to be any doubt—I'm a Yanks girl through and through. I work fine with Mets fans, but that doesn't mean I've got to like them."

"Yankees man right here," Boris said, jumping up from his seat for a high five.

"You talking crap about my team?" Garth grinned and dangled a Mets keychain.

"I just want you all to know where I stand. Transparency is important to me," I said, returning his smile. "We'll save the real shit-talking for happy hour."

"There's an idea," Vance said, lighting up and turning to me. "The guys always go for a drink at the end of the week. Why don't you join them?"

I hesitated. While work-social events such as mixers, dinner meetings, and conferences were George's arena, happy hour could potentially veer into personal territory. I didn't think I could successfully make the transition from work to play, so I never tried if I could help it. "Maybe some other time," I said.

I shifted feet, and Sebastian gave me a once-over. "Got better plans?" he asked.

My plans involved a hunky Great Dane, an appropriate amount of junk food to ease first-week-at-a-new-school stress—a ritual that had carried over into adulthood—and switching the channels between reruns of *Flipping Out* and *House Hunters International*.

I wasn't sure if those plans were *better*, but they definitely sounded more appealing. My ex had gotten our friends in the breakup—more like he'd stolen them using the tactics that made him such a great salesman. He'd convinced them I was a drama-hungry liar, and he'd had to end things to stop enabling me. So, reality TV it was.

I dipped my head in an elegant, restrained nod I hoped would convey that yes, indeed, I'd already committed to a posh Upper East Side dinner party, a hip Williamsburg gallery opening, or candlelit yoga overlooking the Hudson.

And then Vance once again opened his big mouth, proving that while Sebastian was *Modern Man*'s greatest liability, Vance might be *mine*.

"What's the matter, Sebastian?" Vance asked. "Afraid your new co-manager will see firsthand how little game you have?"

"I have more game than anyone in this room, and you know it," Sebastian said.

"Actually, we *don't* know that." Justin nodded at me. "Now that we have a new member on the team."

I almost laughed. George could handle herself fine in a roomful of men. Georgina, on the other hand, not so much. What kind of after-work event required game anyway? But in order to earn their trust, I needed my team to believe that I understood men as well as women. "I do all right," I said with a half-smile. "But I try not to pick up dates at a work event if I can help it."

Sebastian laughed and raised his chin. "This isn't a work event. This is drinks at the local watering hole for those who can handle it. No office talk allowed."

The group looked on as Sebastian and I held each other's gaze. He'd posed a thinly veiled challenge meant to put me on the spot, and one I wasn't sure I could afford to turn down.

Vance plugged his ears. "I think this is the kind of stuff HR has warned me about," he said before leaning over to add quietly, "but off the record, this could be a great chance to demonstrate your earlier point."

"Which one?"

"About how using a common interest is a more effective way to meet someone than pretending to be someone else."

"Oh." The irony practically hurt. Who was I to teach anyone about dating? I glanced at my feet. "I don't really work that way. I mean, out in the field."

"If you don't test your theories, how do you know they work?" Sebastian asked.

I glanced up. Judging by the silence and all the eyes on us, Vance's comments hadn't been private at all. If I didn't say something, I'd start blushing.

"I'll bet Georgina can teach you a thing or two," Vance said.

"She'll probably be fighting off guys as soon as we walk in the door," Justin said, winking and nodding as if encouraging me—as if he thought he was being *helpful*.

Sebastian studied me, seemingly curious about my response. A flush began working its way up my neck. "Just another Thursday night," I said, but my voice had lost some of its confidence.

He tilted his head as if he'd caught me in a lie. "Yeah? I'd like to see that. Figure out what I've been doing wrong all these years." His eyes sparkled as my confidence drained.

"I'm not here to teach you how to get a date," I said, which was laughable considering women obviously flocked to him.

"But that's what the magazine is about, and if you're going to come in and start changing things, you should know what you're dealing with," Sebastian said. "We help men level up. Teach them how to refine their palates, decorate an apartment, build the perfect fire, and assemble IKEA furniture without breaking a sweat. If you think we learn these things to impress our friends . . . well, I'm not sure this magazine is the right fit for you."

"It's true." Justin gave me a short nod. "We do all that to get laid."

Vance pointed at Justin. "Comments like that are the reason we're in this mess."

"You make them all the time, sir," Justin said.

"Which is why we need Miss Keller," Vance said. "And not just from nine-to-five. We could all stand to be better men in and out of the office." He clapped his hands together once. "So, happy hour it is."

Crap. How had I gotten myself into this? I wasn't even equipped for a rough-and-tumble night out with these guys, much less proving to them that I could score. Excluding Sebastian, it'd been months since a man had even *tried* to strike up a conversation with me. If these guys found that out, they might not trust me to helm this ship. Yet happy hour was also prime bonding time.

Before I could answer, Sebastian shot to his feet. "Is this presentation over? It was fun and all, but some of us have real work to do."

"It can be fun *and* enlightening," I said, looking up at him. "I'm looking forward to taking this publication in a better direction with you, Mr. Quinn."

"If you're proposing we walk on eggshells to please people *outside* of our demographic," he said, gesturing behind me at the slides, "then I assure you, that direction will be down."

He left the room without another word, and everyone looked at me. I put on a solid smile, even though his dismissal stung after all the effort I'd made to include him. "He must be a Mets fan. They're famous for getting butt hurt."

The men laughed. "Actually, it's worse," Garth said. "He's from Boston."

Boston? Shit. No wonder we'd been butting heads. I should've known, but I'd let his dazzling good looks and spotty reputation blunt my normally keen enemy radar. If

Sebastian rooted for the Red Sox over the Yankees—and if he was from Boston, then he did—that made us natural rivals. For some reason, going up against Sebastian made my nerves flare more than the usual stumbling blocks I encountered at a new job. Was it just because my confidence had taken a hit after my breakup with Neal—or was it that Sebastian had witnessed me in a vulnerable moment before he'd even learned my name?

The thought that he'd already gotten under my skin on the first day bothered me more than anything. He was as much the boss as I was, and in order for this arrangement to work, I needed his support.

Vance leaned over. "He'll cool down. You can smooth it out after the meeting."

As I buttoned up my blazer, one of the men rose to give me his spot. I thanked him as I took the chair. I was on track to earning the respect I'd need for a smooth working environment. Well, mostly smooth.

For now, I just had to focus on making it through the week—or at least to happy hour.

4

I'd stormed out of the morning meeting prematurely.

I returned to my office and sat heavily at my desk. I enjoyed almost everything about my job, even Mondays. Often times, *I* reigned from the front of the room—Mufasa, King of the Pride Lands. I sat up straighter in my seat. If I were an animal, I'd be a lion, commanding the rest of the jungle, watching from a rocky overhang as my kingdom sang showtunes.

I hummed "The Circle of Life" as I opened my yellow legal pad and wrote *Quiz idea: Which alpha male cartoon character are you?*

Next, I took my black leather agenda from a drawer and scribbled a reminder for my assistant: "*The Lion King* Broadway tickets."

I rubbed my temples. This time last week, I'd had no idea what was to come. Within days, Vance would bring in an outsider to do my job. And not just anyone—a woman. For a *men's* magazine. And Vance actually bought into her shtick. I hadn't been worried about the exposé's call to fire me, but Vance had never made a comment to me like the earlier one about restructuring. For years, I'd been revered for taking this magazine from near failure to hit success. I'd thought that was enough to overshadow a few bad quarters, but maybe I'd been wrong.

If Vance needed to try this to prove I was as good as it got, then so be it. It was only eight weeks. Eight weeks of dealing with the brash, rude, Yankees-loving Georgina Keller. Clearly my judgment had been cloudy this morning if I'd mistaken her for shy.

Having her around wouldn't be pleasant, and I'd promised myself I was done with women like her, but this time, it wasn't really up to me.

At ten-thirty on the dot, a knock at my door was almost definitely Justin with a fresh round of donuts and coffee. He didn't do well on Monday mornings, when he was still in weekend mode—or Friday afternoons, for that matter. Or basically any weekday after three o'clock.

My stomach grumbled. "Come in."

The door opened, but chestnut-haired, pint-sized George stepped in. Justin was nowhere to be seen. I automatically dropped my gaze to her blazer, looking for the thin tank top beneath it, for a flash of Yankees blue. She complemented a cheap jersey with Christian Louboutin pumps. I'd noticed those at the coffee shop as I'd snuck a peek at her legs—all my girlfriends had owned a pair of Louboutins or two. Or five. How could I have missed that glaring clue about the type of woman she was?

Ah—this was why. Because at this very moment, Georgina looked the opposite of how she had in the conference room. She wrung her hands in front of herself and worried her bottom lip between her teeth in a way that made me want to *be* that lip.

Fuck. I needed to get my head on straight. Fantasizing about the enemy wasn't a good way to kick things off.

"Um, about this morning," she said. "I wanted to apologize."

"For calling me an entitled asshole? Or implying that I thought I was better than others when I was the only one to stand up for your 'friend'? Or for the way you tried to embarrass me just now in the conference room?"

"To be fair, you embarrassed yourself," she said, the corner of her mouth ticking up. "Storming out like a child —is that how you earn respect around here?"

"I said *trying* to embarrass me. You'll have to work a little harder to pull it off."

"Noted," she said with a slight jerk of her head.

"Is that it?" I asked. "Did you come in here just to *not* apologize?"

"Oh—uh, no." She looked thoughtful a moment. "Since Vance hadn't planned on my services, and my position is temporary, there's no office for me."

"That's a shame," I said, leaning back in my seat. She really did have a nice figure. The old me would've fixated on that. The old me, I figured, might've even found her sharp tongue a turn on. Yes, she possessed characteristics I'd sworn off of, but in some small almost imperceptible ways—the tremor in her voice, the softness in her eyes— she also seemed like what I was looking for: the antithesis of my usual type. But my *usual* type wore Louboutins, spoke down to the help, and had no problem throwing the word *asshole* around.

". . . and I know it isn't ideal," she said, "but I think it'll be good for both of us."

I raised my eyes. "What will be good?"

Her brows knit. "You and me. Together."

You and me. Together. This morning, I would've liked those sentences strung together a whole lot more. "Huh?"

"Did you hear anything I just said? Vance would like us to share an office—"

I shot forward, and my leather chair squeaked. "What?"

She shut her eyes, sighed, and shook her head. "If you have to stare at my breasts, at least try to listen at the same time. Otherwise, this will never work."

My mouth dropped open. Had I been that obvious? I scoffed. "Actually, I was shooting imaginary lasers at your Spankees jersey."

"No, you weren't."

"Modest, aren't we? I assure you, your breasts are safe from me."

"Why's that?" she asked, cocking her head.

I paused. I'd expected something more along the lines of "Thank God for that." "Because you aren't my type."

She glanced away for only a second. "Then sharing an office shouldn't be a problem. We won't have to worry about those pesky non-fraternization rules."

She was *teasing* me. Or was she flirting? Certainly not— she'd be a stickler for the sexual harassment policies. But then what about that skintight top she'd just flaunted? I refrained from growling, angry that she was getting under my skin. "I'm sorry, but I don't have the space."

She gave me a knowing, if not terse, smile. "You have more space than anyone other than Vance."

"Then impose on him."

"He's not even on this floor, and anyway, he wants me in here. Says it makes the most sense since you and I will be working closely together. And I won't be an imposition, promise."

"My desk is organized just the way I like it," I said. "Everything has its spot, and I don't do well with people touching my things."

She glanced at my desk. "Vance is trying to arrange one for me. I mean, it certainly won't be anything like *that*, but . . ."

I frowned. "Like what?"

"Did you blow your first paycheck on office furniture? What is that, mahogany?"

"It is, actually."

She opened her purse and pulled out her phone as she murmured something about overcompensating.

That was the *last* straw. *Overcompensating*? Fuck no.

By city standards, my cock qualified as a small skyscraper.

I had so much junk, the New York City Sanitation Department had tried to haul it away.

The only private dick more famous than mine was Sherlock Holmes.

I started to suggest she dial up *any* of my exes to see if I had reason to overcompensate, but my desk phone rang. I snatched up the receiver. "What?"

"Is George Keller there?"

"Jesus Christ," I muttered. "This is *my* office. Sebastian Quinn."

"I know, Mr. Quinn. It's Mary at the front desk. Is George there?"

I sighed and glanced up. Georgina was trying so hard not to smile that deep, deep dimples formed in her cheeks. Those were new. I might've found them cute if I wasn't sure she was giddy over annoying me. "She's here."

"Will you let her know some boxes have just arrived from her office?"

I hung up. "There's stuff for you at reception."

"Oh, good." Georgina put her phone away. "It's supplies and a bunch of research and data. I prefer paper over digital. Easier to sort through. But that means the boxes get a little . . . heavy."

"Lift from the knees," I said, returning to the notepad in front of me. I'd never claimed to be a gentleman. Well, I *had*. Several times, in my articles, but that was work. In my personal life, I was a gentleman where it counted—like any time I was in the presence of my sister or late mother. Or when I was on a date or trying to get one. It wasn't as if I wanted to sleep with George.

I cringed. George-*ina*.

If I was going to get in the habit of thinking even remotely sexual things about her, I had to stop referring to her as George.

Once she'd left, I flipped the page of the legal notepad in front of me and wrote, *Chivalrous Acts of a Modern-Day Gentleman.*

One—look into her eyes during conversation, not at her breasts. They say eyes are the window to the soul. Crawl through that window and right into her bed.

Two—she made you wait twenty-five minutes on her living room couch while she got ready? Instead of complaining, tell her she looks beautiful. She might bestow you with a quickie right there. This is where the couch shines. It's the couch's moment of glory. All the ass it has to endure, it does it in hopes that one day, you'll get laid on top of it. Do it for the couch.

Three—take care of her during a rainstorm. Give her your jacket if she's cold, hold your umbrella over her, and walk closest to the street in case of splashing. Keep her dry now for the opportunity to make her wet later.

Four—help her move. Moving to a new place, even if it's down the block, can be daunting. Take a day off from Netflix and Chili Cheese Fritos to lend your girl a hand. Lift her literal box to get access to her metaphorical one.

It needed some tweaking, but it would work. And yet,

in place of pride, I felt a twinge of something I couldn't quite identify. Instead of being a gentleman, I'd sat there writing about it. Once again, I wondered what my mom would say about that.

I stood and went to the front, where I found Georgina bent over *her* literal box.

Which looked to be the size of a small house.

"Let me get that," I said.

She glanced up, surprised to see me. "Oh. Really?"

"Sure. I have a feeling I'll be missing arms day at the gym tonight anyway." I'd surely be staying late to try to reverse all the damage Georgina had planned for us. I dropped to a squat and lifted. Behind the box sat another smaller one. "I'll come back for that."

"I've got it," she said, bending over to pick it up.

As much as I liked the view of her surprisingly round, tight ass, I blurted out, "*Knees*, Georgina. I was serious earlier. You'll hurt your back otherwise."

"Knees, got it," she said, crouching to wedge her fingers under the box. As she hoisted it up, she said, "And thank you."

I returned to my office, set her things by the couch, then reassumed my throne to review my notes.

"Got something there?" she asked as she entered the room.

"An article I just wrote."

"Let's hear it."

"Maybe later."

She sighed and dumped the box with a *thud*. "Look, Sebastian. I'm here for the next two months. You don't have to like it, but you do need to accept it."

"It's not that—I just don't share my work until I've had time to perfect it."

"That's a great tenet for a *monthly* publication," she

said, not bothering to hide her sarcasm. "Did you write it in the five minutes I was gone?"

I leaned back in my chair, twirling my pen. "Impressed?"

"Speediness doesn't impress me. I prefer men who take their time."

I caught myself before I laughed—apparently *I* appreciated a woman who could land a good burn. "I take my time where it counts."

Was this the real Georgina, or was it an act? I hadn't missed her discomfort during talk of happy hour—which was why I'd pushed her to accept the invitation. I wanted to know why I kept encountering two seemingly different sides to her personality.

She pulled a Ziploc bag as big as her head from the box, scooped out a handful of gummy bears, and popped them in her mouth. She wandered over to my desk and read my notepad upside down. "The first two—eye contact and couch sex—have nothing to do with chivalry," she said, chewing. "The team can work with the others, though."

"I never said it was a final draft, and anyway, I don't usually open up my pieces for feedback."

"It'll be a good practice for everyone, including you. In fact, let's bring in digital. This would make for a good webisode in the Quickie Series."

I cocked my head. "We don't have a Quickie Series."

"We could." She unbuttoned her blazer and dropped onto the couch like she'd done it a hundred times. "Our unique visits are lagging around a million hits a month. It should be higher for a magazine with our circulation. Just off the top of my head, we could do short videos with tips on how to woo a woman."

I glanced at my notes and crossed off the part about

the couch. If George was going to take up residence on mine, then couches had to remain asexual.

"How to woo a woman?" I repeated. "Pretty sure it's been done."

"Not in sixty seconds. Data shows people are more likely to watch a video that's under a minute."

Being the busy man that I was, I already knew that from personal experience. If I needed help getting laid—which I did *not*—I might actually watch that. Maybe even for fun. Especially if it involved a hot chick. I reviewed the list from a woman's point of view, envisioning top model Aliana Balik on the screen, reading in her Polish accent . . .

"Open the car door for me, and I'll race you to the backseat. Zero to sixty is nothing. I can have you raring to go in ten seconds flat."

Ooph. I saw stars, little Aliana-faced stars. Yeah, I'd watch the hell out of that series, tentatively called *Gone in Sixty Sex*—or better, *secs. Sixty Secs in the City* . . .

The sound of George rustling through her things again derailed my idea train. I wanted to discuss this with Peterson from web, but did I need to go through George now? It was her idea after all, but was scooping her worse than having to get permission? How would that look to my guys?

"What the hell do you have in there besides a family-size bag of gummy bears?" I asked.

Georgina, elbow deep in a box, glanced up. "Office supplies, handbooks, data binders, that kind of stuff. I'm looking for my laptop."

My mouth fell open. "There's enough stuff in there to lose a computer?"

She ducked her head and continued rifling. "No, it's just—sometimes I, like, have a hard time keeping track of things. Must be the George in me. He's messy, like most men."

I grimaced. "I wish you wouldn't refer to yourself as a man."

"I didn't. I referred to the man *inside* me."

It was my turn to go red in the face. Had she seriously just said that? Was she so naïve that she didn't catch the double entendre, or was she just trying to throw me off?

She straightened up, laughing. "I'm sorry. Sometimes, I have a juvenile sense of humor. I'm not as buttoned up as you probably think."

"I didn't say you were. I just prefer you to be Georgina instead of George."

She visibly flinched at that but shut it down quickly with a clearly forced smile. "Wouldn't the absence of breasts make it easier to work with me?"

I slammed my mouth shut. It reeked of a trick question. "Did you know who I was down in the coffee shop?"

She didn't respond right away. "Obviously not."

"Why is that obvious?"

"I would've said something."

"I don't know that. You might've been spying for something to use against me later."

She held up a stapler. "Oops. I don't think I was supposed to take this from my last assignment." She glanced at me. "Do you think I'm out to get you?"

My gut response was no, but I wasn't sure I could trust it. She was proving to be quite the actress—small and meek one moment, then down my throat the next. "I think you like power."

"Who doesn't?" Next, she pulled out a small, diamond-shaped award and studied it. "For an essay I did on the underrepresentation of real women in media."

I nodded. "I have awards too."

Sort of. The soccer trophy on the shelf behind me was from a thrift store. Justin had covered the plaque with a white label and written "Sexiest Beast in the Northeast" in black marker.

"What's a real woman?" Georgina didn't strike me as the type to be insecure.

"Do you really want to know?"

"Why wouldn't I? I love women."

"I don't know you very well, Mr. Quinn, but I get the feeling you don't date or even *know* any real women."

That was a fucked-up assumption. Maybe I didn't have the most diverse dating track record, but anyone who dared call my mom or sister fake was asking for trouble. "Try me."

"Okay. How about this? Five pounds that won't budge for the life of you. Stretch marks. Ill-fitting undergarments. Period stains. Bunions that take your favorite heels out of rotation. Roots."

I struggled to keep up. I'd been with my fair share of women, and had grown up with two, but these weren't familiar problems. Except maybe period stains—Mom had taught me how to remove anything from any garment, sometimes against my will. "What do you mean by roots?"

She patted the top of her head. "You know—if we're not diligent with our stylists, our true colors start to show."

Damn. I studied her. She wasn't a full-on redhead, more autumn day than summer heat, but I'd assumed it was natural, and I usually had good instincts about these things. "You too?"

With a sly smile, she said, "I'm not telling."

George had nice hair, so much that it almost threatened to overpower her. With her back to me this morning, it was the first thing I'd noticed when I'd walked into the café. A cascading blend of chocolate, maple syrup, and mahogany—just a few of my favorite things. I let my eyes wander a little lower. "I don't see five pounds."

"That's because I've perfected my ability to hide them." She laughed. "Or you just aren't looking hard enough."

I'd never heard a woman laugh about extra weight before. If Georgina thought she was up five pounds, most likely they were located in her northern region. As in, her cup filleth over. As in, she had big tits for such a small girl.

The flirt in me was about to suggest she take off her clothes so I could check for any other *insecurities*—such as ill-fitting undergarments or stretch marks, both of which I doubted existed—but I bit my tongue. Now that I knew the situation, there was only one thing I wanted less than to be interested in her, and that was her thinking I might be.

"And no, you cannot check the fit of my bra," she said, calling my eyes back up to her face.

Christ. Not only had she read my mind, *and* stolen my comeback, but she'd caught me looking. Again. I couldn't resist. With attractive women, flirting was a reflex, like fist bumping after a soccer goal, taking a shot placed in front of me, or tearing up during *Titanic*.

Yet, with our conversation, the tension in the room alleviated a little. Our easy banter reminded me of how I was with Justin or the guys on my team, but I couldn't forget how Georgina had shown her true colors earlier at the café—and I wasn't talking about her hair.

5

"Should we get started?" Georgina asked. Seated on my office couch, she'd returned to searching her box for the state of Rhode Island or whatever else she was storing in there.

I looked down at the simple yellow legal pad on my otherwise tidy desk. I'd already started. Without her. Because this was my job and my office. "Be my guest."

"I thought we could call a meeting with your—*our* team. This morning was a good overview, but I want to get into the nitty gritty. Come up with a strategy."

"We meet after lunch."

"Well, let's try things differently today." She brought her laptop over, pulling up a chair to the opposite side of my desk. "I just want to let them know where we stand."

I sat back. "Where do we stand?"

"That's what we're going to figure out." She opened her laptop and tried to power it on before returning to the box. "Hmm, strange. I could've sworn I packed my charger. I'll just have to do it old school."

After what felt like ten minutes of her sifting through

more things, and then her purse, and then a tote bag, even I was exhausted. "Need something to write on?" I asked.

"Yes, please." She came back, smiled sweetly, and took the spiral bound pad and pen I offered. Instead of sitting, she switched off the overhead light and raised the blinds the last few inches. "Do you mind? I can't stand artificial light during the day."

I followed her with my eyes as she returned. "Sure."

"Thanks." She shoved more gummy bears in her mouth and began to pace. "What did you think about what I said this morning?"

I set my elbows on the desk, lacing my fingers in front of my face, and tried to think of a diplomatic response. "I thought it was bullshit."

I'd climbed every rung of my career ladder. I'd spent enough years kissing ass and kowtowing to rich kids to get here. Why was I still biting my tongue? So I could end up taking direction from an amateur?

She stopped walking and glanced up from the notepad. I waited for her reaction, hoping she wouldn't rat me out to Vance, or worse—cry again. Women's tears made me think of my mom and sister and the payback I'd exact on anyone who made them cry. Had my morning been different, and my job hadn't been at stake, I would've gone after Georgina earlier to apologize.

She smiled. "Thank you."

"Why are you thanking me?"

"I work best with people who are direct. I have no time for men who think they might hurt my feelings." She resumed pacing, making a note on her pad as she rushed out, "By the way, this morning was out of character for me, and I assure you it won't happen again. That's why I wanted to apologize."

I lowered my hands from my face but remained wary.

Was this like the time one of our editorial models had told me she was okay with no-strings-attached sex a month before my doorman had caught her graffitiing my front door while I'd been on a date with another woman?

"So which part exactly did you think was bull?" she asked before I could respond.

"There were a few things." I leaned in as if to tell her a secret. "But mostly, we're not a women's magazine."

"I never said you were."

"So why would we market to them? Our female demographic is low because they're not the heart of this magazine. Can't win 'em all, know what I mean?"

"Mr. Quinn—Sebastian?"

I refrained from rolling my eyes. We'd already discussed breasts and stretch marks. She'd accused me of being entitled, and I'd called her an imposition. We'd blown right by formalities before we'd even officially met. I nodded for her to continue.

"Who do you think buys magazines? I've looked over *MM*'s reports, and for the website, focusing largely on the male readership makes sense. Men mostly browse and make purchases online. They subscribe to the magazine, and *typically*, we have them for life after that because they're too lazy to unsubscribe."

"You mean the magazine's too good to unsubscribe from."

"But the decline in print sales could set a distressing trend, and it'll impact advertisers' budgets," she said, ignoring me. "Women are generally the ones out shopping and spending money during the day—grocery stores, malls, bookstores."

"You're not."

She pulled back a little, her mouth opening. "That's because I—"

"Don't you think you're generalizing a bit? And, on top of that, you're not describing the *modern-day* woman."

"Show me your research."

"It's sitting right in front of me. You're a woman in our target age range. I don't see you out shopping on a week-day, keeping house for your man."

"That isn't what I—come on, Sebastian. I didn't pull this out of my ass. My research is based on facts." She returned to the desk for more candy as she fixed her eyes on me. Their crystal-clear lime color was unusual, yes, and a little distracting, but I was a goddamn professional. I'd get past that. "In the United States," she said, "and defi-nitely outside of New York, women are still the primary sex frequenting places magazines are sold. When that data shows something different, we'll have a different conversation."

She shoveled more gummies into her mouth and stepped out of her heels, which probably put us about eye level now considering I was seated. I narrowed my eyes as she resumed walking around the room. She could show me a graph indicating women were responsible for a hundred percent of consumer spending for their households, and I still wouldn't admit defeat. Not after a few measly hours with her. "What about single men?"

"I'm not looking for either-or. I want all relevant demo-graphics. Over forty percent of your readers are married." She hummed to herself as she chewed and swallowed, then scribbled on her pad. "Why are they reading about how to pick up women? Maybe they still like to surprise their wives."

"If we start writing articles and choosing layouts with women in mind, then we're a women's magazine. We'll lose all brand recognition."

"I agree." She stopped at my window overlooking

Eighth Avenue. "I'm not after that reader, but there are subtle tweaks we can make to appeal to women, too. Like you said, we're going after modern women. The ones who're tired of reading about the latest nail polish trend or impossible-to-achieve sex positions. The woman who—"

"Impossible to achieve?" I asked, unable to help the rising corner of my mouth. "Show me your research."

She came and sat down, rolling her eyes. "I'm just saying, when you print an article on the same topic every month, you're bound to get a little *too* creative. Do you honestly think the Double-Fisted Flying Squirrel is doable?"

At the same moment my mouth fell open, my dick twitched. And the scary part was, I wasn't even sure why. There was nothing sexy about squirrels, but I liked the way her mouth curved when she talked about sex positions. "The *what?*"

"That's nothing compared to the *Upside Down* Double-Fisted Flying Squirrel," she added. "You'd have to be a member of *Cirque du Soleil* to pull that off."

This was about the last conversation I'd expected to be having this morning. I'd been counting on steamrolling some middle-aged man by Friday. I openly gaped at her. "Are you making this up?"

"We're getting off track. What I'm trying to say is, there are women out there who want to read about sports or who'd love to learn how to brew their own beer. So why aren't they?"

"They are." My sister got *Modern Man* every month, but was that only because of me? I visited her and her husband in the Boston suburbs as much as I could, and they rarely got into specifics about the issues. Libby wasn't our target audience at all. She ran her own clothing boutique and had a double-wide stroller with kids to put in it. Her clothing staples included expensive leather flats, cardigans, and pearls, and she had a standing appointment for a blowout every week. While I'd been at baseball practice as a kid, she'd "cleaned" houses with our mother as an excuse to spy on rich kids' violin lessons or tea parties or etiquette classes. I wondered for the first time if she actually enjoyed the articles we printed, or if she'd just been indulging me all this time.

"I have lots of female friends who read the mag," I said, "and I've heard no complaints."

"You're not talking to the ones who *don't* read it. They pass over *Modern Man* because they don't know what we have to offer. Because we aren't marketing to them. Because we openly insult them."

Her eyes flickered away with that last part. What she meant was that *I* had openly insulted them, or at least, I was catching all the heat for it. I drummed my fingers on my desk. "I see your point."

Her perfect posture eased. "You do?"

"Yes, but I still don't know what you're suggesting. That we print bylines in script font? Incorporate pink onto the cover? Host a bake sale?"

Her jaw ticked. Finally, we were getting somewhere. She'd been way too cool about all of this when she secretly wanted to tell me to fuck off the way she more or less had that morning.

"Did you hear a word I just said?" she asked. "This isn't the fifties, and I'm not trying to turn you into a chick lit rag."

Justin strolled in wearing a shit-eating grin, but that was nothing unusual. It was his default expression. "What's for lunch?" he asked before he spotted Georgina.

"Lunch?" she asked, checking her watch. "It's barely eleven."

Justin maneuvered around her boxes and flopped onto the couch. He put an arm along the back. "Yeah, but we need to brainstorm about what we're going to eat, and that can take up to an hour."

"Is that so?" Georgina asked, pursing her lips. "Sounds productive."

I sliced a finger across my neck to get Justin to shut the fuck up. He always knew exactly how to make things worse. "Give us a minute, Justin."

Justin raised his palms. "I'm not even here."

"You need a crash course on gender stereotyping," Georgina said, turning back and picking up the conversation as if Justin wasn't even there. "Honestly, I'd really hoped the sexism rumors were an exaggeration, but I'm starting to think they're not."

"You don't know me," I said. "Don't come in here accusing me of things after a few hours. *You're* the one implying women do nothing but shop all day." I loved women. *Loved* them. If I was sexist against anyone, it would be men—I'd kick Justin to the curb in a second for a beautiful woman, and Justin would do the same to me. Beyond that, I treated the women in my life like queens. *Past and present.*

"Oh, please. You just suggested we add pink to the cover and call it a day. As if that's enough to get a woman's attention—"

"You should listen to him," Justin chimed in. "If anyone knows how to get a woman's attention, it's Seb."

"Shut *up*," I told him before looking back at Georgina. I had no idea if it was Justin's comment or our arguing, but she'd worked herself into a tizzy. As if she'd just run around the block or escaped to the bathroom for a quickie, her cheeks had gone pink, her eyes narrowed, breathing labored.

What would she look like, pinned against the locked door of the men's bathroom, legs circling my waist, lacy black bra peeking out from a crisp button-down, hair messy from my hands as she begged me to finish her off?

Fuck!

Why was I thinking about sex? I pushed the fantasy out of my mind . . . even though I had a shameful feeling I'd revisit it later.

"*You* need an education on gender discrimination, and discrimination in general," I pointed out. "You assume that because I work here and look the way I do, that I have no consideration for women—"

"Oh my God." She scoffed. "I mean, *wow*. In a city of arrogant men with overinflated egos, you really take the cake."

That was utter bullshit and proved that Georgina was completely clueless about me and my past. I'd not only battled through overinflated egos but had gritted my teeth as I'd done my best to blend in by faking arrogance and privilege. And I'd managed to keep a level head through all of it. "There you go assuming again about things you know nothing about."

"I don't operate off assumptions. I employ facts, and the *fact* is you've been nothing but a complete jerk since you dumped coffee all over me this morning."

"*I've* been a jerk? *Me*?" My temper rose. *She* was the one who'd run into *me*. *She* had gone from zero to sixty, cutting as deep as she could and without mercy, accusing me first of entitlement and then of sexism. I surged to my feet, my office chair rolling back into a wall. "You think because you read some click-bait article that you have all the facts about me? You don't know where I've been, where I come from, or what matters to me." My voice had risen to an unnecessary level, but I couldn't help it. I pictured my mother walking through the door after work, her hair barely holding in its bun, her spirit broken from a long day of dealing with people who thought they were better than her. I was not and would never be the person who treated others, specifically women, like dirt—no matter what some dumb fucking article said, no matter what Georgina thought she knew. "You called me an asshole this morning, but at least I speak up for the people I care about."

"Sebastian—"

"Justin, I told you to shut up," I shot back.

Georgina's mouth hung open. "I tried to speak up, but you . . . you . . ." She stammered, then seemed to give up on the thought. "I can't believe I gave you the benefit of the doubt. You really do deserve your name in that article."

"Get out of my office. Both of you." Georgina and Justin stared at me. Already, my fury began to recede, but I didn't care. I wanted to be angry. People like Georgina Keller didn't deserve to get off the hook just for being pretty and pouty. "Fine." I picked up my cell and went around the desk. "*I'll* go."

They didn't try to stop me. I refrained from slamming the door on my way out. I couldn't really go anywhere—there was work to do, and I wasn't about to leave it in her hands—but I needed a breather.

I ended up in the men's bathroom, leaning my hands against the sink as I avoided my reflection by staring into baskets of disposable razors, aftershave, and deodorant.

Georgina had performed the rare feat of ruffling my feathers, and she'd done it twice in one day. I considered myself easy to get along with, but she clearly had something against me. It was also possible she just didn't like me.

It was uncommon for me, not only to be disliked, but to return the feeling. Men wanted to be me. Women wanted to be *with* me.

Lots of women.

I finally looked up, caught my eye in the mirror, and cringed.

"You assume because I work here and look the way I do . . ."

George had gone easy on me given that comment. I made a point to take care of myself—went to the gym five times a week, ate right, and as an editor of a men's lifestyle magazine, I got only the best products, usually free. I lifted my chin and inspected my jawline. I'd shaved meticulously that morning. In New York, you had to stay on your game. It was as if Georgina had seen through all that. I'd been treated a certain way since I'd hit puberty, shot up in height, and lost any baby fat. I'd been told enough times that I was handsome and charming, but Georgina didn't seem to care about any of that—not even that I also made an effort to be kind. I'd been living in a world opposite to the one in which I'd been raised, and staying grounded was easier said than done. Since accepting a hardship scholarship to Harvard, I'd gone from flipping burgers to feasting on gourmet Thanksgiving fare at my roommate's parents' mansion on Nantucket. Even if my peers had been forced into summer jobs in customer service or waiting tables, they'd never know the true struggle of a single mother working for, and sometimes below, minimum wage.

Why didn't Georgina see that about me?

And why wasn't I that way around her?

I almost hadn't helped carry her boxes across the office.

"You really do deserve your name in that article."

I'd learned early on that to move up, I had to play a part. I'd blown my first few real paychecks on a custom suit, had networked at every university event I could, and had been with women where dates had felt like a status exchange. My confidence had been hard-earned along with things like an enviable apartment, my playboy image, and exotic travel. I let my peer group and the media believe I was the kind of man who took a new woman home each night, hosted decadent parties in the Hamptons, and didn't mind blowing money on expensive things, but at the core of it, I'd thought I was still clutching to the values with which I was raised. I hadn't had a one-night stand in over a year, I always managed the events I hosted sober, and though I splurged on expensive things, I *did* mind. I only spent what I could expense or personally afford.

But was the exposé true? Was Georgina right? With the way I'd treated her, at some point, had I started to become the image I'd cultivated for myself—and was that the reason for what my mom had asked of me in our last conversation?

Justin burst into the bathroom. "Admiring the view, you narcissistic asshole?" he asked when he caught me staring at myself.

"What do you want?" I grumbled.

"You guys make a real cute couple, you know. I was enjoying the show until your accent surfaced. Then I knew she was in trouble."

I snorted. A classmate at Harvard had once told me he could tell which part of Boston I was from by my accent, and within weeks, I'd neutralized it. It only came out now when I was pissed. "She pushes my buttons, and I'm pretty sure she does it on purpose."

"What reason could she have?"

I pushed off the counter and leaned back against it, crossing my arms. "She's the one who called me an asshole at the coffee shop this morning."

"I figured that out. I think it was because earlier, you said she called you an asshole at the coffee shop this morning . . ."

I shook my head. "It's only been a few hours. How the hell am I supposed to work with her for eight weeks?"

"You're telling me you didn't even get the tiniest bit excited when she unbuttoned her blazer in the meeting?"

"No."

"Just a little? Like the first time a girl tries to finger your asshole? You're grossed out and confused, but you're also a little curious . . ."

"You're a sick fuck, you know that?"

"But I make a good point."

"I was too disgusted by her presentation to be turned on," I lied. Admitting even remote interest in her would be a huge mistake. Justin would run with it.

"All right." Justin scratched the base of his neck, his expression easing. The bastard rarely even wore a tie to the office. "But did she really deserve the hellfire you just unleashed?"

I hadn't moved past the childish stage of wanting to be mad at her. She'd given me plenty of reasons. "Yeah."

"This about your mom?"

I blinked, ready to give Justin a piece of my mind. But I didn't. Justin knew me too well. "Probably," I admitted.

"I figured. A year, man. I know it's been tough."

Tough wasn't even the half of it. If I'd had more time to prepare for Mom's death, would it have been different? Easier? Would I have handled it better instead of dropping the ball these past few quarters, landing myself in this position? I doubted it, because I couldn't imagine any of this being easier.

Justin sighed when I didn't respond. "Give Georgina a

chance, dude. Once she gets to know you, she'll see you're not the guy that exposé painted you out to be."

"She came in with preconceived notions."

"And for some reason, you're playing right into them." Justin frowned. "You're not that guy, are you?"

I hesitated. "No."

"Show her that. Take a minute. Cool off. I think you'll decide she's not as bad as you think."

Justin left the bathroom, which meant I was now alone with his words hanging in the air. This was about my mom. It didn't take a pro to figure that out. Adina Quintanilla was the best woman I'd ever known. For my sister Libby and I to live full, successful lives, she'd taken a lifetime of shit.

She'd worked the kinds of jobs I couldn't even wrap my head around. As a child, I hadn't liked it, but as an adult with money and an understanding of the nasty side of human behavior, envisioning my mom that way sometimes got to be too much.

Even though she would've preferred to shelter me from it, I'd often witnessed it firsthand. Her bussing diners' meals while Libby and I did homework at a nearby table. We'd been too young to stay home alone and too poor for a sitter.

What had I learned at that diner aside from multiplication tables? That some people cared more about their burgers than about being decent human beings. When I'd asked my mom why people spoke to her that way, she'd shrugged it off and tried to hide the fact that it hurt her. Mom had never had much of a poker face, though. Especially not with Libby and me.

Libby. *Fuck.* I'd been avoiding her calls today so I wouldn't have to shoulder her pain along with my own. On the one-year anniversary of our mom's death, it wasn't any easier to be without her. Maybe even harder. Libby and I had not only survived despite our beginnings, we'd thrived. But while money could make my mom comfortable in her home at the end, it couldn't stop cancer.

Mom had known it, and she'd still smiled until the end. Smiled, held my hand, and told me in her thick Mexican accent, "Stop dating girls you know you'll never end up with, *Sebastián*. Find a nice woman who loves you and treats you well. Treat *her* well. Love her. Be nice to her. Please, just find someone *kind*."

Wendy, who I'd been dating at the time, hadn't been that different from the ones who'd come before her. To say Libby and Mom hadn't liked her was putting it mildly. Wendy had been mean to Libby, my mom, Justin, wait-resses and valets, and she'd been mean to me. She'd also been smoking hot and adventurous in bed. That'd been enough for me back then. Not anymore. Now, I'd have given anything to go back in time and introduce my mom to a "kind" woman—someone she and Libby would like. And to be able to assure her that I wasn't alone in this world.

It appeared I wasn't going to find that with the social life I led now—bars, clubs, events, weekend getaways. In one day, Georgina alone had proven that even coffee shops were dangerous. Nowhere was safe, not even happy hour with the guys. She'd be infiltrating that too.

That was assuming, of course, that Georgina and I even made it to the end of the week.

6

I paced the sidewalk in front of Cantina Santino, willing myself to stay calm. As much as Justin had insisted that happy hour wasn't a work event, I needed to believe it was—or else transform Georgina into a completely different person in the next few minutes.

They were just my coworkers. Nothing more. I'd been working alongside them without incident so far. Of course, it helped that the workplace had clear boundaries, whereas happy hour had *none*.

And that Sebastian and I had been doing a decent job staying out of each other's ways.

My phone lit up with a call, and I answered on the first ring. "I'm not sure I can do this."

"Unless the objective is avoiding death or taxes, it can be done," my boss replied.

I checked the screen. I'd texted Luciano to call and talk me off the ledge, but instead, I saw Dionne's name. "Sorry," I said. "I thought you were Luciano."

"I just got back from Italy and wanted to check in. How's the assignment?"

"The men have been resistant," I said, double-checking that I was alone on the sidewalk, "but I anticipated that. I think some of them are coming around. The rest are waiting for someone to tell them I'm not there to burn the place down."

"Let me guess—that *someone* is Sebastian Quinn?" she asked. She and I had been e-mailing the last few days, and I'd briefly filled her in on what I was dealing with.

"Yep. Sebastian and I share an office, which makes it hard for him to ignore me completely," I said, "but we've mostly been working around each other. At some point before the next issue goes to press, he and I will have to collaborate."

"I have faith in you. That's why I put you on this assignment. So, what is it you don't think you can do?"

I glanced at the door to the cantina the men had just walked into. "Happy hour."

"You've been to plenty of those in your life."

"Not like this. It's not a work thing. More like hanging with the guys. Or, I'm afraid, initiation."

"Ah." After having spent enough time with me around Neal, Dionne was familiar with my insecurities outside working hours.

"I'm afraid if I don't bond with them, I'll make this whole assignment harder on myself. I'm not sure I'll ever get Sebastian on board, but at least his team is receptive."

"*Your* team," she said. "Don't let Sebastian push you around. Not at the office, and not outside of it. He'll get on board, because he has no choice."

"It's just that he . . . well, you know his reputation. He's not used to taking orders, especially from women."

"There's more to someone than their rap, Georgina. I don't let others walk all over me and that has earned me the *bitch* label, but anyone who knows me understands I'm not that."

Was Sebastian more than the image he projected, or was he an actual bad boy to handle with caution? I'd seen glimpses of both. Then again, he'd witnessed different sides of me as well. "At work, he's intimidating," I said. "Outside of the office . . . forget about it."

"Fight that feeling," she said. "Remember, he's not Neal. He's just a regular colleague."

She'd obviously never seen him in a suit. Or up close. Or at all. *Regular* guys didn't leave a trail of longing sighs in their wakes.

My phone beeped with an incoming call. "I'll come by the office tomorrow to debrief," I told Dionne.

"Good luck," she said and hung up.

I switched lines, but this time I answered with, "Can you teach me to be a bitch in sixty seconds?"

"I've been trying for years," Luciano replied, "but unfortunately it won't take."

"I don't know how to act in there. They think I'm someone I'm not—someone cool and confident with actual game."

Luciano didn't bother to mute his laugh. "Wait. Slow down," he said. "Where are you, and who thinks that?"

"My new boss wanted me to go to happy hour with the guys, so I'm here. I believe he said I could 'teach them a thing or two.'"

"Why does he think that?"

"I was critiquing their current methods by pointing out better ways to pick up women. My ideas make sense in theory, but I never thought I'd have to test them with everyone watching."

"Relax," Lu said. "Buy them a few rounds of drinks, and they'll forget all about that. And if they don't, just approach a man the way George would—like he's a situation to be handled."

"I *can't* be George in there, Luciano. I'm supposed to show them I can hang outside the office, but I *can't*. I don't want to turn into a wallflower and lose the shreds of respect I've started to earn the past few days."

"So Sebastián is coming around?"

"No, I meant with the other guys. Things haven't progressed with Sebastian."

"Well . . . for tonight, just try to look past the fact that he's drop-dead gorgeous."

"Is the *drop-dead* really necessary?" I asked. Why couldn't Sebastian just be *decent-looking*, or even just *attractive*?

"You're trying to work with him," he continued, "not sleep with him. Unless—"

"Don't go down that path."

"Why not, G? It's been like a year. I think you're officially revirginized."

"Luciano," I hissed, turning my back to the bar as if someone might hear. "It's barely been four months. Rude much?"

"Oh, yeah. I blocked out the part where you let your spineless ex sweet talk you into a 'closure' fuck. He's such a piece of shit."

"Totally," I agreed. During the months I'd been incapacitated by the breakup and prone to making excuses for Neal's behavior, I'd found it helpful to just agree with Luciano.

"You need to erase that experience with someone new," Luciano said. "And don't think I didn't notice you blushing in the café the morning you met Sebastián."

"Don't think *I* don't notice you're saying his name with an accent because it sounds sexier."

"I've been trying to get you to go Latin for years, *mi amor*."

"For your information, he's from Boston," I said. "And his last name is actually Irish. Like mine."

"He's Latin, believe me. If you'd like, I can teach you some Spanish words that'll blow his mind."

I rolled my eyes. "Dionne wouldn't take kindly to me fraternizing with a client. Besides, being 'on' all the time is taking it out of me. I can't wait to go home and curl up with a pint of Mocha Chocolate—"

"Don't you dare finish that sentence. You do not get to choose ice cream over men this often in one lifetime."

"I can't stay long anyway." I checked the time on my phone. "The sitter is about to leave."

"Oh, come on. Bruno'll be fine for a few hours."

"You're probably right. There's a ninety-nine percent chance he'll be sprawled out on the couch and dreaming of tennis balls until I walk in the door, but that one percent . . ."

"How long are you going to keep making excuses to be alone?"

"He's *not* an excuse—he needs me."

"Then I'll go hang with Bruno until you get home," he said. "There's a *Project Runway* marathon on anyway."

"I can't ask you to do that."

"You're not. I'm volunteering for the good of your sex life. Go get a stiff drink and an even stiffer cock."

"Oh my God. I told you, that's so not happening—"

He hung up before I could make a case for a life with just Bruno, a gay best friend, and documentaries about the reign of Catherine the Great.

I almost jumped when Sebastian spoke behind me. "You have a kid?"

I turned. He stood at his full height just outside the

door to the bar, jingling change in his pockets, his tie loosened around his neck. He'd still been at the office after I'd left late the night before, yet he didn't even have bags under his eyes. "I'm sorry?" I asked.

"You mentioned a sitter." He tilted his head as if I'd just posed a complex riddle. "Are you a mom?"

I took a quick mental inventory of my conversation with Lu once I'd turned my back on the bar. Had I said anything compromising? Anything Sebastian could use against me? Had he heard the part about how sexy his name sounded with a Latin accent? "Were you eavesdropping?"

"Just making sure we hadn't run you off already."

If he was teasing me, there was no hint of a smile on his face. "Give me more credit than that. I had a call to take."

He squinted down the street. With the onset of fall, days were getting shorter, but the sun was still setting. "So the kid," he said, turning back to me. Today's tie, the color of a cloudless sky, almost made his piercing eyes look blue. "Are you a single parent?"

"No." I had yet to see Sebastian this interested in me, and his focused gaze made my heart flutter. I tucked my hair behind my ear, almost wishing he'd let up, despite the fact that I'd been hoping for some kind of breakthrough with him. "Well, sort of."

"How is someone *sort of* a mom?"

"My dog." I smiled. "Bruno."

He raised his eyebrows. "You have a *babysitter* for your *dog?*"

I'd shored up this defense before. My ex hadn't understood my devotion to Bruno, or why I'd willingly take on the responsibility of a terminally sick dog. Not even

Luciano got it all the time, and he knew all the shitty details of my situation.

"How long are you going to keep making excuses to be alone?"

I could easily truncate this conversation with the truth, but Bruno's condition wasn't something I liked to talk about. Or think about. Or live through. I certainly wasn't about to open up about it to someone who couldn't care less about my personal life, so I went with another perfectly valid, totally truthful, but possibly less convincing argument.

"For your information, he's a big dog that needs a lot of attention," I said. "Not just exercise but mental and emotional stimulation."

"Emotional . . . stimulation."

"Smart dogs—and people for that matter, though I wouldn't expect you to understand that—need to occupy their brains or they get into trouble. When Bruno gets bored or tired, he chews up stuff or figures out ways to get into things he shouldn't, like the pantry."

"Is this an actual dog or a human?"

Ah. And *that* was the fundamental reason Sebastian and I would never get along. The issue wasn't our opposing management styles, rival sports teams, or clear personality differences. Sebastian was clearly not a dog person, while I would take a bullet for mine.

"There's no human I'd rather spend time with," I said, "so he might as well be one."

"I should've guessed by your unfortunate people skills that you'd be prone to anthropomorphizing, and now misanthropy too."

"And *I* should've known you'd hate animals," I snapped back.

Suppressing a smile, he held my stare and didn't deny the accusation. He dropped his eyes to my mouth. My neck. My chest, hips, and ankles. And still, didn't deny it. He just stood there, inspecting, studying, charting me like a map, or whatever he was doing.

"I can't quite figure you out, Georgina. Sometimes, you're one way . . . and then you go and act like . . ."

"A bitch?" I asked somewhat hopefully.

"*What?*" Sebastian's eyes widened. "I—God, no. You aren't exactly vanilla ice cream on a summer's day, but I wouldn't put it that way."

Plain, boring, and easily run over—was that how he saw me? And why did I care what he thought about me above anyone else, even Vance? Vanilla ice cream—*really?* "Why'd you come out here again?" I asked.

"To be polite and check on you. I know the guys can be intimidating."

"And what about you?" I asked.

"Me? I'm about as menacing as cinnamon."

If Sebastian's plan was to bewilder me into silence, it was working. I wasn't even sure there was an appropriate response to that. "I don't get it."

He shrugged, again jingling keys or change in his pocket. "Just a saying we have in New England."

"I've never heard it." I scratched my nose. "Maybe it's specific to your neighborhood. Which would be . . .?"

"I'm from Boston."

"I know, but I couldn't find much about your background beyond that. And I need to know these things." I sniffed. "To do my job."

He took a few steps back and opened the door to the bar, still facing me. "Knowing the neighborhood I grew up in is pertinent information?"

Knowing *Sebastian* was. And while his past eluded me, I still had a largely incomplete picture of him. "Yes," I said with conviction.

"Good to know." He gestured through the doorway. "Coming in or not? We're all waiting on you."

"Oh," I said, jumping into action. "Sorry."

"Well . . . that's better," he said as I passed.

At one end of the bar, my new coworkers had gathered under a string of paper flags in every color of the rainbow. "What is?" I asked, heading in their direction.

"You, not fighting me at every turn." Suddenly, he was right at my back, his voice lowered. "I much prefer it that way. I call, you come."

Chills traveled up my spine. I almost stumbled but managed to compose myself. Even if he hadn't meant it suggestively, it'd sounded that way—his voice low, warm breath at my ear. He wouldn't be able to see my furious blushing from behind me, but I suspected he knew anyway.

His words alone inspired a thrill I hadn't felt since my early days with Neal. A thrill that lasted all the way until we reached the group. But as the bartender looked right over my head to take Sebastian's order, I saw his comment for what it was—the first compliment he'd given me, and it had *doormat* written all over it.

"Call all you want, and see if I come," I said, walking away before he could respond.

7

Sebastian stayed at his end of the bar. Whether he scowled in my direction or ignored me completely, I wasn't sure since I avoided looking at him.

Justin came and set a shot in front of me. "Hanging in there?" he asked.

I nodded. "Why wouldn't I be?"

"You and Sebastian have put nearly the entire office between yourselves, not just tonight but all week. I was surprised you even showed up to work on Tuesday considering how he spoke to you the first day."

Which time? Sebastian had cut deep both at the café and in his office, and since I'd only seen his mood darken around me, it was becoming apparent I inspired that in him. Either way, I'd definitely struck a nerve in Sebastian Quinn, when all I'd really wanted was to do the opposite. Everyone's lives would be easier if he and I worked together instead of fighting each other at every turn. I even respected that Sebastian believed so strongly in his work and his team that he'd fall on his sword for it. But that was just the kind of thing I'd been hired to prevent. *Modern Man* needed a lifeline, not a deathblow.

"It'll take more than a tantrum to keep me away," I said.

Justin clinked his shot against mine and took it. "I wanted to tell you that Sebastian—he's a really good guy," he said, sucking on a lime. "I'm not just saying that because he's my boss and my best friend. He's a softie inside." His eyes lit up. "He volunteers on Thanksgiving, visits his sister every month, and cries during *Titanic*. He's got some personal issues, but he's good people."

I twirled my empty shot glass, trying to seem disinterested. It wasn't that I wanted Justin to tell me more about Sebastian's personal life, but I *did* have to work with the man. I needed to know if I should keep a straightjacket sized "big and tall" on hand, or if Sebastian was just throwing a hissy fit. "When you say issues . . .? I'm just asking in case I need to be concerned for my safety," I teased.

"Normal stuff. We all got 'em." Justin shrugged. "What're yours?"

I raised my eyebrows at him. "Now who's the job therapist?"

"The more I know, the more I can smooth the way for you and Sebastian. And, you know, whip you each into shape. Or you can whip each other—no judgment."

"Justin," I scolded.

He showed me his palms. "Sebbly's been pretty grumpy since the exposé came out, but I haven't seen him this worked up in a while."

"Sebbly?"

"Tip number one—don't call him that. I have all kinds of nicknames for him, mostly to use behind his back. He's anti-nicknames in general, thinks they're juvenile."

"What else do you call him?"

"I'll ease you in with Sebbly—a.k.a. Silly Seb. I also call him Hump Day Hottie on Wednesdays since he was dumb enough to use that in a piece once, or when he's in a mood, he's Se-*beast*-ian. I think he secretly likes that one."

Justin was the definition of a class clown, but it seemed as if he was also a great friend. "How did you feel about the exposé?"

"It sucked. Made us sound like a bunch of assholes."

"You guys *can* come off as assholes," I pointed out.

"That's the whole idea. Not to look like assholes, but to project an image men want to emulate—cars, parties, women. It doesn't mean we're actually these people. For Seb, it started in college. Networking came in many forms, and for a guy like him, it was crucial to his success. He's mild compared to the bros that went to colleges like ours. It's a wonder we turned out so well."

A guy like him? I was familiar. Luciano often called Neal a slimy salesman, but even before he'd sold insurance, he could get a "yes" out of almost anyone. In Sebastian's world, it sounded as if networking meant schmoozing, and sure—that was a necessary evil for getting ahead if that was important to Sebastian. It wasn't what you knew but *who*, and all that. "You went to Harvard also?"

"Penn State," Justin said. "But it was the same idea. Without a tough outer shell, you got squished by others on their way up."

As the article had said, from Cambridge to New York City, the world was Sebastian's playground—and women likely let him off the hook for everything. I hadn't necessarily pegged Sebastian as the silver-spoon type, but Justin described behavior stereotypical of a wealthy, attractive, Ivy League-educated man. They'd never had to work very hard for anything, and that explained why Sebastian hated having me around to monitor him.

"I'm not here to step on anyone's toes," I explained. Now that I had more facts, I could use them to stay in Justin's good graces—and hopefully work my way into Sebastian's. "I like to have fun at work. We can goof around as long as we meet our goals—goals we set together."

"The atmosphere around there is important to Sebastian. He protects his team fiercely, sometimes at the jeopardy of his own job."

Sebastian was one of the more passionate business-people I'd worked with. Would he actually risk his position for his team, or did a privileged life simply make him feel he was invincible? Either way, it explained why my presence frustrated him so much. Conviction, fear, or both—they were powerful motivators. "He *has* been at *Modern Man* a long time," I reasoned.

"His whole career," Justin agreed. "It was his first internship out of college. The magazine was going under when he took it over."

That much I knew from my research, but the fact that Justin wasn't making a joke of it only emphasized that this was more than a job for Sebastian. In a way, as dramatic as it sounded, it was his life's work. He wouldn't let me take over without a fight.

"It must suck coming into a workplace where nobody wants you around," Justin said. "I get that you're here tonight to be one of the guys, and I think it was the right choice."

My smile faded. Was I that obvious? Being a consultant could be a lonely job. My teams always came with an expiration date. It was my responsibility to come in, make them function better, then release them into the wild while I watched from the sidelines. I preferred it when they liked me, which was why I worked so hard to fit in, but it didn't always play out that way. Being "one of the guys" would make life easier, but it was proving to be as difficult to achieve as I'd anticipated.

"Keller doesn't have a drink," Garth yelled from Sebastian's end of the bar.

All eyes turned to me—even Sebastian's all-knowing green ones.

The owner, Santino as he'd been introduced to me, nodded. "What'll it be, *guapa?*"

On the spot, with everyone waiting, I couldn't think of a single drink, not one. More tequila? Could I order a Guinness, or would that be an insult to Mexican beer? What was a good Mexican beer again? Oh, God. What was wrong with me? All week, I'd not only had the attention of the whole staff—I'd *commanded* it. Why couldn't I speak now? Or think? That was the problem—I was *over*thinking it and making things worse. All I heard was Luciano in my head, telling me to choose something flirty.

"Lemon drop," I blurted.

"What the hell's a lemon drop?" Albert asked.

"It's a fucking *lemon drop,*" Sebastian said from his post. "Is this your first time out in public with a woman?"

Albert scowled. "Go to hell."

Ugh. I could not have chosen a more feminine drink. On a scale of one to girly, I was currently Barbie in a dream house waiting for Ken to pick me up in a convertible. I didn't even *like* lemon drops—Luciano did. I'd been raised in a Guinness-drinking household, my dad a typical Irishman and my mom an Italian spitfire. I just hoped my parents never found out about the order.

"Good choice. I make a mean lemon drop," Santino

said, getting to work. "It's lethal. None of these guys could handle it."

I smiled. The rest of the men ordered bottles of Corona and Pacifico, Mexican beers I'd forgotten despite ordering them myself countless times. There wasn't a Guinness in the bunch and that gave me some comfort. I could certainly take on a gang of non-Guinness drinkers easier than the alternative.

Santino served me a frosty yellow martini glass, and I immediately took a sip. For a lemon drop, it wasn't half bad, only mildly sweet. As the team debated whether Sebastian should get a globe for his office—pros: it looked distinguished; cons: globes were huge and who needed one when there was Google Maps?—it was the crack of a base-ball bat that made me look up. I'd almost forgotten about tonight's Yankees game. The Mariners' center fielder caught a fly ball for the Yankees' first out.

"Oh, come on," I said.

"This season could go either way," said a man in a suit sitting alone at one end of the bar. "Which means we *need* these guys on their game."

"I know, right?" I agreed, slapping the bar. My dad had texted me the same thing hours earlier.

Sebastian turned to look at the guy, then at me. "Easy, slugger," he said.

Slugger? I'd moved right out of Barbie's dream house and into *The Sandlot*. I didn't know which was worse. "Sorry. We—my family—take it personally when the Yankees aren't playing well."

I expected Sebastian to go back to justifying his future globe purchase, something I suspected he wanted so he could spin it really fast and see where his finger landed, but he sat on the stool next to me so we were eye level. "That's the second time you've apologized in twenty minutes and *also* the second time you've done it all day."

I stopped myself from apologizing again. He was catching on to my act, and that was a problem. Why would he respect someone who apologized for existing?

I squared my shoulders, forcing myself to hold eye contact. "It's called being polite. Maybe you could try it sometime."

"I give what I receive. Kindness for kindness." He set his elbow on the bar and circled the pad of his thumb around the rim of his Pacifico. "You scratch my back, I scratch yours."

"That's not what that means," I said.

"You lift me, I lift you." He leaned in. "You go down, I go down—and I reciprocate in spades."

Goosebumps rose over my skin. I knew he'd meant that last one as a threat, but the hint of gravel in his voice, his sizeable hand fondling his beer, and the slight curve at the corner of his mouth sent my thoughts right to the gutter. Neal had *hated* going down. Sebastian's almost drunken expression read as if he was having the same thought I was, and he didn't hate it at all. I liked the look on his face and the attention he paid me.

A lot.

"I can't tell what you're thinking," he said. "You haven't been this quiet since the morning at the café, when I was trying to . . ." His dimples appeared with a sly smile. "Well, before everything changed."

I wished I could say I hadn't thought of that morning since, but I had—frequently. Sometimes fondly at the memory of his flirting. I licked citrus from the underside of my upper lip. "What's the fun if you know what I'm thinking?"

He got even closer. "Good point."

And then, while reliving the moments "before every-thing changed," I remembered how weak-kneed I'd gotten just from one short conversation, and how dropping my guard around my smooth-talking ex had gotten me into this situation—having to become someone else to get through one happy hour.

I pulled back right as Justin appeared next to us. "Oh, man," he said, slapping Sebastian on the back. "She's working you so hard right now."

Sebastian frowned. "What?"

"You're practically falling off your seat. You said she had no game, and now she's spitting it all over you."

"Ah, that's right," Sebastian said, lighting up as he turned back to me. "I almost forgot about the challenge."

"It wasn't a challenge," I said. "Vance simply wanted to get me out with you guys. There was no challenge."

"To 'show us a thing or two'—I think that was how he put it," Sebastian said. "Teach us some game and put your theories to the test."

"I never claimed to have game," I said, trying to quell the panic rising in my chest. "You were the one bragging about it, so why don't *you* show us what you've got?"

"Happily," Sebastian said.

"We've seen him in action enough times," Justin said, winking at me. "How about this? Whoever displays the most game by the end of the night wins."

"*Wins?* But—" I started to protest, but it was too late. The guys had caught wind and were chiming in their agreement.

Sebastian studied me until he said, "I'll take that bet."

"The objective is too vague," I said. "You can't measure game."

"We can," Justin said. "We make a living of it. We'll be the judges."

Judges? A bet? All I'd wanted to do in the meeting was demonstrate how the editors of *Modern Man* could improve, not that I could do their jobs better. Most of the guys looked on with excitement, and how would it look if I tried to back out?

Like I was scared.

By the slight smile on Sebastian's face, I thought maybe he could sense that. He wanted me to back down, either so I'd embarrass myself, or so he could retain his "best game in the office" title. Probably both. As I debated the most convincing way to fake a stomachache, the lone Yankees fan at the end of the bar cried out, "Hell, yeah," his eyes glued to the TV as he began clapping.

I darted my eyes to the screen. We were still behind but had finally scored. "Look," I said, turning to show Boris, but he wasn't there. My eyes landed on the guy down the bar as he took a slug of Corona. Despite a loosened tie and slight bags under his eyes, he was nice-looking with a round, inviting face and an abundance of black hair.

Cute but not the kind of attractive that turned my throat and mouth to cotton.

At least he got points for his choice of team.

Most importantly, he wasn't sporting a wedding ring.

My strategy clicked into place, and I had to dive in head first before I lost my nerve. I shouldered off my blazer and passed it to Sebastian. "Hold this for me?"

He dropped his eyes to my leopard-print blouse and said, "Anytime."

"Thanks." I picked up my lemon drop and walked by him. The crowd parted as I followed the curve of the bar, passing empty stools until I found one next to the Yankee. "Hi," I said, placing my drink on the bar. I nodded at a bowl of nuts. "Do you mind?"

"Have at it," he said.

I picked up a few cashews, happy for something to do with my hands. "I'm Georgina."

He wiped his hand on his trousers and held it out. "François."

"Oh." I chewed on the nuts and shook his hand. "Are you French?"

"Creole. I grew up in Louisiana. You can call me Frank, my friends do."

"You're not an Astros fan?"

"Nope. Still root for the Saints, but even before I moved here for work, I was a Yankees fan."

"I'm from upstate," I said. "It's a tense time at home right now."

He smiled, popping a few peanuts. "I hear Aaron Judge might return to the lineup this month."

"Let's hope." We watched the game a couple minutes, exchanging opinions about the season. When the conversation stalled, I glanced over my shoulder and met eyes with Sebastian, who dropped his to his beer. Most of the guys made no secret of the fact that they were watching. Justin even had out a notebook and pen. What, was he keeping score? He gave me a thumbs up.

They were out of earshot at least, so I turned back to Frank, took a bolstering sip of lemon drop, and said, "Can I ask a favor?"

"Sure."

"Those guys I'm with—who are mostly a mix of Mets and Sox fans, by the way—they made this bet." He eased back on the stool to see behind me, but I said, "Don't look."

He stopped himself and met my eyes with a spark of curiosity in his. He had the kind of ruddy cheeks that made him look cheerful, though at the moment, he just seemed curious. "What kind of bet?"

Having to say it aloud was a little harder than I thought. To keep from blabbering through my nerves, I just said, "They don't think I have the guts to pick up a guy in a bar."

He worked his jaw back and forth a moment. Fine lines formed around his eyes as he thought. "So I'm the target. Did you choose or did they?"

"I did." I shrugged a shoulder. "You're a Yankees guy —I figured I'd find an ally in you."

"Anything for a comrade." He shifted to one side, took his phone from his pocket, and unlocked it. "Can I get your number?"

I smiled gratefully and leaned subtly to one side to make sure the guys could see. I took Frank's phone, opened the phone app, and pretended to type.

"You could actually put it in there," he said.

Oh . . . crap. It was either naiveté, poor planning, or a bit of both, but I hadn't anticipated that my target might actually *want* me to pick him up. If I'd come into the interaction that way, I would've chickened out. I glanced up at him. "The thing is, I just started a new job that takes up all my time, so I'm not really dating right now."

"I only asked for your number, not a date," he said.

"Oh." Flustered by my mistake, I nodded hard. "Duh. Sorry."

"I'm kidding." He grinned. "I actually have tickets to an upcoming game and nobody to take. So, if you *were* dating, then this time, I'd be asking."

The phone dimmed as I hovered my fingers over the keypad. I'd had no intention of actually getting a date out of this. My "common interest" theory had worked *too* well. "I don't know," I said. "I'm not sure I'm in the right place."

"Does this have anything to do with the guy staring daggers at me right now?"

I wrinkled my nose. "Who?"

"Tall, expensive-looking suit, seems like he belongs in a cologne ad."

Sebastian. I could just picture his scowl as I not only beat him to the punchline, but did it in under ten minutes. "That's just my coworker," I said. "His face always looks like that."

"He's not your boyfriend?"

"No, but—"

"Let me see your phone." I hesitated but slid my purse from my shoulder, typed my passcode into my cell, and passed it over. As he navigated to my contacts, he said, "Imagine how much more impressed they'll be that you not only got a phone number, but an actual date too."

I didn't *want* that. I had enough on my plate as it was, and I was still recovering from Neal. Though Frank seemed nice, could I really trust my judgment?

Frank smiled as he finished adding his number. "If nothing else, you'll get to see the Yanks play." Within seconds, his phone vibrated in my hands with a text from my number. He leaned over to read the screen. "There. Now we have each other's info. I'll contact you with the details next week."

"Okay," I said, handing back his phone. The Yankees hadn't even played a full inning since I'd sat down. That had to be some kind of record for scoring a date—it was for me, at least. "I'd better get back so I have sufficient bragging time."

He took his wallet from his suit jacket. "I've got to take off anyway. I'll be in touch."

I slid off the barstool with my phone in one hand and

the dregs of my lemon drop in the other, a little fuzzy about what'd just happened.

When the guys saw me coming, they parted. "Well?" Albert asked.

I set my glass on the bar and unlocked my phone to show them. "I got the number."

"Nice work, Keller," Justin said. "Record time."

Sebastian's eyes darted over the screen, and then to me, barely visible under his heavy eyebrows. "How do we know you didn't just tell him about the bet?"

"Does it matter if she did?" Garth said. "Maybe that's one of her moves."

"That's cheating," he replied.

Justin shook his head. "Judge rules—*not* cheating. The guy would've blown her off or given her a fake number if he wasn't into her."

"And it isn't fake," I said, navigating to my texts. I opened the one from François that read, *Looking forward to the game.*

"What game?" Sebastian asked, reading upside down.

"We're going on a date." I smiled, reveling in the chance to finally be smug. Sebastian's knuckles whitened from gripping his beer bottle. François was right—having the date in my back pocket was much more fun. "My theory works. We bonded over the Yankees, and now we're going to see them together. How's that for game?"

"If the date's for real," Sebastian said, "why would he let you walk back over here right into the middle of a group of men?"

"Because I didn't ask for his permission," I said.

Justin snickered. "It's bright outside the cave, huh, Sebastian?"

"Well, she definitely got his attention," Garth said,

nodding toward Frank. "He's looked over here probably ten times while paying his bill."

"François from Louisiana." Sebastian snorted. "Sounds like he belongs in an Anne Rice novel." There was no way Sebastian could've heard our conversation from where he'd been standing, which meant he'd gleaned Frank's location from the area code. He finished off his beer, put it on the bar, and handed me back my blazer. "Excuse me," he grumbled, walking away.

"I take it he's not good at losing," I said to Justin once Sebastian had disappeared around back.

"Not really," Justin said. "But I wouldn't count him out yet."

8

I n the half hour since I'd gotten Frank's number and sent Sebastian sulking, I'd learned more than I cared to know about *Fortnite* from Derek. He was mid-sentence when he paused and looked behind me. "Looks like you might have some competition, George."

My heart sank. I knew instantly what Derek was referring to. Maybe Sebastian wasn't sulking after all. There were generally only three reasons for a man to separate from the pack—food, alcohol, or sex—and since the bar was fully stocked on the first two, I wasn't surprised to turn and find Sebastian alone at a table with an attractive woman.

A *very* attractive woman with a nose ring, a sleek, winding forearm tattoo most people could never pull off, and long, honeyed hair to match her long, golden-skinned limbs.

"Damn, she's fine," Albert said. "Sorry, George, but Sebastian's going to score higher in that department."

Justin agreed as he made a note in his pad. "Attractiveness of date," he murmured. "Ten out of ten."

I frowned. They didn't have to rub it in, although I suspected they'd given Sebastian grief as well. No wonder he'd looked so cranky after my ten minutes with François. What had I expected, though? I was clearly out of my league. Sebastian had what women wanted, and he knew it. I hadn't needed to experience much of his charm to know its potency. Not to mention his *actual* job was curating a style, conduct, and sex bible for men all over the world.

Did he have all the answers? No, otherwise Vance wouldn't have called me in. But was he miles ahead of the pack? Probably. Exhibit A—he'd been the first man in a long time to spark my curiosity and pebble my skin with just his words.

It was safe to say where women and sex were concerned, he knew what he was doing. The woman's eyes sparkled as she set her elbows on the table and laughed. Sebastian turned her forearm up and traced the lines of her tattoo. She bit her bottom lip and I almost did too just wondering how it would feel for him to touch me with such focus, such interest.

He was making my attempt at game look like child's play, and I didn't have to stick around to watch. Not only was I about to get pummeled, but the jealous thoughts forming in my head weren't going to help anything.

I turned and signaled for Santino to close my bar tab.

Justin leaned over to me. "You're not going to sit back and let him win, are you?"

"This has been fun, but I should get home," I said and thought, *Bruno, Luciano, and Tim Gunn are waiting for me.*

"But he's had it too easy for too long. If I know Seb, he'll have this girl hanging all over him by the end of the night." Justin ducked his head to catch my eye. "Provided he doesn't encounter any, ah, turbulence."

It would take more than a few bumps and jolts to knock Sebastian out of the sky. Justin thought I could still win this challenge, but in order to do so, I'd have to pull out all the stops. I looked back over my shoulder at the new couple that could only be described as beautiful. Had it always come as easy to Sebastian as Justin had said, or had he battled through an awkward stage like the rest of us?

"Is sabotage against the rules?" I asked.

"Hmm, let me see." Justin pretended to check his notepad and said, "Nope."

I had a choice. Slink away like I normally would and let Sebastian win, or prove that my strength carried outside the office. It would've been much easier to resign myself to the life I was clearly meant to have—knitting in a rocking chair, Bruno at my side, empty ice cream pints scattered on the floor. If I were an alien, my mothership would be a Dreyer's pint. And, okay, I didn't knit, but that was a minor detail. I'd have plenty of time to learn. At age thirty, I was probably about halfway to retirement, and then I could really lean in. It wasn't such a bad life.

Unfortunately, the idea of Sebastian winning got under my skin almost as much as the thought of him taking the golden goddess home tonight. I'd had the pleasure of his attention once, and Monday morning was already beginning to feel like a lifetime ago, but I hadn't forgotten how it'd felt to have Sebastian flirt with me. That alone wasn't enough to get me out on a limb, but I'd known this job would be a challenge, and apparently that didn't stop at the office. I owed this to myself.

I racked my brain for a reason to interrupt them. Judging by the way the woman's eyes were glued to his face, it would take a lot to unstick her. When Santino set the bill holder in front of me, I slid it back to his side of the bar. "Never mind," I said. "I'm staying."

"Atta girl," Justin said. "Take that arrogant asshole down."

I couldn't help smiling. "I thought he was your friend."

"I love the guy, but I love to fuck with him more."

I sucked in a breath and started toward them before I could chicken out. The woman looked up first, and then Sebastian. His eyebrows rose higher the closer I got. I grabbed a chair from the next table over, pulled it up between them, and planted my ass right on it. "*Bravo*, Sebastian," I said breathlessly and began to applaud. "That was excellent work. You've come *so* far."

His eyes narrowed almost imperceptibly. "I'm sorry . . . *what?*"

"Oh, no. I'm being rude." I turned to the woman and stuck out my hand. "Georgina Keller."

"Um, hello." She took my hand. "I'm Isabella?"

"Are you?" I asked. I got a scratchpad from my purse, flipped it open, and pretended to read the field notes I'd made a few days back while observing customers in the magazine aisle at Barnes and Noble. "Isabella, can I ask you some questions?" As she opened her mouth, I continued, "On a scale of one to ten, how well would you say Sebastian did at starting a conversation?"

"I'm sorry?" she asked in an accent far lovelier than anyone deserved. Italian, like my mom's side of the family.

Sebastian drew back. "Georgina—"

"God, where is my brain tonight?" I asked. "I should've mentioned this since Sebastian obviously wouldn't. I'm his coach."

"Coach?" she asked. "What does that mean?"

"Sebastian and I have been working on some . . . tactics," I said gently, emphasizing the word as if it were a dirty one. "I'm a renowned pick-up artist—and Sebastian's dating coach!"

The woman's mouth went round. "Did you say *pick-up* artist?"

"I know, I know," I said, waving my hands. "Forget what you've heard. It's not as skeevy as it sounds. People have coaches for everything else. Why not the most important thing there is? Love," I said before she could answer. "I work with those who are, well, for lack of a better word . . ." I smiled broadly at Sebastian and patted his shoulder. "*Romantically challenged.*"

Isabella's eyes darted between the two of us before she fixed her glare on Sebastian. "You were *practicing* on me?"

Seeing as his jaw nearly rested on the table, he didn't respond. I leaned over to Isabella and whispered loudly enough for Sebastian to hear, "Take it as a compliment, sweetheart."

"A compliment?" she asked.

It was working. She looked almost as horrified as Sebastian. The fact that I'd made his jaw drop did more than boost my confidence—it made me want to giggle. I was having *fun*. I leaned back in my seat and addressed Isabella. "By the way, if you know of anyone who could use some help getting dates, you can find me at fromchumptohump-dot-com, formerly fromdisstokiss-dot-com, formerly fromwimptopimp-dot—"

"We get it," Sebastian said through his teeth, then turned to Isabella. "You're not buying this, are you?"

"How do you spell that first website?" Isabella asked me, fishing around her purse, presumably for her phone.

I gave Sebastian what I hoped was an ultra-casual smile. "Sebastian has been one of my best students to date. He's a fast learner." I let my smile fall into a cringe. "You should've seen him just last month."

"All right." Sebastian's nostrils flared. "That's enough."

Isabella squeaked. "What was he like last month?"

"Oh, you wouldn't believe it." I remembered in college reading about an author who'd written a book on how to be a player. I'd never read it, but apparently, I didn't need to. With a little help from Garth's "geek" how-to, the ideas flowed like a river of melted butter. "His mother booked me through my website," I said. "I found him in New Jersey sitting in her basement on a throne of pizza boxes playing *Minecraft*. Not even *Fortnite*! At least that takes skill." I shook my head solemnly and looked at Sebastian. "You'd be surprised what I can do with a man who was recently masturbating to animated women in midriffs."

"Did you say *New Jersey*?" Isabella asked.

I leaned in confidentially. "He was wearing those pajama jeans from Costco."

"Costco?" Isabella stood so fast, her chair nearly toppled over. "You used me, you pig," she said, snatching her purse from the back of her chair before she stormed out.

I grimaced. "The masturbating comment was too far, wasn't it?"

Sebastian glared at me. "What the *hell* do you think you're doing?"

"Did you think I'd just hand over victory?"

"Justin put you up to this, didn't he?"

Sebastian was angry. My instinct was to go red in the face and apologize profusely for interrupting his evening. I'd come this far, though, so I battled through it. "Listen, if you can't come back from that, then you've been resting on your looks too long."

"She ran out! I couldn't even get a word in edgewise."

I shook my head slowly. "You're rusty."

"Really? I can still catch her." He got up from the table but hesitated when I flinched. Quickly, I schooled my expression to hide any disappointment.

"If that's what you're looking for, go ahead," I said, but the confidence I'd just earned faltered. He seriously wanted someone superficial enough to walk out on him over jeggings?

"Fine, I will," he said, but he didn't move.

I didn't want him to go, because I knew he'd talk his way out of this. And then Sebastian and Isabella would probably laugh about it at their wedding while I sat in a corner wondering why I'd ever let him go after her. It was possible I was jealous. Which meant it was possible a crush was developing. Noticing the way Sebastian filled out a suit, wanting his approval, hoping he saw me as a bitch simply because, according to self-proclaimed expert Luciano, men loved them . . . those were classic signs. A crush could not happen. Not only was *Modern Man*, and by extension, Sebastian, my client, but he and I had to co-manage a team without taking each other out in the process.

"Fine," I agreed. "Go ahead."

Our team descended on the table just as Sebastian took off for the exit. "What the hell just happened?" Albert bellowed. "Did Georgina scare off your date?"

Sebastian called back, "Not if I can help it."

"He's going after her?" Justin asked me.

It appeared he was. If I'd asked him not to, it would've looked like forfeiting. This way, at least, I'd lose with a shred of dignity.

As time ticked down, the guys took bets as to whether Sebastian would get her back in—the general consensus being that would make him the winner. My stomach was in knots, but not about losing. I hated the idea of him taking her home. Maybe they were already in a cab. I tried not to stare down the door.

After a few minutes, Sebastian strolled back in. By the

swagger in his step, I assumed she was hot on his heels, but he was alone. "No luck," he said, shrugging. "She wouldn't give me the time of day."

"Then I guess we have a winner," Garth said, handing Sebastian a beer.

"Bullshit." We all turned to Justin, who had his head cocked as he studied Sebastian. "You're forfeiting."

"Do you see her by my side?" Sebastian asked.

"No, but you're a shit liar with one dead giveaway that never fails. And don't ask me what it is. I'm not stupid enough to tell you. Give me your phone." Justin held out his palm to Sebastian while glancing at me. "Sorry, George, but like you said, a bet's a bet."

"What do you mean?" I asked.

Sebastian passed over his cell. "She's not in there, dude."

"What was her name?" Justin asked.

Justin thought Sebastian had gotten Isabella's number and might still have this. I bit my bottom lip, then released it as soon as Sebastian glanced at my mouth. "Her name was Isabella," I said.

Justin went through Sebastian's contacts. "Hmm. Don't see her."

"Then that settles it," Sebastian said. "Georgina wins this round."

I sent up a quick prayer that this was the *final* round. I wasn't sure I could handle another go at this.

"Wait a sec," Justin said and scrolled the opposite direction.

"Justin," Sebastian warned, finally looking away from me. "Leave it alone."

"A-*ha*." Justin held up the screen. "Cantina Santino Isabella," he read off the screen. "It was under 'C'."

Sebastian rubbed his brow, his eyes on me. "Ah, yeah.

But that was from earlier, not right now—she gave me her number *before* Georgina blew up my game."

"Wow," I said. "You work fast."

"You're not so slow yourself." He tipped his head back for a sip of beer, glancing at me. "I always get the number right away. As you can see, Justin has burned me in the past."

Justin side-eyed Sebastian before checking the notebook. "Sebastian failed. Judge rules—Georgina wins."

Garth put his hands on my shoulders from behind and squeezed. "Nice work, boss," he said. "You bested a pro."

"Next drink's on me, Keller," Albert added.

I'd bested the best. Who would've thought? Happy hour was a success. I'd not only survived it but had come out on top. I'd been correct in assuming I'd make more headway with the guys tonight than I had all week at the office.

"No need, Al," Sebastian said. "I'll get Georgina's next drink. After all, we never set any stakes."

I wasn't sure that was true. It seemed that the stakes had been set the first time I'd been introduced to Sebastian as my new co-boss. He wasn't willing to make room for me in his office, much less in his world. It was me or him, and neither of us would go down without a fight.

fter a quick pick-up game of basketball with my sister's husband in their driveway, Libby called us in for brunch. Sturdy trees with changing leaves flanked their Colonial-style home in Newton, a suburb of Boston. Aaron tossed the ball onto the lawn as we entered the house through the garage. My nephew sat on a stool at the kitchen island, picking lox off a bagel while Libby buzzed around him, setting out fruit, cream cheese, hummus, Bloody Mary mix, and more.

"How was the drive?" she asked when she saw me.

"Hardly any traffic," I said, popping a grape as I sniffed the air. "Are you wearing perfume around your own house?"

"We just got back from synagogue. If I don't dress to the nines, everybody thinks I'm the kids' nanny."

At five feet tall, my twin sister looked much younger than her actual thirty-three years. It was the same dark hair and complexion as mine that often got her mistaken for the help. Only our height and eye color set us apart—

otherwise, Libby and I looked the same, talked the same, and saw most things the same way.

"It probably doesn't help that you carry a jar of home-made *salsa verde* in your purse," I said.

She checked a skillet on the stove. "When I was a kid," she told her son, "your *abuela* made *chilaquiles* all the time for me and your uncle."

"She made them for me too, Mom," José answered. "I wasn't a baby when she died. I was already four."

Libby made the sign of the cross the way Mom used to. "Don't play with your food."

"I hate lox."

"Have one bite." She took a bowl with Saran wrap over the top from the fridge.

I peeked in and made a face. "You're serving guac *and* lox?"

"I have culture coming out of my ears," she said, stopping in the pantry for a clipped bag of chips. "Unlike some people, I'm proud of my Hispanic heritage. My children will be too."

Libby's jabs were never subtle. By *some people* she meant Mom and me. There'd been times we as a family had tried to hide our background to make things easier on ourselves, but Libby had never subscribed to that—especially when it came to names. She'd given her husband no choice but to defend their children's traditionally Mexican names to his Orthodox parents. She'd convert to Judaism for him, but damn if she wouldn't put our family's stamp on things. She'd even been using her full name, Libertad, since Mom's death.

Aaron balanced Carmen on his hip, dragging her playpen into the kitchen. "Things calmed down at work yet?" he asked me.

I visited Libby whenever I had a free weekend, and

every time they asked about work, I answered with some version of "the usual." Today, my mind went to Georgina. She was a disruption to my routine, a routine I liked and one that had served me well up until recently.

"Why are you hesitating?" Libby asked as she plated the food.

She and I weren't the kinds of twins who finished each other's sentences but sometimes, she was a little *too* in tune with me. "Work has been better."

"It hasn't been very long," Aaron said, one-handedly mixing Bloody Marys as he carried Carmen around the kitchen. "Don't let all that stuff bring you down."

"What stuff?" My first thought was Georgina, but there was no way they could've known about her.

Aaron lowered his voice. "Your sister set a Google alert for your name."

The fucking exposé. I hadn't mentioned anything about it to Libby, hoping I could avoid the exact look she was giving me now. She clucked, shaking her head. "I can't say it surprised me," she said, setting a hot dish in front of me. "What *Modern Man* prints is mostly inoffensive, but sometimes things slip through that have me scratching my head."

"You're just saying that because everyone else is," I said after a bite. "I never heard any complaints from you before."

"Your sex advice column—"

"Is called *Badvice* because it's *bad advice*," Aaron explained. "It couldn't be more obvious. I don't understand how people don't get that, or why it wasn't detailed in the exposé."

"*Thank* you," I said, throwing up my arms. "They misprinted the name to make it look as if my column was titled Bad-*Vice*, with a capital V, when it's a portmanteau of bad and advice."

From the enclave desk in her kitchen, Libby picked up a magazine I'd hoped I'd never have to see again. "I've got it right here."

"Oh. Fantastic." Feeling a character assassination coming, I took my niece from Aaron's arms and hugged the nineteen-month-old like a shield.

Libby spread out the offending feature on the island and slipped on her reading glasses. In most ways, my sister had me beat. She and I had spent our formative years around Boston's upper crust, and while Mom had cleaned, Libby would sneak into piano lessons, ballroom dancing, book clubs, or whatever other extracurriculars were on tap for the school year. She'd used all that to start a business, a boutique nearby. At least I'd one-upped her in one way— my vision had always been twenty-twenty.

Libby flipped through the magazine until she found a pull-quote from *Badvice* to read aloud. "'Date a coworker. In fact, date two or three. The office is an unfairly maligned breeding ground for men who don't want to work too hard to get dates.'" She glanced at me over her glasses and continued reading. "'An excerpt from *BadVice*, a monthly sex advice column aimed at men, curated and often written by Quinn, a notorious womanizer.'"

"That was a joke," I said. I knew that. Everyone at work knew it. Our readers knew it. But my vilification was no picnic to hear aloud. Especially knowing these kids, and my own, might see it one day.

"What about the intern who showed us behind the curtain?" Libs asked, sliding her food across the island. "It says here she'd taken off her shoes after a long workday and gone to the breakroom. When she returned, she caught an editor fondling them."

I chuckled to myself as I shifted Carmen to my hip and picked up my drink. "Classic."

"Why are you laughing?" she asked as she chewed. "That's disgusting!"

"That's *Justin*," I said. "He wasn't fondling them. He was trying to hide them."

"Dude," Aaron said. "How is that better?"

"You have to understand the history there. They had a thing going, and he was over it. The last woman he'd ended things with had thrown a heel at him and nearly given him a concussion, so he never breaks up with a girl while she's wearing shoes."

"That is so utterly ridiculous and immature," Libby said. "And sounds exactly like something Justin would do."

"Look, we're not perfect," I admitted. "We've got some changes to make. But everyone's acting like the sky is falling."

Libby closed the magazine and picked up her fork. "This is bigger than *Modern Man*, Sebastian. You guys need to get with the times and have somebody hold you accountable."

"Oh, believe me," I said, "we're being held accountable."

"By your editor-in-chief?" Aaron asked.

"The board hired a consultant." Talk of Georgina had a history of riling me up, so I lowered my niece into her playpen. "Also known as a glorified babysitter."

Libby raised an eyebrow. "A publicist?"

"She calls herself a 'publishing consultant,'" I said, "but I call her a pain in the a-s-s."

Aaron laughed, but Libby didn't even crack a smile. "I think you could use some pain in your ass, *hermanito*."

I nearly rolled my eyes. She only called me "little brother" to irk me. I'd been born six minutes after Libby and four after midnight, which technically made her a day older. A fact she never let me forget. "What's that supposed to mean?"

"It means sometimes, I worry you've forgotten where you come from." She turned to Aaron. "Did you know he once paid twenty dollars for a cocktail? And that he and Justin are considering renting a place in the Hamptons next summer? And that he's been on *three* dates in a single night?"

She had a point about the cocktail. Twenty dollars was excessive, especially for a drink that'd been tossed in my face. Come to think of it, that'd been the night of the three dates, but that was well over a year ago. "That shit-for-brains 'journalist' called me a womanizer," I said defensively, "but I've barely dated since . . ."

Libby and I had already done the anniversary thing over the phone, and I didn't want to bring up Mom's death again.

Neither did Libs, it seemed. "He used to be scrappy and pinch pennies," she told Aaron.

"Wasn't this countertop like a hundred dollars a square foot?" I asked.

"This is my forever home." She stood and moved the skillet from the stove to the sink. "And we're not talking about me."

"Mommy," José said, twisting on the barstool. "I want ice cream."

"Not until after supper," she said automatically, and then to me, "So you're *not* a womanizer?"

Aaron moved his Bloody Mary as his son tried to dip a finger in it. "Don't get on Seb's case or he'll never bring anybody over."

Libby picked up her dishes along with Aaron's. "The day my brother introduces me to a girlfriend who isn't five-foot-ten and a hundred-percent full of herself is the day I'll back off."

I shrugged. "There's a motive I can work with."

"So, is the consultant helping?" Aaron asked.

"Of course not. *She's* not the one responsible for the bottom line. Georgina wants to implement these pie-in-the-sky ideas supported by her own research—obviously, it's going to be biased."

"Georgina?" Libby asked, perking up like a dog offered a bone.

"Yeah. Her proposed changes will send readers fleeing and leave me to clean up the mess with advertisers. We publish what sells. *Modern Man* never claimed to be hard-hitting news."

"Can I please, *please* be excused, Mom?" José asked.

Aaron finished off his cocktail and stood. "How about another game? Uncle and nephew versus the dad?"

"Sebastian's going to help me clear the table," Libby informed her husband.

"I tried," Aaron muttered to me before herding José out back.

Libby stooped to get plastic wrap from a drawer. "You're sensitive today."

"How? I'm just answering your questions."

"Normally you shrug me off with a joke." She recovered the bowl of guacamole. "Something's bothering you. I can tell. It's the whole twin telepathy thing."

"We don't have that."

"Of course we do, Sebastian. You can be so cynical sometimes."

I stacked Aaron and José's empty plates by the sink to avoid Libby's side-glances. It was no coincidence that she was piling on today, accusing me of forgetting my roots—it seemed as if I'd been called into question or questioning things myself ever since the exposé. Was I really such a bad manager that the magazine needed a handler to help me run things? Would everyone forget the work I'd done if Georgina's plan succeeded? And after the way I'd spoken to her in the café and at the office, did Georgina doubt my character like everyone else seemed to?

"Do you think I'm a different person than I used to be?" I asked.

She moved fruit from a platter to Tupperware, pausing to bite into a strawberry. "Of course."

I frowned. "You answered that really fast."

"We're both different. Especially after Mom's death." She leaned her elbows onto the island and had another strawberry. "You can be in touch with who you used to be and still be different. The idea is to keep getting better."

"And you think I'm not?"

"Since when do you care what I think?" she asked, tossing the stems into the garbage disposal before capping the Tupperware. She knew full well I cared what she thought. More than anyone else in the world, now that it was just us. "Tell me about this Georgina person."

Oh, for fuck's sake. I'd mentioned her *once*, and now Libby was peering into my eyes, trying to read my thoughts. I wanted to look away, but then I wouldn't be able to read hers. "I already did. Like I said, she's a pain."

"How so?"

"How long do you have? For one, she's fucking messy. She's always losing stuff, walking around my office barefoot while she eats gummy bears of all things, and she can't even read her own handwriting. Last week, she handed me *her* notepad and asked if I could decipher her last entry."

"And could you?"

"Yes, but that's not the point."

My sister smiled to herself. "Cute."

"*Cute?*" I gaped at her. "What's cute about trying to turn the whole office against me?"

"I highly doubt she's doing that," Libby said.

"Want to bet? During her first meeting, she read excerpts from the exposé to everyone, then at happy hour, she drops a bomb on my game in front of all the guys." *Fuck.* As soon as the words left my mouth, I understood my sister had just tricked me into revealing too much information.

With an annoyingly smug smile, she finished moving perishables into the fridge. "So, a new girl shows up at your office, questions your work and your character, and now you're asking me for the first time in years if I think you've changed? Is she pretty?"

"It's not the first time in *years*."

"Whenever I ask about your personal life in Manhattan, you go monosyllabic. So, most of what I know comes from Justin or what I see in the society pages." She plugged the sink and turned on the faucet. "Then this exposé pops up . . ."

"Not true. We talked about my love life after what Mom said those last few days," I said. "You agreed I need to settle down and meet a nice girl."

She squirted dish soap into the rising water. "Is Georgina a nice girl?"

I snorted. "Not in the least. Exactly what Mom warned me against."

Libby tilted her head. "Really? Your usual type?"

"*No,*" I said before I realized that answer was contradictory—and would only incite Libby's curiosity.

"Was she like your last girlfriend—what was her name? Wenchy?"

I rolled my eyes. "Sure, Georgina is like *Wendy*—minus several inches, plus a real job. And if Wendy dyed her hair red, had freckles, wore suits, and was fucking rude."

"Wendy *was* rude."

"So is Georgina."

"To you or to others?"

"Both."

"Then if she's a bitch, forget her." She pulled on yellow rubber gloves. "What's bringing all this up?"

"Take your pick." Scratching under my chin, I listed, "The one-year anniversary of Mom's death. For the first time in my career I've stumbled, and now I have a handler. I'm entering my mid-thirties. Given all that, I'm allowed some introspection."

"Okay, so what have you been introspecting?"

"I work hard, Libs. Mom taught us the importance of that, but she never reaped the benefits. I tried to get her to retire, but she wouldn't. So why are people on my case for enjoying what I've earned?"

She began scrubbing the dishes. "Your values will change once you meet someone. Everything I do is for Aaron and the kids."

"I don't have that yet. When I do, I'll settle down."

"It's the other way around—start settling now, and you'll find someone, but she's not going to fall into your lap."

"You never know," I said. "I've had a few girls land in my lap."

"Isn't there anyone at work who *isn't* there to model? I've heard the office is an unfairly maligned place to meet women. Maybe a woman like . . . Georgina?"

I shook my head with a sigh. "She's not a bitch, by the way. Just . . . frustrating."

"How so?"

I rounded the island to take a dishtowel hanging from

the stove handle. "She's called me entitled, arrogant, a jerk, and an asshole—some of that before I even knew her name."

"Back up." She handed me a plate. "How is that possible?"

"We met in a café before work," I said as I dried. "I had no idea she was the new consultant. *She* ran into *me* while I was in a hurry, then called *me* an asshole when my drink spilled on her."

"Well, that's understandable. Girl hadn't had her coffee yet."

"That's an excuse to call a stranger names?"

"I know it's rare for you to ever spend a morning with a woman, but just ask Aaron. Anything that happens pre-coffee doesn't count. And wasn't it her first day on the job? Maybe she was nervous."

"Why are you making excuses for her? You don't even know her."

"Because I can't think of a time in recent history you've volunteered the name of the girl you're dating, or even talked about one this much."

"We're *not* dating."

"Just pointing out that you've brought her up several times."

"Because I vehemently disagree with everything she stands for. She's silent when she should speak up—like when her friend, the barista, was getting shit on by a customer—and she's a know-it-all when she should sit back and listen, like at our meetings."

"Aha." Libby's eyebrows met in the middle of her forehead as she moved the remaining dishes into the soapy water. "I think I understand. You've always had a weird thing about how people treat the help."

"But Wendy was as stuck-up as they come."

"And for that reason, you knew things could never be serious with her. You could run when things got messy. That's why you date women like that. When you care about someone, you don't tolerate rudeness, and you're as loyal as a dog."

"Are you seeing that therapist again?" I asked.

"Yes, and he agrees you're subconsciously sabotaging your love life."

"Was," I said. "I *was* sabotaging it until Mom made me promise—" I shook my head. What the fuck? My sister had witchy ways of getting me to admit things that'd never even crossed my mind. I doubted my subconscious was even evolved enough to recognize self-sabotage. Her psychoanalytic subterfuge was distressing enough that getting back to venting about Georgina somehow felt safer. "I only used that example to demonstrate Georgina's character. Her position at the magazine is a waste of time and resources—and Vance won't stop singing her praises. She rolled into the office as if she had all the answers. Did I mention she was hired on a Wednesday and started Monday? I've been working there for *years*."

"She had under five days to prepare and Vance is that impressed?"

I ran my hands over my face and looked at the ceiling. "*Ay, dios mío.* Give me strength to deal with the women in my life."

"Oh, don't be so dramatic. What's the matter?"

"The same thing that's always the matter." Something I would never admit to Georgina after the way I'd peacocked over my experience with women. "One minute, I think I understand your gender perfectly, and then? I realize I don't know women at all."

Libby wore what looked like a secret smile. Surely she

was amused by the fact that Georgina had stumped me. "I'm guessing this Georgina falls into the latter half."

"I just don't get her. I don't know how to work with her."

"Do you think Vance will ask her to stay on permanently?"

"God, no." It hadn't even occurred to me. "I'd quit."

"She's that bad?"

No, she wasn't. I knew that. But there was no reason for Georgina to stay on as co-manager, except if I was doing a shitty job on my own. And then, why wouldn't Vance just give her *my* job? He'd already unofficially warned me I was on thin ice. Was it possible that was Georgina's endgame?

"Yeah," I said. "It's that bad."

"Well . . ." Libby sighed as she handed me a pan to dry. "If you really want her gone, I can tell you exactly how to make it happen."

I massaged the headache forming in my temples. How the hell did some people have all the answers? I'd been mulling this over since the day I'd heard Vance was bringing in a consultant. "Tell me."

"I will, once you answer my question."

"Which one?" I asked.

"Is she pretty? Or better yet, do you find her attractive?"

Who wouldn't find a girl like Georgina attractive? She was small but mighty, ambitious but not malicious, and feisty with a streak of sweet, both in her personality and manifested as freckles on her delicate nose. But so were lots of women in this city. I just had to find out where *else* to meet them.

"Like I said, she's not like the girls I typically go for," I said with a firm nod.

"What concerns me more than the fact that you think you can deflect with me, is that you think you're good at it."

"You're full of constructive criticism today, aren't you? What do they serve you at that synagogue?"

She shut off the faucet and leaned her hip against the counter to face me. "Walk me through it. What popped into your head when you first saw her?"

How my hands would feel in her silky auburn hair. That was *before* I'd caught her post-thunderstorm scent. Then, of course, the way she'd shivered when I'd barely touched her leg. All that'd been enough to make me forget I was on the phone with Justin. But if I was honest, now I was most captivated by the fact that I'd have her pegged one moment and then doubting everything I knew about her the next.

Happy hour, for instance. Georgina, a pick-up artist? She'd been convincing. And quick. And creative.

From chumptohump-dot-com . . .

Far from where Georgina could bust me for it, I smiled. It'd been a good prank. She'd pulled it off seamlessly, then had looked so vulnerable at the bar when she'd thought I'd win the bet anyway. Just when I thought I knew her, a softer, shyer side of her personality surfaced. The side I'd seen those first few moments at the café.

"Okay, scratch that question," Libby said, turning her back to put away drinking glasses. "The way you're smiling, clearly your first thought was not PG."

I sighed. "She's attractive."

"Mom didn't mean for you to find someone quiet and meek, Sebastián." She dumped the remainder of Aaron's Bloody Mary into the sink and submerged the glass. "If this Georgina has a little spice and can put you in your place, that's not the same as being rude and vapid."

Spice. That was one way of describing Georgina. Cinnamon, spice, and everything nice. One of the most irritating things about her was the smattering of goddamn freckles across her nose and cheeks. They were cute and innocent when she was anything but, and it made me angry. At her for having them, and at myself for wanting to know where else they peppered her body.

"Maybe she's been trying to impress you," Libby said. "Have you considered she might be interested in you?"

"She's not. In fact, she's apparently going on a date," I said. "A Yankees game with some finance bro." With a look from Libby, I added, "And no, I didn't say it that way because I'm jealous."

"Sure. Sounds completely platonic."

I'd never admit it to Libs, but there was a chance I was a *little* jealous. Watching Georgina exchange numbers with the wannabe vampire had annoyed me, and it'd had nothing to do with our bet. The bet had been bullshit anyway. What Georgina hadn't known, and what Justin had suspected, was that I'd thrown the game. I'd actually caught up with Isabella outside the bar, and within minutes, had her hanging on my tie, asking me to walk her to her subway stop. In New York, that was an intimate thing after a date and could end with a kiss. All I'd been able to think about was Georgina back in the bar, mostly how nervous she'd looked about losing in front of everyone. So, I'd straightened my tie, put Isabella in a cab, and lied about calling her later.

The worst part wasn't even that it was my own fault Georgina had gotten the date in the first place. What really annoyed me was that I cared, and it was partly why I'd been steering clear of her since happy hour. Maybe I couldn't help being attracted to Georgina's hot and cold personality, but acting on it wasn't an option. Not only was she the first person to threaten my career in a long time, but I'd vowed to remove any ice from my life. It was only warm, nice girls from here on out.

"I haven't seen you this worked up in a while," Libby said in her maddening know-it-all tone. "Don't rule her out yet."

"I don't see the logic in that," I said, hoping to annoy her back. "If Georgina was interested in me, she wouldn't be going out with another guy."

That made Libby laugh with a little too much enthusiasm. "Oh, Sebastian. If you're treating her like she's got the plague, why *wouldn't* she go out with someone else? It's her only option."

I ran the dishtowel through my hands. "How do you figure?"

"Either she's not interested in you and randomly accepted a date from a nice guy, or she *is* interested in you and wants you to notice. You better hope that date doesn't go well, or it'll mean you blew your shot."

I'd come to Newton that weekend certain Georgina hated me. Now I'd gone and missed my shot with her? Did I even *want* a shot?

Libby focused on cleaning the skillet she'd used to make the chilaquiles. "I was thinking . . ." She hesitated. "You want to take a drive?"

I rubbed the bridge of my nose, knowing full well where this conversation was headed. "No."

"The lawyer has been calling."

"My position hasn't changed," I said. "We're not selling Mom's house. We don't *need* to. I'm taking care of the mortgage."

"It's not about the money, Sebastian—if it was, we'd fix it up and rent it. We don't need to keep it just to know where we came from."

"It's where we grew up. You're the one talking about staying true to our roots."

"There's a difference between honoring your heritage and living in the past. Without Mom in it, it's just a rundown pile of bricks."

"It might not be all of this," I said, gesturing around the custom kitchen, "but it's all we have left of her."

Libby turned off the faucet and tapped a foamy, rubber index finger against my chest. "She lives here," she said, "not in that house. Not anymore."

"I hear you," I said, or else this conversation would continue in circles, "but my answer is no. I'm willing to pay the mortgage. I'm not willing to sell."

"When was the last time you were even in Eastie?"

She knew the answer to that—a year ago. Mom had wanted to spend her final days at home, so we'd arranged it. I'd spent that week making sure she was comfortable, then maintaining my sanity by fixing rain gutters, cleaning out the shed, or touching up the exterior.

I couldn't even attend her wake. I hadn't been back to the house or anywhere near downtown since the funeral. "Any time I've come out, it's been to see you. Here."

Libby might've lived in Newton now with her white picket fence and driveway basketball hoop, but gritty East Boston was our home. Only a year after Mom's death, I couldn't understand how Libby was ready to give that up. Without that, who were we? Without my past, was I anything other than the New York City playboy persona I'd meticulously created?

"I'm glad she didn't see the exposé," I admitted.

Libby shrugged and wiped down the counters. "She'd have called the reporter a *gringo*, then turned around and given you an earful. She was the only person allowed to talk shit about us."

I smiled. "Then she would've told me how to move on."

She looked over her shoulder at me. "You know, good advice is genetic. Not for you, clearly your advice sucks, but I'm great at it."

"And I suppose you'll give it to me whether I want it or not."

"Look at this exposé as an opportunity to make some changes, Sebastian. Both at work and at home. If you listen to this woman—Georgina—and do as she says, you win either way."

"How do you figure?"

"Either she's right and you're better for it, or she leaves."

I cocked my head. "Leaves?"

"That's the secret." She peeled off her rubber gloves and draped them over the lip of the sink. "You wanted to know how to get rid of her? Be so good that the magazine doesn't need her anymore."

Well, *that* was fucking simple. I couldn't believe I hadn't thought of it. I'd been putting up a fight about everything, even if it was just to disagree with her when I had a nagging suspicion she was right. But was getting rid of her still what I wanted? I couldn't shake Libby's suggestion that another guy had potentially taken my shot with Georgina.

Finally, I had exactly what I needed to take her out. Now I just had to ignore the disturbing thought that I might rather *ask* her out.

10

Justin sat in front of his computer making a case for watching Netflix at his desk. And the strangest part was—I agreed with him. Then again, not much about this working environment had been routine.

It was the most engaged I'd seen him yet. Apparently, he'd even arrived before Sebastian today. I'd found him feet up at his desk halfway through season two of *Ray Donovan*. "It's research," he explained. "I want to profile Anthony Pellicano."

"The private investigator," I said.

"And real-life 'fixer.' His life story has sex, violence, and Hollywood scandal."

I was glad I'd nixed Justin's story on the manliest floaties to bring to a pool party. Even though it took a certain kind of skill to write fifteen-hundred words around Shamu references and breast implant jokes, I'd had a feeling Justin could do better. "You have my blessing," I said. "In fact, we can make this a five-page spread."

"We rarely do more than four pages," he pointed out.

"I want to see more thoughtful, in-depth pieces that're

still sexy—like this—and less filler junk," I said. "Quality over quantity."

Justin ran a hand through his blond hair, and I thought I detected a hint of doubt, but he nodded. "I can do that."

"Good." I smiled. "And make it grizzly."

"You got it, boss." He leaned back in his office chair to see behind me. "Look who it is—boss number two."

I glanced back. As Sebastian approached with his laptop bag slung over one shoulder, I crossed my arms to show my disapproval. In what I'd thought was a rare stroke of generosity, last week, he'd offered to order me a temporary desk from IKEA. That morning, I'd been pleased to find it built and ready for me—with a pink *Girl Power* mousepad on top and drawers stocked with purple stationery, *Hello Kitty* stickers, and multicolored gel pens. In the top drawer, a Post-it stuck to a box of Crayola glitter markers read "*Harder to lose in a box*" in block letters. Sebastian's neat, contained handwriting made mine look like scrawl. It definitely belonged in the sleek black leather notebook where he was always making notes. Even Broadway tickets to the *The Lion King* sounded severe in there, with a sharp *w*, and the dots of his *i's* perfectly aligned with their stems.

Yes, I'd stolen a peek at his playbook. As long as Sebastian treated me like an enemy instead of an ally, I'd have to resort to snooping for intel.

"Good morning," I said, checking the clock to emphasize that it was already past ten.

"Morning." He nodded at Justin. "Boss number *two*? Really, dude?"

Justin shrugged. "She lets me watch Netflix at work."

Sebastian turned to me. "May I see you in my office?"

"Yes," I said. "You may see me in *our* office."

We walked through the cubicles toward the corner. As

with every morning, Sebastian's chiseled features hit me like a Louis Vuitton duffel to the face, but I did my best not to stumble in his presence. Problem was, there was more to him than soulful, green eyes and a strong jaw. He had conviction. He stuck to his guns. He didn't cave under pressure. I'd be attracted to that if it didn't frustrate me so much.

"Imagine my surprise when I tried to get to my desk this morning," he said as we approached the closed door to our office.

"Imagine *my* surprise seeing *my* new desk and its contents."

"You're welcome," he said. "I was here until after midnight putting it together." He swung the office door open. Bruno, lying at the foot of Sebastian's desk, lifted his head. "At least my surprise couldn't *kill you*."

I entered the office and kneeled beside my sleek, blue-gray, utterly lovable Great Dane. "Bruno's a gentle giant."

Sebastian closed the door behind himself and walked to his desk to put down his bag. With a *squish* that made me look up, he slow blinked and lifted his foot to look at the sole.

"Oh, no," I said. "Did Bruno have an accident?"

"An accident?" Sebastian grunted. "On the contrary, I can't help but think this is intentional."

"Or karma, more likely."

"For . . . ?" he asked, removing his shoe to show me it was vomit, not poop.

If not for everything up until today, then perhaps karma was evening the score for the girly desk, and the *other* Post-it he'd left on the stationery. It read, *Enough to last you 'til the end.*

He was counting down the days until my departure.

"Not sure," I answered him. "There must be lots for her to choose from."

"Well, karma can thank her lucky stars these seven-hundred-dollar oxfords were a gift from Ferragamo."

I tried to get Bruno back onto the dog bed I'd dragged all the way from Brooklyn. It was never easy to see him get sick, especially because this meant I'd have to go through the process of giving him his pills again—a chore even on easy days. "Sorry about the smell," I said, lowering my proverbial weapons since this *was* a shared office. "I'll clean up the vomit in a minute."

"Did he eat something bad?" Sebastian asked.

I wasn't in the mood to get into details; he probably didn't care, anyway. Dogs were just animals to him, and I was no more than a temporary nuisance. I stood and took my purse from the couch. "Must have."

"You don't think he might be more comfortable . . . anywhere but here?"

Of course he would. Coming to the office was clearly too much excitement for him. "My sitter had an emergency, and I needed to be here today."

"Ah, right. The sitter."

I fished out the orange, blue, and white labeled canisters with Bruno's pills and set them on the desk. Bruno made his way over to his dog bed, where he dropped down with a sigh. Next, I pulled out a small jar of Trader Joe's peanut butter and a plastic knife.

"You carry that in your purse?" Sebastian asked.

I'd hoped I wouldn't have to give Bruno his meds at the office, but when he was with me, I never left home without them. I got to work covering each pill in peanut butter. "It's his favorite," I said. "And my last resort in getting him to take his pills."

Sebastian's silence was so long and so rare that I glanced back at him.

"What're they for?" he asked.

I wasn't thrilled about letting Sebastian into what was a very significant and sometimes painful part of my life, but I was even less interested in wasting time fabricating a story. "He has an enlarged heart," I said. "As much as I try to pretend it just means he has more love to give, it doesn't. It means his heart works harder and less efficiently. And that he's very sick." So as not to invite any more questions, I added, "But we manage."

I squatted by Bruno, teasing the concoction in front of his nose until he licked his chops. When he started to drool, I gave him the pills and rested my elbows on my knees, praying he'd swallow them. He spent a full twenty seconds sucking all the peanut butter off before he spit out the diuretic. Then the supplement. Then the rest. I dropped my face in my hands. "Damn it."

Sebastian came over. "Did you try—"

"I've tried everything," I said, not bothering to hide the frustration in my voice. "I made him chicken and rice this morning and he took his pills then, but as you can see," I gestured toward Sebastian's desk, "he threw them up."

"Does that happen a lot?"

I lifted my head to look up at Sebastian. From my angle, he seemed to hit the ceiling. "Some mornings are fine, others are impossible."

"Sounds like it could get expensive."

Of course, Sebastian's first concern was money as Neal's had been, but he wasn't wrong. Bruno's illness, in addition to supporting myself and my ex for years, had eaten up my savings. From consistent check-ups to daily medicine to alternative therapies, there was no cost too high to keep Bruno alive, but it did require a steady paycheck and personal sacrifices on my part such as turning one dinner into two when possible and regularly opening up my closet to eBay. "The meds keep his heart working and fluid out of his lungs, so I don't really have a choice."

Sebastian removed his suit jacket. "I'll clean up the mess."

"You don't have to do that," I said, but he picked up his shoe and left the room. I faced Bruno. "Okay, big guy. I tried to play nice, but here's how it's going to go—I'm going to stuff them in your mouth, and you're going to swallow. It won't be pleasant, but it's the only alternative you've left me. And it's for the best. Got it?"

Bruno cocked his head.

I picked the pills out of the carpet, stood, and pointed at a spot next to my feet. "Come. Sit."

Bruno groaned as he got to all fours, then dropped his haunches at my side. Slowly, so as not to spook him, I straddled him from behind. He wagged his tail then looked up and back at me, as if we were about to play. I scratched his chest until he thumped his back leg. "Good boy," I said in my most soothing voice, then quickly pried his mouth open, tossed the pills back, and held it shut. My vet had shown me how to do this, assuring me it wouldn't hurt him, but I usually left it as a *last* last resort anyway. He wrestled with me until I was forced to release him. Within two seconds his meds were scattered at my feet.

"Come *on*," I said, plucking them off the ground. Bruno sensed what was coming and backed away. "No," I said, gesturing for him to come back. If Sebastian saw this and thought Bruno was a distraction, he'd go to Vance, and I'd be forced to take Bruno home. I lunged, chasing Bruno around the office. Luckily, Sebastian had shut the door, or I had no doubt Bruno would be bounding through cubicles right now, jumping desks and dodging my coworkers like he was on an obstacle course.

I pushed two of my boxes, still partially unpacked, next to Sebastian's mammoth desk, then went around to the other side. Now that Bruno was trapped, I rested my hands on my knees, partly to look him in the eye, and partly to catch my breath. The most exercise I'd had lately was sprinting from the subway after work to catch my favorite taco truck before it left for the night. "Finally, this overcompensating hunk of wood is serving a purpose," I said to Bruno.

"Hunk of wood?" Sebastian asked as he reentered the room. "Should I be flattered or insulted?"

I looked back over my shoulder. Sebastian held a bowl of liquid with a spoon sticking out, along with a roll of paper towels under his arm.

"I was talking about your ridiculous desk," I said.

"Ah." He grinned. "The word you're looking for is *under*compensating."

"That's not a thing." I shrugged as best I could while bent over. "I see something like that, and I have to draw my own conclusions."

"Without all the evidence, your conclusions are simply hypotheses."

I nodded at the colossal piece of furniture that would probably qualify as a small boat. "This is all I have to work with."

"That's all you *choose* to work with. If you'd like me to invalidate your assumptions, all you have to do is ask."

I frowned. Had he just offered to show me the goods to disprove my overcompensation theory? Sensing my distraction, one of his many humanlike abilities, Bruno made a break for it. I pounced, caught his collar just as he tried to escape through my legs, and straddled him from behind as

I worked my fingers between his clamped teeth. "It's for your own good," I said, panting. "Swallow the pills. Swallow the pills!"

"Keller—"

"Stay out of this," I said to Sebastian. Bruno wriggled underneath me. "You want a treat?"

He opened his mouth, and I shoved the pills in just before he bucked me off. I toppled on my ass, flopped back on the ground, and covered my face with my forearms. "I can't do this today."

Bruno nudged his snout under my arms to lick my face. "Leave me alone," I said, but of course he didn't. He was preternaturally good at knowing when I needed comforting, even if he was the cause of my distress.

Sebastian sighed heavily. "That's enough wallowing."

I didn't move, reluctant to face the reality of everything he'd just witnessed. Dog puke, me getting winded after a minute of running around, and a breakdown that had brought me to the ground. All things which could, and surely *would*, be used as ammunition to embarrass me at a later date. I peeked at Sebastian from under my arms. He was on his knees soaking a towel in the bowl he'd brought, then pressing it against the stain. "What is that?"

"Dawn dish soap, hydrogen peroxide, and baking soda."

"How do you know how to do that?"

"You think he's the first to puke in here?" he asked.

I laughed without thinking, then stopped when he checked the stain. The towel in his hand crunched, because it wasn't a towel, but something fluffier and stark white. "Is that . . . a diaper?"

"Yep. Soaks up better than a towel."

"But how do you *know* that? And where did you *get* it?"

"Dixon Media has a pregnancy magazine a few floors below us. I work with Justin—this isn't my first rodeo."

I blinked at him. Did he have a secret life as a dogsitter? Was he a *dad*? It wasn't that far-fetched considering his playboy history—surely, he was no stranger to pregnancy scares—and it would explain his intensity when he'd grilled me about whether I was a single parent. None of my research had turned up a family, but maybe he'd intentionally kept it hidden.

"Just out of curiosity," I started, "have you ever, you know, held a newborn? Or a baby bottle? Been required to keep a human alive overnight?"

"Huh?" He checked the carpet, then continued pressing the diaper to it. "Just my niece and nephew."

Ah. Of course—his sister. That was why he knew about vomit stains and sanitary shortcuts. "How old are they?"

"Five, and nineteen months." He stood, dusting off his hands. "It also works with a pad."

"What?"

"A menstrual pad. But I didn't want to get busted raiding the women's bathroom."

"Good to know." I eased myself into a sitting position. "I'll hit up the store later."

"Go through this a lot?" he asked.

"Yes, but usually at home. If I can't get Bruno to cooperate, then the sitter takes over. He's a vet student and the only other person who can handle the tantrums."

"Bruno." He chuckled. "Suits him perfectly. We can let this sit while we air out the smell. Where's his leash?"

"In my tote bag," I said cautiously. "Why? We already went for a walk this morning."

"We could all use some fresh air." He got hand sanitizer from his desk. "I'll call janitorial to come get the trash while we're out."

"We?"

"Yeah." He squirted enough goop in his palm to sanitize a small child, then rubbed his hands together. "Bruno's not the only one who needs morning Zen."

"And you think we'll find that downstairs, blocks from one of the world's top tourist destinations?" I asked, cringing at just the idea of the crowds clogging Times Square.

"I know we will." He went through my "Dogs are Good, but Danes are Great" tote bag. Bruno jumped to his feet and ran over, whining and wagging his tail as Sebastian hooked the leash onto his collar. "Bruno and I are going to de-stress. You coming?"

"*De-stress*? What happened to anthropomorphizing?"

"Have it your way. We'll see you when we get back."

Walking Bruno could be a dangerous endeavor. Nobody ever did it except me, Luciano, or Bruno's sitters. He wasn't some easily controlled lap dog—he'd been through several rounds of behavioral training but could pull me across a sidewalk in a flash. Especially when there was a female dog involved.

Because sadly, Bruno played right in to Luciano's theory—he *loved* bitches.

I got off the floor. No way was I letting them go alone. Bruno needed me, almost as much as I needed him.

And though neither of us needed Sebastian, in that moment, I had to admit—I was glad he was there.

11

With Bruno's leash in hand, Sebastian opened the door to our office, stuck his head out, and looked left to right.

"Maybe I should take his leash," I said. "He can be a handful."

"I've got him, and you're only allowed to come with us if you promise to relax."

"Fine," I said, crossing my arms as I waited behind them. "What are you doing?"

"Checking that the coast is clear."

"I already approved this with Vance."

"It's not Vance you need to worry about," Sebastian said. "It's Scaredy-Cat Jones."

I took a wild guess. "Justin?"

"He's scared of dogs. And heights. And women's shoes. And intimacy. The guy's a real piece of work. We keep the floor pet-free so we don't have to deal with more of his neuroses."

"He'll change his tune when he meets Bruno."

Sebastian looked back at me. "Considering this dog

would come up to Justin's stomach, I don't think so. Can Bruno army crawl?"

"Uh . . . not on command."

"Never mind. Flank Bruno's other side, and let's go." Sebastian strode out of the office. I scurried to keep up in four-inch heels, shielding Bruno from the left as we wound through the cubicles. "We're good," Sebastian said, easing up when we reached the elevators. "Justin must be on the shitter."

"Is everything about pooping with you two?"

Sebastian punched the call button. "Everybody does it, Georgina. Don't be a prude."

The elevator dinged, and the doors slid open to reveal Justin with a box of Dunkin' Donuts. "They were out of jelly," he started, "so I got us extra glaze—"

Bruno, most likely having caught a whiff of the pastries, bounded into the elevator and leapt for the box, ripping the leash from Sebastian's hand.

Justin stumbled back against a wall. "Monster!"

I jolted forward, but my heel caught on the carpet, and I face-planted into Sebastian's back. He didn't budge an inch, but spun around and grabbed my arm. "Whoa—"

"My heel, it's stuck," I rushed out as an apology. "I can't get it—" Reflexively, I kicked my foot to free myself.

Justin had abandoned the box of donuts and was trying to escape as my shoe, stiletto up, flew into the elevator. He threw his hands over his face and ducked into a corner as the heel narrowly missed his head. "What's happening?" Justin asked as Bruno licked his face. "Is this hell?"

My heart hammered, both from my near fall, and because Sebastian's big, stupid hand felt so good around my bicep. "Are you okay?" I asked Justin.

"He's fine," Sebastian said, releasing me to grab

Bruno's collar. He pulled him off Justin and passed me the leash. "The dog's friendly."

Justin peeked out from behind his arms to glare at me. "What are you, some kind of high-class assassin?" he asked me. "You almost killed me with a Jimmy Choo."

"Justin, take your fucking donuts and get out of here," Sebastian said, stooping to pick up my shoe.

"How am I the one getting yelled at?" he asked, side-eyeing the dog as he scraped the fallen donuts back into the box.

"You're a drama queen," Sebastian said. "It was about time you faced your fears."

Justin maneuvered by us, gripping the crumpled box as sweat dotted his temples. "You think I'm cured now?" he mumbled on his way to the office. "That only made things worse."

I hobbled onto the elevator with Bruno as Sebastian held out my Choo to keep the doors open. I traded the leash for it and angled to slip it back on. Without thinking, I steadied myself on Sebastian's bicep. As if the muscle wasn't hard enough to jar me into realizing what I'd done, an electric jolt spurred me to jerk my hand back and grab the elevator railing instead.

"Need help, Cinderella?" Sebastian asked, looking amused as he hit the button for the lobby.

"I'm fine." I straightened my shoulders. "What's Justin's shoe thing about?"

"He's been nailed by one before." Sebastian pinched the bridge of his nose and muttered, "Incidentally, it was also Jimmy Choo."

"That's some bad luck."

Sebastian nodded gravely. "If you hear him tell the story, he almost lost an eye."

I started to laugh. Sebastian also gave in to a deep chuckle. "Why are you being so nice to me?" I asked.

"Because you brought your *sick dog* onto the battle-field," he deadpanned, as if I should know what that meant.

The elevator stopped at a floor, and I moved closer to Sebastian and Bruno as people boarded. "What are you talking about?"

"It's like when you're gaming at a friend's house, and his mom comes in with snacks while you're talking shit. I have no choice but to lower my weapons and be nice."

"So I wasn't that far off base with the whole basement-dwelling nerd on a headset."

Sebastian ruffled the top of Bruno's head. "I have no idea what you're talking about."

I smiled to myself as the elevator opened and we passed through the lobby. Sebastian nodded at one of the security guards. "I can't believe you let this one in the building," he said, thumbing over his shoulder at me.

"Sorry, Mr. Quinn," he said. "She said he was an emotional support dog."

"Emotional support," Sebastian said under his breath as he glanced back at me.

I shrugged and tried to look sheepish. "A white lie that doesn't hurt anyone. Except Justin."

Sebastian shook his head and turned back to security. "I wasn't talking about the dog. I mean the Yankees fan."

"Oh-ho-ho," the guard said, slapping his forehead. "I had no idea, or I would've turned her away."

Since we'd just lost four games in a row against the Sox, I couldn't even retort. "It's not enough that we're giving it up to you on a regular basis?" I asked. "What are you traitors even *doing* in New York?"

"She's got a point," security said, shooting us a wave as

we exited onto a busy sidewalk. I followed Sebastian as he turned right, leading us through the first wave of a weekday lunch rush. It wouldn't be long until lines curved around food carts and strangers ate on shared benches. I balled my hands into fists to keep from taking Bruno's leash back amidst all the activity. Aside from him taking off after a bitch, a squirrel, or a UPS truck—he detested anyone who delivered mail—I worried about him getting too excited. It wasn't good for his heart, which was why I ensured he was rarely alone.

"Thanks for your help with the mess upstairs," I said. "Where'd you learn how to do that?"

Sebastian stopped to let Bruno sniff a tree trunk. "You mean . . . clean?"

"Don't you have a housekeeper?"

"Fuck no," he said with enough vehemence that I wondered if I'd hit a sore spot. "And I never will."

"I just can't picture you on your hands and knees scrubbing down your Fifth Avenue bachelor pad. Or is it simply that you researched a How-To on caring for a date who boozes too hard?"

"If you must know," he said, "I wasn't raised the smooth-talking, bespoke-suit-wearing gentleman you're acquainted with."

Surely, he was messing with me, because that didn't add up. Sebastian held himself with the poise of someone who'd grown up with Emily Post spines in the study, cotillion during the week, and an assurance that he'd never spend a night without a roof over his head. "But you went to Harvard and 'summered' on Nantucket as a kid."

"You know where I went to school, how I spent my summers, and the location of my apartment?" He rolled his wrist to wrap the leash around it. "What are you, some kind of stalker?"

"No," I said defensively, except that one night after a bottle of wine, a futile hour on Tinder, and a particularly combative workday with Sebastian, I *had* maybe succumbed to some stalker-like activities that went beyond what I'd needed to know for the job. "I did some research. Know thy enemy and all that."

"Enemy, huh?" Bruno tugged on his leash to get to a discarded takeout carton, but Sebastian pulled him forward. "What happened to getting to know your team so you could therapize us?"

Damn. That would've been a much more rational explanation. "You say *therapize* like I'm trying to lure you into a dark alley and rob you blind." I checked my hair in the reflection of a store window. "That could be what I'm doing for all you know, seeing as you have yet to schedule one-on-one time with me."

"Aha," he said. "I see what you're up to now. You planned this to get me into a Georgina Keller therapy session."

"You think I made my own dog throw up?"

"I don't know what you're capable of."

Bruno stopped to poop, and Sebastian cleaned it up before I could even offer. "You're derailing the topic," I said.

He tied the plastic bag. "Which is?"

"Me trying to reconcile your past with your present."

"I'll tell you one thing as long as you keep it between us." We turned a corner. "I never 'summered' anywhere, and my extensive cleaning knowledge is thanks to generations of Mexican matriarchs."

So he *was* Latino as Luciano had suggested. I'd tried digging into his heritage, but there was scant information out there about his past. The few clues I'd uncovered hadn't pointed to anything other than a charmed life. It made me wonder exactly how much information Sebastian put out there, and how many blanks had been filled in by the public.

"Why do I need to keep this between us?" I asked.

"It would be greatly appreciated."

"By who?"

"By *whom*," was all he said.

I waited for him to give me a reason. When he didn't continue, I said, "I thought you were Irish."

He snorted. "I have the opposite complexion."

"Not everyone in Ireland has red hair and pale skin," I pointed out.

"I'm half Mexican, half Caucasian."

"Oh. Considering Boston's strong Irish population, and that your last name is Quinn, I assumed . . ."

"Ah," he said and got quiet.

"So then is your dad—"

"Look." He nodded ahead of us. "We're here."

Maybe I should've known this would be a touchy subject, but I wasn't an *actual* therapist. I was only pretending to be one, and an occupational one at that. I kept my eyes on him a moment longer, then looked forward. We'd reached Bryant Park in record time—or maybe talking to Sebastian had just made the walk feel short.

"This is your Zen?"

"I come here to unwind when work gets to me," he said.

"*Unwind?*" I asked, feigning shock. "Whatever you do at the office all day, it looks an awful lot like unwinding to me."

He snorted. "I'm not exactly what you think, Keller."

"You don't know what I think."

"Well, you just accused me of goofing off on the job."

"Okay, so you *do* know what I think."

He gave me a look as he squatted to remove Bruno's leash. "Go on, boy. Have at it."

"Wait," I said, seizing Sebastian's bicep. Either he responded by flexing, or he was made of stone. "You can't let him off leash."

"Why not?"

"For one, it's illegal outside of the dog run."

"Do you see the K-9 unit around?"

"Like the bomb sniffers?" I asked. "You know they aren't the *actual* dog police."

"It was a joke. Never mind. Will he run away?"

"I couldn't lose him if I tried."

"Is he dangerous?" he asked. "Would he eat a small child?"

"No . . ."

"So, what's the problem?"

I took a deep breath and looked around. The park had a lot of green grass Bruno would love, but it wasn't fenced. And he really needed to be monitored during exercise. "Too much excitement is bad for his heart. I never let him off leash outside."

"Well, shit," Sebastian said. "How does he play?"

"We take long walks every day and do mental exercises like—"

"Georgina, do you see the size of this guy? He needs to get his zoomies out."

"Zoomies—?"

Sebastian unclipped the leash, and Bruno bolted across the lawn. "When pets get a burst of energy and act all crazy. There's a whole Reddit thread dedicated to them."

I let Bruno get about fifty yards before I called him. Maybe he had the zoomies, but Mom had the panics. It *was* fun to see him go wild, but I preferred he did it closer. He skidded to a halt and sprinted back to us.

Sebastian slid out his wallet. "You hungry?"

"Not yet. I have lunch at the office."

"I'll be right back."

As he walked away, I watched Bruno zigzag between benches, wrought iron park tables, and other dogs. If only I'd brought his pills, I might've been desperate enough to steal someone's sandwich and turn it into a cocktail of heart meds. Once I'd gotten enough dirty looks, I squatted and whistled for him. He came bounding back and plopped down in front of me.

"Hey, you're not really going to a Yankees game with that guy Francis, are you?" Sebastian asked from somewhere behind me. "If you want to drink beer, eat hotdogs, and root for a bunch of losers, we can do that at the office any day."

I looked up once I'd latched Bruno's leash back on. Sebastian waved a bunless hotdog in a paper tray at me. "It's François," I said. "And why wouldn't I go out with him?"

"He's clearly some overworked finance bro who got lucky. Right place, right time."

"Who said anything about finance? Or getting lucky for that matter?"

"He's a bro, trust me. I've got radar for these things. The point is, you made your case, but there's no reason you have to go through with the date."

"There is a reason," I said, standing. "You guys have all these fancy ways of trying to get laid when the answer is very simple."

"Oh, yeah?" He was freakishly close to me for some reason, and I had to tilt my head back to see his face. "Enlighten me, Georgina."

"I already did. He and I share a common interest—baseball." I tugged Bruno and started walking. "Catching a game sounds like the perfect date to me, and on top of that, he was a nice guy."

"He just assumed you were single, despite the fact that you were at a bar with six guys?" Sebastian asked, catching up to me in a few long strides.

"No. He asked if you were my boyfriend."

"He did?" Sebastian tore the hotdog in half. "Me specifically?"

"Yep. That reminds me—you guys published an article about introducing a new girlfriend to your friends."

"Hmm." Sebastian closed one eye. "Yes. February 2015."

"What about trying that from the girlfriend's point-of-view? Get a guest writer with a crisp comedic voice. Meeting a guy's friends is ripe for humor. Plus, it brings the female presence *Modern Man* desperately needs."

Instead of pointing out the flaws in my idea, he seemed to consider it, which was progress. But then he said as he tore the hotdog into little pieces, "I wonder what made him think of all the guys, *I* was your boyfriend."

I wasn't sure whether he meant that as an insult, but he had a point. Sebastian and I were least likely to partner up. Then I realized with a start that I'd forgotten to fear this time away from the office with Sebastian. And that we were almost behaving like friends.

"*What* are you doing to that hotdog?" I asked when I noticed he hadn't eaten a bite, just torn it up in the paper tray.

He reached in his trousers pocket and pulled out Bruno's meds. I hadn't even seen him pick them up. "For the brute."

"You brought his pills?" I asked.

He stuffed them into the hotdog chunks and fed them to Bruno, who swallowed them right down without a fight. We'd done the hotdog thing plenty of times before, but always at home where I boiled them myself.

"Wow," I said, not even trying to hide my awe. "Good boy."

Sebastian smiled, clearly pleased with himself. "Thank you."

I didn't know how to respond to this new side of Sebastian. In the span of one morning, he'd cleaned vomit, taken care of my dog, and gotten us outdoors for some vitamin D. My mood had improved considerably seeing Bruno run free for the first time in a while. "No, thank *you*," I said as I stepped outside the park. "Did you have pets—"

"Watch out," Sebastian said, grabbing my arm to pull me backward.

"To your left," a bike tour guide said into a small, handheld megaphone as he dinged his bell at me, "you'll see a busy New York power couple grabbing some rare alone time on their lunch breaks."

Bruno barked at the fleet, and Sebastian's hand remained firmly on my bicep, even as the last cyclist pedaled by. A tornado of leaves followed, swirling around our feet. Bruno fell silent. A breeze blew my hair into my lipstick and Sebastian glanced at my mouth, then back up. New York City had many personalities. With the fall sun and a moment of quiet, it became serene. Maybe even a little romantic. I could see now that Sebastian's eyes weren't as green as I'd thought. They shaded into blue like the calm waters of the Mediterranean. Stillness in the city, and also in his eyes, was so rare and unexpected, that it almost felt wrong. Was this the calm before a storm, or were we standing in the eye of it?

As if Sebastian's thoughts had followed the exact same course, his face smoothed, and he shook his head. "You have all these little fucking freckles," he said. "It's like someone sprinkled you with cinnamon to serve you up as breakfast."

I gaped at him, but was his statement really that surprising? Like ninety-nine percent of redheaded children, I'd grown up being teased about my freckles. And as an adult, Neal would often compliment my skill for covering them up with concealer.

"Ex*cuse* me," I said, pulling my arm back to cross it over my chest. Instantly, the warmth of his hand receded. I repeated my mom's words of reassurance to me. "They give me character."

"You already have enough characters for a George R.R. Martin novel."

If Sebastian was implying I had multiple personalities, well, that might've been true, but what gave him the right? He wasn't my therapist or my mother or even my friend. "Whatever." I scoffed. "We should get back to the office."

"Tell me the truth. Did you ask François to ask you out?"

I turned on my heel to head back. "Do you want me to tell everyone you're acting like a sore loser?"

"I'm not asking because of the bet. I just don't want you to feel obligated to go through with this 'date.'" He made exaggerated and *highly* insulting air quotes. "What do you think, Bruno? Should she just cancel?"

"I'm not canceling a date I actually want to go on," I said. "Geez. You'd give anything to see me suffer, wouldn't you? You probably keep a notebook of things that annoy me."

"Like your freckles and cinnamon."

"Cinnamon doesn't annoy me. Being likened to a cinnamon bun *does*."

"And then there's me," he said. "I obviously top the list."

"So, you do have a notebook."

"Of course not. I keep the list on my phone for easy access."

I trained my eyes forward but heard the smile in his voice.

We paused for a cab rounding the corner, then crossed the street. "I'm going to need proof of this alleged date, you know," he added.

"Fine," I said. "That shouldn't be a problem."

His smirk gave him away. He didn't believe there *was* a date.

Well, if proof was what he wanted, I'd find a way to give it to him. That gave me even more reasons to not only go on the date, but to spite Sebastian by enjoying it.

12

I t was entirely possible my "common interest" revelation was a dud. I would've thought two baseball fans at a Yankees game would have lots to talk about, but with several innings left, François and I were struggling to keep the conversation going. Or *I* was struggling. He was just watching the game.

"Do you like beer?" I asked him.

In a Yankees cap and Louisiana State polo shirt, an odd combination I still hadn't gotten used to, François leaned his elbows on his knees as the opposing team's first baseman moved to the batter's box. "I was drinking one when we met, remember?"

"Right." I waited for him to catch on to my line of thinking, but he just eyed the mound as if *he* was up to bat. "I can go get us one," I volunteered.

"I don't typically drink before the sun sets," he said, glancing back at me. "Do you?"

"Well, no," I said. Did brunch cocktails count? "But it *is* baseball. The rules are different on the diamond, François."

"Call me Frank." He rubbed his nose. "I don't want to be fuzzy for the rest of the game, but go ahead if you want."

I hated that Neal popped into my mind on my first date since our breakup, but he'd said that same thing a lot—*if you want*—and in a way that made it clear he disapproved. We could hire a cleaner *if I wanted*, even though we wouldn't have an issue if I just picked up after myself more. Skipping the gym was fine *if you don't mind those extra pounds*, but he'd be cycling the length of Brooklyn. *If that's how you want to spend the little money we have* he'd say in the same tone when I'd look up Cliffs of Moher cruises.

I doubted Frank had meant it that way—it was my own issues that made it feel combative—but how had I gotten mixed up with a guy who was too tightly wound to day drink? Baseball was not the kind of sport that required a lot of concentration, even for the most devoted fan. And it was usually better with beer because the innings could drag sometimes. But maybe I wasn't being fair. Getting buzzed alone didn't sound all that appealing anyway.

"I'm good," I said, "I'll just grab something later."

"How about these seats?" he asked, clapping through a play. "Pretty great, right?"

"Better than I'm used to."

"How'd you get into baseball?" he asked.

"My dad." I'd already mentioned that partway through the first inning, but Frank had been distracted. "I grew up in Buffalo, so it was a big deal to drive in for a game."

"You already told me that, didn't you? Sorry. My attention's a little divided."

"It's okay, totally fine," I said, even though I was starting to question why he'd asked me to the game. It seemed as if he might enjoy it more alone. "We never had seats this close. We were usually in the bleachers. It's cool to actually see the players' expressions."

"This is the only way I'll come to a game. I can't sit farther back than this."

"There's actually a weird sense of camaraderie in the nosebleed section . . ."

François groaned at a bad call and turned forward. I should've considered how long a baseball game could go on. It was my first date in a while, and this wasn't making a case for doing it again anytime soon. Silence made me just as uncomfortable as stilted conversation. Was he not interested enough to learn more about me? What if we ran out of things to talk about at some point?

I wiped sweat from my upper lip. I was starting to regret my long-sleeved shirt. It'd been cold when I'd left my apartment, but the sun was right on top of us now. Apparently, the weather was still making up its mind. "So, did you stay in the city this summer?" I asked.

"I spent some time at my parents' beach house in Florida," he said. "You ever been?"

I perked up with a fresh topic. "Just Miami. Is that where their house is?"

"Boca Raton. Did you go for work?"

"No, a bachelorette party with some girlfriends for a weekend."

François looked back at me and winked. "Sounds like a *fiesta* I'd like to attend."

He hadn't shown much physical interest in me since we'd met outside the four train before the game, so I wasn't sure how to take his comment. Friendly? Suggestive? Creepy? I didn't think I'd make it through the rest of the game without a drink, but as he'd pointed out, we'd met in a bar. I didn't want him to think I needed alcohol to have a good time.

I tried to think of something else worth mentioning. Frank had gone monosyllabic when I'd brought up Bruno, and my dog was probably my favorite subject. "On my way here," I said, wrinkling my nose, "a guy on the subway offered me half an avocado. Isn't that strange?"

Frank smiled over his shoulder. "Subway?"

"I mean, that's not an ideal place to eat anything, especially avocado. And then to offer me some?"

"You mean the sandwich place?" he asked. "They offer me avocado all the time."

"No, no. A man *on* the subway offered me half."

"Oh, got it. Yeah, weird," he agreed, turning forward again.

Weird, yes, but maybe not enough to mention. I should've gone with the silence. I had all sorts of interesting work anecdotes and factoids to stimulate conversation, but this probably wasn't the right audience to inform that magazine covers with the word *climax* sold better to women than ones with *orgasm*.

After five minutes that felt like thirty of watching the game, two hands appeared from behind me, one holding a loaded hotdog, and the other a full beer. Condensation dripped over the long fingers of a large male hand attached to a brawny, dark-haired forearm.

How I knew that it belonged to my frustratingly gorgeous and just plain frustrating coworker, I wasn't sure. I turned in my seat to meet Sebastian's amused green-blue eyes. From beneath the shade of his baseball cap, he gave me a megawatt smile, showing off nearly all of his straight, white teeth. "Thirsty?" he asked.

I just stared at him, opening and closing my mouth. "What are you doing here?"

"I told you I'd need proof."

Sweat trickled down my temple. I'd already been

warm, but with Sebastian's presence, the afternoon seemed to get a few degrees hotter. "I thought you meant a selfie or something. You said you only go to Sox games."

"Did I?" He thrust the food and drink at me. I took it, but only because I'd never been more grateful for a cold beer. "We noticed you weren't drinking, and that concerned me . . . *us*."

At the top of the steps, Justin balanced armfuls of hotdogs and beer. He started to wave and nearly fumbled it all, catching himself at the last second. "Where are you guys sitting?" I asked.

"Same section as you." Sebastian gestured a few rows behind us. "What're the odds?"

Shit. The only thing worse than a boring date was Sebastian *witnessing* a boring date. He couldn't know how bad I was at this, or I'd never hear the end of it. I had to make more of an effort. "This is François," I said.

Frank shifted around in his seat and held out his hand. "Nice to meet you."

"Sebastian."

François lowered his hand. "You're brave to wear a Sox hat around this place."

I pulled back and sure enough, the Boston Red Sox logo looked back at me. "You can't wear that here!"

"I'm not." Sebastian removed it and dropped it over my hair. "*You* are."

I shook my head hard since my hands were occupied. "Take it off. I wouldn't be caught dead—"

"You need it, Keller. You're starting to look like a stick of cinnamon gum."

"I don't care how I look. I'm no turncoat."

"Come on, now, nobody'll even notice," he said, adjusting the cap as he settled it on my head. "Small price to pay to maintain such flawless skin." He winked, then turned and met Justin four rows directly behind us.

"The nerve," I growled, turning forward again. Cinnamon gum? Flawless skin? Did his sarcasm know no bounds? "Can you *believe* him?"

"You want my hat instead?" François asked. "You are a little red . . ."

I sat back in my seat. I didn't want François's hat, because—I hated to admit—I liked wearing Sebastian's. It was like being back in high school, and the quarter-back had just draped his letterman jacket over my shoulders.

"It's fine," I said. "It's just a hat."

But it wasn't just a hat—and the beer in my hand wasn't just a beer. They were exactly what I needed in that moment. What did it say that my enemy was taking better care of me than my date?

As the game rolled into the next inning, I began to cool down with the help of the beer and the baseball cap. Except now, I was faced with a different kind of heat— Sebastian's eyes on the back of my head. Was he watching me or the game? Why *would* he be watching me? Why did I care? Now that I'd wondered it, I couldn't think of anything else.

Frank glanced at my beer. "How was it?"

Too small, I thought since I only had a few sips left. Based on his earlier comments, though, I assumed he'd judge me for having a second one. "Satisfying."

He smiled at me. "You're cute."

"Really?"

"Don't sound so surprised."

"Well, I just . . ." I hesitated. "I was worried you weren't having a good time."

"I'm having a great time." He put an arm along the

back of my seat. "This is my kind of date—Yankees and a sweet girl. Now, if only we were winning."

"Want me to go down there and have a chat with them?"

He laughed. "How's someone like you still single?"

"I, um . . . just got out of a relationship."

"Ah. Me too. I wasn't planning to get back out there so soon, but here I am." He angled toward me. "Honestly, I was shocked when you asked me out. My ex never would've done that—too shy."

If I'd been the type to set the record straight, I might've pointed out that I hadn't really been the one asking—only pretending to. Because I *was* his ex. I never would've approached Frank if I hadn't been forced to.

"You even look good in a Sox cap," he said, wetting his lips. "That's something." Nothing about the moment screamed *first kiss*, but Frank dropped his hand to my shoulder and brought me closer. I didn't even have a chance to pull away before the bill of his cap knocked into mine. I laughed nervously and silently thanked Sebastian for saving me from afar.

"Hey, Keller," Justin called from behind me. "You on a date?"

I glanced back at a grinning Justin. Sebastian had his eyes on us, his knee bouncing a mile a minute. Without his hat, his hair was messy, and he was dressed as casually as I'd ever seen him in a hoodie, gray t-shirt, and jeans that definitely did not double as pajamas.

"What's with those guys?" Frank asked. "You told me at the bar that guy was your coworker."

"He is. They both are. They just like to mess with me."

"They came all the way here to hassle you on a Saturday?"

"I don't know how, in a stadium this size, they ended

up right behind us, but whatever. Don't pay any attention to them."

"All right," he said, playing with my hair. "I'll pay my attention elsewhere."

This time, I recognized the look in his eyes—and then he removed his hat. He hadn't given up on the kiss.

As Frank reached to remove Sebastian's cap from my head, Sebastian called down to us. "Georgina."

I needed to take my own advice and ignore him—after all, he was probably interrupting us on purpose to annoy me. Except that I was more relieved for the save than anything. Frank paused as if he was also deciding whether or not to acknowledge Sebastian.

I looked back. "What?" I asked.

Sebastian pushed his sleeves from his forearms to his elbows as he glanced between the two of us. "Come up here a sec."

I had a decision to make. I'd told Sebastian once I wouldn't come when he called—but it was either that, or stay and get kissed.

13

If François had felt confident enough to go in for a kiss before the fifth inning, I could only assume Georgina's date was going well—and thanks to my big mouth, I was about to find out.

Georgina followed me up the stairs toward concessions. Behind me, she said something, but the chatter between innings drowned her out. I angled sideways, putting a hand on her upper back to urge her in front of me. "What'd you say?"

"I asked where we're going."

I leaned down to her ear as we reached the concourse. "Beer."

"I must look pretty thirsty," she said.

I caught her drift. I'd picked a fine moment to interrupt the date. I'd tried to convince myself witnessing the kiss wouldn't bother me, but I couldn't tell if Georgina had invited it or had been trying to pull away. When François had reached a grubby hand for the hat I'd put on Georgina's head—*my* hat—I'd reacted without thinking and blurted out her name.

In line at the concessions stand, I got out my wallet. "What're you having?"

"I'm not sure I should drink any more."

"How many have you had?"

"Only the one you brought me, but Frank seemed weird about the fact that I was day drinking. How would it look to get drunk on a first date?"

I refrained from telling her it was a bad sign if he was already making her feel guilty about something—only because I didn't want her to think I was judging. "Who knows," I said, "he might start to look better."

"Is that why Justin is drinking?" Georgina asked while we waited.

Jokes about Justin and I dating were a dime a dozen, but ruffling Georgina's feather was a rare opportunity I wasn't about to pass up. The cashier called us forward. I ordered two beers, then leaned down to Georgina's ear. "You have a point there. Justin and I haven't even bumped hats yet."

She shifted feet. "That wasn't what it looked like."

"No? It *looked* like he tried to kiss you. So why didn't he?"

She looked back at me, holding my gaze until the register's cash drawer popped open with a *ding*. She was saved by the bell—for now. I paid for our drinks, picked them up, and steered us to a two-top table when she tried to walk back toward the stands. "Want to sit?" I asked.

She took her drink. "I'll stand."

I took a tall stool to put us at eye level. "So, why didn't you kiss him? Bad breath?"

She gasped into her hand. "My breath is fine."

"I meant his. I'm sure yours is pure relish on a hotdog."

She made a face. "Gross."

"I happen to love relish," I said. "But does François?"

Each time I said *François* with flourish, she flinched. I didn't care. Something about him bugged me—I just couldn't put my finger on it.

"We didn't kiss because you interrupted us," she said.

"So? If I were in his position, and we both wanted that kiss, I wouldn't let anyone stop me."

"*Frank* and I are clicking," she said, scowling. "There was even mention of spending time at his summerhouse."

"Hamptons?"

She coughed into her fist. "Boca Raton."

The idea of Georgina spending a summer with a closeted vampire in Boca Raton was tragic enough that I almost smiled. I got the sense she was playing up the date. If it was so great, why wasn't she sitting here with him? And why was I more relieved than smug about that? "Meanwhile, Justin and I will be clamming in Montauk."

"You two should really just make it official and announce your love to the world."

"But then I wouldn't get to flirt with pretty girls."

"For someone who pretends to have as much game as you," she said, "I still haven't seen you successfully flirt with *any* girls since I've known you."

"How do you know I'm not flirting with you right now?"

The slight tint of her cheeks was worth stepping out on a limb. "I said *successfully*," she retorted.

I didn't mean to ask it, but the question had come out, a natural response. Because flirting came easy to me, and I *had* flirted with her once. Before I'd known who she was. I'd been wondering whether I'd jumped to conclusions about Georgina since my talk with Libby, and I couldn't forget she was a threat to my job—but could she be more than that too? The way her personality flipped on a dime, I still couldn't tell. Seeing how someone her size handled Bruno, not just physically but shouldering the weight of his illness, caring for him the way she did . . . it aligned with the strength she'd exuded in front of a roomful of strangers. But it also hinted at the sweet, vulnerable side of her I'd only gotten glimpses of. Which had left me only more confused about who Georgina really was.

At the moment, she was pink-nosed, sweet smelling, and throwing snark in my direction. "What was that?" I pretended not to hear her so I could scoot to the edge of my stool.

"I said I still haven't seen you flirt *successfully*."

I set an elbow on the table. "Maybe I ought to come down and get some tips from Mr. Boca Raton. Or you could ditch him and come sit with us."

"What would be the fun in that?" she asked. "I know you and Justin are having the time of your lives analyzing my first-date moves."

I wasn't sure about that. Watching them had made me want to interrupt, the same way I'd had to refrain from interjecting when they'd met at happy hour. Was it just François who got under my skin, or was it her *with* him? That sounded an awful lot like jealousy.

"Can I give you your hat back now?" she asked.

If her flushed cheeks were any indication, Georgina burned easily. Those little freckles were endearing, but there was nothing cute about skin cancer. "Not 'til the sun goes down, buns."

Her mouth fell open. "*Buns*? What does that mean?"

"Your nickname."

She gasped and covered the seat of her jeans. "Did I sit in something?"

"Buns doesn't have to mean butt. It can mean hotdog buns, hamburger buns, sticky buns."

"*Man* buns," she offered, her eyes glimmering. "*Oh*, I know. This is because I tried to wear my hair in a bun the other day."

"I remember that." She'd come to work in glasses with her hair spooled on top of her head looking like she'd walked out of the sexy geekette spread Derek had been trying to get us to run since her PowerPoint. I reached up and fingered some strands of her hair. "Little pieces kept falling out . . ."

"I was running late that day, and I ran out of time to . . ." She seemed to lose her train of thought as I twirled the hair around my index finger. "Have you guys been calling me that the whole time?"

"It's not a bad thing. It could also mean honeybuns." *Honeybuns*? Christ, I was cheesy and nearly on the edge of my seat, but I couldn't seem to tear myself away. I released the tendril. "Or my personal favorite—cinnamon buns."

"Your fascination with cinnamon borders on troubling."

Tell me about it. Dunkin' Donuts made a mean cinnamon bun, but it was the sprinkles dusted on her nose that had my attention.

"*Cinnamon doesn't annoy me. Being likened to a cinnamon bun does.*"

I'd never called her one, and damn if her response hadn't been cute, especially with her pouting over it the way she was now.

"You're not seriously going to call me that in public?" she asked.

Of course I wouldn't. Justin would string me up if he ever heard me wax poetic over a pastry. I kept my voice low. "We can keep it between us if you like."

"But you hate nicknames."

"Says who?"

"Justin."

I sniffed, easing back a bit. "He only thinks that because my sister complains that I refuse to call my niece *caramela* instead of Carmen."

"Why won't you?"

"Because she's not a piece of candy."

"So how come you can't see the rest of us that way?"

The exposé had blasted me for referring to women as food. I was about to tell Georgina she shouldn't believe everything she read—obviously, I didn't *actually* disregard her as some empty-calorie breakfast treat. But I had called her that when I wouldn't do the same to my niece, so maybe she had a point. "Does it make you uncomfortable?" I asked.

"To be seen as a lowly cinnamon bun?"

"Nothing lowly about it." I leaned in. "Don't tell anyone, but most days, I prefer buns over donuts."

She sighed. "It doesn't bother me, because I don't think it's coming from a malicious place. But you can see how some women might find it belittling."

I'd wanted to best Georgina, challenge her, run her out of the job—but I never wanted to make her feel small. "Yeah," I admitted. "I guess I can see that."

Her eyebrows shot up. "Are you only agreeing to get me off your back?"

"No." If it wasn't her job to *be* on my back, having her there wouldn't have sounded too bad. I didn't relish the idea of admitting I'd been wrong, but I got where she was coming from. "I hate nicknames because I grew up with them," I explained. "As a twin, and with a Hispanic surname, sometimes they were cutesy and other times derogatory. So I do understand."

"Oh. I'm sorry." She tucked her hair behind her ear,

sliding her fingers under the edge of the hat. "I wouldn't have thought *Quinn* would give you any trouble."

It'd given me plenty of trouble all right. "It's Quintanil-la," I said. "When my sister and I entered middle school, my mom chopped it off. Kids made fun of it. Teachers couldn't pronounce it. She worried it would hold us back."

"I . . . I had no idea."

"Nobody does." I looked her over. I'd shared something with Georgina, someone who could possibly end me, that only my immediate friends and family knew. "It isn't public knowledge."

She hid her hand in the sleeve of her shirt and asked, "Why are you telling me this?"

It was a valid question without an answer. Nor could I explain why I'd gone overboard just to tag along on this date with her. I searched her eyes, and though the idea of Georgina scared me in more ways than one—both what she meant for my career and the fact that she'd brought out a side of me I didn't like—I wasn't afraid of the person I saw right then. We were even closer now. Had I moved, or had she? She wore the same alarmed look that'd crossed her face near the end of our walk in the park. Fear that I might kiss her? Or anticipation? The old Sebastian might've taken what he wanted, consequences be damned, but I was trying to be better. For my mom. For my job. "I don't know why I told you that," I said, except I did. I trusted the Georgina in front of me. It was George at the office who made me wary.

"Your sister's name is Libby, right?" she asked. "She still lives in Massachusetts?"

I pulled back in surprise. "Yeah."

"You light up when you talk about them. And Boston too. Do you think about moving back there?"

Maybe I lit up over my family, but not the city itself.

Since Mom's death, Boston remained a dark cloud over my memories. "No," I said. "Except to visit my sister's family in the suburbs, I'll never go back to the city."

She tilted her head. "Never?"

A couple guys passed us on the way to the counter and said, "Nice *Red Sucks* hat." One sniffed at Georgina. "Go back to Boston."

As the guy turned his back, Georgina paled. She took off the hat and glanced up at me. "I'm a Yankees fan."

"I know. Why are you telling *me?*" This was what I didn't understand. At the office her first day, she'd practically told us, a group of men she barely knew, to love it or shove it about her devotion to the Yankees. Yet, she struggled to do the same to some drunk chowderhead. I crossed my arms. "You want to say something, say it."

"What if they get mad?"

"Not while I'm standing here."

She put the hat back on and spoke a little louder. "I'm a Yankees fan."

The guy turned back. "Not with that shit on your head. A true fan wouldn't be caught dead in that."

"For your information, the hat is so I don't get a sunburn. I'm a born-and-bred Yankees girl, but I'll wear what I want."

"Whatever," he muttered as his friend paid the cashier. "Poser bitch."

I stepped around Georgina. "What the fuck did you say?"

"It's okay," Georgina said, grasping my bicep as if she could hold me back. "I take *bitch* as a compliment, especially from this turd."

Turd? I gaped at her, unsure whether to laugh at her attempt at an insult or pound this idiot.

"Ignore him, he's drunk," the guy's friend said as they got their beers. "We don't want trouble."

I stared them down until they were out of sight. Georgina deflated beside me with a soft sigh and I glanced back at her. Her back went straight as if I'd caught her doing something wrong. "We showed them, huh?" she said.

I studied her a moment. "That took a lot of effort for you, didn't it?"

She attempted a casual shrug, but I couldn't help noticing her chokehold on the beer. "Nobody likes confrontation."

"Yet, if I'd called you a bitch, you would've put me six feet under."

"Maybe. Maybe not."

I arched an eyebrow at her. "Come again?" I asked. "You nearly took me out at the café for far less."

"I hadn't had my coffee yet. Should we go back?" She picked up her bag from the table.

I took it, set it back down, and guided her onto a stool by her shoulders. She wasn't getting off that easily. "You and I are going to have a little chat, Georgina."

"About?"

I'd had enough back and forth from her. She'd done an admirable job of keeping me on my toes, but I needed both feet on the ground where she was concerned. Maybe it was the beer or the fact that we were far from the office, but I sensed she'd open up now if I pushed her. "How come you were quiet and shy at the café before our collision? And why was it so hard to speak up for yourself just now? And why is it okay for *anyone* to call you a bitch?"

She sighed. "You know what they say. Men love bitches."

"Who says that?"

She hesitated, clearly uncomfortable. "Listen to this," she said. "On the way here, a man offered me half an avocado. On the subway."

"Are you serious?" I asked. "Why?"

"I have no idea."

"Did he at least give you something to eat it with?"

"No," she said and smiled in a cute way that made me forget what we were supposed to be talking about. Which I supposed was her plan.

"How'd you respond?" I asked.

"I told him no thanks—I only eat the bad kind of fat."

I laughed. "Why is this relevant? Did he call you a bitch?"

"No. I just wanted to see if you thought it was strange."

"Definitely strange."

She relaxed, setting her elbow on the table and her chin in her hand. "How come you always call me Georgina?"

"What should I call you?"

"George, same as everyone else."

"Not everyone uses George," I pointed out.

"Everyone does sometimes. Georg*ina* is exhausting."

I would've steered the conversation back to the issue at hand, but I had a feeling we were somehow circling the heart of it. In her eyes, was there some differentiation between George and Georgina? I stayed standing, looking down at her as I chose my words carefully so she wouldn't get defensive. "You think Georgina is burdensome to others?"

She blew out a breath, meeting my gaze. "It's a mouthful."

"If you think that, why not call me Seb? Or 'hey you,' which has less syllables than Sebastian. My name is longer than yours." She furrowed her brow as if tallying the letters, so I saved her the mental strain. "Yours has eight, mine has nine."

"Okay, I'll call you Seb, *Seb*."

"I still won't call you George."

"Because George feels like your equal," she reasoned, "whereas Georgina is easier to see as an inferior."

"Jesus, no." I pulled back. That had nothing to do with it. Her name could be fucking Fido but while we were both humans, I'd see her as an equal. An equal who potentially held my fate in her hands. The only way to dig my way out of this was the truth. "When I met you—let's just say, I had impure thoughts."

With the way her eyes widened, I couldn't keep the hint of triumph off my face. It *was* fun to surprise her. "About me?"

"About you. And since then, I refuse to picture you as George."

"Well . . . that makes things difficult," she said.

"Only if you yourself favor George over Georgina."

She opened and closed her mouth. "I—I don't know what that means."

"Yes, you do."

With a quick glance around me, as if searching for an exit, she stood. "I should get back to—"

I put my hand on the table to block her with my arm. "You're like one of those complex, jumbo puzzles with hundreds of pieces. Even when I manage to put a corner together, I can't help feeling further from completing the picture."

"You're wrong." She moved around me, but I caged her against the table.

"Am I?" I couldn't ignore the way her cheeks flushed as her breathing sped. She didn't look happy to be cornered in more than one way, but I wanted answers. Not just the job kind anymore, like if Vance had said anything to her about my work, or whether my fate rested on her shoulders —*now*, I was curious about other things too. Like exactly which nerve I'd hit in the café to make her blow up at me. And why she allowed François and the loudmouth Yankee to treat her one way, but she never let me get away with shit. "I'm not even sure I'm playing the right game."

"Try checking the box," she said. "If it says 'ages three and up,' you probably are."

We narrowed our eyes at each other without so much as a blink between us.

"Do *you* see Georgina as inferior?" I asked, my eyes on her full, pink mouth, just inches from mine.

She dropped her gaze to the zipper of my hoodie. After a couple seconds, she said, "Not inferior, just . . ."

"What the hell is taking so long?" Justin appeared out of nowhere, causing each of us to flinch. "And where's my dr—oh. Shit. Am I interrupting?"

I straightened up, and Georgina stepped out from under me. "No," she said, relief passing over her face.

I watched her closely. She *really* didn't like me poking around her head. That only made me want to do it more, especially now that I was getting somewhere. But I owed Justin a beer, and he wasn't going to let me off the hook until he got it. I took my wallet from my jeans. "What d'you want?"

"Whatever you're having," he said.

I walked away. If I *had* been hitting on Georgina, this would be the perfect opportunity for Justin to fuck with me. So, it shouldn't have surprised me to overhear him say to her, "Well, well. It's a fine line, isn't it?"

If Justin wasn't careful, I was going to knock the smug right off his face and onto the baseball diamond. It was the second time since we'd returned to our seats that he'd caught me watching Georgina and François instead of the game.

Justin's face split with a grin. "Enjoying the view?"

"Of course not. I'm at a *Yanks* game."

"That's a pretty big sacrifice you've made for Georgina. You told me we were coming here to judge her dating skills."

"What do you think I'm doing?"

Justin folded his hands in his lap and shrugged. "I think you're trying to figure out how you feel about her. And seeing her with another dude is making it pretty clear."

I looked back at François's arm around her, tempted to go down there and *interrupt* one more time. The last time. "I'm just going above and beyond for my job," I said. Justin might've been right, but he already had all the ammunition he needed. "Making sure Georgina is up for the position she took on."

Justin adjusted his sunglasses. "You're telling me you betrayed your precious Red Sox *and* gave the people in these seats a two-hundred-dollar gift card to Peter Luger just to make sure Georgina sucks at her job?"

"To make sure she sucks at *my* job," I pointed out. "You forget my ass is on the line here. Vance warned me I was on thin ice, meanwhile he can't stop fawning over Georgina."

Justin glanced over at me. "You think she's gunning for the creative director position?"

She wouldn't be the first to try, but judging by Vance's reaction to her, she could be the first to succeed. She'd never mentioned wanting to stay on full-time, and she didn't run the office as if she planned to stay, but it'd be a lie to say it hadn't crossed my mind. Tussling with Georgina could be many things, including fun, but I'd given everything I'd had to this job, including my reputation. I'd never give it up without a down-and-dirty fight. "Maybe."

"Don't get paranoid," Justin said. "I happen to like her. She's smart, funny, and looks cute in your baseball hat, don't you think?"

She looked *adorable* in the hat. I grunted my assent.

"What do you think she's like in the bedroom?" Justin asked. "All business, or you think she'd let you take the lead?"

Unprepared for the vivid image of sheet-wrestling with a bossy Georgina, my throat locked up—and then my balls. Georgina and I might've been on a level field in the office, but our entire relationship had been a power play. I wanted to be on top. So did she. I imagined that would carry over into the bedroom as well, but taking it to the sheets sounded way more fun.

The more pressing question, though, was whether she was having a good time with François. We'd arrived at the game to find her shoulders square. She'd looked tense and neglected without food or drink. This guy seemed more into the game than her, but some chicks dug that. They liked to work for the attention—I knew from firsthand experience dating an actress here, a model there. The less attention you showed, the harder they tried to get it.

"How long are we going to sit here?" Justin asked. "This is like watching sports in slow-motion."

I rubbed my jaw, not even trying to hide the fact that this time, I *was* looking at Georgina. "We stay as long as they do," I said. "You think it's fun for me listening to everyone root for a rival team?"

"Fun? No. But clearly a price you're willing to pay."

I ignored him. I didn't have the patience to try to throw him off the scent. "What were you saying to her when I went to get your beer?"

"Just commenting on how cozy you two were."

"You nosy fuck."

"You know, I don't think I ever got a 'thank you' for the lengths I went to so you could sit here and stalk her." He crossed an ankle over his knee. "My spies aren't cheap."

"Yeah? How much did you pay for this info?"

"It cost me three trips to the vending machine before my operative was able to get a clear view of Georgina's phone screen while she was waiting for a bag of chips."

I heaved a sigh. "Sometimes I can't believe what I've been reduced to."

"Man, don't worry. The date obviously isn't going well, and now you not only have something over Georgina, but you also get some peace of mind about her dating life."

I craned my neck as François leaned over to say something near Georgina's ear. "She made it seem like she was enjoying herself. You really think it's not going well?"

"Can't you read her body language? She's stiff as a board. You should know what that looks like."

"Fuck off," I said, but I was secretly pleased. Because Justin was right, but not only about her body language. As if me braving a Yankees game hadn't made my feelings clear enough, seeing Georgina with François did.

And I realized what it was that bothered me about him. I wanted to be sitting where he was.

14

Justin reclined in his chair and crossed his ankles on Sebastian's desk. "Destiny's Child, 'Bootylicious.' *Boom*. I know all the words, and the dance too. This one time—"

"Get your shoes off my desk," Sebastian said.

"Relax, I just took them from wardrobe," Justin said but sat up immediately, removing his feet.

"It's the fashion department, not wardrobe," Sebastian said as he reviewed the next issue's flat plan with a red marker. "This isn't a movie set."

"Whatever. What was I saying?" Justin asked.

"Your favorite song to sing in the shower," Boris supplied.

"Yeah, but I had a story." Justin scratched his temple. "Lost my train of thought."

Sebastian sighed. "More like the conductor's asleep at the wheel."

I stifled a laugh—not my first of the morning. Sequestered at my small desk across the room, I'd been trying to answer e-mails for the last hour when I wasn't distracted by the guys.

"How about you, boss?" Boris asked, unwrapping a stick of Trident.

Sebastian pointed a paperclip he'd bent between his thumb and index finger. "Easy," he said. "'American Woman.' Guitar and all."

Warmth crept up my chest as I pictured Sebastian, tall, trim, and unabashedly naked for his shower guitar solo. If I remembered correctly, the song had its fair share of grunting. When he caught me staring, I averted my eyes back to my computer screen.

"You *wish* you were Lenny Kravitz," Justin said, working a toothpick through his teeth. "Last time we did karaoke, you were all about *NSYNC. You didn't even need the prompter for 'Tearin' up My Heart.'"

"It's a classic." Sebastian brushed what I assumed were invisible crumbs off Justin's side of the desk. He'd already thrown out all the wrappers from lunch, called janitorial to get the trash, and wiped down his desk. "How about you, Georg*ina*?"

I didn't miss the way Sebastian drew out my name, probably to remind me of my embarrassing admissions at the baseball game. I was pretty sure I'd hinted at having multiple personalities.

I tapped a fingertip on my upper lip as I waited for data from my office to load. "I always get Ace of Base stuck in my head."

"Maybe it's a sign," Justin said.

"It's definitely *The* Sign," I said, humming a few bars. "Or that one from Fifth Harmony, 'Work from Home.' I catch myself singing it some mornings when I'm getting ready."

"I can't imagine why," Sebastian said, glancing at

Boris, who wiped sauce from his mustache with his sleeve. "Who wouldn't want to come in to this dream team every day?"

"Actually, you guys have been making me laugh all afternoon." I shut my laptop. "And I've decided *Modern Man* needs a podcast. *You* need a podcast."

"Us?" Boris asked.

"Well, Justin, Sebastian . . . and friends," I clarified. I wouldn't listen to Boris for an hour unless I was getting paid. "You have a great rapport. Our readership needs to hear from you—and then tell their friends."

"We already have Peterson's team working on the webisodes we laid out last week," Sebastian pointed out.

"Then they'll have to work a little harder. What're some reader questions you have left over from *Badvice*?" I asked.

"Oh, *now* you want to bring it back?" Sebastian asked.

"No, but this could be what *Badvice* should've been— readers getting thoughtful, humorous, legitimately *good* advice."

"Goodvice?" Boris suggested.

Sebastian ignored him, opened his phone, and started to scroll. "Here's one. 'Do women ever *shave* each other?'"

"Shave?" I was afraid to even ask for clarification. "As in . . ."

Sebastian shrugged. "That's the whole question."

I put my face in my palm. I was discovering that men had many misconceptions when it came to women, particularly anything involving sleepovers or our bathroom buddy systems, but this was next level. "Who's spreading this myth that we shower together?" I asked. "That's the dumbest question I've ever heard. Next."

"All right, geez," he mumbled, flicking his thumb over the screen. "You're going to hate all of these."

"Try me," I said.

He sighed. "Greg H. from Madison, Wisconsin says his ex would never let him touch her during her period, but his current girlfriend is begging for it. He wants to know if women like sex on the rag and how to do it." Sebastian raised his eyebrows at me. "I've brought it up with the team, and . . . there seem to be conflicting schools of thought."

All the guys turned to me. "That could work, actually," I said. "It's debatable from both sides and both genders. Use it for your debut podcast episode, but take out 'on the rag.' Nobody says that anymore."

Boris cleared his throat. "But what's the answer?"

Sebastian sat forward and put his chin in his hand. It was the most interested he'd looked since lunch had arrived. Suddenly, my throat was dry. As a talking piece, the question worked well; opinions generally landed on one side or the other. It would rile up listeners, but as long as we tackled the issue from both the male and female perspective, the discussion could be healthy and informative. We could even touch on biology, and maybe—just maybe—the listeners would *learn* something.

But that wasn't what the guys were asking.

Sebastian, in particular, looked as if he wanted to know my response. And of course now, I couldn't seem to speak. "It's a . . . personal preference," I said. "There's no one right answer."

"But in general?" Justin asked. "I've always heard women are extra turned on while menstruating."

"You also told me BDE stands for 'bestest day ever,'" Sebastian said.

"What's BDE?" I asked.

Justin's mouth slid into a smile. "Yeah, Sebastian, what

is it? You should be the one to tell her since, according to *New York Magazine*, you've got it."

I frowned. "Is it some kind of STD?"

"Jesus, no," Sebastian said, nearly lurching out of his chair. "It stands for 'big dick energy.'"

Oh. I didn't need any more clarification. From a biological standpoint, Sebastian was unequivocally male—tall, broad, full head of hair, enviable jawline, mesmerizing light eyes to lure in prey . . . but there was more to it than that. He oozed confidence, virility, and moved with the kind of ease I rarely saw in other men. All that in one man was partly what'd drawn me to him in the café.

I could only suspect, based on the facts, that he had the goods to back it up.

Justin held up his hands about a foot apart, subtly nodding at Sebastian as he grinned at me and whispered, "You won't be disappointed."

Sebastian threw the paperclip at Justin's head. "Dude."

Mortified, I squeezed my eyes shut to get the image out of my head, but it was replaced with Sebastian playing air guitar in the shower again—only with one much more *favorable* detail.

"Aw, come on," Justin said. "George's no prude. She's seen things."

"But has her counterpart?" Sebastian asked.

I couldn't blame Justin for looking confused. He didn't know that Sebastian was talking about Georg*ina*, not George, because around here, only I knew there was a difference. Until now, it seemed. Sebastian was on to me, and my denying it over beers hadn't thrown him off the scent. I thought back to the game, the way Sebastian had almost sounded jealous that François and I had "bumped hats." The way *Sebastian* had trapped me against the table to kiss—or strangle—me, and how I wouldn't have stopped him. Not with my hair curled around his finger and "buns" on his tongue. Why was I the only person Sebastian was willing to nickname?

Would he have kissed me if not for Justin's interruption?

The thought made my heart pound the way it had in the moment. I would've let him, but I couldn't forget that Sebastian had considered me an enemy up until this point, and maybe still did.

"Hard at work, I see," I heard from behind me. We all looked over at Vance in the doorway of the office.

"We're practicing for our podcast," Justin said.

"Podcast?" Vance looked to me. "Your idea?"

Sebastian made an exaggerated red slash on the spread in front of him.

"Not really," I said. *What?* Dionne would have a fit if she heard me giving credit when I should take it. But it wasn't as if I'd worked hard for it. All I'd done was smile and laugh enough to make my cheeks ache—and recognize that Sebastian and Justin's back-and-forth was something special. "After listening to these two bicker for weeks, it was a natural connection to make."

"It was her idea," Sebastian said, his eyes down.

Vance nodded toward the hall. "George, can I see you in my office?"

"Oh. Sure." I was sixteen and getting called to the principal for too many tardies. I shut my laptop and took a notebook and my phone. Sebastian watched me stand, his eyes jumping between his boss and me.

I followed Vance to the elevator. We usually met once a week, but this was the first time he'd come looking for me. "Is everything okay?" I asked.

"Everything's great." We rode up a few floors, where

he gestured me toward his office. "Can I get you anything?" he asked as we passed his assistant.

"No, thank you. We just had gyros."

"Don't feel as if you have to keep up with their greasy food habits," he said as he sat at his desk. "Wouldn't want you wasting as much time at the gym as Sebastian and Justin seem to."

I took a chair in front of him and crossed my legs. For someone my height, it wouldn't take much to get fat, Neal had said once in front of his family when I'd gone for a second helping of Christmas dinner. Vance was hedging a little too closely to unsolicited advice on my figure, so I moved us back on track. "How can I help you?"

"How do you feel things are going?" he asked, opening a drawer.

"Great." I'd said as much in our last appointment. "I'm very happy with the team's progress."

"And we're very happy with you." Vance took out a *Modern Man*-stamped notepad and matching pen. "It'll be a while before we have any firm numbers, these things take time, but don't think we haven't noticed the impact you've made these last several weeks."

"Thank you," I said. "But I'm only doing my job."

"The online analytics are already showing results. Surprisingly, the female demographic is actually growing."

I opened my notebook. "My team at the agency has been working closely with the sales department on their targeting."

He shifted in his seat. "And who would've thought something as simple as changing the name of the magazine would make such a difference?"

I had to admit, adding *A Gentleman's Guide* underneath the masthead was one of my better ideas, and perhaps the only thing Sebastian hadn't fought me on. "It's all about honing our image," I said.

"The focus groups you've run were very positive too." Vance doodled circles on the paper in front of him. "The board has noticed, and we all agree the magazine is headed in the right direction."

"How would you describe the progress we've made?" I asked, taking notes.

"Still *Modern Man* but more refined and with broader appeal. We're starting to reach the men who think with their big head more than their little one."

Not exactly how I would've put it, but I looked forward to sharing a laugh over that with Dionne. "Anything else?"

"The 'women who drone' webisode is a great example. Strong, shareable content that's supportive of women while appealing to both genders."

"Glad you liked it," I said. "A friend of mine posted footage while working on a film in Toronto, and people went wild over it. It was an easy leap to get her on board."

"That's the thinking we need." He leaned his elbows on his desk. "Look. At the end of the day, we're a business."

"Of course."

"Sebastian was exactly the person to grow this magazine quickly. To capture the attention of millions and launch a sensation. But those tactics aren't working anymore, and he's been distracted the last year. I'm not sure he has what it takes to adapt."

"Our team has shown great progress since I arrived," I said carefully, hoping to send the message that this was *my* team too, and everyone held value, including Sebastian. *Especially* Sebastian.

"My point exactly. Sebastian didn't even recognize that we *had* a female demographic, much less appeal to them, and he either didn't see or refused to admit that we were losing our more sophisticated readers."

I opened my mouth to say that wasn't true, but hadn't I skewered him for those exact reasons during my first presentation?

Vance continued, "He had a year to turn things around but couldn't. Not until you."

"He needed a little guidance," I said. "Which is exactly why you brought me in. When the compass breaks, I simply right the ship."

"It's more than that, George. The men respond well to you. Even that ADHD case Justin. Even *Sebastian*. Though I see him fighting it, he's made improvements as well."

"So we both agree."

"It seems we do. I want to bring you on full-time."

"I'm practically here full-time as it is," I said, sitting back. "I still need to be at my office one or two days a week in order to—"

"No, no. I mean we'd like to hire you, Georgina. As creative director."

Oh. "That's Sebastian's position," I said dumbly. Sebastian didn't just work as a creative director—he *lived* the job title. "Are you . . . are you promoting him?"

He hesitated. "Sebastian is welcome to stay on the team—your team—if you decide to keep him. That would be your call."

That didn't sound like a promotion. In fact, it sounded like a *demotion*. "Sebastian is very nearly back on course," I said slowly. "Trust me. He's got this."

"It's obvious that a change in perspective has done everyone some good," Vance said. "Against the advice of my peers, I gave Sebastian more editorial control than customary for this industry because I had a feeling about him. It worked in my favor. I have that same feeling about you."

I wiped my palms on my slacks. "I'm very happy with the position I'm in now," I said. "In fact, there are opportunities within my current agency."

"That so? What kinds? I'd at least like the chance to match them."

It was only partially true. I'd heard rumblings from everyone except my boss about the possibility of expansion, from hiring new agents to opening an office out of state to introducing a new department. Yet, any of those options would be, at best, a lateral move for me. "I'm not at liberty to discuss them," I said.

"Are you at liberty to discuss salary?" He glanced at the notepad, then cocked his head and scratched out what he'd written. He hadn't been doodling but writing zeroes. "I suppose I'll need to up my game if I've got competition." He wrote a new number and skated it across the desk. "Here's what I'm authorized to offer. If anyone asks, you negotiated me here."

I widened my eyes. It was nearly double my current salary, which was already very decent—at least, for those who lived anywhere but New York City and didn't care for a terminally sick dog. A strange sense of pride settled over me. I'd taken on this job unsure of how I'd wrangle an office full of "bad boys." Clearly, I'd succeeded. My boss had believed I could do it, just like she'd cultivated my drive since day one. Yet, it'd been some time since I'd been promoted. At my current position, job satisfaction came from challenging assignments such as *Modern Man*, but considering Dionne had founded the agency, my position lacked upward mobility. Had my ambition plateaued as a result? I wasn't sure how I felt about staying on as creative director, but it hit me that Vance was offering the *more* I'd never get where I was now.

And I did want more. That was how I'd grown into George, and it was how I took care of my loved ones. Money *had* been tight ever since Neal had stopped working and left me to handle our bills, including the seemingly never-ending vet visits. Once I'd started to fall behind, I hadn't been able to catch back up, and the debt had been mounting for a while. The number in front of me would not only allow me to cover Bruno's healthcare expenses but upgrade them. *And* put a serious dent in my debt. *And* leave some for myself.

"You're speechless," Vance said. "That's what I was going for. We'd love to bring you on as soon as you're able to get free of your current situation."

"I . . . I'm not even sure I'm legally allowed. I'd have to look over my contract."

"Well, find out," he said, ripping off the top slip of paper and crumpling it. "Take the weekend to weigh your options. And of course, keep this between us. It won't be easy breaking this to Sebastian, but I'll handle him. It shouldn't come from anyone but me." He grumbled as he tossed the notepad back in a drawer. "If he storms in here one more time making demands, he'll get an unwelcome reality check."

Sebastian. He'd been running the show successfully for a long time. What'd happened this last year to throw him off his game? Perhaps I could've gotten to the bottom of it if he'd ever indulged me in a one-on-one session like I'd requested. But he hadn't thought it was worth his time.

Could I do this to him knowing how much he'd dedicated to the position?

Dismissed, I exited the office in a daze and headed back downstairs. I went straight for the restroom, where there'd be no chance of running into any of the guys. I needed a moment to process this, and peace and quiet was hard to come by anywhere but the ladies' room. As soon as I turned the corner, though, I nearly ran into Sebastian on his way out of the men's.

"Hey," he said, leaning against the wall and blocking me from the moment alone I desperately needed. "What'd Vance want?"

"What?" I stalled. *Vance wants . . . me. Not you.* "Oh. Nothing. Just a check-in."

"Don't you do that Fridays?"

"Yes, but as we get closer to the end of my assignment . . ." I tried to swallow without gulping. "I guess he needs to touch base more."

"Ah. Makes sense." Sebastian's damn shoulders were so broad, I couldn't even see around him. That made it easy to notice when they eased from around his ears. Did he suspect something was up? I gestured behind him. "I just need to—"

"I've barely seen you all week," he said.

I held my notebook to my chest. "I had some work to catch up on at my office," I said to explain my absence since the baseball game.

Which could very well be my old *office soon.*

Was Vance testing the waters, or had that been an official offer? And was it firm? The salary was generous, but I'd never leave any job or position, especially one I loved, without negotiating for the best.

Sebastian tilted his head. "Well?"

"Sorry, what?" I asked.

"I said, how's *François*?"

"Um." I scratched my eyebrow, trying to glance around Sebastian's irritatingly large physique to signal that it wasn't the best time for a chat. I needed to digest the news, and I certainly didn't want to be talking to Sebastian until I'd decided how to broach this with him . . . or if I should at all. "I don't know. We haven't spoken since after the game."

Sebastian glanced over my head. "*After* the game? Justin said you went straight home."

I cocked my head. Justin had already teased me mercilessly about François. He'd peppered me with questions even after I'd told him with exasperation that *yes*, the date had been fine, and *maybe* we would go out again and *no*, François had not kissed me at my train stop. A first kiss in a subway car with onlookers would've been only slightly less awkward than one in front of Sebastian and his sidekick at the game. But why would any of that have come up between Justin and Sebastian? "I did go home," I said. "But we took the train together until his stop."

Sebastian's eyebrows lowered. "He couldn't even see you to your door?"

"He would've had to ride all the way to Brooklyn, walk three blocks, then backtrack home." I caught myself fidgeting with my notepad and stilled, not wanting my anxiety to show. Sebastian making non-hostile conversation for once wasn't helping my budding guilt over the fact that I'd been offered his job minutes earlier.

"You only live three blocks from the subway?" he asked. "What're your cross streets again?"

"I live on Pineapple." This conversation was going nowhere. Couldn't we be having it *after* I used the bathroom? "But again," I said, "it would've made no sense for Frank to—"

"Pineapple. Cute," Sebastian said, smiling like it was an inside joke. "If it were *me*, I would've walked my date home—at least to see how the hell her Great Dane fits in a one-bedroom. Or is it a studio?"

Despite my desire to escape, I smiled a little at that. "One-bed. We go on lots of walks."

"Hey, Bruno and I are good on walks. Any time you need some extra muscle, let me know."

"Sure." With a higher income, Bruno and I could move closer to a park. Apparently, I really was considering Vance's offer, but I couldn't decide how to feel about it while Sebastian was being so *nice*. I moved to get around him. "I need to—"

"I'm available weekends," he teased. "This one, in fact."

"Sounds good." I ducked to the right.

"You have plans with François?"

"No plans," I called over my shoulder and finally took cover in the restroom.

I locked myself in a stall, leaned back against the door, and exhaled a breath. It wasn't as if I owed Sebastian anything. Not an explanation for considering the position, or exploring the idea that I might want it.

It wasn't the first job offer I'd ever gotten from a client, but it was the first that would be such a big step up. And the only one I'd taken seriously. I'd loved reconfiguring *Modern Man* because I was passionate about problem solving, but neither the magazine's content nor its message inspired the same excitement in me. If the publication continued on the path I'd set, I'd remain a casual reader, but at the heart of it, I wasn't the director the team needed. One of the best parts of my job was that no two days were alike, and once I started to get comfortable in an assignment, it ended for another.

At the same time, I knew firsthand that the creative director position regularly presented unique and complex problems. Regardless of how I felt about coming in to the same office each day, it wasn't a dull job by any means. I hadn't gotten this far in my career by walking away from challenges—or opportunities to advance. I prided myself on being a smart and savvy businesswoman with more drive than the person behind her.

And then there was the money. I could hear Neal in the back of my head . . .

"Who in their right mind would walk away from double the salary? You'd be stupid not to take it, and you're not stupid, Georgina. Are you?"

His condescension was still, at times, too loud to ignore. I *had* been stupid for all the times I'd second-guessed myself around him, even though this was one of those times.

If I wasn't moving forward, though, was I going backward?

15

B runo did not respect hangovers. Or late nights chasing Turkish dramas and delights with wine, which was what Luciano and I had done until he'd fallen asleep on my couch around one.

Schlepping down the block with Bruno's leash in hand, I thanked the powers that be for oversized sunglasses to block harsh sunlight and for hats to hide unkempt hair. *Sebastian's* hat, to be exact. I'd meant to return it to him after the game, I really had, but he hadn't asked for it, and it smelled so good—like him. And me. *Us*, if such a thing were to ever exist.

Bruno perked up and took off, pulling me after him, but this time, it wasn't a squirrel that'd caught his attention, nor the UPS truck, or even the neighbor's ugly-cute French bulldog that drove Bruno wild. It was a man tall enough to high-five the changing leaves and sexy enough to stop traffic with tousled dark hair and muscles that stretched his charcoal-colored sweater—and to top it all off, he sported not only a wide, devastating smile but two Dunkin' Donuts coffees.

"Finally," Sebastian called as he headed in my direction. "I've been wandering the street for fifteen minutes. You didn't pick up your phone."

No no no. He had to be a mirage.

I was *braless* under my sweatshirt.

With pimple cream on my chin.

And sleep crusting the corners of my eyes.

And him? His smooth-shaven jaw looked sharp enough to cut glass, and his easy, confident energy justified his swagger. If he was a mirage, he was a pretty attractive one.

Bruno wagged his tail as he ran over to Sebastian. Was it too late to pretend I hadn't seen him? Was I clever enough to convince him I was not, in fact, Georgina but her doppelgänger? Could I escape into a manhole like a comic book villain?

"I have a mocha latte with your name on it," Sebastian said when my gaping became uncomfortable. "Literally."

"What are you doing here?" I asked.

He thrust the drink at me. "It'll get cold."

There wasn't much sadder in this world than cold coffee, so I took the latte, which had either been very hot, or had been kept toasty by Sebastian's sizeable hand. "Um, thanks," I said, looking up at him from behind my sunglasses. "But why are you here?"

"What do you mean? I told you at the office I was coming over to help walk the brute . . ." He paused, glancing over my head. No, *at* my head. More specifically, at my *hat.*

Oh, no.

I was wearing his baseball cap like a lovesick schoolgirl. By the way his mouth slid into a knowing smirk, he obviously took pleasure in busting me, but at least he had the decency not to mention it.

"But how do you know where I live?" I asked.

"Pineapple." He nodded behind him. "It's not a very long street, so I took my chances. I told you I was coming, remember? For muscle?"

I wrinkled my nose. "I had no idea you were serious."

"I was. I am." He glanced at my sweatpants. "I assumed you'd sleep in, which is why I came at eleven."

"I'll have you know I was up at six this morning."

"To take Bruno out?"

That, and to see Luciano off to work. "Yes, but——"

"Did you go back to sleep afterward?"

I scowled. Since when did he know my address, habits, and the exact time to catch me at my worst? "You live thirty minutes from here. You're a bridge and a subway stop change away. We're not even in the same borough. There's no way you came all the way here to walk Bruno."

He squinted down the block. Sunglasses stretched the neckline of his sweater. I sipped my mocha. It was just the right temperature, damn him—not scalding, not luke-warm. Some people, like Sebastian, led that easy life. I could only imagine I'd surprise someone with coffee the same day they'd sworn off caffeine.

Bruno finished peeing on his usual fenced tree, then started toward the next block, where he'd sniff and mark his other spots.

As we walked, Sebastian cupped his coffee with both hands. "Actually . . . I've got a favor to ask."

"The mocha latte tipped me off." I sighed. "Go ahead."

"I want to run a story idea by you." He paused. "I mean, I guess I *have* to run it by you."

That made me think of brainstorming sessions, which turned into the memory of Vance's offer. Luciano and I had spent half the night weighing the pros and cons. The offer was tempting, but the job itself wasn't something I would've sought out. Not to mention it belonged to *Sebastian*. When I'd brought that up, Lu had reminded me of how putting Neal's dreams before mine had resulted in a broken heart, a pile of debt, and a serious confidence problem. The creative director position could be a chance to mend at least two of those issues. If my breakup with Neal had taught me anything, it was that I had to put myself first.

I tuned out my unsettling thoughts. "Okay," I prompted. "What's the idea?"

"Since the common interest date worked out *so* well for you—"

I did not appreciate his sarcasm. For all he knew, François and I were getting serious.

"—let's try it with a spin. I want to demonstrate how a guy can use a hobby to get the attention of a girl who wants nothing to do with him."

I twisted my lips. I couldn't really knock the common interest thing after the way I'd sung its praises. And it wasn't a bad idea. Industries had been built on the underdog trying to win over his dream girl.

"Who's the subject?" I asked.

"Me."

I tried not to laugh. "Is rejection a problem for you?"

"Sometimes."

"Give me one example of a woman who didn't surrender to your charms."

"Well, gee. There's . . ." He raised his eyebrows. "*You*."

I pulled back. "Me?"

"You told me yourself—you've never seen me flirt successfully."

Well, sure, I thought, *that's called a white lie.*

"The article has to be convincing, and who better to

give me hell than you? I just have to do my best to win you over. All for the article, of course."

"For the article," I repeated. I could see where he was coming from. And it *would* make for an interesting piece. But playing Sebastian's date for a night sounded as dangerous as it did fun. He thought I was immune to his charm? Hardly. I was just good at pretending to be. "Is there anyone else you could experiment on?"

"Not unless you can find me a dog lover who can't stand me in the next hour."

"You want to do this *now*?" I asked.

The corner of his mouth quirked. "Did I leave that part out?"

"Do we actually have to go out?" I asked. "Or can you walk me through how it would go?"

"Depends. Are we publishing fiction now?"

I rolled my eyes. "Fine, but I'm supposed to give up my Sunday for a fake date?"

"You're looking at it wrong. I'm giving you full clearance to critique my first-date moves—for the benefit of our entire readership, no less."

I *did* like that idea. I chewed my bottom lip. "First of all, I'm in no state to do anything. I'm wearing sweatpants."

"With 'Royal Pain' printed across the butt," he added.

I scoffed, covering my backside with my free hand. "They were a gift, thank you very much."

"Welcome, buns."

I ignored him. "Secondly, my dogsitters don't work Sundays."

"First," Sebastian countered, ticking off his defense on his fingers, "I can wait. Bruno and I will hang out while you get ready. Second, Bruno's coming with us."

"Ex*cuse* me?"

Hearing his name, Bruno nudged Sebastian's leg. Sebastian automatically squatted and scratched his chest. "It's a dog date. You love dogs, Bruno and I are pals, so I'm using that to make a connection."

A dog date? Yes, *please*. I'd never been on one of those. And I wasn't *going* on one—because this wasn't real. At least, it wouldn't be for Sebastian, but could I spend the afternoon with him and keep my mask in place? Just because Sebastian and I were learning to get along didn't mean I was any defter at navigating men outside the office. "What makes you think I don't have plans today?"

"Mostly that you told me you didn't."

I wrinkled my nose. I did not remember saying that or giving him my address. I was running out of excuses to skip something I wanted to do, even if I hated to admit it. I looked back toward my apartment. If Luciano found out I'd declined a date, even a pretend one, for a day on my couch with pub food, craft beer, and season two of *Can't Cope, Won't Cope*, he'd never let me live it down.

"I can wait down here if your apartment's a pigsty," Sebastian said.

I groaned inwardly. Now I *had* to invite him up to prove it wasn't. Fortunately, my apartment was presentable if you didn't count the evidence of my night with Luciano. Even my bedroom was in decent shape, a miracle considering I could be as messy as I wanted. Nobody except Luciano ever went in there . . . *ever*. Not since Neal. Even my dogsitters steered clear. I sighed at the thought.

"This is what you asked me to do," Sebastian pointed out, probably thinking I'd sighed in protest. Bruno's back leg thumped the sidewalk as Sebastian continued to hit his sweet spot. "It's about how men can do better, be better, and maybe even have a shot with someone they thought was out of their league."

This was one of the best parts of my job—the break-through. It seemed despite his resistance, I actually had been getting through to Sebastian these past several weeks. How could I go and cut his progress short? "Where are we going?" I asked.

"Let me worry about that. You'll have to trust me."

Famous last words. "All right," I conceded. "Mostly because you got to critique my first-date moves, so it's only fair I see yours."

"You aren't only going to see them," he said, standing as we turned back for my apartment, "you're going to get the inside track."

An up-close-and-personal look at the inner workings of my arch nemesis and a notorious playboy? I showered and shaved my legs faster than Justin could make a room uncomfortable.

When I came out of my room, Sebastian was seated on the couch with Bruno's head in his lap. He didn't even cozy up to Lu that way. I passed behind them on my way to the kitchen, where I picked up the dog bowl. "I just have to feed Bruno and give him his pills, then we can go."

Sebastian lowered the issue of *Poised* he'd been reading. I'd been collecting stacks of magazines over the past several weeks, anything marketed specifically to both men and women. "Did it and did that, too," Sebastian said.

I stuck my head into the living room. "Did what?"

Sebastian turned his head over the back of the couch. "I figured I'd pitch in since you're doing me a favor."

"You fed Bruno? His pills too? But how'd you know what to do?"

"I checked the color-coordinated schedule on the fridge and saw that Bruno gets a third meal on Sundays around lunchtime along with his pills." He shrugged. "Bruno showed me where to find the pill box, and since each day is already divided up and Sunday's meds were untouched, I put two and two together."

"He showed you where his pills were? Who's anthropomorphizing now?" I teased, although my heart doubled in size at the way Sebastian looked after Bruno. Even if it was part of his act, it didn't matter as long as Bruno was happy —and he clearly was, as he completely ignored me to sit with Sebastian. "How'd you get him to take his pills?"

"That's our secret." Sebastian tossed the *Poised* aside and stood as Bruno jumped off the couch. He turned and paused, blinking at my outfit.

"Is this okay?" I asked, my bangles jingling as I smoothed out the flowy floral dress and straightened my denim jacket. "I have a scarf in my bag. Since you won't tell me where we're going—"

"Yeah." I didn't miss the way Sebastian's eyes scanned my bare legs down to my suede booties, and I didn't mind it, either. "It's just . . . I've never seen you in a dress like that. One that wasn't, you know, for work."

"This is what I'd wear on a first date."

"It's not what you wore to the game," he pointed out.

"That was a different kind of first date." I took Bruno's leash from a hook in the entryway. I didn't even have to say the word *walk*, and he was already loping around the apartment. I got a tote bag from the hall closet, cursing as I reached into the side pocket.

"What's wrong?"

I pulled out my hand to show him my gooey fingers. "My gummy bears melted."

"Do you carry them everywhere?"

"I told you, they help me think."

He sighed, waiting as I packed Bruno's emergency items, then said, "There's one thing I should've warned you about before you agreed to this."

"Okay," I hedged and whistled for Bruno.

"I have many irresistible qualities," Sebastian said, "and lots of charm, and I can't just shut that off."

I rolled my eyes as I hooked Bruno's leash to his collar and whispered, "Here's hoping his *best* quality is that he knows when to stop talking." To Sebastian, I asked, "Your point?"

"Try not to actually fall for me today."

"I'll do my best," I said wryly.

What Sebastian didn't seem to realize was that I was already doing my best—and had been for a while.

16

Sebastian had sent me for a second round of coffee so he could "pick something up." With my bag of Bruno essentials over one shoulder, I carried two cups and walked Bruno to the corner where Sebastian had told me to meet him.

Possibly due to nerves from being on a pretend date with someone who considered me his enemy, I was already halfway through my mocha latte when Sebastian rounded the corner.

With a dog.

A brown, white, black spotted—and utterly *adorable*—dog. "Georgina, Bruno," Sebastian called, "meet Opal."

Bruno's and Opal's tails wagged furiously as they sniffed each other head to butt. "Sebastian . . ." Like any time I encountered that level of canine cuteness, I crouched for kisses. "She's precious, but *please* tell me you didn't adopt a dog to impress a date."

"I volunteered to take her for the day," he said as I handed him his coffee cup so I could pet her. "Irresistible quality number one—I'm charitable with my time. Two—

I'm creative. I'll bet you've never been on a date with a mutt."

I glanced up at him. "And I'd be lying if I said I haven't enjoyed the first hour of it."

"You're sharp today, Keller," he said with a lingering look. "We can mark that in *your* 'irresistible quality' column."

I focused on fixing Opal's twisted collar to keep from blushing. "Where'd you get her?"

"A shelter nearby. She's a two-year-old beagle-foxhound mix."

"I feel the need to ask this," I said, reading her dog tag, "they *do* know you have her, right?"

"You're accusing me of stealing her?"

"You weren't gone very long."

"I have a friend on the inside, and she helped me arrange it beforehand." He grinned. "Irresistible quality number three—I'm prepared."

Opal licked my cheek, which was good because I was giving into the flush that'd been working its way up my neck. "By the fact that this *friend* is still speaking to you, I assume she's not an old fling."

"Actually, she is—not all my exes hate me, believe it or not. We can call any of them up now and ask if you like."

"You must be superhuman to keep them all straight." When he didn't jab back, I wondered if I'd gone too far. But *he'd* made the bed that was his reputation. Why shouldn't he have to lie in it?

I stood and rubbed slobber off my dress. A dog date was fun in theory, but I wondered if I should've worn something more appropriate for handling two dogs. Like a garbage bag. "You know dogs can't go on the subway unless they fit in a carrier, right?" I asked.

"Of course. Everyone knows that."

Flanked by Bruno and Opal, we walked. Brooklyn Heights had tree-lined streets, alternating busy avenues and sleepy cafes, and a promenade that overlooked the East River. There was plenty to do, but it wasn't really a date destination. "Then where are we going if we're not taking a car or the subway?" I asked.

"I already told you, it's a surprise."

"Some women love to be surprised, others hate it, but we all want to be dressed appropriately."

He glanced at the spot where my dress brushed above my knees. "So I should've mentioned that we'll be rock climbing?"

"Yes, because then I would've worn underwear."

Sebastian's expression remained passive, but he almost ran into a chalkboard sign advertising cannabis lattes. I also schooled my face against surprise at my own bravado.

"That was a bold joke," he said.

"What makes you think it's a joke?"

He narrowed his eyes on me. "Is it?"

Since Sundays were normally reserved for laundry, my underwear selection was down to special-occasion lingerie or gag gifts. While my "doggy style" briefs and their matching paw-print bra had been tempting, I'd gone for some lacy boyshorts instead. Still, I shrugged. "I guess we'll find out once we're on the wall."

Sebastian swallowed as a look I couldn't quite decipher crossed his face. It could've been disgust . . . could've been lust. Perhaps there was a fine line between those too.

Sebastian glanced over when I adjusted the tote on my shoulder. "What've you got in there, a year's supply of poop bags?" he asked. "You make fun of my desk, but that pocketbook is the same size as you. Doesn't your back hurt?"

"Bruno and I need everything in here—including the

poop bags," I said defensively, side-eyeing his easy, unencumbered stride. "Do you have any of those for Opal, or do the women in your world never go number two?"

He snorted. "I've got one in my pocket, thanks, and I'm not that squeamish. Nobody asked *my* opinion on period sex, but I'll give it to you if you want. The opinion, I mean."

Oh my god. I didn't even know what to say to that. If nothing else, Sebastian had a knack for throwing me off my game—but were we even playing still? I realized then, in the midst of our fencing, that I'd completely forgotten to fret over whether to be George or Georgina today. What did it mean if I was actually *comfortable* with Sebastian?

We turned onto a busier street, parting for a throng of rosy-cheeked young women who looked as if they were either coming from or going to brunch. The hipsters, in muted scarves, retro sunglasses, and leather backpacks, fussed over Opal while I stood at the corner, waiting to cross. I was jealous. How could I not be? Usually Bruno was the one getting fawned over. Opal zigzagged around Sebastian's legs until she'd wrapped him up in her leash. He turned in a circle, detangling himself as if he did it all the time.

With a little more swagger in his step, he sauntered toward me. "I could get used to being a dog owner."

"It entails a lot more than just picking up women and going on fake dates," I said.

"Enlighten me, buns."

Buns. Only Sebastian could get away with that nickname. He said it with a knowing grin, probably as he thought about cinnamon, and almost made it sound *flattering*. "Dogs need to be exercised every day, not just when it's convenient," I said. "Rain or shine, even if the weather could melt or cryopreserve us, I have to walk him. Some days, I get my ten thousand steps in before most people have had their morning coffees."

"Huh," Sebastian said as we stopped at an intersection. "Have to say, I took you for a late riser. Maybe it's the way you suck down caffeine."

As we neared the water, trees made canopies of green lace against the cloudless sky. I sighed. "I was, and I am, but that was mostly B.B."

"Before Bruno?"

"Yep."

"Is he from a shelter?" Sebastian asked.

"I adopted him from friends of my ex. They were going to put him down because they weren't sure how long he'd live." We crossed the street to the East River, walking along a promenade that wound along the water, separating Brooklyn from the city. "My neighbor growing up had a Great Dane, and I'd always thought they were so elegant."

"Bruno was sick when you got him?"

"Yes." Even though I'd always known what was to come, it was never easy to say aloud. "It'll eventually lead to congestive heart failure."

"I'm sorry. I'm assuming there's no cure."

"No, it's progressive." Absentmindedly, I ran my finger-nails through Bruno's fur. "I took him to one of the best veterinary heart specialists—in Boston, actually," I said, glancing up. "All we can do is manage it."

"Does your ex still see him?"

"He wasn't really a dog person." We parted as two young boys in matching sweaters ran between us. "My decision to adopt was actually a point of contention for us."

"How come?"

"Neal didn't want a dog at all, let alone Bruno. He thought he was weak." At least, that's what my therapist and I had worked out. Neal had a penchant for zoning in on a person's failings—and sometimes exploiting them. Sebastian and I paused at a cart of books the park had set up along with bright green bistro tables and chairs for reading. "Then there was the process, costs, shorter life-span. The fact that he wasn't a puppy. It didn't make sense to Neal, and I guess it wouldn't to most people, but . . ."

Across the water, the shimmering Financial District skyline rose tall behind Sebastian. "But?"

"It didn't seem fair to put down a dog because he was going to die anyway. He could still live a fulfilling life." I traced a couple book spines. "It's not the reason Neal and I broke up, but looking back, I always resented him for trying to talk me out of it. And I'm glad I didn't let him, because Bruno's still here, years later."

Sebastian held open a copy of *1776*, but his eyes remained on me. "Why'd you break up?"

My weaknesses. I'd boiled it down to that through therapy, and Sebastian would eventually make the connection too. For now, it was too embarrassing to admit.

Sensing my hesitation, he added, "I'll tell you why I broke up with my last girlfriend."

My first reaction was to make a joke, but as soon as the temptation passed, curiosity took its place. "I'm not sure that's a fair trade. Your last girlfriend was probably in and out in a week."

"Believe me, it's a fair trade."

It was something I never would've shared with Sebastian before today. Maybe even before this moment, so I gave him the easy answer. "He left me for someone else."

His eyebrows cinched as if I'd responded in Greek. "Did he cheat?"

"Not according to him." I hoped I could blame my reddening cheeks on the sunny day. "She was his study partner. He fell for her 'spirit.' I think that just means she knew how to say no to him."

Sebastian caught Opal gnawing on a bottom shelf book spine and tugged her away. "He might like that now, but he won't forever."

It gave me some comfort to have Sebastian side with me for once. "He didn't. They weren't even together two months. What was your reason for breaking up with . . . ?"

"Wendy," he said as we continued walking. "My mom didn't like her."

I refrained from laughing. After the battle of the sexes we'd been through, I wouldn't have pegged him as a mama's boy. While it was noble, I wondered why her approval meant that much to him. "That was the only reason?"

"Nah, it's a bit more complicated than that."

"I had a feeling," I said.

"I have a feeling there's more to your story too."

Tit for tat. I wouldn't get an explanation if I didn't give one. And I wasn't sure how I felt about confessing how weak I'd been—all the reasons Neal hadn't seemed to think *I* had spirit.

Ahead of us, a crowd cheered. Docked between piers, a boat with a yellow-and-white striped awning was full of people our age in coats and sunglasses, all holding cocktails. Some gathered at the bow, looking over the side, and others crowded around the bar in the center. "It's a boat that's a bar," I said.

"Up for a drink?"

We headed for a grassy hill under a tree. "There's no way they'll allow dogs."

"Then we'll tie them up for a few minutes."

I smiled. "Over my dead body. Bruno has separation anxiety."

"Bruno? Or you?" Sebastian squatted to tie Opal's leash around a trunk. "It'll be good for Bruno," he said. "It's like that thing new moms do where they let the baby cry in their crib to toughen them up."

"It's *nothing* like that," I said, "and that's cruel."

"My sister said the same thing until she had a newborn. Now she swears by it."

"You guys are twins, right?"

"Yep." Sebastian knotted the leash and stood. "So, what do you say?"

"I'm pretty sure the shelter would have your head if you left Opal unaccompanied," I said.

"She's not, though. She's with Bruno." He grinned. "Fine. How about if I bring the bar to you? What's the maritime equivalent to a lemon drop?"

"I . . ." I cleared my throat. "I have a confession to make."

He arched a dark brow. "You're not really a baseball fan."

"No—"

"You *do* shower with other women."

I swatted his arm, and Opal whined. "*No.*"

"Hmm." Sebastian pinched his chin, dropping only his eyes to me. "You hate lemon drops?"

"How'd you know?" I exclaimed.

"Call it an inkling. Why'd you order one at happy hour then?"

"The truth?" I nudged the toe of my boot into the grass. "Everyone was looking at me, and I blanked."

"Who would've ever suspected George Keller might be susceptible to stage fright?" He laughed. "So what's your poison?"

"Guinness," I said, "but I don't suppose they've got that on the boat."

He looked impressed as he got out his wallet. "Nice poison. Is it the Irish in you?"

I nodded, going for my purse. "My dad's side of the family."

"How about your mom?"

"Italian. It can get heated in our house when both families visit for the holidays."

"Sounds nice." He smiled to himself as if lost in a memory. "I take it your parents are still together."

"Twenty-seven years next spring."

He closed one eye, pretending to count. "Either you're younger than I thought, or . . ."

"They had me out of wedlock. Both sides of the family are Catholic, so their outrage united them against my parents." I grinned. "It made everyone closer, so it worked out pretty well. Are your parents still married?"

"Never were in the first place," he said, eyeing my wallet. "Put your money away."

"I want to get the drinks," I said, unzipping it. "You already picked up two of my coffees."

"Don't bother." He covered my hand with his to stop me, and the suddenness of it made me freeze. I hoped he didn't notice the way the hairs on my arm rose from his touch. "I took petty cash from the office since the date is research," he said, taking his hand back to tug at his collar. "So, whatever I spend now comes out of your share of dinner."

I couldn't help a small laugh. "Won't it be awkward for you to eat while your hungry date watches?"

"Good point." He smirked. "Nothing worse than feeling awkward on the first date."

"I think you're lying about the petty cash." At happy hour, Justin had claimed Sebastian had a tell. Thanks to the tip, I'd been watching closely and had figured out that when Sebastian wasn't being forthcoming, he usually touched his neck or the knot of his tie. I held up a twenty. "So let me get this round."

"Naw. I'll cover it. I wouldn't look good in the write-up otherwise."

I rolled my eyes as he walked away. Of course, this was meant to be all about the magazine, even if it was starting to *feel* like more . . .

I stopped the thought in its tracks. Wondering if this could be something other than make-believe was just asking for trouble. And danger. And disappointment.

I refocused on the piece we were working on. No doubt Sebastian would make himself look like an angel. Should I have been taking notes? Using a rating system? Would he need pull-quotes for the piece? As I watched him walk away, I thought, *Four out of five doctors recommend that ass.*

Sebastian stopped to talk to the boat's very pretty hostess.

And the one doctor thinks he is an ass.

I pretended not to watch Sebastian lay on the charm as I unfurled a linen throw onto a park bench and sat.

Opal sniffed the base of a tree trunk, then squatted and peed.

"Don't worry," I said, as Bruno lay at my feet. "*I* wouldn't leave either of you alone for a cocktail."

Bruno didn't seem to care. He kept his eyes glued to Opal as she explored the immediate area, then finally settled a few feet from him.

Had Sebastian actually planned anything beyond a walk outdoors? What more could we do with dogs in tow?

If he really was keeping me out until dinner, then we still had plenty of time together—and topics to cover. I realized then how effectively he'd cut off our conversations once they turned to his family. Either he wasn't ready or wasn't willing to share that part of himself with me. If only he knew that the mystery around them made me even more curious about how he'd grown up. Because the more I uncovered about Sebastian Quinn, the less I believed what I'd read about him.

And the more I wanted the truth.

17

Sebastian returned from the boat—after flashing the hostess a panty-dropping smile—gripping two paper bags in one hand and a large cup in the other. "I think Bruno's found himself a girlfriend," he said, nodding at the dogs. "He might like Opal better than you."

I scowled. Bruno *had* been noticeably distracted since she'd come on the scene. "He's just blinded by a pretty face. You know how that is."

He set down the cup—full of water—between the two dogs and passed me one of the paper bags. "You mean the crew member?" he asked.

"Here's a tip for your article," I said, peering in the paper bag at a can of Coors. "Don't hit on other women while you're on a date."

Sebastian sat on the bench next to me. "I wasn't hitting on her."

"Deny it all you want. I saw it with my own eyes, and I'm afraid I'll have to dock you for it in the article."

"I was smoothing the way to sneak our beers out." Sebastian rolled the bag down enough to expose the lip.

He took a sip, then sat quietly a moment. "That girlfriend I mentioned? It was about a year ago that we broke up. Before her, I dated casually, like any other person my age." He shifted on the bench to face me a little more. "I had a certain type, and maybe they photographed well, and maybe their attitudes allowed me to keep them at arm's length, but you should know . . . I'm not the womanizer I've been made out to be. I don't sleep with every woman I go out with. I've never broken someone's heart on purpose."

I stared straight ahead, shocked into silence. "Why are you telling me this?"

"Because I've certainly never set out to make a woman feel anything less than cherished when we're together. I *wasn't* hitting on her."

I studied the paper bag, slightly ashamed I'd jumped to conclusions. "I'm sorry," I said, "but you can't blame me for thinking that. You don't have the cleanest record."

"I should've explained all this your first day, but I have an image to uphold. People think I'm capable of running a men's lifestyle magazine because they envy *my* lifestyle, and I let them because of my career. But that has its downfalls."

"Such as?"

"People also think I'm an ass. People like you."

People like me. Someone like me. It always sounded like an accusation, even when it wasn't. I tried not to let the words take me back to Neal.

"You made a comment earlier about how I keep all the women straight, but I've never had that problem. I'm not the player you think I am—I only play one in the media."

"Why do you care what I think?" I asked.

"I always have, Georgina. You have power over me."

That Sebastian ever gave me a second thought both surprised and flattered me. "I do?"

"Of course. What you say and do influences my team and my boss. In a way, my career is in your hands."

My heart dropped.

More than he knows.

"You underestimate others and yourself," I told him. "You don't need all that to be good at your job."

He rubbed his nose. "Years ago, when I'd still been a style editor, I went to a party in the Hamptons. A friend of mine from college was there, and she'd recently married some bigwig producer. She drank way too much and I'd barely had one, so I took the keys to her Ferrari and drove her home."

"I read about this," I said.

"Everyone did. Leaving the party, I swerved into a ditch to avoid a drunk driver and totaled the car. The headlines ran wild. According to the press, I was having an affair with a married woman. I was a drunk and off to rehab. One gossip columnist even speculated my friend and I were conspiring to get her husband's money."

It was one of the first stories that'd come up when I'd searched *Sebastian Quinn*. "What happened when you set them straight?"

"I didn't. My name was everywhere. Vance noticed. My coworkers started high-fiving me in the halls. Social media took an interest in my love life. It was natural for me to run with it because I'd already been putting on a persona since college. Within a year, I was promoted to creative director-at-large."

Hearing him use his full title, one that might be mine soon, formed a pit in my stomach. "You believe your rep got you to where you are."

"I know it did. And now it's threatening all of that."

I shifted on the bench. Vance had sworn me to secrecy, and technically, I owed him my loyalty, but having this conversation was beyond uncomfortable. "It doesn't have to," I said. "Drop the bad boy act. You don't need it, and I don't believe you ever did."

"You don't know that, Georgina."

"You've got to let go of the notion that some stupid gossip item got you here instead of the truth—it was your talent."

"I'm not doubting my talent," he said. "I'm saying a fuckload of people in this city have that. You need more to get noticed."

"Sebastian." I sighed. "You're already at the top."

"That doesn't mean I'll stay there."

Vance's warning rang through my thoughts. *If he storms in here one more time making demands, he'll get an unwelcome reality check.* I wasn't sure I could keep Sebastian from reacting impulsively to the information I had, but I *could* open his eyes to the fact that the persona he'd crafted was hurting more than it was helping.

The question was why I wanted to. If Sebastian changed course and delivered what *Modern Man* needed, would Vance rescind my offer? Why should I consider Sebastian's feelings at all? My first day, it'd taken a lot of guts to show up and present to his team, and his support would've smoothed the way immeasurably. Instead, he'd gone out of his way to make it hard on me. He'd thought I was a joke. For all Vance's faults, at least he'd always taken me seriously.

Sebastian squinted and let out a whistle. Bruno lifted his head as Opal jumped up, her entire body wiggling as she found her way between Sebastian's legs. She launched her front paws into his lap to lick his face.

I never would've pictured the debonair man I'd met at

the coffee shop laughing through kisses from a mutt. Then again, he'd just started to reveal another layer, one that showed he wasn't necessarily the person he projected.

That was why, as much as I wanted my own success, I wanted his too. I'd brought fresh perspective and ideas like I'd been hired to, but Sebastian had put in the work, however grudgingly. He was still the right man for the job, and unlike me, he actually *enjoyed* it.

"Steer the magazine in the direction it needs to go," I said, picking at a notch in Bruno's leather leash. "If you take over, I become obsolete. Walk in with me as a united front tomorrow morning."

"Bringing you in made everyone think I failed to save the magazine," he said, smoothing both hands over Opal's head as she panted at him. "Once I submit, they'll *know* I did. I don't want to lose the respect of my team."

I was all too familiar with that fear. I became a different version of myself each morning to secure respect. Even now, I was afraid to open up to Sebastian about why Neal had left, and why I warred with myself every day, due to the possibility that he might see me as weaker. "We don't have to fight each other at every turn. We can work together. It's not too late."

"Too late for what?"

Shit. I hesitated. If I decided to risk my assignment, and this new opportunity, by telling Sebastian about my meeting with Vance, it would also end the date immediately. And I didn't want that. What I wanted was to see if there might be anything more worth exploring between us.

"Not too late to dispel the rumors," I said. "Fix your rep. Admit you were wrong. You and I have made a lot of progress, and my assignment's almost over. It's time for me to take a back seat and let you run the show. There'll be no question of respect."

"What do you think, Opal?" he asked, playing with her ears.

"She likes you," I said when he didn't respond, wondering if the topic was closed to further discussion.

"I like *her*. I don't know if I want to return her." He glanced at me. "Maybe I ought to adopt."

It was, perhaps, the sexiest thing he'd ever said. He was already verging on the perfect date—chivalrous, vulnerable, handsome . . . but adding dog dad to the list? That was next level.

Still, I knew firsthand that owning a pet wasn't without its rough spots. It hadn't been convenient for Neal. "It's a lot of responsibility," I warned. "With a dog at home, you can't stay out all night. They need potty breaks and training and lots of exercise. They're expensive. And you can't pick up and leave town whenever the urge strikes."

"A year ago, I would've said I liked my freedom." He tilted his head at Opal, and she cocked her head back. "Lately, I've been questioning whether having some attachments would be so bad."

Despite the fact that the two of them seemed to be having their own conversation, I got the feeling we were no longer talking about adopting a dog. "What happened a year ago?"

"Hmm?" He didn't look as if he planned to answer, but he never got the chance to anyway. His phone chimed, and he got up to check the screen. "He's here."

"Who?" I asked.

"Get your things. We're on to the next stop."

"I thought *this* was the date," I said, standing to bundle up the throw.

"I told you, you're stuck with me until dinner. Unless things go south, in which case I have Justin on standby to call me with an emergency."

If I hadn't been tossing the water bowl in a nearby trashcan, I would've smacked his arm. "You're not supposed to tell your date that. What if there really *is* an emergency? I'll think you don't like me."

"You already think I don't like you."

He had a point there. With both leashes in hand, Sebastian started back the way we'd come. When we reached the street, a car with dog ears on the roof honked from the curb, and a young guy waved at us over the hood. "I'm Kenny, your Ruff Ride driver."

"Our what?" I asked.

"Your wagging wagon," Kenny continued, "your pet-ty cab, crate on wheels, driving miss doggy, muttmobile." He took a breath. "I'll be your chauf*fur* this afternoon, your pupp daddy, David Barkham—"

"We get the idea," Sebastian said.

"You ordered this?" I asked him.

"While waiting for our drinks." Sebastian opened the car door for Opal and Bruno. "After you, Lindsay Lohound and Shia LaBowow."

The dogs just looked at him.

"Who wants to go for a ride?" I asked. Bruno perked up. He knew what it meant considering we regularly took a Zipcar out of town to see my parents, but if I'd asked if he wanted a colonoscopy in the same tone, he would've been equally as excited. Bruno and Opal hopped in and each one took a seat by the window.

I bent at the waist to look inside. "Where do the humans go?"

Kenny opened the driver's side door. "Usually backseat with the pups, or you can sit up front if you like."

Sebastian stuck his head through the other window to look past the dogs at me. "We could always do the lap thing."

I scoffed. "I'm not sitting on your lap."

Sebastian grinned. "I meant the *dogs* go on *our* laps."

I tried to look indignant as I squeezed in, forcing Bruno to give up the seat he'd already claimed. He stepped on my thighs, and I gnashed my teeth under his weight to keep from howling. Opal was small enough to curl up on Sebastian's lap, but Bruno sat his haunches on mine and stretched his front legs toward Sebastian.

Sebastian leaned through the gap between the front seats. "We're a little behind schedule."

"Say no more." The tires screeched as Kenny put the pedal to the metal.

Sebastian reached toward me. Startled, I jerked back. "What—"

He pulled my seatbelt across my body and snapped the buckle. "Safety first, Keller. Wouldn't look good for my date to end up in urgent care."

"I suppose not," I said wryly.

He stayed where he was, a glimmer in his eyes. "You know, if I were François, this would be the awkward point in the date where I'd try to kiss you."

"*Ha.*"

"You don't think I would?"

"Nope."

"Why not?" he asked.

"Easy," I answered, gripping the seat in front of me as we barely made a yellow light. "You don't want to."

"Are you only saying that so I'll prove you wrong?"

Not even the blast of his cool-fresh-spice scent could pierce my frustration. First, he'd played with my hair at the game. Now, he was getting up close and personal. His nearness stole my sense, and I needed my wits about me. I tried rolling up my window, but it wouldn't budge. Kenny must've turned on the puppy lock.

"Are you just flirting to see if I'll take the bait and reciprocate?" I asked.

"You got me," Sebastian said. "But then again, you've just described every incidence of a man flirting with a woman *ever*."

"I meant that you're trying to *trick* me into reciprocating," I clarified.

"Why would I do that?"

"I don't know—so you can hold it against me at the office? I wouldn't put it past you to announce it at Monday morning's meeting. 'Georgina wants me and I can prove it.'"

"So you want me?"

"About as much as I want Montezuma's Revenge."

"Traffic is light," Kenny called back as we passed under the Brooklyn Bridge. "We're making great time."

Sebastian scowled, ignoring Kenny. "I've been nothing but chivalrous to you all day, and you're comparing me to diarrhea."

It'd been an automatic response. It would be mortifying for Sebastian to take me on a fake date and find out I wished it was real. I shrugged, looking out the window. "If the shit fits."

Kenny took a corner so fast, Bruno and I went flying across the seat toward Sebastian. He shifted to look around Bruno, who panted in his face. "So, if I were to point out that we've been having a pretty great second date—"

"Second?"

"Oh, come on," he said. "You had more fun with me at the game than with François—I call that a date."

I rolled my eyes. Typical of Sebastian to believe he'd scooped another man's date out from under him. "When you say things like that, you only encourage Justin. You know what he said to me at the game?"

Sebastian searched my face. "Whatever it was, he probably read it on the back of a cereal box . . . and still confused the details."

"It was more of an observation," I said.

Well, well. It's a fine line, isn't it? According to Justin, Sebastian and I hadn't just been fighting since day one. We'd been fighting something *between* us.

"Do you agree with his observation?" Sebastian asked.

I needed to move back to my side of the seat, but I didn't want to. Sebastian wasn't pulling away, either. I couldn't forget why we were really here, though. The moment I started seeing Sebastian as anything other than a colleague was the moment I could no longer trust my judgment around him.

I slid away from him. "I don't think so," I said.

"Oh, Keller." He sighed. "For someone so smart, you can really be clueless on some things, can't you?"

"I am *not* clueless." Justin had clearly shared his thoughts with Sebastian, so I could only assume by his reaction that he agreed. Or was it that he'd finally figured out there was more advantage to making a friend than an enemy of me?

I hoped it was the former, and that scared me. As did my hope that it *wasn't* the latter. Could I trust myself to keep a clear head and not fall for someone who had no plans to cross the line from hate to love?

Kenny screeched to a stop. "Nine-and-a-half minutes. That's got to be a record." He turned in his seat to look back at us, panting as if he'd run a marathon. "Maybe don't mention this in my review. My boss won't appreciate the rush order, if you know what I mean."

"Thanks, man." Sebastian stopped me as I went for my door. "Come out my side. Yours opens into traffic."

I slid out after Sebastian as he jogged off with the dogs.

"Come on," he called over his shoulder. "It already started."

As eager as I was to find out what *it* was, I rarely jogged for anything that wasn't a traveling ice cream cart. I followed them into McCarren Park, where a large group of people—and their dogs—took various positions on rubber mats. A couple instructors walked through and arranged the dogs in what looked like stretches.

"When I asked about what to wear," I said as I approached Sebastian, "you might've mentioned this."

He arranged four mats in the back row, squatting to unroll them. "Why the hell would I?" he asked, glancing up to scan my bare legs from the hem of my dress to my ankles.

Piano played in the background. I helped Sebastian position each dog between us using treats from my Bruno bag to get them to stay. Bruno sat on his haunches, panting as he looked around, probably trying to determine the nearest source of food.

An instructor came by and set bowls of water in front of Opal and Bruno. "Welcome to the class," she said. "I'm Michelle."

"How does this work?" I asked, removing my booties.

"We're here promoting the new doggy gym and daycare facility we're opening in Union Square," she said with a smile. "Today, we're just having fun. Dogs get exercise, treats, and some special attention from me and my partner. Humans get a free class."

"Don't tell her it's free," Sebastian said, trying and failing to touch his toes. "I don't want her to think I'm a cheap date."

"Sorry about that," Michelle said, positioning herself behind Bruno. "Set an intention for the day, then get into the downward-facing dog position like my colleague at the front."

"Since I'm in a dress, I think I'll stick with upward-facing dog," I said, lying on my stomach so I wouldn't give the crowd of onlookers a show.

Sebastian leaned forward on his outstretched arms, extending his legs behind him. "But I've been dying to see what kind of panties Georgina Keller wears—if any."

"You should've asked. *George* wears boxer briefs like most guys."

Sebastian scowled, obviously uncomfortable in his position. "Very funny."

The teacher got Bruno to roll onto his back, then took his paws and stretched him. I looked past her. "Here's something you can use in the article. The right girl won't care if you spend money on her," I told Sebastian. "That's the point of planning around her interests. *That's* what'll impress her—not how much you paid for Pilates."

"*Pup*lates," Sebastian corrected me.

"We just call it yoga for dogs," Michelle said.

"Really?" Sebastian frowned. "Not even doga?"

"No."

He *tsk*ed. "Missed opportunity."

I arched my back, lifting my head to the sky.

"Nice form," Michelle said before returning to the front.

"Very nice," Sebastian agreed.

"Thank you." Feeling Sebastian's stare on me, I fixed my dress and pushed my hips back over my heels for child's pose. "For the record," I said, "I'd prefer a fun, 'cheap' date to a boring, expensive one any day."

"Yeah?"

"Earlier, when you said that stuff about having an enviable lifestyle . . . do you only see it as a way to advance your career? Or do you also use it to impress women?"

"Of course I do. Mostly because I didn't have much growing up. At least in a material sense."

With my arms stretched to the top of the mat, I peered at him from under my bicep. He'd alluded to that last time we'd been at a park. Though my curiosity grew, it didn't seem like the right conversation while he had his ass in the air.

"It won't matter to the right girl," I said.

"Salary doesn't matter to you?"

"When dating someone?" I made a slightly above average income and had *still* been taken advantage of. I'd never mooch the way Neal had done to me. "Nope."

"No—*your* salary. You asked if having money and status is important to me. Is it to you?"

The moment Vance had brought money into our meeting, my outlook had shifted. It wasn't the number itself that tempted me, but the security of it. "I'm not trying to prove you wrong," I said. "Do you *want* to meet a girl whose interest in you correlates to what you spend on her?"

Watching the instructor at the front of the lawn, Sebastian kept his palms on the mat as he attempted to walk his feet to meet them. He gave up and skipped ahead, standing with his hands turned out at his sides. "In my experience, it's not a good sign."

Instead of feeling superior that I'd made my point, I just hated that Sebastian had experienced that at all. Maybe the women he'd dated were used to a certain lifestyle and had made him feel he had to support that. "I'm sorry I assumed you were something you're not," I said as I touched my palms in front of my heart.

He didn't respond right away, mirroring my hands.

"I'm sorry I dismissed you before I'd even officially met you."

I pressed the flat of my right foot against the inside of my left knee. "I'm sorry you're putting yourself through puplates for me."

"I've gone through worse to get laid," he said in a wobbly tree pose, and my balance faltered.

I knew Sebastian well enough at this point to recognize the teasing in his voice, but it seemed the wall between us could be coming down. The question was what we'd find on the other side—and what we'd be to each other without a line to separate us.

18

F ollowing an afternoon of playing in portable sprinklers, mastering the dog gym's mini obstacle course, and giving Bruno more treats than he normally got in a week, I parked on a bench to clean up and feed the dogs. Bruno took his pills with a little peanut butter, too exhausted to fight with me.

Sebastian had excused himself twenty minutes earlier, and when he finally returned, I almost didn't recognize him in a crisp, black button-down, jeans, and his hair styled off his face. Only the beginning of his five o'clock shadow gave him away as the same Sebastian I'd started the morning with. He carried a wicker picnic basket and what looked like Pendleton blankets rolled under one arm.

Sitting on the bench with Opal between my legs, I curled my toes in my boots. He looked so *handsome*. "What's going on?" I asked.

He held up the basket. "I promised you supper."

Sebastian looked like the kind of date I'd expect to find at my front door. "Did you say *supper?*"

"Yea, sometimes the Boston in me surfaces. First-date

jitters." He held out his hand. "Come on. This is the last night of the outdoor film series."

I glanced past him to see people setting out blankets under a screen at the opposite end of the lawn. I'd been to my fair share of movies in the park, but never on a date, which was arguably the height of romance in the city. Sebastian had really pulled out all the stops to change my opinion of him. Was it just for the article, or was there more to it than that?

I took his hand tentatively. Were first-date jitters even a thing for someone like Sebastian? Because hearing that, now I had them too. "What do you think the feature is tonight?" I asked as we crossed the lawn with the dogs.

"Surely some kind of fairy *tail*."

"You mean like *The Little Furmaid*."

He snickered. "*Brokebark Mountain*."

My heels sank in the grass, so I stooped to remove them. "*Love in the Time of Collars*," I said. "Featuring Sandra Bulldog and Drool Barrymore."

He stopped to wait for me. "Don't forget Tommy Flea Jones."

"*Titanic*," I said.

"*Titanic*? I don't get it . . . oh, wait." He narrowed his eyes in thought. "Kate Wins*let* the dogs out?"

I resumed walking in my socks. "There's no play on words. I'm just wondering if you like that movie."

Realization crossed his face. "Damn it. I know what you heard, and it's not true. Justin claims I cried, but the truth is that I have an inordinate number of eyelashes. Sometimes they cause trouble in the eye-watering area."

"Sure." I grinned, squinting ahead. "Looks like *You've Got Mail*."

"For the record, I requested *Lady and the Tramp*," he said, "but that only got me the side-eye."

"You did not."

"I one-hundred percent did." At the edge of the crowd, he stopped and set down the picnic basket. "Made some last-minute calls and said it was for a piece I was working on. So *You've Got Mail* feels like a huge 'fuck you,' to be honest."

My laugh came out sounding awed. He had this dating thing down to an art. I could almost convince myself this felt real to him too. "Seriously, where'd all this come from?"

He unfurled a blanket onto the grass. "Never ask a magician for a peek behind the curtain."

"I've never had anyone go to these lengths for a date." I squatted to pull the edges taut, and my words hung in the air. Maybe I should've kept that to myself. "I mean, the thing is," I continued, testing the waters, "we could probably end the date now and have plenty of material."

"Not unless you're sick of me."

I smiled inwardly. "If I wasn't sick of you four hours in, I wouldn't be after six."

"I've never been on a date this long. You?"

I stuck each of my boots on diagonal corners of the blanket. "Only if you count weekend getaways."

"With your ex," he guessed, opening the basket. "Never done that. Now, I can say my first getaway date was a trip to Greenpoint."

"Sorry, but mock dates don't count."

"Ah, I see," was all he said.

Thankfully, the dogs were already lying in the grass, half asleep. Bruno needed rest. Today had been more activity than usual for him, and his heart condition was never far from my mind.

Sebastian passed me the second blanket. "It's getting chilly."

I sat cross-legged and covered my lap with it while he unpacked a bottle of red wine. "This is from that stash the Spanish vineyard sent over."

"For the natural wine piece?" I took the bottle from him and read the label. "Looks fancy."

He sat next to me. "The most impressive part is that I remembered a corkscrew."

I looked up. "Since I've been with you all day, I can only assume you packed this before coming over this morning, which was risky."

He pulled out several takeout containers. "How so?"

I tried to peek at the contents, but the lids had steamed over. "Considering our history," I said, "it would've been a safe assumption that I might not have agreed to help you today. What if I'd slammed the door in your face?"

"I wasn't taking no for an answer." He took the plastic top off some mixed greens, and my stomach grumbled at the promise of food. "I'm persistent," he said. "Irresistible quality number four. Or was that five? I'm losing count."

Sebastian had known I'd say yes. In truth, I hadn't put up much of a fight. He and I had butted heads since practically the moment we'd met, and yet I'd given up a Sunday to go out with him. Was that romantic, I wondered, or foolish?

The din of the crowd lowered slightly as the movie started. He uncorked the wine and poured us each a stemless glass of red. "*Salud*," he said, raising his drink.

I clinked my glass to his and took a sip. His attention was even headier than the wine, and I was glad I'd agreed to come. I didn't regret a moment of the day, but it would've meant even more to know if he was feeling the same.

"Georgina?"

I licked the underside of my top lip. "Hmm?"

"I asked what you think of the wine."

"Oh. It's fine."

"How does it compare to last night's?"

I wrinkled my nose, wondering if I'd missed something else he'd said. "What?"

He set down his wineglass, looking into it as he worked his jaw back and forth. "Are you still talking to Frank?"

As if the question wasn't random enough, his use of *Frank* over *François* got my attention. "We haven't been out again if that's what you mean."

"What about . . . staying in?" He peered at me. "I saw the empty wineglasses and Pinot bottle at your apartment this morning. And I haven't stopped wondering about it all day."

The way he said it, brows heavy, it was almost as if the thought of Frank spending the night bothered him. "Do you really think I'd invite a date, even a pretend one, upstairs when I'd spent the previous night with someone else?"

"Georgina." He gave me look. "You can't honestly tell me you still believe we're on a fake date."

My heart skipped. Happiness bubbled up so quickly, I had to stop myself from breaking into a grin. I'd been trying to bury my instinct that this was real, but deep down, I'd known it was. I'd just been clinging to the lie out of fear of the truth. As Neal's dark cloud crept back over me, my excitement subsided. Some days, our breakup didn't feel that long ago. I *felt* ready to move on, but was I really? I worried it wouldn't take much for those insecurities to surface—or for me to fall into old habits. I had reasons to be skeptical of Sebastian's intentions, but I wasn't. I trusted him. Or was it only that I wanted him enough to ignore red flags as I had in the past?

"Oh, no," he said when I didn't respond. "You *do* still think this is for the magazine."

"I—"

"There's no article." He worked his fingers under the lid of the largest container, then popped it off. "I didn't want to risk you turning me down. But clever as you are, I would've thought you'd have figured it out by now."

I watched as he scooped spaghetti and meatballs onto a plastic plate. "I guess I'm still learning how to read you," I said.

"I'm complex. Another one of my qualities. Though I imagine that one falls under frustrating as well." He served me pasta and salad. "So, now that you know the truth, you know why I'm asking if Frank spent the night. And why I hope to hell that answer is not a fucking chance."

"Luciano and I had a sleepover," I said, secretly awed that he sounded *jealous*. "I haven't talked to Frank in days."

"Good."

"*Good?*" I asked.

"Yes, good. Why haven't you spoken?"

"I don't know. Life, I guess." I took a bite. "This is still warm. How'd you put all this together?"

"Even Santa Claus has helpers."

Justin. It had to be. He really was a good friend. "Does your elf know this isn't make-believe?"

"Of course. *Lady and the Tramp* was his suggestion—I think he's hoping for a spaghetti kiss."

I blushed, my stomach suddenly full of butterflies that hadn't been there before. At least not since I'd run into him outside my apartment. Now *this* was the right moment for a first-date kiss—the setting sun, wine, good conversation. Frank could take a few notes from Sebastian.

"We weren't really a match," I said.

Sebastian seemed to know instantly that I was talking about Frank. He nodded. "Why not?"

I twirled spaghetti onto my plastic fork. "A few reasons, but there were a couple things he said that actually reminded me a little of my ex."

Sebastian hummed. "And I take it that's a bad thing."

"My ex was . . . patronizing. More interested in what others thought than what I did. I second-guessed myself a lot around Neal, and it turned me into sort of a . . . pushover." I exhaled a long breath. There, I'd said it. "I would end up deferring to him on everything."

"I have a hard time seeing that," Sebastian said, studying me as he took a bite of pasta.

"That's because, you've mostly only seen me as . . ."

He tilted his head as he chewed and swallowed. "George," he finished.

Maybe I should've been more surprised that he'd figured it out, but the difference between George and Georgina had to be obvious. "You asked earlier why Neal and I broke up. Another woman was only half the truth. He saw me as weak, and I realized when it came to him, I was."

"Weak how?"

"I give up my seat on the subway. I let others have the last slice of cake at a party. He'd say mean things about me while we were dating, and I'd believe him." I traded my fork for my wineglass. "He slandered me to our mutual friends assuming I wouldn't put up a fight. Most of them don't even speak to me anymore."

He swatted at a fly hovering over a meatball. "Why *didn't* you put up a fight?"

I shrugged. "I have Lu, Bruno, my family, and my work. Neal, he needs people around him who make him feel important. Honestly, if our friends believed what he told them, they weren't friends anyway."

"Georgina, you aren't a pushover." Sebastian smiled gently at me. "You're kind."

"That's not all," I said, fiddling with my bracelets. "I supported him so he could go back to school. And as soon as he'd graduated, he left me." Would Sebastian see me differently after this? As someone without a backbone? I glanced at my hands. "I didn't realize how bad I was until he came back a couple months later and talked me into forgiving him. At least for a few hours."

He reached out and stilled my hands. "I'm still not convinced you're anything other than a good person."

"People don't respect good," I said. "They respect bitches."

A slow smile spread across his face. "Don't you hear how ridiculous that sounds?"

"Saying it out loud . . . maybe I do. But it's what Luciano always says. He opened my eyes to the fact that I lost myself in that relationship." I paused. "I don't want to make that mistake again."

"Then you have to date someone who doesn't want to lose you, either."

I didn't want to lose *Sebastian*. Not when I'd finally found him. "Are you suggesting . . .?"

His eyes gleamed in the reflection of the movie. "I regret how I spoke to you the morning I met you. *I* was patronizing. I should've just told you the truth. That you're beautiful."

I glanced into my drink. I'd been called *cute* and *pretty* plenty in my life but rarely *beautiful*. Hearing it was like trying on a hat I loved but one I couldn't get to fit quite right.

He lifted my chin with his knuckle. "You know that, don't you?"

I bit my lip. "*Beautiful* is such a big word."

"And yet it describes you so well."

I believed Sebastian when he said it. I wished I hadn't come to question that over my time with Neal. "That morning, when I flew off the handle? It wasn't directed at you. I'd already been berating myself for not sticking up for Luciano, so when you called me out for exactly that, I responded out of hurt and guilt."

He frowned. "I overreacted, Georgina. Would you believe me if I told you I had a good reason?"

I already knew why. I nodded. "You were on the phone with Justin, and you looked angry. I can only imagine it had to do with me, even though neither of us knew it in that moment."

He wiped his mouth with a napkin and balled it up. "It wasn't about work. Well, not entirely. It had more to do with my mom."

"Your . . . mom?"

"She immigrated from Mexico when she was eighteen, poor, and pregnant. Made it all the way to the east coast on her own."

"Wow." I moved my plate away, adjusted the blanket over my lap, and hugged my knees to my chest. "She sounds resilient."

"She had to be. When she arrived in Boston, she worked as a cleaner."

I tried not to show my surprise. For a while now, he'd been hinting at a past that didn't line up with what I'd read about him. Judging by Vance's offer, Sebastian did very well for himself, and I'd uncovered that his sister owned a successful clothing store in Chestnut Hill. "Until when?"

"That was all Mom ever did, under-the-table jobs.

Cleaning for fast food restaurants when I was really young, then a higher-end department store. She eventually worked her way up to five-star hotels and rich people's homes."

"*That's* why you 'summered' on Nantucket."

"Yeah. We lived in the maids' quarters."

"That's so bourgeois," I murmured.

"Wasn't as bad as it sounds, to be honest. At least people weren't rude to her the way they'd been at her other jobs, sometimes right in front of me." He paused for a bite. "At the café, when that woman disrespected Luciano, it triggered something in me. Rudeness usually does, apparently."

His comment came rushing back to me.

"You'll call a stranger an asshole, but you can't even stand up for your supposed friend?"

Everything clicked. "I didn't defend him."

"Yeah, so I took it out on you. Especially since that day in particular was . . . tough."

"Because I was starting the job?"

"No." He reached out and cleared some hair from my cheek. After a few moments, he said, "You're just the kind of woman my mom wanted me to meet. I wish I could bring you home."

"Where's home?"

"Gone," he said.

One word sent chills down my spine. My response came out as a strangled whisper. "Gone?"

"The day I met you was the first anniversary of her death." He took his hand back.

The misshapen puzzle that was Sebastian's personality finally clicked into place. *Mom* was the piece I'd been missing. She was why he'd stood up for Lu in the coffee shop and had called me out for not doing the same. "I'm . . . I'm so sorry, Sebastian. What happened?"

"She . . . when we were saying goodbye . . ." He paused, swallowing. "I made her a promise to be better. She wanted me to settle down and meet a nice girl, so I've been trying to make some changes."

She was behind his sudden change in lifestyle too. I'd doubted the integrity of the exposé in the first place, but now the lack of research over things like the car accident and Sebastian's background angered me. "The exposé must've been a huge setback," I said.

"I'd never felt like such a disappointment."

His reaction to my presence, and to being maligned in the press, made more sense now. "You've been under pressure since the day I met you."

"And my mom was the one I went to for anything," he said. "Always."

"You're not a disappointment," I said. "How could you be? You're kind, smart, generous, successful. If *I* of all people know that, your family definitely does."

"Was that a compliment?"

"It was four. You called me beautiful."

His expression fell. "You should know, my mom would've had my hide for how I've treated you. She didn't raise me that way."

"I understand so much better now."

"Do you?" he asked. "I need you to know I'm not Neal."

The vehemence with which Sebastian said it told me he comprehended the damage Neal had done. And that was enough to prove they were nothing alike. I nodded. "I know that."

"A few minutes ago," he said, "you said you forgave him, but not for long. What happened?"

I hugged my legs more tightly, clasping my elbows. "It . . . when he asked me to take him back, I assumed he'd realized what he'd had in me. And he did, but not what I'd thought." I rested my chin on my knees. "He said he never should've left *someone like me* for a stronger woman. To him, I wasn't loyal or devoted—just easy to control. He was the first person to ever make me feel so meek."

"And I was the second." Understanding dawned on Sebastian's face. "I came along and said you'd get run over in this city."

"Before Neal, I would've brushed it off. But you hit a nerve."

"Georgina, you aren't meek. For one, you *didn't* take him back. Secondly, you wouldn't let him bully you into not adopting a pet that needed you."

"That was for Bruno, not myself."

He shook his head. "You're drawing non-existent lines. What matters is that you were strong. For him and for yourself. You're both George and Georgina. *You* got up in front of a room that first day at *Modern Man* and gave the shit out of your presentation—no one else."

It was such a simple concept that I was embarrassed to admit I'd never really thought of it that way. *I* was still the one standing at the front of the room, not some version of myself that I could return to a box later . . . even if it sometimes felt that way.

And of course there was the fact that I'd forgotten to be either version all day. I'd just been myself.

"Now, since I can't kick my own ass," Sebastian said, "tell me where to find that cocksucka Neal so I can make him sorry he ever opened his pie hole."

Smiling, I pushed Sebastian's shoulder. "I have to admit, it's a little sexy when your accent surfaces."

He caught my wrist, sliding his hand down until he held mine. "I'm serious. I don't like how he treated you. Not at all."

"You don't have to worry about him."

"And Frank?"

My insides pulled, sending a twinge of excitement down between my legs. Sebastian wanted me all to himself. I hadn't pegged him for the possessive type, but I recognized my own jealousy in him, which had quietly formed seeing him with Isabella, June, or in photographs with other women. "There's nobody else," I said. "You?"

"Not even close." He squeezed my hand and let it go, leaning back on his palms. "Did you give Bruno his meds?"

"Yes. Thank you for asking."

"See?" He grinned. "I'm a natural at this dog thing."

"It's easy to think that when you don't have one. From the outside, it looks like lounging in Central Park, cuddling on the couch, and posting cute videos. But there's a lot of shit too. Literally."

"You keep trying to talk me out of adopting Opal," he said.

"It isn't something you can decide on a whim. What if she chews up your furniture? What if you want to leave town? What if she gets sick and needs treatment?"

Sebastian flinched. "Then I'd take care of her. Who's going to return a dog because she's sick? What a load of shit."

"Neal would've."

Sebastian looked as if I'd sucker punched him.

I hadn't meant to compare him to Neal after I'd just finished explaining that was why I wouldn't see Frank again. "I didn't mean—"

"Give me more credit than that, Georgina."

"There's no glamour in taking care of a sick dog. His care got in the way of vacations and nights out and even nights in." Bruno's legs twitched as he surely dreamed of chasing squirrels and a certain attractive beagle-foxhound mix. "You never know how you'll react until you've been in that situation."

"I do know. I have been in it." He briefly clenched his teeth. "My mom had cancer."

My breath caught, and I instantly regretted everything I'd just said. He hadn't said how she'd died. No wonder he'd been so helpful with Bruno. I covered my heart. "Sebastian."

"Don't say you're sorry," he said, his expression easing. "You and Bruno deserve better than to be abandoned that way. Opal too. I wouldn't do that."

"I know," I said softly. It was nice to hear that from someone other than my therapist, mom, or Luciano. "I'm sure she was so proud of you. You were a great son, and you'll make a great dog dad."

He glanced at the movie screen. "How's your food?"

I wanted to probe further about his relationship with her, but I let him change the subject. "Good," I said. "Really good, Sebastian. It's not too good to be true, is it?"

He smiled. "Tony's makes a mean spaghetti and meatballs."

"That's not what I mean."

"I know."

"My guard is down. You know me now, better than anyone else at the office—better than anyone lately, aside from my family and Luciano."

He sat forward, brushing grass off his hands. "Is that a bad thing?"

I tried to configure my thoughts in a way that wouldn't offend him. I didn't want to be rude or skeptical or accusatory. I also didn't want to trust blindly and end up in another Neal situation. "This isn't a game anymore."

"This was never a game for me, Georgina. I was scared for my job. I still am. It was never personal."

It was either the best or worst moment to bring up my talk with Vance. The date had gone from simulation to reality, and that meant I had more to lose. I wasn't entirely sure Sebastian would understand if I told him what I knew, but I *was* sure I didn't want this night to end here and now.

"Can we really go from hating each other to dating each other?" I asked.

"Justin's convinced it's the best way to do it."

"Justin sure has a lot to say about it."

"If he were here, he'd be handing me a spaghetti noodle right about now."

I laughed, spinning my bangles around my wrist. I wasn't in the habit of discussing a kiss before it happened. I couldn't decide if that made things more or less awkward.

Sebastian set his empty dish aside. "All done?" He piled my plate on top of his, and he moved closer, dropping his eyes to my mouth. "I'm actually pretty annoyed with myself that I'm not your only, and not even your first date this week."

I shivered, both excited and nervous at the prospect of finally kissing him. "But you were the best one."

"You cold?" He took the blanket from my lap and wrapped it around my shoulders. Pulling me closer by the edges of it, he kissed my cheek and whispered, "For the record, I never hated you. But if you thought that, I'd like to make it up to you."

If anything, my shivering increased with his words. "How?" I asked breathlessly.

"Candy." He released me and looked into the picnic basket. "What's your favorite go-to chocolate movie snack?"

His nearness had stolen my wits. I pulled the blanket closed around me and tried to think straight. "You won't find it in there."

"Try me."

"100 Grand."

He glanced up, blinking at me. "Are you kidding? Whose favorite candy bar is 100 Grand?"

I shrugged. "There's something about that crispy rice and caramel combo."

"Well." The contents of the basket crinkled as he sorted through them. "I don't have that, but it's okay. I've got something even better."

I twisted my lips. "I'll be the judge of that."

He pulled out a Butterfinger. "If you like crispy, this is the one. The crumbly peanut butter flakes . . ." He groaned. "Nearly as good as sex."

I took it from him and inspected the wrapper. "Not the sex *I* have."

His expression darkened, and he took the bar from me, tossing it aside. "And just like that," he said, getting closer, "I'm hungry for a different kind of dessert."

Instinctively, I lay back, and he followed, propping his elbow on the blanket and his head in his hand. He made no move to kiss me, just stared. I'd never observed him up close this long. Maybe it was his thick black lashes that'd once distracted me into thinking his eyes were green when they actually had hints of blue. Perhaps it was his unfairly sharp jawline more than anything that'd gotten me so riled up that first morning at the coffee shop. "We're missing the movie," I said finally.

"I don't miss it at all."

My cheeks practically ached from a day of smiling and laughing. Several hours on, and I wasn't ready for our dog date to end. I wanted *more*. To learn not only his fears, but to understand them inside out so I could soothe him. To be there on the next anniversary of his mom's death—equipped with Dunkin' Donuts and a shoulder to cry on instead of harsh words over spilled coffee.

I could picture it clearly, and if that was the future I saw for myself, I could kiss it goodbye if I took his job. He'd never forgive me. I wouldn't do that to him anyway, now that he'd let me in and showed me what'd driven him to work as hard as he had.

Vance had offered me something more, but today, Sebastian had painted me our potential future. Was I willing to lose that over a job? The answer was obvious.

Sebastian was the more I wanted.

There was only one way to wave the white flag. Perhaps because I'd fought my attraction to him for so long, it now overwhelmed me. I tilted my chin with as subtle a pout as I could manage. I could've begged for a kiss just then, but pillowy lips said more than words ever could.

Sebastian cupped one side of my face. "You want me to get a noodle?"

I would've laughed, but cozied up in the blanket, with him pressed up against my side, I was oddly calm—and content just to lean into his palm. He trailed his hand down my side, resting it on my waist, then lowered his mouth. I closed my eyes as his rough tongue landed on my cheek.

Wait.

I squealed as slobber covered the right half of my face. Bruno nosed his way between us, pushing us apart. He rested his head on my chest and stared at Sebastian.

Sebastian flopped onto his back, scoff-laughing. "You've *got* to be fucking kidding me," he said, his eyes on the sky. "Bruno's even nosier than Justin."

"At least Justin *wants* us to kiss. Bruno, on the other hand . . ." I put my hand on my dog's soft head. "I think this might be his way of saying he likes you as a friend but nothing more."

Sebastian turned his head, locked eyes with Bruno, and sighed. "I've never had to work this hard for a kiss, but if Bruno doesn't approve, then I'll just have to keep at it." He moved a strand of hair from my cheek, then thumbed the bridge of my nose, over my freckles. "You know what they say."

"There's a thin line between love and hate?" I asked.

He smiled, punctuating one cheek with his semi-colon dimple. "The best buns are worth waiting for."

19

On the doorstep of my apartment building, Bruno ensured Sebastian and I stood one Great Dane's length apart. After the movie, we'd returned Opal, and Sebastian had insisted on walking me home.

He leaned against the doorframe, admirably collected under Bruno's side-eyeing. "So, how'd I score today?" he asked.

"By my calculation . . . you haven't yet."

"Yet?" Sebastian raised both eyebrows. "Was that an invitation upstairs?"

I resisted an enthusiastic *yes!* Sebastian was first and foremost my colleague. Wasn't he? After what he'd planned for me today and what we'd each shared, our relationship had shifted. No, he was definitely more than a colleague.

"Do you think it's a good idea?" I asked. "We still have to work together."

"I'll quit," he murmured, moving closer, undaunted by Bruno's growl, "if it means I can come up."

My heart skipped and my insides tightened, excited by his persistence. "We haven't even kissed."

He leaned in, wine and mint on his breath. "That's because I've been waiting for a moment when I wasn't at risk of getting my junk bitten off, but . . ."

I laughed nervously and pulled Bruno back by his collar, taking the next few seconds to collect myself.

Sebastian Quinn and I had gone on a date.

Sebastian Quinn wanted to *come upstairs*.

And me? I wasn't ready to say goodnight.

"What do you think, boy?" I asked Bruno as I got out my keys. "Should we let him in?"

Bruno cocked his head and barked.

"He says it's all right as long as you cool it with the dog puns," I said and unlocked the door to the building.

Sebastian followed me in. "He's showing me his teeth. You sure?"

"No." I hit the elevator call button, and the doors opened. "But I'm willing to take the risk."

We boarded the car. "Did he give your ex any trouble?"

"Not really," I said, "but Bruno and I have been on our own the past six months. Plus, Neal was sort of . . . non-threatening."

"That would imply *I'm* threatening."

"What I mean is that he and I had a different kind of chemistry. We went through the honeymoon phase like anyone else, but it wasn't that intense. Or that long."

"Aha." Sebastian nodded, fixing his eyes on me as we ascended. "And Bruno is picking up on our . . . *threatening* chemistry."

"He's very intuitive."

"That, or I'm emitting a pretty strong I-want-to-fuck-your-brains-out vibe."

My breath actually caught in my throat, and my involuntary squeak turned his eyes hooded. "He's picking up on your BDE," I suggested.

"If there was ever a moment for it, it would be now." He wet his lips. "But I guess I'll have to take it slow until Bruno's comfortable."

"When have you ever taken it slow?"

"It's been a while since I liked anyone enough to get to know them better."

I stayed on my side of the elevator until we arrived on my floor, even though what I really wanted was to go to him, cancel let's-take-it-slow, and dive in head first.

"I was afraid opening up to someone would endear them to me," he said. "And I was right. I want to tell you all my secrets."

At my door, I let Bruno in and turned to Sebastian. "You can, you know."

"I could," he agreed, "but then I'd have to kiss you."

"You'd *have* to kiss me?"

"Or kill you. Your choice."

"If you were any other guy, I'd accuse you of hyperbole," I said, "but I'm sure you've wanted to do both at some point."

Sebastian shrugged. "As Justin would say, there's a fine line between kissing and killing."

I stepped inside and flipped on the living room lights. "There's the title of your feature," I said, removing my booties.

Sebastian paused in the doorway, his broad shoulders nearly blocking the light from the hallway. "Still want me to come in?"

"Do *you* want to?" I asked.

"Yes. But that doesn't answer my question."

I toed my muddy, grassy-soled, dog park sneakers under the coffee table—the same one hosting the wine bottle and glasses—and straightened a stack of magazines, which included the latest issue of *Gauntlet*. "If I say yes, does that make me a traitor?"

He cocked his head, scanning me head to toe. "To whom?"

The lamps weren't the only thing warming the space between us. The apartment was stuffy, and having Sebastian there wasn't helping. He took up the whole entryway, giving me looks that made me sweat. "We're supposed to be enemies," I said. "Don't you feel like you're betraying yourself?"

"We were never enemies." He entered the apartment, closing the door behind him. "You frustrated the hell out of me. Got under my skin in ways I didn't like. Threatened my life's work."

Well. There was no need to rehash every dirty detail. I went to the window and started working on the rusty latches. I rarely locked it because it stuck, but I had that morning knowing Bruno would be out with me.

Sebastian strolled around the living room, his hands in his pockets as he passed my TV. He stopped to look at my Nintendo. "You really do play video games?"

"Of course." Well, as of a couple months ago, so I could fit in with the guys. Up until then, I'd only ever played for fun at Luciano's.

"Huh." At my bookcase, he glanced at the spines before moving on.

"Here's another tip for the article you're not planning to write," I said. "Books are a window into the soul. You can learn a lot about your date by what she reads."

"What does it say if she reads *Gauntlet*?"

"That I'm doing my job."

"By giving my competitor money?"

"It was research," I said. "I don't have to tell you —*know thy enemy*."

He was quiet a few seconds. "What about if she reads *Unleashing the Bitch Within?*"

My cheeks flushed. How had he even *seen* that from where he was standing? I finally got the latches unhooked and pushed up the window. "That one's about dogs."

"Liar," he said. "I read the back cover."

I scoffed. "It's in the corner of the bottom shelf. You snooped earlier."

"Like you said, books are a window to the soul. I wanted to make sure I got a complete picture before our date. Good thing I find self-improvement sexy." Sebastian came over and squatted to inspect the window. "All that work to open it a couple inches?"

"That's as high as it goes."

He positioned his palms under the frame and pushed. It didn't budge.

"Told you," I said.

Bruno ambled over on his long legs, sniffing the air around us. Sebastian inhaled deeply before trying again, the frame denting his palms as his face reddened. Bruno wagged his tail, sticking his nose out the window as it rose one inch and then another. By the time Sebastian blew out a breath and dropped his hands, he'd opened it enough for Bruno to get his whole head out.

"Wow," I said. "I didn't think it opened that far."

Sebastian sat on the ground, tracing a finger along the white window frame where I'd made notches with dates in colored pencil. "Is this Bruno?" he asked.

"Since I didn't have him as a puppy, we never really got to do the measurement thing." I squatted and pointed to the first date. "This was when I got him at three." I moved my finger a smidge. "Six months later."

A deep chuckle rumbled from Sebastian's chest as he touched the frame. "Four," he said, his finger basically on top of mine. "Four-and-a-half. How old is he?"

"Almost five. I'll measure again in January."

"My sister does this with her kids in the laundry room. Do you own this apartment?"

"No, I rent. You?"

"Own, and I still wouldn't mark up the walls." He dropped his hand and turned out the window. "I don't even paint."

"They're just white?"

"You say that like it's more unusual than measuring your full-grown dog on another person's windowsill."

I shrugged with a smile. "I don't plan to move, but if I do, I can paint over it. Life is too short not to be where you are, even if it's a rental."

"That's something my mom would've said. We always had the cleanest house on the block, but somehow it was still lived in. I miss that. Home." The way he said *home* made me wonder what else he'd lost when his mom had passed. Knowing the truth about his past, and how he'd gotten here, made me feel closer to him than ever. If not because I understood him now, then because I doubted he often shared the way her death had affected him.

A breeze from the window blew hair over my face. He reached out and tucked it behind my ear. "I think I might feel attached to you now, Georgina," he said and thumbed the corner of my mouth. "Which would make it hard to kill you."

"So I guess you'd better kiss me instead."

He glanced at Bruno, who still had his head out the window, then slid his hand around the back of my neck. He pulled my mouth to his, stopping when we were an inch apart. "Stay very still," Sebastian whispered. "Or you'll wake the beast."

"Don't worry, he can spend hours looking for squirrels, even in the dark."

"Not *that* beast," he said, a hint of gravel in his voice. Slowly, he pressed his lips to mine and inhaled. The night air cooled my skin as his kiss warmed me to my core. He stayed there—testing our chemistry? Savoring the moment? Awaiting my permission? I stilled, not breathing. It was something I'd fantasized about but had never thought would really happen—Sebastian's hands moving into my hair, my heart speeding with anticipation, our mouths opening to each other.

Chills spread over me, the kind that came with a skipping heart, like witnessing a perfect pitch down the center and the crack of a bat that sent a baseball over the fence. He rounded first base as our tongues met, one hand in my hair as the other grazed my upper thigh.

He hesitated, his palm hot on my skin—and unmoving. If he didn't steal second soon, I would.

He released me. "Fuck, Georgina."

"What's wrong?"

"What's wrong? Nothing." He looked almost pained as he got up and brushed off his pants. "Everything. If this were a normal date, right now's about when I'd be asking to see your bedroom."

I stood and pulled my denim jacket more tightly around myself. "If this were a *normal* date?" I asked. "What do you mean?"

"Maybe I shouldn't've come up. I don't want to revert to the man in the exposé."

While Sebastian's chivalry was appreciated, it wasn't necessary. From my perspective, it felt as if we'd been on one long date since the moment we'd met. He hadn't given me a goodnight kiss just now—it'd been an *un*-goodnight kiss. The kind that started a night, not ended one. "That's not what this is," I said. "I want this, and I have for a while. Arguing is our foreplay, and I'm ready for release."

"Yeah?" he said and finally smiled, dimples and all. "I want to hear more about that."

"As much as you frustrated me, I've been fantasizing about you from the moment you opened your mouth."

"Then you made it minutes longer than me."

"So if you think about it . . . we've actually waited a very long time for this."

He flexed his hands as if trying to stay them. "You make a good point."

I took off my jacket and tossed it on the couch. When the strap of my dress fell over my shoulder, I resisted fixing it. "So, if this *was* a normal date, what would come next?"

"It's no secret what would happen, Georgina. Use your imagination."

"I don't want to." I pretended to scratch under my jaw, grazing my fingertips down my neck. "Tell me what you'd do next. After all," I teased, "how would it look for the article if you forfeited in the final inning?"

"I thought backing off was the right thing to do. I'd assume your advice would be not to sleep with a girl on the first date."

"My advice is to ask. Don't assume what pace she wants to go."

He tracked my hand at my throat, then blinked his gaze to my left shoulder. "What if she just told me her ex treated her like a pushover? What if she felt I was doing the same?"

"Ask her," I said, noticing the hoarseness of my voice. "*Ask.*"

"Is staying here tonight treating you the way he did?"

He ran a hand through his hair. "I can cool it, Georgina. We can go at any pace you want."

"I've taken it slow with all my exes, Sebastian. It never made a difference. I would say you and I have taken it slow enough."

"Then . . . I'd slip the other strap of your dress over your shoulder." He swallowed. "Every time you removed your jacket today, those damn straps fell."

"They're flimsy," I said, brushing the other one down. I wanted to fall against him, to feel his arms around me. "*I* feel very flimsy at the moment."

"And I feel strong. Like I might break you if I'm not careful."

I zipped the pendant of my necklace along its chain. Luciano had told me once I had pretty, slender hands, and that if I put my mind to it, I could use them to direct a man's attention wherever I wanted. "You won't."

"No matter what you wear to the office," Sebastian continued, "I imagine what it would be like to take it off. Jacket. Blouse. Skirt. Stockings. Even your jewelry, like that necklace."

Sebastian had built a career on an adeptness with language, so it shouldn't have surprised me his words aroused me as much as finally feeling his lips against mine. "You don't have to imagine anymore."

He frowned. "I want this, Georgina. You know I do. I'm trying to be good."

I reached back and unzipped my dress just enough to loosen it. "And I'm saying you don't have to be."

"What happened to being shy?" he asked.

It was a valid question. I'd spent most of our acquaintance fumbling the line between bold and bashful. "I guess you bring out the George in me."

He groaned, covering his face with one large hand.

"Why would you say that? I told you, I can't fantasize about someone named George."

"What about someone named George who wears lingerie?"

He slatted his fingers to peek at me. Turned out I could talk the talk—but did I, as myself, without a mask or a character to play, really have the guts to seduce Sebastian? For now, I left my dress where it was.

He dropped his hand. "I like you, but I'm scared of fucking it up. I don't want to treat you like a one-night stand."

"How do you know you like me if we've only been out on one date?" I asked, because in order for us to proceed, Sebastian needed to vocalize it for himself as much as I needed to hear it.

"All day has been an adventure," he said. "And ever since you walked into my office, I've been trying to be better. For you, or to beat you, I don't know. A little of both. But in the end, you challenged me when nobody else would."

Something he'd hated me for. And now? The way his eyes roamed over my body, then back to my face, it didn't look as if he hated me at all. Maybe he never had. Maybe he'd meant it when he'd said there'd been no game.

"You make me laugh," he continued. "You make me *crazy* with your messy desk and melting gummy bears and the fact that one of your video games requires a PlayStation you don't seem to own."

I crossed my arms. "That's why the plastic wrap is still on. I have three days left to return it."

"Meanwhile, you're creating color-coded schedules for your dog and reviewing my team's ideas and personal lives with a fine-tooth comb. I can't figure you out—I never could. You make me mad in a bad *and* good way. Just because I didn't ask you out until today——"

"You didn't *technically* ask me out at all."

"See?" he said. "You can't just let me finish my sentence. You do that all the time, nitpicking over details, and yet you keep your sunglasses in a Ziploc bag."

"The cases are too bulky," I said defensively.

"But a plastic bag, Georgina? Really? They're all scratched up."

I sighed and walked to him, my shoulders straight but my straps sagging. "Believe it or not, those are the reasons this will work——unless we both decide we don't want it to. We were enemies first, but we *still* want to kiss. That means something."

"You were never my enemy," he repeated.

I'd certainly felt like I was, but I couldn't say he was mine, either. "I'm not some girl you picked up at a bar or club, or wherever you pick up women."

"The theater," he said. "Industry event . . . at the park. On the subway. Sometimes even the sidewalk——"

"Okay. I think my point is made."

"The office." This time, *he* came to me, eliminating any remaining space between us. Although I'd been doing my best to be brave, his closeness had my heart pumping and my brain fuzzy. "I've never picked up a colleague before."

I arched an eyebrow. "Seriously? How is that possible?"

"Mostly because it's forbidden."

For the first time, I remembered Vance's warning in our initial meeting. Fraternization *was* against the rules. I didn't have much time left at *Modern Man*, but I did have a reputation to uphold. Whether it was the beginning or end of an assignment, Dionne had a clients-come-first business model.

And I didn't think *this* was what she'd meant by that.

Sebastian slipped his arms around my waist, walking us backward toward the bedroom. "Tell me you want this, Georgina."

I didn't even hesitate. Maybe I should have, but this didn't feel like being a pushover. It *felt* like taking control. "I want this, but——" As he leaned in to kiss me, I held him off with my palm on his chest. "I completely forgot that fraternization is, as Vance put it, *strictly forbidden*."

He stopped walking. "Don't tell me now that I've given in, you're having seconds thoughts."

"I'm not. It's just . . ." If I'd thought earlier was a bad time to bring up Vance's job offer, now was even worse. Even though I'd decided to turn it down, was keeping the information I had to myself enough to sour things between us? It wouldn't matter if I was Aliana Balik, Sebastian's celebrity crush—he'd still see me as someone who could put his job in jeopardy. I wasn't sure that would change just because we slept together. "I just don't like to break the rules," I said.

"Then I'll break them for you." He tightened his hold on my waist and lifted me as I gasped. He headed briskly down the hall as if I might protest again. "If Vance asks, I'll tell him it was all my idea."

I wrapped my arms around his neck, my bare feet dangling at his shins. "I'm there to ensure you're *better* behaved around the office, not worse," I said with a sigh.

"If I go home now," he said, opening my bedroom door, "you won't get to try bossing me around until we're back at work in the morning."

"You like to *think* I boss you around because it gives you something to complain about."

"Trust me, since you've shown up, I've had plenty to complain about." His eyes sparkled. His expression, part playful, part challenging, had to have mirrored my own.

"Put me down," I said.

"Nope."

"You said I could boss you around."

"I said you could try."

"What are you going to do, hold me up all night?"

Something different sparked in his eyes, darkening his gaze as my stomach dropped. "If that's what it takes," he said.

I hadn't meant it sexually, but the thought of Sebastian and I getting creative on our feet made me squirm. A few steps into my room, he set me down but kept ahold of me. He had to stoop to lower his forehead to mine. He looked about to speak, but as I sighed, he made a noise akin to a growl and took my mouth for a rougher kiss than before.

I hugged his neck for support, to get closer to him, trying vainly to match his height. He pulled me up, lifting me to my toes, bringing me to my full height, kissing me until my legs were so weak, he was holding me up. His five o'clock shadow scraped in the best way. I sucked his bottom lip between my teeth, and he answered by biting mine.

Bruno whined from the doorway, and I pulled away, gasping.

"Georgina," Sebastian warned. "If he thinks my BDE was threatening before—"

"I'll handle it," I said, wiggling out of Sebastian's grasp. I squatted to Bruno's level, scratching behind his ears. "Listen, buddy. You know you're my number one guy, but tonight, you're on the couch."

Bruno put his paw on my knee with a groan.

"Anthro—" Sebastian coughed into his fist, "—pomorphizing."

"Don't listen to him," I said to Bruno. "I know you understand." Well, Bruno at least knew the word *couch* since Neal had screamed at him to get off of it enough times for Bruno to think he was in trouble. Guilt panged in my chest sending Bruno away. He'd only ever slept in the living room when I was out of town. Neal or Luciano would send me a picture of Bruno in the entryway, waiting for me to come home. But this was the only way Sebastian and I would get any privacy.

I led Bruno out by the collar and shut the door on him. Before I'd even turned around, Sebastian was at my back, lifting my hair off my neck to place it over my shoulder. "I'm sorry," he said. "I'll make it up to him. Promise."

His fingertips brushed my skin and stole my response. He unclasped my necklace and set it on my dresser, then slipped my bangles off one by one. With his cheek against mine, he said, "I've wanted to kiss you since I saw you that morning in the coffee shop. I've had to wait weeks and weeks. I don't want to wait that long to be inside you, Georgina."

I held my breath as I shook my head. "I don't want that."

"Don't want me inside you," I felt his smirk near my ear, "or don't want me to wait?"

I no longer had any reason to deny my feelings for Sebastian. I wasn't entirely sure how he'd made his way into my heart, or I into his, but it didn't matter anymore. "Wait," I said. "I mean, don't wait. Option two."

"Say it, Georgina."

I bit my bottom lip where his teeth had just done the same. "I don't want to wait anymore."

20

If Sebastian's and my earlier kiss had been the first stop on a home run, our second kiss was a race to home plate. I turned, rose onto the balls of my feet, and brought his mouth to mine a second before he hoisted me up to press my back against the door. My legs circled his waist, our tongues meeting quickly, lashing and sparring like practiced enemies.

He gripped the outside of my thigh with one hand and slid the other up my nape. "When's the last time you were properly kissed?" he asked.

He took a handful of my hair so I couldn't move my head. He had me right where he wanted me. "If this is proper? Never."

"This is how you should always be kissed at the end of a date . . ." He nudged his nose against my cheek and took my earlobe between his teeth. "Hard. Hungry."

Pinching that small, soft flesh sent an electric current down between my legs. "Then we should go on more dates."

He groaned and sucked the spot he'd just bitten. "You're right, we should've done this earlier."

My dress, partly unzipped, sagged to expose the nude, lacy line of my strapless bra. "That would've been difficult considering we could hardly stand to be in the same room."

"That isn't true, and you know it." He pulled back to look me in the eye. "I'm just as turned on by you now as I was watching you around the office."

I exhaled, all breathy desire. "You watched me?"

"How could I not? You took over, pacing in bare feet, always tugging the hem of your skirt down and your damn neckline up." His hand moved beneath my dress, curving against the sensitive, neglected skin under my thigh. "As you'd lean over my desk to show me something and hold your blouse to your chest, depriving me a view of your gorgeous tits."

"*Oh* . . ." Sebastian wasn't exactly known for his restraint, but even when he'd taken aim, he'd always been polite about it. To hear his unfiltered thoughts made me lock my ankles and move against him.

"Yes, *oh*," he teased, meeting my rhythm with his hips, making his erection known. "*Oh*, you know just how to get under my skin."

"It's not one sided."

"No, it isn't. I haven't always been nice to you," he said, dropping his voice until it was all gravel, "but I haven't been mean, have I?"

I didn't want to fight anymore, and at the same time, all I wanted to do was fight. To give him what he came for. "Not yet," I said.

"Not *yet*?" He delivered a light slap on my ass. "How's that for mean?"

I bit my lip. How did I tell him he didn't have to be nice just because we were finally getting along? "Not bad."

He dropped his eyes to my mouth. "You like it. I wish I'd known. I've wanted to discipline those buns on many occasions."

I exhaled a laugh as I wiggled against him, his meanness as welcome as his teasing. He hissed, clasping my body flush to his as he took my mouth again. I pulled at the buttons of his shirt, my patience thin as he grew even harder between my legs. He traced the edge of my panties with a fingertip and caught my stuttered breath with his mouth.

"I want to see you," he whispered, gripping my waist to lift me. "Don't deprive me anymore."

Reluctantly, I loosened my legs so he could set me on my feet. With a knuckle under my chin, he lifted my mouth, stooped, and pecked me. Before I could attempt to deepen the kiss, his lips moved to my throat. My collarbone.

I only had to shimmy to let my dress fall.

He groaned. Dropped to his knees. Looked up at me as he took my waist. "Here's another *should*—I should not have called you anything as simple as *beautiful*. It's too mild a word. You're the stuff of dreams."

"I'm not," I said softly. "I'm real." I should've been self-conscious baring myself to Sebastian—after all, he'd spent the last several weeks scrutinizing my weaknesses and flaws, as I'd done to him. He'd been with many women, and *beautiful* didn't describe them, either. Sebastian's own magazine used words like *modelesque*, *lithe*, *angelic*, and even *gazelles of the human race*. But I only saw truth and admiration in his upturned eyes, and I couldn't help but doubt my own fears over his compliments. "*You* are beautiful," I said.

"And *you* are pure torture. Show me, Georgina," he

pleaded. "Your bra barely holds them in, they're so fucking perfect."

As I undid the hook, he reached up and took the bra. Wetting his lips, he thumbed my nipples until they pressed, hard and resolute, into the pads of his fingers. "So pink. So full. And god, are you inviting."

I missed the heat of his lips on mine, but I was soothed by a new kind of warmth—his mouth on my right breast, and then my left, teasing each nipple to make it rock hard, sucking until the sensation had brought me to the tips of my toes.

He kissed his way down my stomach and tugged the elastic band of my lacy boyshorts. "Did you wear these for me?"

"Mmm." I was glad I'd gone for sexy over silly underwear. "Yes."

"Please tell me these have something written across the butt too."

"Sorry. All you'll find back there are two buns in need of a hotdog."

I'd meant to make him laugh, but instead his jaw set. He pushed his hands under the waistband and around to my backside, taking two handfuls. "Don't tease me like that."

"I have some cinnamon in my pantry if you want to sprinkle it on them."

"Christ." He dropped his forehead to my stomach, undeterred by my silent laughter. "*Christ.*"

I worked my hands through his hair to tousle it. Now that my restraint had broken, now that I no longer had to deny myself, I wanted to touch all of him. "Sebastian."

"Am I going too slow?"

"No."

He yanked down my underwear and I gasped.

Shackled by my ankles, I was bared to his eyes, prisoner to his touch. "Too fast?" he asked.

Lazily, with my bottom lip clamped between my teeth, I shook my head. "It's just right."

"Okay, Goldilocks." He pressed a soft kiss on my lower tummy and said with a warm exhale, "Then I'll blow, blow your house down."

I shivered. "You're mixing childhood fables."

"Not to mention defiling them," he said. There was nothing innocent about the way he tossed my panties aside to free my ankles. Or how he spread my thighs to nuzzle between my legs. Breathed me in. Placed gentle kisses over my mound. "This little pussy went to market."

I gripped his head and said, "Enough, enough. Please."

"I've never heard anything sweeter than that word from you in this moment."

"*Please*," I repeated and used his own words against him. "Don't deprive *me*."

As if that flipped a switch in him, he put his mouth on me, tongue lapping at my wetness, teeth grazing my swollen lips. My hips bucked, and he put a long finger inside me, slid it out, and added another. I clutched the doorknob to keep from falling to my knees. He parted my lips wider with a thumb and laved my clit, eliciting my audible gasp. Was he smiling? I thought I felt his delight against me. I didn't have long to wonder. Sebastian pushed my hips back against the door and fingered me harder, his rhythm unbreaking, his tongue alternately hard and soft on me.

Did he . . . intend to make me . . . come . . . like *this*? "I don't," I said breathlessly, my hands still in his hair. "I can't."

He pulled his mouth away. "You *can't*?"

I shook my head up at the ceiling. "I never have, not like this. I need . . ."

"What do you need, Georgina?"

It was an embarrassing request to make. I wished it was as simple as saying I needed to be kissed or fucked or spanked to orgasm, but what would truly tip me over the edge was harder to ask for—intimacy. "More," was all I said.

Sebastian took my hand from his hair to lace our fingers together. "Then I'll need you to look at me."

I'd never liked asking for *more*. I'd learned that just saying it aloud didn't necessarily mean I'd get it. But I forced myself to meet Sebastian's eyes. His fingers slowed, stroking every inch of me as he slid them in and out. He looked to me for approval, and I nodded. He picked up his pace, curling his fingertips into spots that got him moans. His touch was no less pleasurable for his restraint, but it was more deliberate. No less firm but more intimate as he held my gaze.

I rested my head against the door and ground onto him, eyes closed as I urged myself over the edge. I could do this. I *wanted* to do this, for Sebastian to be the first man to bridle my orgasm any way he pleased.

"Georgina," he grated out, "I want to give you more."

"You are."

"Then *do not* look away."

I tilted my chin forward. Sebastian's brows drew together in yearning or focus, maybe both. I couldn't see his hand, buried between my thighs, couldn't really see anything but him. His eyes, intent on mine, told me this was love not war. He had me where he wanted me.

He had me.

I squeezed his hand, gripped his shoulder, and did my best to hold his stare, keeping my timidity at bay as he coaxed me over the edge. It wasn't until I was tumbling into my climax, into him, that my eyes fluttered shut, my ears ringing as my body vibrated with all-consuming currents of pleasure.

When it had passed, I was still in that position, holding onto him, my breath coming hard as I recovered. He let me float down from the moment until, loose-limbed and boneless, my knees buckled. Sebastian caught me, encircling my waist as he stood and lifted me to meet his height. "You don't, huh?" he asked. "You can't?"

I hid my face in the crook of his neck as he crossed the room. "I didn't think I could if I wasn't . . . you know."

"I don't know. I'm new at this. You'll have to spell it out for me."

"You're not new at this," I said, inhaling his skin's slightly briny scent. "You do it for a living."

"Mmm. But someone once told me I don't understand women. That I can't score more than one night. Maybe writing it and living it are two different things."

I pulled back to look at him. "She sounds very wise."

At the foot of the bed, he nipped my bottom lip. "Don't make me spank you the way I've fantasized."

My insides tightened. I wanted to hear every detail of my counterpart's daydreams. "What was the subject again?"

"You didn't think you could orgasm without . . . ?"

My excitement fizzled. Sebastian already knew the answer, so it wasn't as if I could feign ignorance. "Love," I said.

"Love," he repeated, as if trying out the word.

"I usually only orgasm if I'm in love and only during sex. Not from oral, and not with a fling."

"Ah, I see," he said.

The words had sounded much more matter-of-fact in

my mind. Aloud, they were weighty with meaning. "I'm not trying to say that I—oh, no." I squeezed my eyes shut. "I didn't mean that I *am* in love."

"I'd have nobody to blame but myself seeing as I *am* exceptionally talented at this. All those how-to articles I researched must've paid off."

I rolled my eyes as my embarrassment vanished. "Here's one: 'How to Make a Girl Instantly Regret Sleeping with You.'"

"We haven't even slept together yet. At least give me a chance to make you regret it." He feigned dropping me on the bed but froze midair. "Georgina. Is your neighbor *watching* us?"

I gasped, throwing my arms around his neck to hide my chest. I *always* drew the curtains as soon as I walked in the room because nosy Renee's window was so close, I could nearly count the curls on her head. Some nights, she'd wave at me from her reading chair. "I *completely* forgot—"

He strengthened his hold on me and turned his back, presumably to hide me, but now *I* was looking out the window at *her*. "Not this way," I hissed in his ear. "We just made eye contact!"

"Well, I'm not turning around so she can get a show."

She shook out *The New York Times*, but who the hell read newspapers in the evenings? Snoops, that was who. She was clearly pretending so she could sneak glances at us. "We have to close the blinds." I readjusted my legs around him, starting to feel like a baby koala. "Walk backward," I said. "Now her *dog* is at the window. This is getting obscene."

"Was she planning to watch us have sex?" he asked as he reversed.

When I was within reach, I pulled the tie holding back one curtain. "She probably still is."

"I think she had popcorn."

"She does not," I said as he moved to the other side. "What do you care anyway? You're still completely dressed."

He let out a low growl. "I don't like to share my buns."

I untied the next sash. Renee lifted a hand just as the curtain fell shut. "This isn't the time for jokes," I said.

"You're right. It's *time* for you to catch me up."

Alone again, I drew back to look at him. "What?"

"My clothes, Georgina."

Ah. I focused on the tanned skin I exposed with each button I undid, avoiding his heated stare as he walked us to the bed. He lay me back on the mattress, and I smoothed my hands over his chest to slide off his shirt. He closed his eyes as I continued down, down, down over each abdominal muscle. "I always knew you were difficult," I said, "but I had no idea you were this *hard*."

"You haven't even gotten to the hard part," he promised.

21

"There's something I've been wanting to ask you," Sebastian said.

My nerves flared. What was it about having me naked and at his mercy that made him think this was the Q&A portion of the night? Then again, this was stubborn Sebastian. He wouldn't become someone else just because we were taking off our clothes. "Ask," I said from under him, lowering his zipper.

"On second thought—" He inhaled as I tucked my hand into his underwear to feel him. I stroked the full and impressive length of him—it came as no surprise that Sebastian had the dick to back up his energy. "Maybe this isn't the right time," he said. "My mind just went to mush."

"Or this is the *perfect* time."

"You're nothing like the other girls I've known."

"If you're about to insult me, remember that I have your cock in my hand."

"Fuck." He thrust his hips in a way that seemed involuntary. "Say that word again."

I'd meant it as a joke, which was the only reason I'd

blurted out *cock*. But he was asking me to be serious now, and there was something more urgent in the way his eyes devoured me. Apparently, there was a thin line between teasing and cock-teasing. "You go first."

"Cock," he said.

"No." I smiled at his earnest expression. "Finish what you were saying."

"Since I met you, I've been feeling . . . more like myself than I have in a while. I put on an act to try to impress most women. Not you."

I would've been *impressed* if I'd held him earlier, all smooth skin, steel, and girth on my palm. "And?"

"Because of that, I can be myself. I *am* myself. But what about you? Do I make you better?" He paused. "Can you see yourself with me?"

If I wasn't mid-handjob, I would've hugged him. It was such a sweet, honest question to not only wonder, but ask. "The fact that you care enough to bring it up is your answer. Of course you're good for me too."

"How?"

It was a lot to ask when I just wanted to *finally* consume and be consumed. There was urgency in his question too, though. How had he made me better? For one, I'd begun to wonder if I still needed the security of putting on a personality to get through the day. "Where others see weakness, you see kindness," I answered quietly.

"I do," he answered. "An abundance of it."

"You've shoved me out of my comfort zone. You might think I do that on my own, but I was in a rut before I met you. I just didn't want to admit it. Now, I want more. You improve my life because you challenge me—and because you have a nice *cock*."

He took a sharp breath, nudged my legs wider, and

kissed me harder than before. "Condom," he grated out. "Back pocket."

I felt around his ass for his wallet, tossing it aside once I'd extracted the condom. "Can I put it on?"

"I don't know, can you?" he asked, maneuvering out of his jeans. "You have such small hands."

I watched in awe as he stripped down to a pair of white boxer briefs, his erection straining against the cotton. "Tell me you're wearing a cup," I said.

"A cup? Why would I . . ." His brows knit as he looked down at himself. "That's all me, Georgina."

It was bulging, reaching for me, almost hostile. I'd obviously been distracted when I'd had my hands down his pants just now or I would've feared for my safety. "Welcome to the major leagues," I murmured as I opened the foil packet.

He laughed, his eyes glued to me as I reached into his underwear and began to roll it on. The period and parentheses that normally softened his face faded, leaving the sharp jawline and focused eyes of a man who knew what he wanted—and was looking right at it.

He scanned my body. "So many," he murmured.

So many. I knew at once what he meant, because until tonight, it was one of the only comments he'd ever made on my appearance. "Counting the number of offending freckles?"

"Offending?" he asked.

"That day at the park, you were disgusted by them."

"I don't remember what I said, but I was hardly disgusted."

"Word for word, 'You have all these little fucking freckles. It's like someone sprinkled you with cinnamon to serve you up as breakfast.'"

He laughed as if I'd repeated a joke back to him. I kept

a straight face. I'd been annoyed by it then, and I was annoyed now. I covered my chest. "I'm sorry if you don't like them, but they're not going anywhere."

"*Don't* like them?" He was still laughing. "God, I guess in a way, I don't. Because I love them."

"That makes no sense."

"If I sounded angry when I said that, it was simply because they weren't mine." He moved one of my hands away and traced a fingertip over my collarbone. "I didn't have access to them, and I wanted it." He kissed a few of the spots that dotted my chest, and I moved my other arm away. "I knew it," he said with reverence. "You *taste* like cinnamon too, on a cold night."

I squirmed under his regard. "All this time, I thought you hated them like my ex."

"Now I *know* he's braindead. I'll only hate them at work, when they're driving me crazy from across the conference table." He worked his way up my neck and ran the tip of his nose along the bridge of mine. "When I want to kiss the ones here. And count the ones lower, on your knees."

"I don't have freckles on my knees."

"You have a few," he said. "I looked that first morning. They're so fucking sexy."

"Sexy?" I asked a little louder than I meant to.

"Mmm. During tomorrow's morning meeting, I'll be fantasizing about my mouth on each and every one of them. I'll taste cinnamon."

I wrapped my legs around his waist and slid my toes under the waistband of his boxer briefs. "Can we take these off?" I whispered.

He pushed them down, removing the final layer between us. I couldn't look. It'd been so long since I'd been with anyone, and just the outline of him was intimidating.

Sebastian positioned the head of himself between my legs. "You are so . . ." He stared down at me. "Whatever words exist past *beautiful*."

"And you call yourself a writer."

He pressed into me. "Dazzling. Strong. Beautiful *ad infinitum*."

I inhaled deeply. Sebastian was big, and Lu had been correct—I might've been revirginized. At least, it felt that way in the moment. I couldn't take him all at once, but "beautiful ad infinitum" wasn't a bad way to be opened up, to marry big and small, hardness and softness.

Once he was halfway in, he drew back and pushed deeper. "Is it too soon to ask about the Double-Fisted Flying Squirrel?"

I couldn't keep the smile from my face and my body eased for him. "Ask all you want."

His expression turned serious. "You good?"

He was offering the intimacy I needed from him. We had inside jokes about things like sex positions and faux dates. Even cinnamon on a cold night could make me laugh as I swooned. I put my hand to his cheek and nodded. "I'm happy to be here."

"I like that." He grazed the tip of his nose against mine. "Happy to be here. So am I."

We met lips, my mouth mirroring his for a slow, sexy kiss. As my body warmed to him, he began to move inside me, easy at first until his glides became thrusts. He got up onto an elbow and glanced between us. Knowing he was watching us come together exhilarated me. It was the cease-fire to end all battles. His abs flexed as he dropped his mouth to mine and picked up his pace, pounding into me. Wrapped up in him, I arched my back, my orgasm building until it was suddenly there, bigger than life, looming on the cusp. Had I ever come this soon? Ever been so lost in someone else? I curled my hands into his chest. "Don't stop," I breathed. "I'm there. I'm *here*."

"Already?" He paused, then pulled out and sat back. "We'll have to teach you some self-control."

I got up on my elbows, panting. "What are you doing? I was on the edge!"

He gave me a rakish grin. "It's going to be a long night, honeybuns. You can hold out a little longer."

Nicknames wouldn't get him out of this one. I threw a pillow at him, and he caught it, laughing as he said, "You just gave me an idea. Turn over."

I flipped onto my stomach—anything to get the train back on its tracks. Sebastian situated the pillow under my hips and moved higher between my legs, thumbing me open from behind. "Nice and pink and wet. *Christ*, so wet, Georgina. You want an orgasm?"

"Do *you*?"

He got the hint. If I wasn't coming, he wasn't, either. "I promise, I'm not trying to torture you. It's just that I—" He pressed the sheathed tip of himself to my opening. "Want to come—" He drove into me. "*With* you."

"Oh, god." I moaned for the way he filled me, for his impatience, for the mere thought of our mutual climax. "Sebastian."

He closed his body over mine, propping a hand on each side of my waist. As he let go, his thrusts hard and deliberate now, I writhed under him. My clit throbbed with pleasure as I ground into the pillow while he took me from behind.

"I like when you talk to me," he said. "Tell me how to fuck you, Georgina."

"Just like that," I said, and thank god it was true—I couldn't articulate anything more. "Just . . . like . . . that."

"Don't fall without me, understand?"

I gripped the top of the mattress, half holding on, half using it as leverage against the pillow. "I'm almost there."

"Good girl," he murmured. "That's good—but not until I say." He grabbed onto my shoulder the way I held the bed and pulled me back into each plunge. He lost any restraint, working himself into the same frenzy I was trying to hold off. I wanted to come with him as much as he wanted it, so I thought of anything not to finish.

Baseball diamond. Dirt-caked cleats. Second base, third, a fucking home run. Fly balls, leathery gloves, a girthy, wooden bat as thick as—

"Now," he commanded, lowering his mouth to my ear as he slammed into me. By some miracle, I'd held off nirvana just long enough. "Come, Georgina."

I pressed my cheek into the bedspread and stopped fighting. I tumbled into my orgasm as Sebastian groaned behind me, pleasure washing from him onto me. It felt so good, so right, so hard-earned to have him come apart on top of me. He collapsed over me, pressing me into the mattress. After a few labored breaths, he shuddered and nuzzled my neck. "Tell me you're here with me."

I emptied my lungs in a long, satisfying sigh. "Where else would I be?"

It was only when he rolled to the side that I realized we were both sweating. He rubbed my back, gathering my hair off my neck and holding it off my skin. "I think I'm actually looking forward to winter for once."

I turned my head to rest on the opposite cheek and face him. "How come?"

He tied off the condom and tossed it on the floor. "An excuse to stay indoors and sweat with you."

I hoped I was warm enough to hide my blush. Winter wasn't far off, and yet in terms of our relationship, it seemed like ages. I'd been brave earlier because I'd wanted him at any expense. But did I really have what it took to tame a Manhattan player?

By the way he looked at me, it was possible. Maybe even likely. "I'd like that," I said. "Although Bruno usually keeps me warm."

"I don't doubt that." He leaned on his elbow, his head in his hand as he watched me. "You might have to upgrade your bed to a king to fit us all. Or we can go to my place."

"I get to see your place?" I asked.

"Yeah." He hesitated. "Except I've been thinking of putting it on the market, actually."

"How come?"

"Compared to this, it feels . . . I don't know. Stark. I like it here, where there are pictures on the walls and plants and—"

"Fraying fabric on the couch, drawers dedicated to poop bags, vomit stains on the carpet—"

"Height charts on the windowsills and fresh flowers from the community garden." He smiled. "I mean, I'm clearly not suggesting we move in together after our first date—"

"Also known as our faux date," I inserted.

"But I think I've outgrown my bachelor pad."

"If you have a revolving bed or Marvin Gaye on tap, I won't hesitate to make fun of you just because we slept together."

"You'll have to come over and see for yourself. How about next weekend?"

The abruptness of his invitation stunned me into silence. This seemed like seventeenth date territory for someone like Sebastian. I hated to turn him down, but I had to. "Can't," I said. "I have plans."

"Can you cancel?"

"I already promised my parents I'd come home. I have

a standing date in Buffalo each month to play gin rummy with my grandad."

I braced myself for Sebastian's teasing, but truthfully, I didn't care. I'd lost time with my family while I was with Neal. He hadn't liked to visit them and didn't want me to leave him on the weekends. Forget holidays. Since we'd broken up I'd been making an effort to drive up there at least once a month. Canceling on them for a guy was out of the question.

"You play gin rummy . . . and call him grandad?" Sebastian laughed, but not in a mocking way. "Cute," he said, tucking a pillow under his face. "You are such a good girl, Georgina. Good, and cute, and beautiful ad infinitum."

Describing me so eloquently would've sounded sarcastic coming from Neal. Sebastian and I had had our moments, but in this one, he wasn't joking around. It felt good. Maybe *too* good.

"As much as I'd like to keep you in bed next weekend," he continued, "there's nothing more important than time with family."

That wasn't quite the response I'd expected. Teasing, yes, and maybe reluctance to let me go. But not something as emotionally adept as encouraging me to spend a seemingly dry afternoon playing cards with my grandad. I thought of how fondly he'd spoken of his mom, sister, niece and nephew. Did family come before anything else for him too? I moved from my stomach to my side, readjusting my pillow to look him in the eyes. "What about your dad?"

"Never knew him."

"I'm sorry," I said. "Who was he?"

He hesitated. Just as I worried I'd pushed too hard, he said, "Some teenager from San Francisco visiting

Mexico City with his family. My mom chose Boston because it was about as far as she could get from California."

That must've been why Sebastian didn't talk about him. With a family as supportive as mine, I couldn't imagine not having my dad to rely on. "Quintanilla was your mom's maiden name?" I asked.

"Yeah." Something like frustration flickered in his eyes, but eventually, his shoulders relaxed again. "My sister, Libby—or Libertad as she goes by now—started using Quintanilla again at eighteen. She accused Mom and me of trying to erase history. I only ever used my full name officially, like on college apps, which, ironically, helped me. Otherwise . . ."

I bit my lip, waiting. This must've been the source of whatever had crossed his face just now. "What?"

"I liked being a Quinn. I know it's fucked up, but Mom was right. It was easier."

"It's okay to want easy," I said, "especially when you didn't have that growing up."

He shook his head. "I'm ashamed to admit it. I *am* proud of my heritage, and yet, I haven't even claimed it in the most basic way. I've thought a lot about changing it back, but I'm afraid now I'll draw attention to the fact that I hid it."

"We can do it if you want," I told him, letting my enthusiasm through. "I can spin it, no problem. You don't need to be this version of yourself anymore, Sebastian. You just told me there was no divide between George and Georgina, nor should there be one between Quinn and Quintanilla."

"I don't want to risk involving my family in all the bad PR this job has brought on."

I put my hand on his chest, and he covered it with his.

"I'm sure your mom was proud of the work you did," I said.

He shook his head. "At the end of her life, all the things I'd done for the magazine . . . all the things we'd printed . . . just felt trivial."

I fought the urge to comfort him with a kiss in case it turned into more. Who knew how long it might be before I could get him to open up like this again. "And what about since?"

"Turning around the magazine the first time had been exciting. But during her final months, I took a lot of time off, and that was when things started to go downhill at work. This time, trying to save it felt pointless. I didn't care, and I got complacent. That's why we're here now."

It was the most honest he'd been about the magazine's situation since I'd met him. Sebastian and I weren't so different, becoming other people for jobs we wanted but also needed to support our loved ones. "Have you ever wanted to do anything other than journalism?"

"In college, I thought I'd go into sports broadcasting," he said. "That's what I was working toward, but I would've taken any internship I got. *Modern Man* was my first offer."

"Have you thought of leaving?"

"The mag? Not seriously, no. And with my reputation, I don't know who'd want me."

"We're working on that," I reminded him. "And even if we weren't, there's life outside of this city. There are lots of publications that would kill to bring on a New York City big leaguer."

"I can barely picture life outside Manhattan," he said. "Much less the tristate area."

"I hear Boston has sports."

The corner of his mouth crooked. "I couldn't. Reminds me too much of what I've lost."

"But your sister's there."

"Don't remind me. She gets on my case about it. Wants us to clean out and sell Mom's house."

"If you don't want to go back there, why does it matter?"

He shrugged a little. "It's not my home anymore, but it was hers."

"Was she sick long?"

"She kept it from us until she couldn't anymore." Remembering his earlier comments about how he hadn't bared his soul to many people, I flipped my hand on his chest and laced our fingers together. "I got her on the most comprehensive healthcare I could once we found out," he said, "but by that time, it was too late."

"That was when you made her the promise?"

"It was one of our last conversations. Find someone who was good to me and to others. I wanted money because I'd never had it growing up, but looking back . . . it would've meant more to her if I was a good man over a wealthy one."

"You *are* good, Sebastian."

"Not always. I went to Harvard on a need-based scholarship, so to blend in with my wealthy classmates, I let things become important that weren't. I thought that was the only way to get ahead, and maybe it was, but for what? My big salary couldn't cure cancer."

"From what you've told me, it sounds like what mattered to her was you and your sister—and that she raised you right. Am I wrong?"

He glanced at our hands and ran his thumb over my knuckles. "You're never wrong, it seems," he said with a small smile. "I suppose I'm the one holding onto her possessions for dear life."

"When's the last time you were home?"

"In Boston? Her funeral," he said. "She passed in her own bed. I haven't returned to the house since her body was removed."

My heart ached for him. I squeezed his hand. "No wonder you don't want to go back. And even though it makes me sad, I understand why those are the memories that've stuck with you."

"Most of the time, it's the first mental image I get of her. In bed, taking her last breath. It's weird . . ."

I glanced up at him. "What is?"

"When home is no longer home." He sifted the ends of my hair through his fingers. "My sister worries I'll forget my roots, but I can't help feeling they've been ripped out of the ground."

My grandad's health had been declining for some time, but I hadn't quite come to terms with the possibility of his death. Losing my parents, though? And with them, my access to our family history, and any sense of home? Tears sprang to my eyes. "I'm sorry."

"You ever lost anyone?"

"A grandmother, but I was young." I snuggled closer. "My grandad's in his eighties, so I try to spend as much time with him as I can."

"Ah," he said. "That explains the upstate gin rummy. You like taking care of others, don't you?"

I looked up at him. I wasn't sure I'd ever recognized that in myself. I'd seen it as a weakness with Neal, and a privilege with Grandad. And of course, the same was true for Bruno. "I've got some bad memories in Boston too, you know. Bruno and I have been to the vet there several times, and while he might've been stable or doing well, his prognosis never changed." I paused, thinking back to all the tears I had shed in their waiting room. "Still, it made me more appreciative that the sun was shining. Of how friendly the people were. Home is still there, Sebastian. It's in the good memories. Maybe you can try to replace the bad ones with them."

"I probably could," he said. "But I don't know if I'm actually ready to let her go."

My voice broke a little as I said, "You'd only be letting *it* go."

"Semantics, Keller." He pulled my arm until I was forced to roll onto his chest. "Know what else?"

"What?" I whispered.

"I'm not letting *you* go."

I wanted it to be true, and for this time, with him, to be different. I wanted to be strong for him and for myself. I glanced at the stubble filling in his jaw. "Is that why you're here now?" I asked softly. "To fulfill your promise to your mom?"

He angled his head to catch my eye. "That, and many other reasons, Georgina. The fact that my mother would've fallen in love with you would be reason enough for me to . . . to do the same. I can tell you why I'm not going anywhere, or I can show you if you'll let me."

I inhaled a breath to keep from tearing up. I nodded. "I'll let you."

"Good, because you're stuck with me now."

The thought made my heart skip with hope. I didn't have to ask myself if I wanted to be stuck. Being physically intertwined felt overdue for us, like snapping in the final piece of our complex, jumbo puzzle. It made me wonder when exactly I'd gone from falling for Sebastian to *fallen*.

I was too far gone to wonder if I even needed a safety net.

22

I woke up for the same reason I did every morning—Bruno, the living alarm clock. Only today, it wasn't his big body shaking the bed, his cold nose in my face, or his monster-sized paw on my head. He scratched at the door, sniffing under it almost as loudly as he whined.

I'd fallen asleep in the crook of Sebastian's arm, but during the night, I must've gravitated back to my side of the bed. I turned over just as Sebastian came out of bathroom in nothing but a towel.

"Morning," he said, scrubbing a hand over his wet, chocolate-colored hair.

Given our history, it should've been awkward to wake up with him. Maybe it would be once I stopped staring at his broad, sculpted, glistening shoulders. I sat up against the headboard, pulling the sheet up under my arms. "I'm sorry if Bruno woke you."

"If you're going to apologize for anything, it should be for stealing the sheets."

"Did I?" I asked innocently. It was a complaint I'd heard before.

"Or your bathroom. Between the baskets of half-used makeup on the counter, and the army of nearly empty beauty products in the shower, I could barely turn around," he said, then grabbed a handful of his tousled hair, "much less do anything about this."

I tossed a throw pillow at him. "I don't believe in being wasteful."

His words had always gotten under my skin easily, something I'd mistaken for rivalry. Now, I saw it for what it was—compatibility. I didn't worry Sebastian would try to twist my words or use them against me as I had in the past.

He flashed me a devastating smile, dropped his towel, and picked up his underwear from the floor. "Remember what happened when you threw a pillow at me last night?"

He'd stuck it under my hips and screwed me on it. Now, he stood here gloriously naked. I tried not to look as stunned as I felt by his maleness. Or his statuesque beauty. My thighs quivered as I remembered taking all of him last night. I almost whimpered as he dressed.

"Luckily, I run warm and carry my own comb," he said, pulling on his pants next but leaving them open. "Do you sleep on one side of the bed even when you're alone?"

"I can't get myself to stay in the middle," I said. "It feels weird."

"Not for me. I'm a spreader." He winked and checked his cell on the nightstand just as Bruno barked from the hallway. "Can I let him in?"

"Yes, please."

Sebastian opened the bedroom door and Bruno zoomed in, tail wagging, tongue out. He launched himself on the bed, turned in a circle, and lay right where Sebastian had been.

Loyal as they came. I patted his haunches.

"*Et tu, Brute?*" Sebastian shook his head and picked up

his dress shirt from the ground. "That right there is why you have a side."

My alarm rang, and I leaned over to the nightstand to turn it off. "You could've waited for me to shower, you know."

Pulling his arms through his sleeves, he came around to sit on my side of the bed. "Believe me, I struggled over whether to wake you. But I knew if I did, we'd never get to the office in time."

I twirled a piece of my hair around my finger. "We could be late for once."

"You didn't let me finish. I meant I wouldn't even get to the office in time *to place a lunch order*." He squeezed above my knee. "My mornings are insane."

"How come?"

"This is when I check the news outlets, brush up on industry trends, and review our social media to make sure everyone's doing their jobs. You?"

"I sleep as late as possible and do that stuff at night."

He chuckled. "Sorry to break it to you, but not tonight, my little flying squirrel. I still have hours' worth of *Poised*-approved positions to try on you." He slipped his hand up my leg, lowering his voice as he leaned in. "I figured instead of getting cozy now, we'd sneak out of the office early and come back here for takeout."

"Is that a euphemism for something else?"

He kissed me once. "As they say, keep your friends close and your enemies between the sheets."

I bit my bottom lip, partly from the warmth of his hand through the thin sheet, and partly because the real world was encroaching. Sebastian had assured me we were never enemies, but I still had information that would hurt him. If we were no longer at odds, then weren't we on the same side? I touched his hairline, and he closed his eyes as I ran my fingers through his damp hair.

"Will it be weird at the office?" I asked.

He pecked me again, then sat back. "No weirder than Justin makes things on an average day."

"I'm serious," I warned. "You better talk to him. This has to stay a secret."

"It's not as if we have to keep it long." He buttoned his shirt. "Shouldn't be a problem."

I could've stayed in bed with him all day, even if it meant jeopardizing my job. That was a first for me. If I wanted his success as much as my own, I had to be honest with him about what was coming. But Sebastian had been wary of me just for showing up, and being offered his job would only validate his concerns. Would he blame me? I didn't think I'd ever felt this way this quickly about anyone. There was no question he'd be angry, but would he see this as a betrayal and end things before they'd even begun?

He patted Bruno's hip and stood to do up his pants. "I'm going to try to get in early so you and I can take off right at five. See you there?"

The prospect of Sebastian finding out from someone else at work, even Vance, was enough to put things in perspective. Since I hadn't had a chance to officially turn down the position yet, I couldn't risk Sebastian thinking I was going to accept it. He had to hear the truth from me. Now that he and I had potential to be more, the meeting no longer felt confidential, just secretive. "Sebastian," I started.

The corner of his mouth quirked. "Proceed at your own risk. If I don't leave in the next few seconds, I can't promise I won't climb back into bed with you."

I shifted against the headboard, pulling the sheet more

tightly under my arms. "Actually, there's, ah, something you should know."

"Yeah?" he asked, tucking his chin to fix the back of his collar.

Sebastian and I were past the bullshit—no use in drawing this out. "When Vance called me into his office the other day, it wasn't just to touch base. He wanted to talk to me about a permanent position."

He lowered his hands and studied my face. "Which position?"

My palms were suddenly sweating. "Yours."

He went still as a statue, not even blinking. "Mine?"

"I didn't know if I should tell you, but—"

"Of course." He shut his eyes and inhaled deeply. "On some level, I knew this could happen. But after all my years there, I assumed he'd have the courtesy to warn me first."

By the set of his jaw, he was angry or getting there. Though I'd expected it, it made my stomach churn. He pinched the bridge of his nose much the same way he had in the café that first morning when he'd stepped away to take Justin's call.

"He swore me to secrecy so he could tell you himself," I said. "I just . . . after last night, I couldn't keep it in any longer."

His glare had me shutting my mouth. I doubted he'd even heard what I'd said. Naked in more ways than one, I knew I'd never be able to channel George in this moment. I had to try to stand my ground and explain things from my side, but I could already feel a tremble working its way up me.

"Unbelievable," he finally said.

"I wanted to tell you yesterday, but . . ."

"Jesus. I'm so tired of his shit." He hung his towel over my reading chair and said, "I'm sorry, Georgina."

I wasn't sure I'd heard him correctly through the pounding of my heart. "You're sorry?" I asked.

"Yeah. Vance never should've put you in that position." He went to the other side of the bed and checked the screen of his phone. "I wish you'd mentioned it yesterday," he said, "but I suppose I can't blame you for thinking you were on a fake date most of the day. Thanks for being honest."

I hazarded a smiled. His understanding felt almost too good to be true. "I didn't say anything because I was afraid you'd get angry and end the date."

"I don't think anything could've torn me away from you last night." He returned my smile. "Don't get me wrong—I'm pissed. But I'll take it up with him."

"Not today," I warned. Bruno rolled onto his side and groaned sleepily, clearly put out by our conversation. "Vance said if you went on the attack, he'd fire you on the spot."

Sebastian shook his head and slipped his phone in his back pocket, trading it for a comb. "I'm not sure I give a fuck."

"You might feel that way now, but promise me you'll wait until you've cooled off."

"I don't know if I can." He stooped to the mirror above my dresser and fixed his hair. "I should go hand in my resignation just to fuck him over. Then he'd have nobody." He scoffed. "I'd like to see him put out a decent issue without either of us."

I relaxed back against my headboard, relieved I wouldn't be the one to feel Sebastian's wrath. Until his words registered—Vance would have nobody? What about *me*? I wasn't taking the job, but I hadn't said that yet. "Sebastian—"

He glanced at me in the reflection and tilted his head.

"Christ, you're pale. You really thought I'd explode, didn't you?"

I was feeling a bit clammy. "You've never wanted me there. I figured you'd blame this on me."

"Why would I?" he asked, putting the comb away. "You didn't ask for the job, and it's not like you'd ever take it."

I frowned, my heart rate slowing. Putting aside the fact that I deserved the opportunity for the way I was turning *Modern Man* around, why shouldn't I want to advance my career? What made Sebastian so sure I'd turn it down? "I never said whether I accepted it," I pointed out.

"Yeah, but I know you well enough now. You wouldn't do that to me." He turned, leaning against the dresser as he crossed his arms. "You're one of the sweetest, most caring women I've ever met, Georgina. You'd never take my job, especially after last night."

I wasn't sure what to say to that. *Especially after last night* almost sounded dirty, as if sex had somehow secured my loyalty to him above anyone else, even myself. Vance's offer was more than an enormous bump in salary—it was vindication that I'd done a good job after all the resistance Sebastian had given me. That I was necessary. That my work mattered. Sebastian had just assumed I'd put him above all that? Of course he did. He thought I was "sweet." "Caring." And, I couldn't forget—easily run over.

My face flushed. With this news, Sebastian had only considered what I was doing to *him*. Not what this opportunity had meant for *me*. He'd expected me to limit my career to help his.

"Well, I guess you're right," I said, irritation hardening my words. It occurred to me that while there'd been no good time to bring this up, it certainly wasn't while I was naked. "Can you hand me a shirt from the first drawer?"

He opened it and pulled a faded black, extra-small Jem and the Holograms t-shirt from the top of the pile. "Is this yours?" he asked, holding it up.

"It's from when I was a kid," I snapped, gesturing impatiently for it. I made a mental note never to sleep with a guy on laundry day again.

He tossed it to me, narrowing his eyes as I struggled to pull on the too-small shirt while shielding myself with the sheet.

"Is . . . something wrong?" he asked.

"Yep." I yanked the hem down. "Did you even stop to consider what this could mean for my career?"

"Um . . . no." He furrowed his brows. "I'm at risk of losing my *job*, Georgina."

"A job I'm far too 'sweet' and 'kind' to take—do I have that right? Too 'caring' to put my career above yours?"

"It's a compliment, for Christ's sake. I'm trying to say you're not the kind of person to fuck me over like that."

In other words, *someone like me* would never put herself first. I'd heard some version of that before. "I'm too much of a doormat is what you mean."

"Oh, god." He ran both hands over his face. "Not even remotely what I said."

I easily tugged the top sheet free of the mattress since it'd come untucked during last night's activities. Bruno jerked, jumped off the bed, and ambled away, most likely to the kitchen since it was breakfast time. "You didn't have to say it," I said. "I can read between the lines."

"Let's keep a little perspective here, shall we? You wouldn't even be at *Modern Man* if it wasn't for my fuck-up."

"Right, so why's it so surprising that I'd be the right person for the job?"

"Because *it's not yours*. You didn't kiss ass and bust ass

just for a chance at an internship. You weren't there from day one when the whole operation was an organizational disaster. You didn't spend countless late nights over several years to bring it back from the brink." His knuckles had whitened from balling his hands. "You did a good job of getting us back on track, I admit, but you don't have what it takes to weather the long-term."

I pulled back. After the last couple months, did he honestly think that? "I don't have what it takes?"

"No, because you don't *know* what it takes. I built our readership from the ground up."

"And then you jeopardized it."

His jaw ticked. "Do you think I need that pointed out to me *every damn day*, or do you just enjoy holding it over me?"

"I didn't bring this up to debate who would be better at the job. I wanted to be honest with you." I stood and wrapped the sheet around my waist. "I'm going out on a limb and putting my reputation on the line to prepare you for what's coming."

"Oh, then I suppose I should thank you. *Thank you* for diminishing the work I've done so you can feel good about being offered a job you're not qualified to do."

I winced and immediately wished I hadn't shown how much his opinion meant to me. "Do you think I stumbled into your office by accident?" I asked. "I've done my homework. I studied the mistakes you made, researched what failed, and came to you with solutions—solutions that *worked*. Subscription rates are finally starting to rise. The female demographic is growing. College educated, high-income readers that we lost are returning. Don't you dare tell me I don't know what I'm doing."

"You're good at *your* job," he said steadily. "But no way in hell are you the best person for mine. *I* am." He paused, his expression cooling. "Wait. Are you trying to tell me you're actually considering it?"

"That's not the point." I started to pick up the sheet to storm off, but apparently I had more to say. "You just assumed I wouldn't take it and never considered what this could mean for my career."

"*Your* career? What about mine?" He pushed off the dresser and gestured behind him. "This is my job, and you wouldn't just take it. It's not who you are."

Who exactly did he think I was? Because it was starting to feel as if he saw me the way Neal had. *Weak. Agreeable. Pushover.* "A job you said was no longer fulfilling."

He studied me, shaking his head. "Is this why you were encouraging me to reconsider going to Boston? So you wouldn't feel guilty accepting Vance's offer?"

I gaped at him. What a slap in the face after the way I'd been nothing but supportive while he'd finally shared his background with me. "Of course not. I was trying to help. *You* said you were feeling complacent."

"Great," he said wryly, stooping to pick up the pillow I'd thrown earlier. He tossed it on the bed. "Now you're going to use my fucking words against me."

"I'm just pointing out that maybe leaving *Modern Man* wouldn't be such a bad thing."

"Well, that's convenient, isn't it?" He grabbed my dress off the floor next. "I'm starting to regret that I opened up to you."

"Oh yeah? Me too. Here's a fairy tale pun for you —*Hansel and Regretal.*" I gathered the sheet in my arms and took off for my bathroom. How had I let myself get so wrapped up in Sebastian mere months after I'd been through this with Neal? I spun back. "I assume I don't have to tell you to leave."

"Georgina, come on." He sighed, still gripping my dress. "What'd you expect me to say? Congratulations?"

"I expected you to react like the rational, supportive person I thought I was getting involved with. You can't tell me the possibility of losing your job never crossed your mind."

"Of course it has. Why do you think I'm not more surprised? I knew my ass was on the line."

"Then it must've also occurred to you that Vance might replace you with me." Still stung that he'd thought I might try to use our heart-to-heart the night before against him, I added, "So how do *I* know you didn't plan yesterday so I'd feel loyal to you?"

He looked taken aback. *Good.* Now he knew how it felt to have his intentions doubted. "Are you kidding me?" he asked.

"You spent weeks hating me and then out of nowhere, you show up on my doorstep offering me a truce. What am I supposed to think?"

He clenched his hand around the fabric, then discarded my dress on the bed. "You were supposed to see how I was trying to do better, Georgina. *Be* better."

"Maybe. Or maybe you figured sex was one sure way to guarantee I'd never take your job."

"What the *fuck*," he said slowly, "does that mean?"

"You knew what last night would mean to me. I'm not saying it didn't mean the same to you, but . . ." Unexpectedly, my throat thickened. *Intimacy.* The problem with getting it meant it could be taken away. "How do I know there wasn't a part of you that recognized you could use my 'kindness' against me?"

"That's not goddamn fair." He fisted his hair. "I'd never do that, and you know it."

"I *don't* know it. I thought I did once, and I was wrong. I won't make those same mistakes again."

His gaze darkened. "You're going to compare me to your piece-of-shit ex after everything you told me yesterday? Don't even *go* there." He inhaled, his nostrils flaring though he seemed to try to calm himself. "I'm not trying to bend your will in my favor," he said deliberately. "I'm just stating the facts—this is my job. My *life*. I wouldn't give it up to anyone without a fight, and I certainly wouldn't get into a relationship with that person. Would you?"

"Would I? Here's what I would do." I clutched the sheet at my hip with one hand, held up a finger, and counted off. "Spend nearly two months trying to save the job of a man who hates me. Invite him to my home. Introduce him to my dog. Spend my Sunday falling for him. Turn down a great opportunity and a salary I could really use. All for him, when he clearly wouldn't even give me a second thought."

"Nowhere in there did I hear that you actually want the job."

"I don't," I cried. "I don't want it. I'm not going to take it, but you never even gave me the chance to say that."

He stared at me, his shoulders loosening along with his fists. We held each other's gazes, something sizzling between us. The light of day only served to remind me how that chemistry could be as dangerous as it was sweet.

"Then we don't have a problem," he said.

"*Oh*, we have a problem," I threw back at him. "I told you to go."

"Look," he said, stepping toward me. "This doesn't need to come between us. I like you, Georgina. I haven't said that to someone and meant it in . . . I don't even know how long."

I shook my head. "If that were true, you would've

considered me the way I did you. Instead, you assumed I'd automatically back down to give you what you want."

"If I assumed anything," he said gently, "it was that you'd do the right thing, which doesn't make you a doormat. It makes you a good person."

"It makes me a sucker. What if taking the job *was* the right thing—just not for you? What then?" My face heated as I recalled that I'd been standing in the same spot when Neal had told me he never should've left me for a "stronger" woman—one who hadn't put up with his shit for more than a couple months. "You were so sure I'd do what's best for you, you never once stopped to consider if it's best for me. I'm sorry, but I'm not doing this again."

"What are you saying?" he asked.

I couldn't say it, so I showed him instead. I went into my bathroom and slammed the door on him. On *us*. I turned on the faucet to brush my teeth, but instead stared at myself in the mirror.

After a moment, he knocked. "Georgina."

We're over. Done. I tried to get myself to say the things I should've said to Neal a million times. "Please go."

"No. We're not done talking about this."

I didn't *want* him to go. I *wanted* him to be the man for me, but how could I ignore the warning signs after wasting years of my life already? My confidence had only just begun to recover. It would be so easy to open the door and continue getting to know Sebastian as something other than a rival. But would I look back one day and wonder how I could've made the same mistake twice?

If he kept pressing, I worried I'd give in, so I took a deep breath and opened the door just enough to face him. "We're professionals, so I trust we can finish out my time there in peace."

Hurt flashed in his eyes. "You can't be serious."

"I'll see you at work," I said. I closed the bathroom door, leaned back against it, and took deep breaths to attempt to slow my pounding heart. If this was how it felt to be a bitch, I wasn't sure I liked it, but I either had to choose myself or lose myself. When there was no more hate, only love, where was the line?

And had I just crossed it?

23

Love was a bitch. And Justin was a bastard. He'd never beaten me to work before Georgina had come along, but evidently, today was the second time he'd managed it in a few weeks. I found him in *my* office, leaning back in *my* chair, feet on *my* desk and arms behind his head. "Well, well," he said, making a point to check his watch. "Look who decided to show up. Late night?"

"It's barely ten," I grumbled, furtively checking Georgina's desk. It was just as she'd left it Friday afternoon. She must've been running behind this morning as well.

"So, how'd it go?"

"What?" I asked, dropping my briefcase next to his feet. He was mining for details about my night with Georgina, but after our argument that morning, I was in no mood to shoot the shit.

"You stopped answering my text messages after the movie last night," Justin said, "so I can only assume . . ."

"You know what they say about assumptions." I kicked the rolling chair so his feet fell.

He jumped up. "What the hell, man?"

"I've told you a million times to keep your grimy shoes off my desk."

"Jesus. For a guy who just got laid, you're in a pretty shitty mood."

"Yeah, well." I took my rightful throne. "I got some bad news earlier."

"Really?" Justin asked as he moved his plebeian ass to the couch. "Just completed my morning rounds for office gossip and didn't hear shit. What is it?"

I was still reeling, even though I'd suspected this could happen. I wasn't sure what pissed me off more—that Vance had told Georgina before me, or that she'd had the audacity to accuse me of manipulating her with sex. Maybe it was how she'd treated me like her ex when I'd only wanted to convey that her kindness was a strength, not a weakness.

I got up and shut the office door before returning to my desk. "Vance offered Georgina my position."

"*What?*" Justin shot forward on the sofa. "How are you not throwing things right now?"

"Georgina and I already had it out at her apartment this morning." I *had* thrown out some words I regretted, but the strange part was that I hadn't been as angry about potentially getting fired as I'd expected. That'd only come once she'd started in on me. "At least, we began to until she slammed the door in my face."

"The whole point of having sex was to release the tension you two have been forcing on us for months. Where does she get off being mad at you?"

The argument had happened so fast and gone downhill so quickly, I was still trying to figure out what the fuck had happened. "She's upset because I didn't consider what the job could do for her career. Instead, I just assumed she wouldn't take it, but what the fuck was I supposed to think? It's *my* job, and she knows what it means to me."

"I'm guessing by her reaction that it also means something to her."

Not the job itself, but maybe what it represented—confirmation that she'd succeeded in the position despite the environment I'd created for her. Calling her unqualified had been below the belt. It wasn't true. She deserved the offer, I just wished it wasn't at my expense.

The worst part was that it'd even *occurred* to her I might exploit the thing I liked most about her—her authenticity, generosity, the way she considered others. I didn't know how anyone could see that as weakness, but that was what Neal had taught her.

I had a lot to apologize for when she got in.

"She's not planning to take the job," I told Justin. "At least, she wasn't before this morning. Who knows now."

"Ah." Justin extended an arm along the back of the sofa. "I wonder if that's why she's talking to Vance."

I froze in the middle of booting up my computer. "Right now?"

"Yeah. She didn't even put her stuff down, just went right to his office."

"Fuck." That was it, then. I'd pissed her off enough to accept the position. I'd barely had time to process all this, much less dust off my résumé.

Who was I kidding? I'd worked my way up as an intern. I didn't have a fucking résumé anymore.

And yet, as Georgina had pointed out, maybe moving on from *Modern Man* wouldn't be such a bad thing. It had certainly opened my eyes finding out that, after I'd sucked it up and played ball when they'd hired Georgina, I still wasn't valued by Vance or the board.

I rubbed the inside corners of my eyes. "I should go

in there."

"I wouldn't." Justin shook his head. "Let her cool off. Maybe just keep your mouth shut until she comes to you."

"That's not how dating works," I said. "You ever heard of communication? Honesty?"

"Dating?" Justin arched an eyebrow. "So yesterday must've gone pretty well if you're still thinking about her that way."

All this time I'd felt threatened by her presence, assuming the worst-case scenario would be losing control of the magazine.

Losing Georgina, though? Somehow that seemed worse.

I hadn't wanted yesterday to end. No question, I'd never been on a better date, and to top it off, I'd woken up happy and ready to do it all over again. Especially the part where I'd had her gorgeous, naked body ready and willing underneath me.

If I was mad about anything, it was that I'd barely gotten one last glance at her mouth-watering tits before she'd covered them up with a child's t-shirt.

I steepled my fingers in front of me. I could tell Justin to fuck off and mind his own business, but I didn't want to. He was my closest friend and when something was important to me, he was part of it. "I like her, man. I really do. I know you'll say you told me so—"

"No need," he said, "as long as it's established that I did."

I sighed deeply. Georgina had been a pain in my ass since I'd met her. It shouldn't have surprised me that that hadn't changed simply because we'd slept together. She'd also pushed me in ways nobody had in a long while. She'd gotten me to open up about my mom, something I usually reserved for Libby and her husband or Justin.

And there was this one detail I hadn't been able to get over since yesterday—Georgina had adopted a sick dog.

Maybe that had signaled weakness to her ex, but to me, it was pure strength. Losing my mom was the hardest thing I'd ever been through, and since then, I sometimes questioned how I could fully love someone knowing I might lose them too one day. Georgina, on the other hand, had faced it head on. She'd *chosen* it so she could give Bruno a life.

"I don't want to fuck this up," I admitted. "Yeah, maybe things didn't come out right this morning. I was pissed, and I couldn't see much beyond the fact that I was getting fired. But if she wants to take the job, I'm not willing to lose her over it. I'll support her—I just wish that wasn't the only option."

"Man, do you have any idea how awkward that would be? Dating someone who replaced you?"

I ran my hands over my face, sitting back in my seat. Maybe he was right, but what other option was there? Was I supposed to let her go after we'd gotten this far? We'd pushed and pulled each other into this mess, and now I didn't want to be anywhere else but knee-deep in it with her. "It's fucked up," I said, "but what hasn't been about Georgina and me? We've been through a lot already. We could handle it."

"All right, then let's get serious here." Justin leaned his elbows on his knees and lowered his voice. "If you want me to find out what's going on, just say the word."

"Meaning?"

"I have eyeballs, ears, heads, shoulders, knees, and toes all over this place."

"You're a creep."

"You want info or not?" He looked offended. "*Pfft.* I've

got operatives everywhere and dirt on everyone in this office, including you."

"Then I guess they know about my recent, NSFW night in the copy room with your mom."

Justin's face fell. "Why would you say that, man? You know I'm sensitive about that."

His mom had always been a total babe, which had caused him some problems in high school. "You make it so easy."

"Whatever. You want me to have the nerds in IT hack Georgina's e-mail?"

"First of all, 'nerds'? You wish you knew how to hack someone's e-mail. You can't even dial out on the first try."

He flipped me off. "It's a new phone system."

"Secondly, do not *ever* hack an employee's personal e-mail."

"Got it. Just work then."

"Not that, either. Stay far away from IT."

Justin pointed to his ear and then to the ceiling, indicating that we were being listened to. "Understood, boss."

"I'm not giving you some secret go-ahead. Stay out of Georgina's business."

He winked. "Loud and clear."

I rolled my eyes. "Get out of here."

"It's Monday. We have a standing date to do some dickstorming before the meeting. We could do it undercover in the men's bathroom so Georgina doesn't know."

"You realize how gay you sound right now?" I asked. "Dickstorming is done. For good. We don't need it—we can do better."

I expected Justin to sulk, but he just nodded. "Sounds good, boss. Do whatever it takes to get back on George's good side."

"That's not why I'm banning it, and I'm not on her

bad side." She was upset with me, but we'd gone head-to-head plenty of times over the past couple months. She'd get annoyed. I'd get frustrated. We'd duke it out. Except unlike before, now we had the bonus of making up afterward.

I'd get myself out of this.

I stood and gathered the mockup poster boards my team had dropped off Friday and rounded the desk. "Let's go to the meeting."

On our way into the hall, Justin slung an arm around my shoulders. "You really like her, don't you? Never seen your confidence this shaky."

That was just what I needed to win Georgina back—shaky confidence. Women loved that. *Fuck.*

I squared my shoulders as we entered the conference room.

Vance stood at the front. Georgina had pulled a chair off to the side behind him. Using her closed laptop as a surface, she scribbled in a notebook, then paused to fix the collar of her blouse, some silky cream thing with tiny sparkly buttons that looked like they'd pop right off in my hands.

She glanced up. I gave her my best remember-how-you-screamed-my-name stare, which she held for a few moments before returning her eyes to her lap. Was she shy or still genuinely pissed? Maybe I was wrong, and this situation didn't call for confidence. After the way she'd asked me to drop the act last night, I'd *still* resorted to peacocking to get her attention—and *still*, Georgina was immune to it.

Vance fumbled with the projector as I approached. He nodded at the conference table. "Why don't you have a seat, Quinn."

It wasn't a question. Was it my imagination, or were Georgina and Vance giving me the cold shoulder? I set the boards against a wall and sat far enough from Georgina so as not to seem threatening, but close enough that I could still count—or *re*count—the sexy freckles on her knees. I hadn't been bluffing the night before. Georgina's freckles *had* frustrated me. They'd been one of the first things I'd noticed about the utterly adorable and off-limits woman I'd instantly disliked. They'd tempted me. Teased me. Called to me when I'd had to keep my distance.

And her ex had hated them? I'd better not ever come face to face with the emotionally abusive asshole.

Georgina crossed her legs and pulled her skirt down. That was as clear a message as any. Eyes to myself.

I'd been shut out.

Even now, I was being heckled by freckles, made worse by the fact that I'd tasted them.

I needed to cool down. I reached for the tray at the center of the conference table and poured myself a glass of water.

Vance called our attention to the head of the room. "Morning."

Laptops opened all around me. I uncapped my pen and opened my notepad to a rough outline for today's meeting. "Hope everyone had a nice, relaxing weekend," I said.

"Not as nice as yours," Albert said to me. "I hope you had a great fucking-weekend."

He said it with a knowing smile, as if a *fucking-weekend* were an event I'd attended. Which meant he knew about my date. Justin had probably opened his fat mouth.

I'd gotten my wish. Georgina's face got so red, her freckles disappeared.

"What do you mean by that?" I asked Al, injecting a healthy dose of irritation into my tone so he knew better than to answer honestly.

"Nothing, boss," he said. "Just being polite."

"You have the manners of a caveman." I tapped the capped end of my pen on the page in front of me. "First item of the day—"

"Hang on, Sebastian," Vance said. "Georgina and I have something to say."

Well, fuck. They wouldn't have a secret meeting, decide to fire me, and then announce it this way—would they? Just how badly had I pissed her off? I stuck the end of my pen in my mouth and sat back in my seat.

Vance twisted back to Georgina. "Would you like to speak?"

She smiled brightly. "Thank you for asking but go ahead."

He turned forward again. "With this being George's last week, she and I just debriefed. She wanted to let me know how impressed she is with how you've all handled this difficult transition."

"With the exception of Albert, of course," Georgina added. "For him, I recommend a very skilled and patient therapist." Everyone at the table laughed, myself included, but the usual small smile Georgina wore when she landed a playful insult wasn't there.

What exactly was happening?

Whether or not we'd *actually* become the good boys Georgina wanted wasn't the issue. We all wanted to hear that we'd been cleared of our charges and were better men now. We'd only needed Georgina to say it to believe it.

Vance frowned. Was it sadness? Disappointment? Was he losing something—*me*? Her? "Georgina believes you lot have made some of the greatest progress she's seen in this amount of time."

"Easy, Chewbacca," Justin whispered behind me. I'd gnawed my pen cap to a pulp.

"I'm grateful to you all for making this work," Vance continued, "and to Georgina for taking on what probably sounded like an impossible position."

Justin snickered and whispered, "No less possible than the one she was in last night."

I glanced back at him. He was on his phone, scrolling Facebook. As revenge for getting me in even hotter water with Georgina, I took his cell, updated his status to "When everyone keeps telling you you've got Little Dick Energy :(" and dumped it in the pitcher of water.

"Hey, what the fuck?" Justin dove in after it. "You better hope this shit is waterproof."

"Guys," Vance warned. "I just complimented you on how mature you've been. Don't make me take it back."

"Thank you for the kind words, Vance." Georgina held a tight smile in place. "I'm only as good as my team."

She had molded us into something better, and she *did* have what it took. She was qualified. I inhaled a breath and tried to think of how I could possibly respond to being fired in front of everyone who'd counted on me the last few years. She kept any emotion from her eyes as they roamed the room, grazing right over my head, giving me nothing.

"Well?" I asked.

"All right, all right, Sebastian," Vance said. "I know you're eager to get the meeting going. We just wanted to thank you all. Georgina's going to start wrapping things up around here, so if you have any final questions or concerns, see her in the next day or two."

She was leaving?

She was leaving.

Right on schedule, if not earlier.

"But you can always e-mail me about anything," she said. "If things go smoothly today and tomorrow, I'll be out of your hair even sooner than planned." She finally glanced at me. "That's how much confidence I have in you all."

Her words from the night before hadn't left me. *"If you take over, I become obsolete. Walk in with me as a united front tomorrow morning."*

She'd been looking out for me instead of herself, and after her history with Neal, no doubt that scared her.

"I've got a breakfast meeting to get to," Vance said. "Over to you, Quinn."

Over to me—if I still even wanted that. She wasn't taking the job. It was all mine. Why didn't I feel relieved?

The answer to that was right there in her expressionless eyes.

I had no idea where I stood with her.

After the meeting, Georgina hung back to talk to Nicole. I didn't want to wait another minute to hash out this morning's argument and move on, but the longer I lingered, the more desperate I seemed, so I returned to our office to wait for her.

I raised the window shades. The office became an oven in the afternoon when they were that high, but Georgina liked natural light, so I'd gotten in the habit anyway.

I'd outlined most of our talking points for the first episode of the podcast we were set to record next week when my impatience got the better of me and I went looking for her. Not only did I need her help on this podcast thing, but I wanted it. This was the closest I'd gotten to sports broadcasting, what I'd thought I'd do after college. For the first time in a long while, I was nervous in my role at *Modern Man*.

I checked Justin's cubicle first, simply because he hadn't

bothered me in the past hour, which meant he was either annoying someone else or napping. Oddly, I found him hunched over his laptop working on an article Georgina had assigned him about male aestheticians.

"Need something?" he asked, glancing up only long enough to take a sip of coffee.

Despite the fact that the article would require Justin to get his back waxed by a dude, the topic was bizarrely fitting. He'd been more engrossed in his work lately, and it was all thanks to Georgina. I wasn't about to jeopardize that. "No, just seeing if you needed a refill."

"Sure, I'll take a—hey!" he said, but I was already on my way to the breakroom.

That was where I found Georgina, posted at a small round table and surrounded by the meeting's notes. Her laptop lit up her face and the shiny buttons of her blouse.

I went to the vending machine closest to her table and dropped in some change. "You should be careful in here," I said. "People can see your laptop while they pretend to buy Starbursts."

She brushed two fingertips down the trackpad as she scrolled. "I have nothing to hide."

"Yeah? Then why are you camped out in the back corner of a dark room?" I punched my order into the keypad. Sadly, there was no 100 Grand, so I went for what I hoped was the next best thing. "No windows in here."

"I'm not hiding. I'm avoiding."

Surely, she didn't mean me. You didn't just come out and tell someone you were avoiding them, right? I went to stand in front of her with my peace offering. "Want some candy?" I asked, showing her a Butterfinger. "A wise man once told you it's as good as sex."

"A wise man does not call himself a wise man."

"Touché." She still hadn't looked up from her work. "Who are you avoiding?"

"Not who, what. I'm avoiding an awkward conversation. An uncomfortable workspace. An unwelcome truth." She took a breath. "I think it's best if I just work in here the next couple days."

All right, maybe she *was* talking about me. "What unwelcome truth?"

She began typing.

"Georgina, what happened in your meeting with Vance?" I asked. "Why are you leaving early?"

"You don't need me anymore, and your job is safe—"

"Fuck the job. What about us?"

Her fingers froze. Finally, she lifted her eyes to mine. "There's no us. There's you, and there's me. *You* are staying on as creative director. *I* am moving on to my next assignment."

"That doesn't answer my question." I tried to keep the irritation from my face. "We had an argument this morning. So what? Let's figure it out."

"How do you think it made me feel to realize that the man I'd just woken up next to, a man I'd gone against all my instincts to trust, would hold me back to keep himself happy?"

"Pretty shitty, if that's how you took it," I said.

"You called me unqualified. You said I don't have what it takes."

"And you *know* that was my anger talking. Nothing more. Of course I want you to succeed and your career to flourish. I think you're good at this job—hell, you're better at it than I am."

She looked down and muttered, "That's not true."

"Look. I've been on edge about all this ever since you

started. This morning, it came to a head, but I didn't mean the things I said."

She sighed back against her chair and fidgeted with a tiny button near her throat. "Thank you, but . . ." She lowered her voice. "We have to be honest with ourselves. The unwelcome truth is that last night was a mistake."

"You can describe last night a lot of different ways, but *mistake* is complete and utter bull, Georgina." I scowled. "No argument could convince me of that."

"Sleeping with a coworker is never a good idea, but especially for us. We were at each other's throats on day one. We're just not compatible."

"I don't buy that."

"I'm not selling anything. I'm simply saying how I feel."

It occurred to me that our roles had flipped. Now, I was the one at the front of the room asking to be let in, and she was pretending she didn't care—the same way I'd dismissed her at our very first meeting. Why had I treated her that way? Out of pure fear. I'd been terrified of change, loss, and failure. "You're scared," I said.

She slammed her laptop shut. "Yes, I am. Of repeating my past."

"The last thing I want is for you to think I tried to exploit your kindness," I said. "You know that's one of the things that drew me to you in the first place." She opened her mouth looking ready to protest, but I cut her off. "*Not* weakness. Kindness."

"And what happens if I forgive you this time? What if I pick a restaurant or neighborhood or vacation spot you don't like?" She opened her hand on the table. "Will your first instinct always be that I should sacrifice so you can have what you want? Will mine be to give it to you?"

I clenched my jaw. That fucking hurt. "After the day we

had, after I cut myself open and bled to you all the things I can't talk about, you're going to keep treating me like Neal?"

Her cheeks reddened. "As soon as I admitted I had feelings for you, I started acting the same way I did in that relationship."

"You're acting chickenshit is what you're doing," I said.

She pulled back. "This is *my* life, and I'm not going to second-guess myself because you don't understand it."

I took a breath, an attempt at composure as she burrowed deeper under my skin. "I'm trying here, Georgina. What I'm failing to articulate is that I'm not ready to call it quits. I made a mistake this morning, and I'm apologizing because you're one of the best things that has happened to me in a long time." I shoved a hand through my hair, looking for a way to ask for what I wanted while being sensitive to her fears. "I want this to work. Does me telling you that feel like I'm pushing you?"

She glanced at the table. "No."

"Then that's what I want." I paused. "And if you're walking away from something *you* want because *I* was an idiot, then you're still letting a man dictate your decisions."

"That's ridiculous," she said, anger threading her words.

"But true." I tossed the Butterfinger on the table. "For when your *cravings* hit tonight."

I returned to my office, leaving her to glare after me. Did the truth hurt? Good. At least she wasn't indifferent. I'd been in the enemy zone for months and the relationship zone for a night. But indifference? Give me death. Because it was true what they said—there *was* a thin line between love and hate, and while it existed, I still had a shot with her.

24

I trudged up the steps of my apartment building cursing the fact that our ancient elevator seemed to need servicing every other month. I didn't think I could get any more tired after falling for, making love to, and breaking up with Sebastian in under forty-eight hours. Seeing him at work today had been hard and avoiding him was even harder.

Especially since I always wanted to know where he was, what he was working on, and who he was with.

As usual, Bruno heard me coming. His nails clicked the wood floors inside as I unlocked the door. One step in and he was circling me, wagging his tail and whining for attention.

"Hi, baby boy," I cooed, ruffling his fur. No matter how my week was going, this would always make it better. I kissed the top of his head. "How was your day?"

I dropped my keys in the handmade ceramic bowl my mom had sent me for my last birthday and headed into the kitchen. Fortunately, Gordie had been able to stay late so I could finish up at work. I'd gotten so much done without

Sebastian around, there wasn't even much left to accomplish.

When I noticed Bruno's food bowl was full, I pulled Gordie's note from a magnet on the fridge. "Couldn't get him to eat tonight."

At my side, Bruno nudged his face into my hip. Unlike most dogs, he didn't go crazy over his meals, but he didn't skip them that often. "You hungry?"

I picked up his bowl, added a little more wet food on top, and set it back down. Once he'd sniffed it and began to eat, I unzipped my skirt and flopped onto the couch with my trusty remote. I'd only managed to turn on the TV when Bruno wandered out of the kitchen and jumped onto the couch. He put his head in my lap.

"There's no way you ate that fast," I said to him. "What's up, buddy?"

He sighed, raising big gray-blue eyes.

I pet his head. "You're needy tonight. Maybe I've been neglecting you lately."

Apparently, ignoring the ones I cared about took it out of me. Or, maybe like me, Bruno was just missing his new friend Sebastian. As if trying not to think about him wasn't hard enough, he'd already called once since I'd left the office.

I wasn't ready to talk. My emotions were still running high, and that would only get me into trouble. I wasn't smooth like him—I'd proven myself susceptible to giving in to others when I didn't even know I was doing it.

My cell rang, and despite the fact that I was still avoiding him, my heart leapt with the thought that it might be Sebastian. I got it from my purse, slightly disappointed to see my boss's name. She rarely called after eight o'clock, so it had to be important. I muted the TV to answer.

"Georgina?" Dionne said. "I'm glad I got you."

"Is everything okay?"

"Yes." She hesitated. "Well, maybe. I'll get right to the point. I caught wind that *Modern Man* is going to offer you a job."

I sighed. "They already did."

"I see." She blew out a breath. "You know I'd never keep you from doing what you need to, which is why there's nothing in your contract that says you can't leave to work for a client. But I hope you'll give me a chance to convince you to stay."

"I'm not going to take it," I told her. "But you and I need to have a meeting about salary. What Vance offered me made me realize I should be making more."

Dionne hummed. She couldn't really argue considering she'd taught me to constantly reevaluate my worth. "We don't need to meet," she said. "I'm going to pay you more anyway, considering you'll be running the agency for me."

I blanched. "What? Where are you going?"

"We're opening a second location in Boston. It was between there and Philly. There's been a lot of demand, what with some media companies being priced out of the city."

"But what about you?" I asked. "Are you moving there?"

"No way, just getting things up and running for the next six months or so. I'm already interviewing people to manage that office so I can begin training as soon as I arrive."

I picked through the couple gray hairs around Bruno's snout. "What happens to my job when you get back?"

"You'll go back to what you're doing now, but at the new, higher salary. We can discuss that once we see how the next few months go."

I should've been elated that I'd be getting more money

to do the same job, not to mention a change of pace, but was she only handing me this to keep me from leaving? I hadn't even argued a case for why I deserved it.

"I appreciate it, I really do," I told Dionne, "but I think I need . . . more."

"More money?" she asked. "We haven't even discussed—"

"No. Just more." I took a breath. It felt weird to say since I'd been pretty content up until recently. I supposed I had Sebastian to blame for reawakening this in me after Neal had killed it—the urge to do better. Be better. "I don't know what that means yet. I'm happy to take your spot while you're away, but when you get back, I need something else. Something to push me. I'm afraid I've gotten too comfortable."

"Something like Boston?" she asked. "If you're looking for a challenge, you could always go open that office instead of me."

That wasn't what I'd meant, but the suggestion made me pause. "Open it as in . . .?"

"Move there and run it," she said simply. "Why not?"

I'd thought there wasn't any higher to go under Dionne, but managing my own branch was certainly a step up—maybe several. "You're serious?"

"Absolutely. Now that I think about it, you'd be a great fit, Georgina. With the aptitude and knowledge you bring to each assignment, plus a process you've honed over the years, you could easily take this on." I heard her smile over the phone. "How does the idea of assembling your own team sound?"

"It sounds . . . interesting, if not a little daunting."

"You never back down from what I give you, even if it feels like too much. You know you're a natural leader."

I tried the designation on for size. Hadn't I led *Modern*

Man away from the brink, along with many other companies? I didn't often think of my role in those terms because the teams I joined were always temporary and usually had their own leaders, like Sebastian.

"Would I still get to work with clients?" I asked.

"I should hope so. Only the ones you choose to, since you'll eventually get to know the strengths and weaknesses of the people under you. And who knows, Georgina. Maybe you'll be lucky enough, like me, to find someone to mentor."

A leader and a mentor. Maybe those were the ways to enrich my career outside of promotions and money. What I got out of my work wasn't just a paycheck, but a sense that I had helped. If it weren't for me, perhaps some of these companies would've gone under by now. Along with their employees.

"I like the sound of it," I admitted.

"I'd certainly sleep easier knowing you were there, and maybe it's selfish, but I'd prefer not to have to leave New York."

Leave the city? I'd never even considered it. It'd been my home since my early twenties, and the thought of starting over somewhere new made my heart pound. I loved it here, but I'd never really been anywhere else. I'd gone from my childhood home in Buffalo to college upstate to the city. If I wanted a challenge, leaving the life I knew was one way to do it.

"Can I think about it?" I asked.

"Absolutely, but not too long. Things are already in motion. You said you're about done at *Modern Man*, so why don't you take Bruno and spend a few days in Boston, see how you like it."

"We've been," I said.

"I know, but you've probably never looked at it through the lens of living there."

Me. Living in *Boston.*

Home to my rival team.

To a top veterinary cardiologist in the country.

And the one place Sebastian would never go.

I pushed that thought from my mind. This wasn't about him—it couldn't be.

I hung up with Dionne in a daze. "What do you think?" I asked Bruno, playing with his big old floppy ears. "Could you see yourself in Boston? Maybe a change would do us good."

I wiped a white string of slobber off my skirt. No wonder I spent so much on dry cleaning bills. I couldn't get more than one wear out of an outfit while Bruno was around. "And of course, I'd make more money," I added. "Sounds good, doesn't it?" I angled to look at him. "Bruno?"

There was more slobber on my leg than before, only now it was foamier. His breathing became labored as he stared off into the distance. Before I could even register what was happening, he started to whine, his eyes darting around as if he didn't see me. He convulsed a few times.

His body went stiff.

The air around me vanished, my vision sharpening on Bruno's twitching whiskers, the pink insides of his eyes, the moisture on his nostril. This couldn't be happening. Not now. Not already. We still had time left, we . . .

My throat thickened as the room tunneled. My muscles locked up.

And I sat there with no clue what to do.

No, I *knew* what to do, but I couldn't remember.

My vet had run crisis drills with me, but I'd never had to put any of them into practice.

Tears sprung to my eyes. My heartbeat took over my entire body. This was it. My worst nightmare playing out in front of me, and I was frozen in fear.

I couldn't freeze, though. Couldn't fuck this up. It wasn't an option.

Bruno whined again. Or were my ears ringing? Was he having a seizure? Why was he so still?

I squeezed my eyes shut and forced myself to think back to my conversation with Doctor Rimmel. If this was a seizure, nothing could be done until it was over except to make him comfortable. His eyes were open, though, and he'd stopped jerking, only his paws spasming as if he were dreaming.

I took a deep breath and slowly picked up my phone from the couch. "It's okay, baby," I said, bile rising in my throat as I unlocked the screen with shaky fingers. I ordered a cab from the company that normally took us to the vet just as Bruno's eyes rolled to the back of his head and he lost consciousness.

"Oh my god," I said, shaking him. "Bruno?"

When he didn't respond, I jumped up, ran to the entryway with a stack of magazines, and propped open the door. Hitching Bruno's emergency bag over my shoulder, I shoved my feet in my heels and hurried back to Bruno while zipping up my skirt. "You're okay, baby. We're okay." I kneeled beside him. "I'm going to pick you up now —just relax."

No response.

If I'd had time, or courage, I would've checked for a pulse. I slipped my arms under his body and lifted, but he didn't budge. "No," I whispered so he wouldn't wake up to the despair in my voice. My body couldn't fail me now. Bruno weighed almost as much as I did, but so fucking what? Couldn't a jolt of adrenaline give me superhuman strength? I tried again to no avail and stood, running my hands through my hair. I bolted into the hallway to bang on the door of my six-foot-something neighbor who always seemed to be coming home from the gym.

After a few seconds, I rushed back into the apartment. I dialed Luciano—no answer. I tried Bruno's dogsitter next —nothing. I steeled myself, bent my knees as I slipped my arms underneath him, and put everything I had into it.

It wasn't enough.

I fell back onto the ground as a sense of helplessness flooded me. I wouldn't cry. I *couldn't*. Bruno needed me to keep a clear head.

For maybe the first time since my breakup with Neal, I felt truly alone. Maybe bad friends and a worse boyfriend were better than nothing at all.

My phone buzzed with a text message from Sebastian. I grabbed it to call him just as Bruno stirred, woke up, and began to squirm.

"Shh," I said, latching on his leash a second before he jumped off the couch and stumbled toward the door. I didn't even have time to feel relieved; I kicked the magazines aside on our way out so the door would close as I steered Bruno toward the elevator.

Once we'd boarded, I kneeled to face him. His eyes held either fear, confusion, or both. The lack of recognition made a lump form in my throat. In the strongest, clearest voice I could manage, I said, "Good boy, Bruno." I touched his warm forehead and swallowed painfully. I wanted to curl into a ball on the ground. To be at the vet five minutes ago. To break down, when I couldn't even afford to fracture. "Good boy," I repeated. "I'm here."

I could get us to the hospital with my eyes closed, but fortunately I wouldn't need to. When the doors opened, I sprinted for the cab.

It turned out life was full of thin lines. They formed tenuous tightropes between loving and hating, mating and dating . . . life and death. One misstep, one nudge, could knock you from one side to the other before you realized it. Before you were ready.

I woke up curled onto a cushioned seat with my face smashed against a muscular, denim-clad thigh. My eyes focused on a vending machine as stale coffee perfumed the room. Holy shit. I'd fallen asleep at the *vet*? I shot upright and cursed when I banged the top of my head.

"*Oww*, G!" I recognized Luciano's voice. "What the hell?"

I covered the welt forming and blinked sleep from my vision. "Lu? What are you doing here?"

"You texted me to come." He rubbed his jaw with one hand. "I found you sleeping all contorted on the chair with your pencil skirt halfway up your thighs."

"Oh my god." I yanked it down and threw my face in my hands. "*Bruno*."

"He'll be all right," Luciano said in an uncharacteristically gentle voice. "He has to be."

I rubbed my eyes. "What time is it?"

"Almost eleven. You weren't out long."

"I can't believe I fell asleep. I had such a long day. What if something had happened?"

"They would've woken you. Don't beat yourself up. Bruno will need you when he's released, so you should rest now."

I pinched the corners of my eyes until a wave of tears subsided. I hadn't let myself cry yet. Not with an audience. Not without news. Not when I needed to be strong for Bruno. "I can't believe this. I thought it was a seizure, but Doctor Rimmel said it's more likely that he fainted. Something about his heart restricting blood flow to his brain." I nearly choked on the words. "He's never fainted before."

"You're prepared for this, Georgina."

I'd frozen up. All Bruno's life I'd known he could go into crisis, and yet I'd almost messed up. What if the seconds I'd sat there staring had been the difference between saving or losing the brightest light in my life?

"You should've seen his eyes," I said, shuddering. "He looked so scared."

"I doubt that. I'll bet with you there, he felt nothing but safe." Luciano put an arm around my shoulders and kissed the side of my head. "Remember that time I showed up on Halloween in a Freddy Krueger mask and Bruno nearly mauled me?"

I hiccupped, halfway between a sob and a laugh. "I wouldn't have blamed him. You were hideous."

"Or how about when he cost me the *Wii Tennis* championship?"

I nodded against him. Luciano and I had gotten so worked up during the final moments of the last game of our set that Bruno had jumped on Luciano and knocked the controller out of his hands. It was the only time I'd won. "It's just like you to blame a poor, innocent dog."

"Right." He snorted. "Try poor, innocent *beast*."

I looked at a clock on the wall across from us. "It's getting late. I wish they'd just tell us what's going on."

"Why was it such a long day?" Lu asked.

He was trying his best to distract me, so I let him, considering the alternative was worrying myself to death. "Where do I start?" I said, sighing. "I slept with Sebastian."

He gasped. "Julia Roberts in a bubble bath!" he cried. "Warn a girl before you blurt out something like that."

It felt good to laugh. "I knew you'd get it out of me in the next few minutes anyway."

He seized my shoulders to push me back into my own seat. "When was this?"

"Last night."

"Spill everything."

"Not much to say. It ended about as quickly as it started."

He grimaced. "Already?"

I caught Luciano up on everything that'd happened since he'd slept over, from Sebastian ambushing me outside my apartment for a faux date to doga in the park to our thwarted spaghetti kiss. And how one of the best days ever had turned into an even better night.

"That sounds like the date of a flipping lifetime," Luciano said. "How the hell did things go bad?"

I tugged my skirt down as far as it would go. It was too cold not to have tights on, but I hadn't had a moment to change since work. "When we woke up, I felt guilty for keeping the job offer from him. So I told him."

He sat back. "Oh. Shit."

"Yeah. You won't believe his response."

Luciano shook his head. "I'm imagining all kinds of curse words. Was he at least clothed when he flew off the handle?"

"He was. I wasn't." I picked at my chipping nail polish. "Not that he really flew off the handle at all. I was actually the one who got mad."

"Did you?" Luciano looked impressed. "Why?"

I dropped my hands in my lap. "I told him I got the offer, but I never said I wasn't taking it. He just assumed I wouldn't accept out of loyalty to him. I was 'too good of a person' to steal his job, which is more or less the patronizing way he put it."

"Ah." Luciano nodded slowly. "And even though you weren't going to take it, it felt like he expected you not to."

I nodded. "It all went downhill from there. He said I wasn't qualified for the job. I accused him of sleeping with me so I'd be easier to manipulate."

"Jesus, G. Do you really believe he'd do that?"

I twisted the pendant of my necklace. I *didn't* think so, but after he'd asked if I was trying to ship him back to Boston, it'd felt like a fair comeback. "Maybe," I said, because I wasn't done being angry. "But it doesn't matter. We're over."

"Hmm." Luciano sighed. "Were you worried it'd become a Neal situation all over again?"

"Obviously," I said, scratching my temple. Except, even though I'd insinuated Sebastian was like Neal, he'd never really *intentionally* made me feel like I didn't matter. Neal had employed manipulation to control me. For a moment, in the breakroom with Sebastian, I'd retreated into a memory of a similar argument with Neal over where to spend Thanksgiving—only in that one, I'd backed down. With Sebastian, I fought. Had I regained my strength, or was it simply that I wasn't afraid to be myself with him, no matter how hard we argued?

"Actually, Sebastian's not like that," I admitted. "I don't really believe he planned the date with bad intentions. Even though he tricked me into going on it in the first place."

"I see. So if I have it right, you ended things, not him? What'd he say to that?"

"He apologized . . . with a Butterfinger."

"Girl, that can't mean what I think it does." Luciano pursed his lips. "You're not that experimental."

I shoved him. "I'm talking about the candy bar."

"In under forty-eight hours, he took you and Bruno on a date, gave you the best sex of your life, and brought you chocolate. And you're upset—*why*?"

I bit my bottom lip. "I never said it was the best sex of my life."

"I've only met the man once, but his BDE is off the charts."

"Geez, are they passing out pamphlets about it or what?"

Luciano laughed. "So was it the best sex or not?"

I thought of how Sebastian had brought me to the brink of orgasm, then flipped me over to get the job done. He'd looked me in the eye and hadn't shied away, even when intimacy had overwhelmed the moment. "It was the most, I don't know . . . connected," I said. "It was special, and I have a feeling we only scratched the surface."

"If you want my advice, which you do, don't write him off so easily. We can't ignore that he apologized, which Neal never would've done."

I picked at invisible lint on my skirt. "I thought you'd be proud of me for sticking up for myself."

"I am, I just don't want you to go the opposite direction and let your past with Neal scare you into being alone. Then it's kind of like you're *still* not calling the shots, you know? He is."

I looked up, eyes wide. "That's like what Sebastian said before he walked out of the breakroom. That by running away, I was letting my fear make my decisions for me."

"He has a point."

I chewed my bottom lip. The fact that I'd been so tempted to forgive Sebastian in the breakroom had only scared me more. He could've walked when I'd pushed him away, but he'd stood where he was and given it right back to me.

He made sure I knew he wanted me in his life.

And if I was honest, I wanted him in mine.

It was the simple truth, but now, things were even more complicated than they'd been that morning. "That's not all," I told Luciano. "Dionne offered me a new position."

He perked up. "A promotion?"

"Yes. All the way to Boston."

"What?" he screeched. "*Why?*"

I covered my ears with a light laugh. "These past couple months got me thinking about how I'm ready to take on new challenges, but where I am now, there's not much room for me to grow. I told Dionne all that earlier tonight, and she wants me to go to Boston to open a new branch."

"Like, permanently?" He sounded worried.

I nodded. "But, Lu, lately I've been feeling like a change would be good. Maybe different scenery, maybe learning some new things."

"Don't you know enough already?" If not for Botox, wrinkles would've formed between his eyebrows. "You can't leave now. We finally became official New Yorkers."

I wrinkled my nose. "When?"

"It happens automatically once you've been here long enough to not only map out but pee in every acceptable public bathroom between fourteenth and thirtieth."

"We've done that?" I asked.

"Probably." He pouted. "Do you actually want this? Or could it be that something else is missing?"

"I think I might want it," I said and purposely didn't ask about the "something else" he was referring to. "Besides everything I already mentioned," I reasoned, "I'll make more money and get more space for what I pay now. Plus, I'll basically be my own boss."

Luciano narrowed his eyes. "I'm not convinced. Something stinks here, and it's not that grandma perfume I warned you not to buy."

"*Hey*," I said, sniffing my wrist. Damn him and his keen sense of smell. The commercial for the fragrance starred Aliana Balik, the model on Sebastian's desktop and the one woman he'd never been able to score for the cover of *Modern Man*. It wasn't that I wanted to *be* her, but it wouldn't hurt to at least smell like her.

"This is all a little too convenient, Georgina. You were on the verge of starting something new and fabulous with a luscious Latin man—"

"I don't see how that's relevant—"

"And suddenly you have to leave?" He took a deep breath, his expression sobering. "Are you sure you're not looking for ways to sabotage this relationship before it starts?"

It wasn't as if *I'd* picked the one place Sebastian would never return. Or had even *asked* to be promoted. "Yes, it would be easier to leave town than risk getting hurt again, but that's not what I'm doing. Maybe I was wrong this morning, but does having feelings for Sebastian automatically mean I shouldn't take this opportunity?"

"I just want to make sure you're making this choice for yourself and not because Neal scared you. I tell you to be a bitch because I already watched one guy undermine you over and over, slowly draining your confidence." He took one of my hands. "I want you to make decisions based on *your* needs, not others'. Take what you want. Do you want Sebastian?"

If Sebastian had truly meant what he'd said earlier

about making this work, and if he could forgive me for the way I'd treated him in the breakroom, then . . .

I nodded slowly. "I do."

"Do you want the job in Boston?"

I inhaled deeply, thinking back to my conversation with Dionne. Some of it was a blur, my memory short-circuiting from everything that'd come after. But I hadn't forgotten the confidence she'd had in me. "I would have a team, Lu, one I get to assemble, train, and mentor. We'd be entering a new space where there's not really much competition yet, so I'd be on the forefront of that. And I'm not bored with my job as it is, but I'd be taking this next step on my own, moving out from under Dionne's wing after all these years."

Luciano watched me. "Yeah. I guess you do want the job."

I squeezed his hand to say what I couldn't. Leaving wouldn't just mean saying goodbye to New York, but to Luciano and all the memories we'd made here.

His eyes doubled in size.

"Oh, don't get emotional," I said. "I won't be able to—"

"I'm not crying." He glanced behind me. "I, um . . . I'm sorry . . ."

"For what?" I asked as he grimaced. "What's wrong?"

"I probably should've mentioned that Sebastian called while you were sleeping."

"Oh. It's fine." Sebastian's text during Bruno's crisis had been a request to come over and talk. Once I'd checked Bruno in at the vet, I hadn't had the emotional capacity for anything else, so I'd ignored the message. "I'm avoiding his calls."

"You were until I picked up."

I slow blinked. "You talked to him?"

He lowered his voice, looking furtively over my shoulder as he rushed out, "Yes, and I was waiting to see how your story played out before I decided whether to stick around for this, but honestly, he got here much faster than I anticipated."

"He's *here*?" My heart stopped. I whirled around in my seat to see Sebastian striding down the hall with a bouquet of white roses at his side. Still in his suit, his hair was disheveled, his tie crooked. "Why?" I whisper-hissed. "Up until an hour ago, you still thought he was my enemy."

"He didn't sound hostile on the phone when I answered it," he said defensively. As Sebastian neared, Lu quickly added, "He sounded *sad*. Said he needed to talk to you. For a moment, I was worried he'd start unloading on me, so instead, I told him about Bruno."

And here he was. "I came as soon as I heard," Sebastian said, pulling up a chair. With authority in his voice, the sharp angles of his suit, and the crease in his brow, I almost felt as if I was in trouble. He sat across from us, leaned his elbows on his knees, and let the flowers sag between his knees. "What happened?"

25

Georgina and Luciano sat across from me in the vet's waiting room gaping as if I'd just flown in on a pig. "How's Bruno?" I asked when they didn't respond to my earlier question.

Georgina flinched. "What are you doing here?"

I'd been leaving the office when I'd decided to try Georgina one last time. Twenty-four hours earlier, I'd been buried in her in more ways than one, and now I couldn't even get her to take my calls. "Luciano told me what happened. Or at least, the gist of it."

Luciano put a hand to his chest and feigned innocence to Georgina. "I only gave him the name of the hospital and the cross streets," he told her, "but I didn't tell him to come, I swear."

I couldn't muster an ounce of offense that she didn't want me there. Knowing what Bruno meant to her, she had to be in a world of pain. Dark circles under her eyes and goosebumps on her knees and arms told me all I needed to know. Why wasn't she wearing a coat?

"You're dripping . . ." Georgina said.

I glanced down between my feet. I'd bought the bouquet in a hurry from a bodega on the way over, and the wet stems had made a puddle. I didn't even know if she *liked* roses, but it seemed like the right thing to do. "These are for you," I said, passing them to her. "So, is there any news?"

"Not yet," she said, resting the bouquet in her lap. "One minute I was petting Bruno, and the next—" Her voice caught. "He . . ."

"It's okay, just relax," I said, standing up. My intent wasn't to make her cry but to comfort however I could. I pulled a bag of gummy bears from my suit jacket, my other last-minute grab from the corner store. "You must be hungry," I said. "You haven't changed since the office?"

She took the candy with wide eyes. "I didn't get a chance."

I removed my jacket and handed it to her. "Put that on," I said, then went to reception for paper towels and a blanket.

Once I had what I needed, I made my way back to them. Georgina, in my oversized blazer, frantically chewed gummy bears and looked as if she was having a whispered argument with Luciano. They went silent the moment I was in hearing distance.

I unfolded a royal blue blanket and shook it out. "This should work for now," I said, handing it to her. "I can go to your place and get you a change of clothes if you like."

"It's okay," she said almost cautiously as she covered her lap.

"How about a mocha latte?"

"I'll handle that," Luciano said, getting up. "There's a twenty-four-hour deli a couple blocks from here. Sebastian?"

"Black coffee is fine. My treat," I added, getting my

wallet from my back pocket. I didn't think I'd ever live down the fact that Georgina's best friend had seen me snap at her in the café. I sighed, thinking he'd probably volunteer to contribute to my next exposé, and gave him a twenty. "If you don't mind."

"Not at all," Luciano said before walking off.

I dragged my chair forward to sit facing Georgina. "Are you okay?" I asked.

She swallowed audibly, then relayed the details of her evening as remotely as she seemed able. Through a series of staccato hiccups, she attempted to hold back tears when she got to the part about how terrified Bruno had looked. "I almost couldn't help him," she said.

I put my hand over her blanketed knee. "It sounds like you did everything right."

"He had too much activity yesterday. I should've known better. And when it was time to act, my mind went completely blank. I almost fucked it all up, Sebastian."

"But you didn't."

She shook her head, her gaze distant. I could practically read the *what-ifs* running through her head.

"Don't," I said sternly, my eyes darting between her gold-flecked ones. "If yesterday was anyone's fault, it's mine. I practically forced you to go out with me."

"No," she said vehemently. "I didn't mean it like that. Everything you did for us was p-perfect . . ." Her chin wobbled. "I'm the one who should've realized."

"Georgina, look at me." She instantly turned her gaze to me the way she had at my demand the night before. She'd needed to know I was there with her then, and I'd make damn sure she knew it now. I wasn't going to abandon her when things got tough. "Bruno had fun. What was the point of saving his life if he can't enjoy it?

Because you *did* save him. You are, and always have been, Bruno's hero."

She swallowed in a way that looked painful. "I keep picturing him lying on a cold metal slab, possibly fighting for his life back there. We don't know what . . . or if he's even going to . . ."

I took her chin in my thumb and forefinger. "Are you ready to give up on him?"

"No," she choked out.

"Then I demand that you stop thinking of the worst-case scenarios. It isn't helping anything."

"Demand?" she asked.

"And I *request* that you stop trying to be strong and let me take over for a few minutes."

After a few silent seconds, she nodded, whispering, "Sebastian."

"It's okay. Let it out." I thumbed the corner of her mouth. "Nobody's looking."

"*You're* looking."

"I don't count. Not only have I seen you cry, but I've been the cause of it." I fucking hated that. I wished I could do that whole morning over again. It was the only thing I'd change about our time together so far. I moved to the seat next to hers and pulled her into my arms, against my chest.

Her entire body shook as she inhaled a breath and exhaled a sob. And then another. "I miss him."

"He's not going anywhere." I squeezed her even more tightly, my mouth pressed into her hair. "It's all right. I'm here."

Eventually, she lifted her head, touching my collar. "I'm ruining your suit."

"It was too clean anyway," I said.

"Did you come from the office?"

"Yeah."

"Why were you there so late?"

"Screwing around." I cleared my throat. "Working on my résumé."

She glanced up at me, her brows drawn. "Vance said he wasn't planning to replace you. You don't believe him?"

"Would you?" I shrugged. "I figure it's good to have it on hand anyway."

"That doesn't sound like screwing around."

"Once I started researching résumés, I went down a virtual black hole and ended up on Google Earth looking up my mom's house."

She inhaled sharply, shifting in my arms to see me better. That gasp meant more to me than she knew. She realized the magnitude of such a seemingly small thing. "How come?"

"The possibility of losing my job has spurred me into action." I paused, tucking some of her hair behind her ear. "Ever since you came along, I've been thinking more about the future."

Was her heart hammering or mine? I read the fear in her eyes, but it didn't scare me.

"How'd the house look?" she asked.

"I stared at it for about five seconds, trying to convince myself it wasn't that scary. That I could go back, fix it up, and finally sell it." The rundown neighborhood I'd grown up in was gentrifying. I'd been torn between a vivid image of a new family putting down roots, making memories and height charts—and my mom's cold, dim final days. The faded memories of Libby and me fighting over the TV clicker while the aroma of tamales filled the house. Of my visits as an adult when I'd updated the television set, installed a bookshelf in the living room, or replaced her fifteen-year-old mattress with a Tempur-Pedic. "I closed the tab. I can't do it. Not yet."

Her limbs loosened. Maybe she'd thought I'd want to go back to Boston, and that was the fear I'd seen. If she didn't want me to go, then she still had hope for us.

I did. And I wanted to show it to her. Despite her tear-streaked cheeks, she was beautiful. With her mouth inches from mine, I could ease her pain with a kiss. Forget my troubles. Erase the strenuous hours since we'd woken up together. Would that be taking emotional advantage of her?

The last thing I wanted was to be compared to her prick of an ex-boyfriend again.

"You could've called me, you know," I said quietly.

She shuddered. "Even after this morning?"

I picked up the blanket, wrapped it around her shoulders, and held her to my chest. "Even after the last couple *months*, Georgina. Including this morning, yes."

"I almost did when I couldn't reach anyone else."

I set my jaw. I didn't want to come after anyone else, least of all *everyone* else. I wanted to be her first call when Bruno had a seizure. When she was facing the rare thing she couldn't do on her own. When she got a job offer she was excited about. I was tired of being *someone*, of walking into a room and adapting to my surroundings the way I'd moved to New York and adopted a persona. I wanted to be *the* one, a man my mom and Georgina could not only be proud of, but could count on. I didn't know how to say all that to her when she had enough on her plate, so I just rubbed her arm, hoping to warm her.

Luciano returned with a drink carrier, and Georgina's eyes had almost dried when a woman in a white lab coat pushed through the metal doors to make her way toward us.

Georgina jumped to her feet. "Dr. Rimmel."

"How you holding up, Georgina?" She held a clipboard to her side as she shook hands with Luciano and me. "Dr. Rimmel, nice to meet you. You guys caught me right before I left for the night."

"Thank you for staying." Georgina's voice was clear, but she was shaking, drowning in my blazer. My back muscles had tautened with the arrival of the vet, but I did my best to appear calm. I slipped my hand into Georgina's. "Come sit," I said, tugging her back.

She returned to her seat. "How is he?"

Dr. Rimmel hugged the clipboard. "Bruno's doing great."

Luciano blew out a sigh of relief and fell back in his seat. "Thank god."

Georgina had gone pale. "Are you sure?" she asked. "Is there a 'but'?"

"No 'but.' Based on your excellent and detailed reporting, we believe he suffered an episode of what we call 'syncope.' In other words, he fainted." She flipped through her notes. "We did a work up and an ECG, and his health is about on par with his last visit. I feel comfortable releasing him to you."

Georgina sobbed and covered her mouth. "He's going to be okay?"

"He is," Dr. Rimmel said.

I rubbed her back but leaned forward to address the doctor. "Why'd this happen?"

"We're not sure, but it sounds scarier than it is. For now, Georgina and I will continue to monitor the situation. As she knows, Bruno's prone to crises due to his heart disease, but so far he's been pretty lucky."

"Does this mean things are getting worse?" Georgina asked. "Is there any . . . permanent damage?"

"No, but we can review the procedure for crises if you like."

"Should you run more tests?" I asked.

"Let's just keep an eye on things. It could've been a one-time occurrence, so trying to treat it could be invasive and cause more distress than necessary. If it happens again, we'll look at adjusting the dosage of his meds and some other options."

"Was there anything I could've done differently?" Georgina asked. "Anything at all?"

"Nope," Dr. Rimmel said. "You reacted swiftly with awareness and clarity. At least it appears that way to me. Bruno's in great shape and going crazy back there. You ready to see him?"

Georgina pinched the inside corners of her eyes and shook her head. I had a feeling she'd prepared herself for all possible scenarios—except good news. "What if I hadn't been there?" she asked.

"At worst, he could've hit his head or fallen in a dangerous area," the doctor answered. "But odds are he would've been okay."

"If I know Georgina, she's beating herself up because she left him home alone for a few hours," Luciano said. "Please tell her that's allowed."

"It's not my job to tell her what is or isn't allowed," Dr. Rimmel said. "But what I can objectively say is that Ms. Keller is one of the best dog owners I've encountered in my career."

I squeezed her hand as she said, "Thank you, Doctor."

Dr. Rimmel nodded. "I'll go get Bruno. Then we can review what to do if this happens again and some small changes you can make to Bruno-proof your apartment."

She tensed, but before I could ask if she was okay, Luciano stood. "I'll stay for the demonstration too since I dogsit," he said, narrowing his eyes across the room. "Right after I give the cutie at the front desk my number."

Once we were alone, Georgina took her hand back. I flexed mine to keep from reaching for her, not ready to let go yet.

"I'm sorry if my palms are clammy," she said. "And if I look scary."

I moved her hair behind her shoulder. After having unfettered access to her just the night before, it wasn't easy keeping my hands to myself. Likewise, it was hard to resist leaning in to kiss her when I'd had my mouth all over her so recently. "You look like a girl who loves her dog."

She shivered, from the cold or from my touch, I wasn't sure. "You don't have to stay," she said. "I'll probably make the vet go over it with me at least three times."

"I'm staying. I've got a Ruff Ride on standby, and I'm making sure you and Bruno get home in one piece."

"Sebastian—"

Bruno burst through the door with a technician in tow. She released his leash, and he nearly knocked Georgina over with the force of his excitement. Seeing her laugh relieved some of the tension in my neck.

I squatted to get eye to eye with Bruno. "Handsome as ever," I said, scrubbing his head. "Opal will be so impressed."

"Opal?" Georgina asked.

"I talked with the shelter today," I said, glancing up at her. "I'm going to stop by after work tomorrow to start the paperwork."

She started to smile and then stopped herself. Why? Did she still have doubts about whether I'd be a responsible pet owner?

"She's a lucky girl." Georgina backed away slowly. "Can you watch Bruno while I pay?"

"Of course."

While she was at the counter, I scratched Bruno's chest.

"You gave us a good scare, you brute," I said. "Your mom was pretty upset. And me too. I was just getting to know you."

Bruno whined and put his paw on my knee.

I glanced back at reception and Georgina was staring at us, pen in hand, as if she'd turned to stone in the middle of paperwork. Maybe filling it out was too much, and she needed my help. This was what life was about—showing up for the people you cared about when things weren't pretty.

Because fuck, I didn't know when it'd happened or how, but I *did* care about her.

Maybe even more than that.

When she'd resumed the paperwork, I walked Bruno across the street to a patch of grass, assuming he hadn't been out lately. Once he'd relieved himself, we started back and found Georgina out front, watching us from the curb.

"You all right?" I asked her, crossing the street to stand in front of her.

Her hand rested over her heart. With a thick voice, she said, "I *love* the way you are with him."

Relief filtered through me, and I loosened the grip I'd had on Bruno's leash. Maybe I was reading into it, but it almost seemed like her way of saying she loved *me*. Or could love me. Whatever had transpired over the last twenty-four hours, she hadn't given up on us.

"Earlier, I said you could've called me for help," I said. "What I meant was that I *wish* you'd called me, Georgina. I want to be there for you—both of you."

She pulled my blazer closed around her. I should've brought her a damn sweatshirt instead of a useless bunch of roses. "You were right this afternoon," she said. "By trying not to fall into old patterns, I overcorrected and pushed you away."

"I know, but I'm not going anywhere. See?" Behind her, the hospital's neon sign buzzed. The automatic doors opened for a woman in scrubs. "I'm here."

"I can't tell you what that means to me."

"Don't tell me," I murmured. On the curb, in her heels, she was tall enough that I wouldn't have to bend to kiss her. Did I have to wait any longer? "Show me."

She glanced at the ground. "Who would've thought, all those weeks ago, that you and I would be standing here?"

"Not me, but if I weren't here, I'd either be at the office, home by myself, or enduring some insufferable club with Justin." I reached out, took her hand, and kissed her palm. "That's an elaborate way of saying, bad circumstances aside, there's nowhere else I'd rather be."

She threw her arms around my neck and buried her face in my collar. "Me neither."

"So let me take you home and wake up with you tomorrow." I rubbed her back, unfazed by her sobs. If *I'd* had an exhausting day, I couldn't imagine how hers must've been. "After such a short time, your apartment feels more like a home to me than my own," I whispered to her. "What does that say?"

She pulled back, keeping her palms on my chest as if she might pull me in for a kiss at any moment. "Sebastian—"

"Don't fight me anymore. Don't tell me all the reasons you think we can't make this work."

She shook her head. "I'm out of reasons. I want you. You, me, Bruno and Opal—I want that so much. I *see* it. But not in my apartment."

"Where then?" I asked, thumbing away a tear as it slid over her cheek. I wasn't fool enough to deny her anything.

"My boss called me earlier tonight about a promotion." She sniffled, her eyes sparkling with tears. "I'd be really good at it, Sebastian. We're opening a new branch, and I'd get to run it. Choose clients, build a team, call the shots. It encompasses all the things I love about my job now, but it's a step up and it's *more*."

After the angry, not to mention false, things I'd said that morning, there was only one response to that. "Sounds like a no-brainer. If it excites you, accept the promotion. You'll kill it."

Her eyes drifted to the knot of my tie. "It's not in New York."

Fuck. She was leaving?

Not just the job, but the *state*?

I sucked in a breath. I'd readied myself to support her no matter what. I'd steeled myself to combat any excuse she might give me for us not to work.

Except this one.

I should've been grateful she wasn't fighting us anymore but leaving New York was a whole other issue. "All right," I said cautiously, and prefaced my next question with, "I'm just asking this so I understand, not to challenge you . . ."

She nodded. "Okay."

"The options are either stay in your current job or accept the promotion and leave?"

Her throat constricted as she swallowed. "Correct."

I could go with her. The thought came unbidden and wasn't as scary as it should've been. Maybe not right away, but eventually, I *could* leave. What was stopping me? A job that hadn't challenged me in over a year? A boss that no longer wanted me there? A city I wasn't sure I identified with any longer?

I failed to suppress a smile, surprisingly intrigued by the idea. "I'm not opposed to doing long-distance for a while. Where is it?"

She wasn't smiling. "Boston."

I stared at her as the blood drained from my face. Boston was all at once *mine*, and nothing to me at all. I didn't want it anymore, but I could never extract it from myself.

"*Boston?*" I repeated. "But I . . . I can't go there."

She bit her bottom lip and didn't respond, because there was only one way to answer. She already knew that. She knew I was done with Boston.

Tears glossed her eyes. I'd been wrong about her pulling me closer. Her palms on my chest stayed me, putting distance between us. "Sebastian, I—"

I took her wrists and pulled her hands off. "So that's why you want this job," I said. "Because you know I won't follow you there."

"Of *course* not," she said, shaking her head vigorously. "I had absolutely no say in the location."

"Maybe it's subconscious, but this is just another form of pushing me away. Of letting your fear win." Neal must've really done a number on her. I'd been willing to pick up the pieces to ensure she never felt as small with me as she had with him, but how could I when she clearly didn't want to even let me try? I took a step back. "I was willing to make this work no matter what, but I guess I should've suspected you'd find a way out."

"I thought I made myself clear this morning," she said firmly. "This isn't *about* you, Sebastian."

"Bullshit it's not." Anger flared in me. She knew. She *knew* I wasn't ready, and might not ever be, to face my past in Boston. I was barely able to look at it on the Internet. "You're running, and I can't ask you to stay without sounding like a jerk. It's easier to leave and blame it on an opportunity than put yourself out there again."

"That's not true." She crossed her arms and then her ankles, warding off the cold.

I would've taken her inside to have this out, but I could barely stand to stay a moment longer. "I've never even heard you mention leaving. And I thought you were happy in the position you're in now."

"I thought so too," she said. "But a lot has changed in the last couple months. In the last *week*, even. I want to be with you, Sebastian, but I need to try this. If I don't, I'll resent myself. And you."

"I'm not trying to keep you here. You want to move somewhere else? We'll figure it out. But not the one fucking place I can't even bring myself to visit."

"You haven't even *tried*," she pleaded.

"Don't." I showed her my palms, and my hands shook with anger. "Don't pretend to know what the last year has been like for me."

"I'm not doing this to hurt you," she said. "This is what *I* need."

"I hear you loud and clear." I sniffed, backing away. "This isn't enough. Not New York, not your job, and not me. So go."

"*You're* the one who's scared, not me," she shot back. "You can't even bring yourself to question why you won't sell your mom's house. Why you won't even step foot in a city you love so much that you light up when you talk about it, even when it's painful."

I couldn't deny that. I hated that my hometown would always be part of me no matter how much I wanted to forget. I couldn't escape my love for it, my loyalty to it, and still, it continued to hurt me. "I'm not willing to sell because it was my mom's home. Period. It's all I've got left of her."

She shook her head. "It's more than that, Sebastian.

It's deeper. I know it's scary, but you can't heal until you face it."

I didn't want to hear it. Any of it. What did she know about death? About losing not just a parent but a lifeline? A childhood? Healing wasn't as simple as putting my grief on the market and walking away. I wouldn't stand here and entertain the thought of forgetting my mother while Georgina made excuses to keep me out of her life. If she wanted that so desperately, I'd give it to her before I abandoned Mom's memory.

I handed her Bruno's leash, but she just stared at it. "Take it," I said.

"But—"

"Boston was too far. Whether you think it's about me or not, it is on some level. You do what you have to do, but I'm done."

When she didn't move, I took her hand, flipped her palm face up, and put the leash in it. The sleeve engulfed her hand. I couldn't bring myself to ask for my jacket back.

"Sebastian, *please*."

I had to turn away from the tears streaming down her face. She was scared, and I was fucking *done* trying to get through to her. I walked away with her words ringing in my ears.

"It's deeper. I know it's scary, but you can't heal until you face it."

Heal? My mother's death, her home, was the one place in me that would never heal. There'd always be a dark hole in my heart when it came to Boston, and if Georgina insisted on living there, then so fucking be it.

I wasn't going to follow.

But she'd known that.

26

J ustin idled at the curb in a convertible with the top down despite the fact that it was cold as fuck. I tossed my TUMI leather duffel in the back, and Opal leaped in the moment I got the door open. I rarely even had to put a leash on her, she was the most loyal fucking dog.

I hesitated before officially trapping myself in a car with Justin for the next few hours. "Somehow, you managed to convince me to go to the beach in December," I said, "but I'm sure as hell not riding all the way through Long Island like this."

"Don't get your panties in a twist," Justin said. "I'll put the top up. All you had to do was ask politely."

"That so? Let me try." I straightened my shoulders as I pulled off my gloves. "Please, may I skip this weekend?"

Justin glanced up at me as he raised the top. "No, but I really appreciate you doing this for me, brother. Women like this don't come along every day."

It was always about a woman—in this case, a Swiss foreign exchange student whose time at NYU was almost over had invited him to a winter wonderland party in the Hamptons.

I shook my head at Opal as I removed my coat, sat in the passenger's seat, and blasted the heater. "Winter wonderland my ass," I muttered. "I could be sitting in the sauna at Equinox right now."

"That's no way to spend a Saturday," he said, plugging in his iPhone before searching Spotify. "Nice to have a rental car for a change, isn't it? Not at the mercy of the Uber driver's playlist."

"Let's get on the road," I said, trying to take the cell from him. "I can play DJ."

"Are you kidding? You'll never lay a hand on my phone again after you dunk-tanked it last month. Thank Jobs for waterproof electronics."

I sat back in my seat as Ace of Base came through the speakers. It wasn't unusual for Georgina to pop into my mind on the regular, but this time, she was deliciously naked in the shower, scrubbing shampoo in her auburn hair as she shimmied to "The Sign."

I looked over at Justin. "What the fuck?"

He shrugged. "I've had this album stuck in my head ever since Georgina brought it up."

Bullshit. He just liked to torment me. I looked out the window. It'd been weeks since I'd walked away from the vet, but *I* still had Georgina stuck in my head. Not just visions of her showering, but also the way she'd hugged me tightly on the curb, taking solace in my neck as she'd sobbed. I'd thought it was all for Bruno, but as I played the night over and over in my head, I wondered if I'd had it wrong. Maybe she really *had* wanted that job but had known what my answer to Boston would be. Maybe she'd cried knowing she'd been trapped. That I wouldn't be able to come with her and face my past to start a future.

That I wasn't *able* or wasn't *strong enough*?

I'd been asking myself that since I'd left. Why did Georgina think my inability to sell the house ran deeper than saying goodbye to my mom? What could possibly be deeper than that?

We were still at the curb, Ace of Base on the stereo. The road opened ahead of us, Opal panted at my back, and the day was sunny if not wintry. Depressing, if you asked me. A perfect day was just a reminder that I wasn't spending it with Georgina.

Justin had stopped using his phone to watch me.

"Well?" I raised my eyebrows. "What's the hold up?"

"It's a good thing you took my advice and finally shaved. You were getting pretty scraggly. But I have to say, it didn't really work. You still look miserable."

"Well, I am," I said. "But what the fuck can I do about it? It's going to take some time for me to get over Georgina if I ever do. Until then, I'm leaning into it." Opal moved around in the backseat, then stuck her cold nose against my ear. I reached back to pet her. "Anyway, I miss the beard. It kept me warm."

Justin looked thoughtful as he peered out the windshield. I braced myself for whatever words of supposed wisdom he thought himself qualified to impart, but instead he just said, "You can't pull off a beard. Sorry."

"If you don't put the car in drive within the next five seconds, Opal and I are getting out."

"So you can go upstairs and wallow some more?" He shook his head. "Let me pose you a scenario."

Here we go. I sighed, wondering if Opal was swift enough to make a break for it with me, or if she'd hold me back.

"Just because I rented a car for the Hamptons doesn't

mean we have to go there," he said. "There somewhere else you'd rather spend the weekend?"

"The gym. My couch with Opal. Satan's asshole. Literally anywhere else."

Justin chuckled in his knowing way, and it told me all I needed to know. He had something up his sleeve. "Think, Quinn. We can go *anywhere* else within driving distance."

Ah. I got it. This wasn't the first time he'd hinted at taking a trip. "We're not going to Boston."

"Why not? I hear Massachusetts is lovely this time of year. Not to mention you might get your life back there."

A life I hadn't even had a hold on before it'd slipped through my fingers. I'd refrained many times from calling up Georgina or driving out to see her new place. At first, I'd been too angry, but once that'd worn off, I'd stayed where I was because it wasn't fair to either of us. No matter how much I missed her, unless she was coming back or I was going there, what was the point of making things harder? I only knew she was in Boston at all since she and Justin had kept in touch.

"I'm serious," Justin said when I didn't respond. "Why can't we go? I know you've been thinking about it. You're not pissed at her anymore—you understand why she had to go. And your sister told me you've been asking about the property."

"You talk to my sister?"

"All the time, man. We're in a virtual book club together."

"Fuck." I closed my eyes and dropped the back of my head against the headrest. "You're like the chick in that movie *Single White Female*."

"I know." Justin unzipped his jacket and showed me his t-shirt, which read, *I put the hot in psychotic.*

I rolled my eyes, trying not give him the satisfaction of a laugh.

"I'm your best friend," he said, all joking gone from his voice. "And as much as I want you in New York, I think Georgina's right. I think Libby's right. And I think you feel the same. You've put this off too long." He raised the volume on the radio. "So unless you're able to convince me a hundred percent that you're not ready to go home, that's where I'm taking you."

Home. Home was not an unkempt house that was probably in disarray. It wasn't Massachusetts or even Eastie. It was Georgina. Bruno. Opal. The family I'd been too stubborn—and yeah, scared—to allow myself. "I'm not showing up on Georgina's doorstep."

"We're not going there for Georgina," he said, opening the console. "We're going to see the house."

"What about your party?"

"Let's say you owe me one Swiss girl." Justin opened a map of the northeast and pointed to a circle he'd made, the sneaky bastard. I let my eyes wander over the familiar neighborhood in East Boston.

Home.

Four hours, a couple Big Macs, and a stop for fuel and Dunkin's later, Justin pulled up to the fence surrounding my mom's house. From the passenger's side window, I took in the small, two-story Colonial, less imposing than I remembered, even though I'd only been there last year. Despite dead grass and patches of dirt, a row of flowers wrapped along the little porch, and the front door had a fresh coat of brown paint. Libby and Aaron must've been keeping an eye on the place.

I got out of the car and Opal followed, running over to sniff along the line of a rickety wood picket fence. As she lifted a leg, I checked the mailbox. Libby was getting the remnants of Mom's mail, but there were a couple pieces of junk addressed to Adina Quintanilla. This was what remained. I took a deep breath, creasing a glossy card for window washing in my grip.

"So this is it," Justin said, coming around the car. He handed me my coat.

I put it on, having forgotten the cold for a moment. "It's not much," I said, shoving the flyers in my pocket. "Two-bedroom, three if you count the curtain divider Libby installed when we were twelve."

Justin turned around. "Neighborhood looks like it's changing."

Mom's house was in better shape than I'd thought it'd be, but it was still one of the more rundown places on the block. A few had been renovated, others were dated but maintained, and some were up for sale. "It's a good time to sell," I said.

"Libby left a key in a lockbox around back." Justin opened the gate. "I'll grab it."

Opal entered through the fence, looked back at me, and sat in the middle of the walkway. My gaze moved from her to the white, chipped-paint façade. The house needed work, no question. Libby and I could hire that out, but I knew the place inside out. Nobody else would give it the care and attention to detail I would.

Was I up to the task?

I finally had an updated résumé, and if I was honest, I was eager to use it. Things hadn't been the same since Georgina had left, and although that was the point of her time at *Modern Man*, my discontent ran deeper. I no longer trusted Vance, but I'd also been questioning whether I was getting what I needed from the job. The answer? I wasn't. Not since Mom's death. And since I'd begun to realize that the New York City playboy role no longer fit me. But was it too late? Was I already that person?

And if not, who *did* I want to be?

As I looked up at the house, I forced the other questions to the front of my mind that I'd been mulling over lately.

Where did I want to be?

Who did I want to spend my days with?

Opal barked as Justin came back around to the front yard. He'd gotten me here. That was the hard part. The nearly impossible part, I worried, was going inside. But if I wanted any shot at starting over—with Georgina—I had no choice but to confront what lay ahead.

"Coming?" Justin asked, dangling the keys. He jiggled the lock before swinging the front door open.

Opal waited as I walked up the path, then trotted ahead and right into the house. *She* wasn't scared. Maybe, I thought as I entered, she even felt a welcoming presence there as she sniffed her way through the living room. The house was still, musty, and bone cold. I crossed my arms against the chill, my eyes roaming over hardwood floors that needed refinishing, pots without plants, and a staircase railing that looked dodgy at best.

I'd been hit with so many memories over the last year, and I'd been here recently enough, that walking in didn't feel strange or unnatural. Covered furniture remained. Libby wouldn't sort through anything without me. It was the emptiness that struck me most of all. The only life in the room was Opal bounding between the kitchen, living room, and hallway.

"It's okay if you need to cry," Justin said. "Stays between us."

A low laugh rumbled in my chest. "I'm good."

If I'd tried to do this last month, I wasn't sure I could've handled it. But ever since Georgina had reopened the Boston wound—and not only poured salt in it but also questioned *why* it hurt so much—I'd been giving it a lot of thought. I'd been back on Google Earth and had even pushed myself to dust off a photo album of childhood pictures Mom had made of Libby and me a couple Christmases ago, before she'd told us about the cancer. It all stung, but in a way, the photos, memories, and four hours in the car to come to terms with where I was headed had all helped prepare my mental state for this.

"It's not in terrible shape," Justin said, opening a closet of empty hangers. "I've watched a lot of HGTV, and you could probably knock out this renovation in no time at all. Maybe even do an addition."

I gave him a look. "First of all, if HGTV is your only reference point then you know basically nothing. Second, you're such a girl."

"Are you kidding?" he asked, shutting the door. He checked the wiring of the TV I'd installed a few years ago. "Women fucking love HGTV. I don't watch it for the programming—it's my best pick-up line. 'Hey, did you see that last episode of *Property Brothers* when the couple asked for an open floor plan?'"

"Isn't that every episode?" I asked.

"Works like a charm." He shrugged. "You're welcome."

I walked through the white-tiled kitchen, Mom's domain, although Libby was a good cook—I'd never be without first-class *salsa verde*, that was for sure. I smiled a little as I opened a few oak cabinets. It would be nice to live closer to Libs and the kids. Not here, but in the city. Fix up the house on the weekends maybe.

I made my way around the backyard, upstairs to my old bedroom, and came to a stop outside the master.

Justin followed but waited in the hallway. "We can get a hotel and come back tomorrow if it's too much."

I was here. I wanted to get it over with. The sooner I endured the house, the closer I'd be to answers. Could I come back here, and if so, would Georgina have me? It'd only been a few weeks, but I'd let her down by retreating when she'd turned up the heat. Maybe she'd already met someone new. With Bruno, in the park, no doubt she got her fair share of attention.

I shoved the thought away and opened the door. Four white walls, a worn beige carpet, and a door leading to the bathroom. Everything else had likely either been sold or moved into storage. Had I known, I might've railed at Libby for cleaning out the space without me, but standing here now, I was grateful. She wouldn't trash anything of value, and what remained was bearable in that moment. It looked like any other room instead of the one in which my mother had taken her last breath.

I inhaled deeply. I was here. I was facing it. Was this moving on?

My last conversation with Georgina hadn't left me.

"It's more than that, Sebastian. It's deeper. I know it's scary, but you can't heal until you face it."

Was I healed?

I returned to the hallway. Justin kept his distance, hanging onto Opal's collar.

"Now what?" I asked.

He shrugged and made a face as if to say it was my call. "What do you need for closure? Want to sell the place as is? Fix it up? Go home and pretend we never came?"

I sniffed and looked back into the bedroom. In a sense, I'd been pretending this place didn't exist long enough. I'd treated it as a problem I'd get to one day when I had the strength. "I want Georgina, and she comes with Boston. So I need to be done with this."

"Then maybe it's time to put it on the market."

Sell, sell, sell. That was what everyone kept telling me to do. The house wasn't a home without Mom, Libs said. It didn't serve any purpose but a painful reminder. Aaron would add that there was a profit to be made. But who was I without it?

Without a mom?

Who would stop me from turning into the persona I'd crafted for myself? This stupid, sagging pile of bricks and memories was the only thing keeping me tied to my upbringing, my family, my childhood. It was the only thing rooting me to this earth anymore.

That was the deeper—the more that Georgina had spoken of. By letting go of the house, I wasn't just admitting Mom was dead. I was scared it meant the good parts of myself were gone too. That I'd no longer be able to take off the mask—I would become it.

"These are my roots," I said to Justin. "This is who I really am. I'm afraid, now that I'm on my own, this is the only thing keeping me from becoming that guy in the exposé."

"Wow, man. That's heavy." Justin blew out a sigh. "I get it. I really do. But it's a lot to pin on a piece of real estate. Why do you have to *be* anyone at all?"

I turned to him. "What do you mean?"

"You're complicating things. Just be who you are."

We had a saying at the office when brainstorming sessions or design concepts went off the rails—KISS. *Keep it simple, stupid.* From Quintanilla to Quinn, Boston kid to city playboy, I'd been trying to keep those parts of myself separate. To slip those identities on and off. But I was *still* that punk who'd hustled to become the man I was now. I was both. Without Mom to put me back in my place when I needed it, I was clinging to this, an empty shell of a house. "I'm overthinking it," I said.

"You're never going to forget where you came from or where you've been. You're not my friend conditionally, dependent on which Sebastian I'm getting. You're just Sebastian, dude." Justin folded his arms over his chest. "And I'll bet Georgina sees you as one whole man, not in parts."

The way George and Georgina existed only in her head. To me, she was just herself—strong, capable, sensitive, sweet, soft . . . kind.

And mine.

If she'd still have me—as the man I was.

Opal strained against her collar until Justin released her. She galloped down the hall, jumping on me. I crouched and ruffled her fur as I glanced up at Justin. "That four-page spread on Valentine's Day gift ideas for every type of sweetheart—think we can push it?"

"Considering the issue after that will be March, I don't think so." Justin cocked his head. "But we could move some things around if we do it quickly. Why?"

"I need a few pages and some prime real estate on the cover."

Justin shrugged. "Who's going to stop you?"

Nobody, that was who. I'd just faced off with the biggest obstacle in my path. Now that I'd confronted the house, I wanted to go home.

27

My new assistant waved at me through the window of our conference room, and I motioned for her to come in.

"Countdown to the new guy's first client pitch starts now," Tonya said. "I'm making an office Dunkin' run to keep him caffeinated. Want anything?"

I clenched my jaw to stem the emotions that flooded over me whenever I thought of Sebastian. Not even moving hundreds of miles away could distance me from his ridiculous obsession with that place. Or from him. "No, thanks," I said.

Who needed caffeine when you were fueled by the need to forget a broken heart?

I was exaggerating a little. Things had been moving at a breakneck pace since I'd arrived in Boston—my job had been hectic, scary, and oddly fulfilling. It kept me busy, that was for sure, but it seemed there was always time to miss Sebastian.

I returned to the research I'd been compiling on a local TV station. It was currently succumbing to a shitstorm brought on by an opinionated, drunken weatherman. It was a beginner's assignment, but I had about three people on my team I was still getting to know and had to decide who to put on it.

I couldn't focus on the work in front of me. I tried not to think of Sebastian for this reason. Once I started, it was difficult to stop until I fell asleep at night. And hopefully, I didn't dream of him. Or wake up with my thoughts full of him. The fact that I hadn't seen or heard from him since the vet didn't seem to help, either. A clean break had only made my mind messier.

Boston was full of surprises the way New York had been when I'd first moved there. Bruno and I lived within two blocks of Peters Park and still spent plenty of time outdoors despite winter. Finding the right apartment, getting my furniture from Brooklyn to Boston, hiring a staff and team that worked well together—it wasn't easy, but no two days were the same, and I'd met so many people in the short time I'd been here. Plus, word-of-mouth was beginning to spread, which indicated I was doing my job right.

Nothing filled the void Sebastian had left, though. None of it had eased my guilt for pushing him away, even if I'd realized my mistake and tried to bring him back in the end. Every time I was tempted to read his pieces in *Modern Man* or listen to his podcast—each time I picked up the phone to *call* him—I was reminded that I'd already asked him to come with me, and he hadn't. He had his own demons, but he wouldn't face them until *he* wanted to.

After another forty minutes trying and failing to focus, I packed up my things and headed down the hall. Tonya talked into her earpiece, pointing through the door to my office, mouthing something I didn't understand.

I entered the sunlit room, rounded my desk, and

paused. The February issue of *Modern Man: A Gentleman's Guide* topped a pile of mail, but it was about a week early. Aliana Balik clutched a silky red Dior robe over her breasts. The headline read, "Aliana: Mother, Activist, and our First Woman of the Year."

"Tonya?" I asked. "Did this come in the mail?"

After a moment, she rolled to the doorway in her chair and held up a note that read "Delivered by messenger."

An early copy, all the way from Dixon Media Tower—from Vance? Justin? Or Sebastian himself? He'd scored Aliana, and on the Valentine's issue no less. He must've been elated. No doubt there'd been much discussion over which adjectives to use for her. She embodied many—glamorous, buxom, sensual. But that didn't need to be said, because it was all there in her eyes. Show sex, say class. I hoped I'd had a presence in the room when they'd chosen *activist* over *temptress* and *mother* over *model*. From that headline alone, I didn't have to read her feature to know they'd honored her instead of objectified her as Woman of the Year.

The sultry yet festive cover looked severe against my white lacquer desk. I picked it up, my eyes drifting to what my research had revealed as the next most important real estate—a heading right of the middle.

"The Bad Boy Issue (It's Not What You Think)
by Sebastian Quinn (He's Not What You Think)"

I froze. It was rare for *Modern Man* to include a byline on the cover and even more unusual that Sebastian would claim the "bad boy" moniker after what he'd been though. *Why* would he do that? I flipped through the glossy pages and stopped on a full-page candid shot of Sebastian in a tux, augmented by a subheader:

Some final advice from a former fake bad boy. And this time, it's good.

I turned back to page one of the spread and read.

A question I frequently get as creative director of one of the fastest growing men's lifestyle magazines is how a man can get a woman to notice him. In the next several pages, I interview some high-profile men who've happily traded their bad boy statuses for families.

But that isn't enough. I took this pervasive issue a step further and offered myself up on the chopping block to get answers for all of you. I'm ready to make the trade myself, so the challenge: could I win over my dream girl?

Here's what I learned dating a woman so far out of my league, we weren't even playing the same sport.

Clutching the magazine open, the next inset quote knocked me off my feet and into my chair.

She's the stuff of dreams but don't call her my dream girl. She was as real as it got.

My breathing sped. I couldn't help thinking back to the first time he'd spoken to me, how I'd frozen in fear and insecurity that a man of his stature would even look in my direction, much less strike up a conversation with me.

What makes me qualified to give you advice?

*Not much. You might think differently after the headlines that've been printed about me, but you're about to find out I was never a bad boy. I'm just another schmuck trying to get a girl to look in my direction. More on that in a moment—what you need to know now is that I've given a lot of advice in my life, and even more bad*vice, *but there's no harder way to learn life lessons than by falling for someone.*

Because I met 'the one' while looking for anyone else—and then I lost her.

I'm going to tell you how not to make the same mistakes, and we're starting with the basics.

You don't know what women want.

I never did, but that's because the answer is as complex as the woman herself.

My heart beat overtime. The skeptic in me stopped to

wonder if this was a ploy to get eyeballs, but the Georgina in me knew the truth. Sebastian was laying his heart on the line—but to what end?

She's the stuff of dreams but don't call her my dream girl. She was as real as it got. A heart and soul girl. A kind person. A woman. At first, I loved to hate her, and then I hated to fall for her, but the truth is I'm made for her. The way gummy bears are made for brainstorming, gentlemen are made of more, and cinnamon is made to sweeten buns.

With a dry mouth, I consumed every word as Sebastian revealed the truth about his past, his reputation, and even his surname. The final paragraph left my heart in my throat.

And it's with this newfound knowledge that I make my departure. My time at Modern Man *has been valuable, eye-opening, and illuminating. I've become a better man for it in some ways and worse in others. I look forward to new challenges ahead and a clean, honest slate with which to approach them.*

He was leaving the magazine.

My phone pinged with a text from Sebastian. The timing was too fortuitous for him not to have sent the magazine. I just didn't know what he was trying to tell me. With unsteady fingers, I opened a message that said "watch me" with a video. In full makeup, and wrapped in the same red robe from the cover, Aliana's high cheekbones, full lips, and almond-shaped eyes filled the screen. "Happy early Valentine's Day from the February cover shoot, Georgina," she said in her Polish accent, waving emphatically. "Sebastian tells me I was his dream girl until you came along and knocked me off the list completely. And, well, he's going to ask you for a second chance. I think you should give it to him." She winked. "It's not every day a woman not only tops the list but totally obliterates it."

She flipped the camera and Sebastian's even more

beautiful face appeared. "Hey, buns," he said, his eyes crinkling in the corners with his smile. "Just wanted to warn you that I'm coming for you, so put down your phone and look up."

I frowned, confused when the video ended. I lowered my cell, and in my doorway stood the most handsome, most intriguing, most infuriating man I knew.

In a peacock-blue pullover that brought out his eyes and his hands stuffed in the pockets of his jeans, Sebastian sighed as if relieved. "You're a sight for sore eyes."

I knew the feeling. Just his presence drained tension from my shoulders I hadn't realized I'd been carrying. "What's going on?" I asked, standing. "Are you really *here*? In Boston?"

"All of what you just read is true." He took a step and warned, "So if you ask me whether I wrote it for any other reason than as a declaration to you, I will come over and kiss you in a way that leaves no question as to my intentions."

My chest rose and fell as I tried to think of one reason *not* to question him if it meant getting that response. Where did I even begin? I picked the easiest of his revelations to tackle first. "You're leaving your job?"

"Left. Once it was in print, there was no turning back."

"But why?" I asked. "What'll you do instead?"

He shrugged. "I wasn't going to sit around and wait for Vance to decide my value. I didn't want to be there without you anyway. As for what's next, I have ideas, but I'm a free agent at the moment."

He'd gone and quit without a backup plan? It didn't sound like Sebastian to flip his perfectly curated life on its side, but I couldn't help but hope that was a good sign. He himself had admitted to feeling complacent. "How does it feel?"

"Weird. Overwhelming. But I can breathe for the first time in a while." He glanced around my bare office, just a desk, computer, and some chairs for now. "It wasn't a shock. Honestly, as soon as you said you were leaving New York, I was already coming up with ideas to make us work so I could eventually follow you—until you said Boston."

I realized it was hope that'd eased my body because it left me again. I'd come here knowing he wouldn't chase me, but that didn't mean I wasn't tempted to go to him now. I held up the issue. "I'm proud of you. It makes for a good story, but what does it mean? Why are you here?"

"You know why. You know what I've wanted for a while, even though there were times I would've jumped off a cliff before admitting it." The corner of his mouth twitched. "You said it yourself—I can't do this without you."

My palm sweat against the glossy cover. I still wanted this—*him*. Enough that in darker moments, I'd questioned whether coming to Boston was the right choice. "Can't do what?" I asked.

"Any of it. Now that I know what it's like to be with someone like you, I don't want anything else. Just you. You make me mad, and for better or worse, I refuse to live without that madness."

Madness, I supposed, was him putting my interests before his so I'd enjoy a pretend date. Showing up for me and Bruno at the vet when I'd tried to run scared. Facing his own fears by coming here. I realized my mind had latched onto something other than "someone like you" for the first time in months. In his eyes, I was a prize, not a consolation.

I inhaled. "You don't have to live without it."

"Good, because I'm here for you, and I'm not going

anywhere. If you need time, I'll give it to you. But I won't give you up."

"But Sebastian . . ." I glanced at my desk, willing myself to keep a clear mind as my heart called for him. When he and I had last been together, my fear of the past had thrown me into overdrive, thinking I had to come first or not at all. Sebastian and I had to learn the art of compromise—but I no longer had that to give. "Are you saying you want to try this for real? Long-distance? I'm not ready to leave Boston. I just got here."

"And? How is it?"

I hesitated, because I didn't want to hurt him. Didn't want to lose him now that I had him back. "I wish I could say I hate it," I admitted, "but I don't."

He arched an eyebrow. "That so?"

"It's something new. And it reminds me of you." My cheeks warmed. "I won't uproot Bruno again, and I won't let Dionne or my team down. This is the job I want to be doing right now."

He rubbed the back of his neck. "How is the brute anyway?"

"Good." I smiled a little. "Bull in a china shop as always."

"Opal misses him. Turns out, she likes a little bull in her life."

"I know the feeling." I was still wary but unable to keep from giving in to the ease of our interactions or the comfort of having him there.

"You were right at the vet," he said.

I had no doubt that was true, and that Sebastian would eventually realize it—but it didn't diminish how good it felt to hear it. I tilted my head. "Can you repeat that, please?"

"You were right that I let fear get in the way," he said, "right after I'd called you out for the same thing."

"I'm not scared anymore, Sebastian." I inched around the desk, my steps muted by the tufted wool rug beneath my heels. Though eager to go to him, there were still things that needed to be said. "When I met you, I'd been trying to hide or overcome my flaws out of shame. Then you came along and told me I was allowed to have them. That I was allowed to be kind."

"Allowed?" he asked. "I *love* that part of you. More than you know. After so long of not having that, you feel like the lifeline I lost." Longing showed on his face. "Don't tell me you're weak. Don't tell me your flaws aren't my blessings."

I swallowed through the urge to cry. To run to him. To let myself fall, finally, into him. But the distance between us kept me from opening my heart all the way. "I'm sorry it had to be Boston," I said quietly. "I wish there was another way."

"And I'm sorry that even though I was looking for a girl like you, it took me so long to see you. To understand that I was holding on to a past that would always be a part of me, even after I let it go. This was my home once, Georgina. But now, you, Bruno, and Opal—that's the home I want, and where that is doesn't matter."

I didn't know whether to laugh or cry as hope crept back in. That was a home I'd envisioned many times since he'd left me on the curb at the vet, but never with any hope. Only as something I'd lost and hadn't known how to get back without sacrificing a part of myself. "You'd come to Boston?"

He opened his arms. "I'm here, aren't I?"

"Standing there is one thing. Can you be happy here? I wouldn't be able to live with myself if it was torture for you day in and day out."

"I have a confession." He dropped his arms at his sides.

"This is my third time here in the last month. I'm sorry I didn't come see you sooner, but I had shit to work through."

I clasped my hands over my heart. He had to *want* to face those demons, and now, he was ready. I silently promised him I'd do whatever possible to be by his side while he did. "You went to the house?" I guessed.

"I did. First with Justin to see if I could do it. Then with Libby to start on the plans to restore it. We're going to sell it." He shifted on his feet, looking like he could use a hug. But more than comfort, he needed to get the words out, so I stayed where I was. "It won't be easy, but I'm going to work through it by doing as much of the labor myself as I can." His Adam's apple bobbed when he swallowed. "Something about physically working on the house feels like a way of, I don't know . . . honoring her. My mom."

I closed my eyes a moment and pictured Sebastian as a boy in the kitchen, his mom teaching him the best way to scrub grease from the stove. Doing homework at the table. Bickering with his twin sister. And then, as a grown man, tearing down the walls that'd protected—but also limited—him.

With my help too.

"Yeah?" he said.

I opened my eyes. I hadn't meant to say it aloud, but I nodded. "Next time you go there, I'm coming with you. I want to help." I hazarded a smile. "At the very least, so it doesn't turn into a bachelor pad."

He grinned. "Bring your colored pencils. I want it to be a house worthy of someone's windowsill height chart."

I nodded. "Then it will be."

He glanced out the window beside me, scratching his chin as silence settled between us. Sensing he needed time to gather his thoughts, I waited until he was ready. "When I stood in front of the house for the first time since her death," he said finally, slowly, "I asked myself some things. Where do I want to be? Who do I want to be? Who do I want to spend my days with? The answer is simple, Georgina."

My heart thumped. I was nearly on the tips of my toes waiting for him to say it, to close this distance between us for good. "Tell me," I implored.

"I want to be a man worthy of spending his days with you, wherever you are."

I couldn't hold back anymore. I started across the room, bolstered by the fact that I had no doubts he meant what he said. When Sebastian cared about someone, he did with all of himself. He fought. He came back. In the end, he didn't run away. The proof stood in front of me now.

"Wait," he said before I reached him, and I stopped. He drew an imaginary line between us with his index finger. "I want that gone completely. If you cross this line, it doesn't exist anymore. Got it? There's only one side."

"Between love and hate," I said, my voice equally soft and rough with unshed happy tears, "I'm on love's side."

"Don't whisper it, Georgina. Get over here and tell me." I took the final steps toward him, and he held my face in his hands as he added, "And say it loud."

"I . . . I love you," I said clearly, overcoming the urge to cry. The confession didn't scare me like it should. More than anything, I was relieved to say it after weeks of holding it in, trying to pretend it wasn't true.

"I'm on love's side," he repeated. "*I* love *you*."

"I knew it when I saw you with Bruno at the vet. The way you were with him. The way you looked at me." It'd hit me all at once, merciless and overwhelming. Along with the truth—that I'd lose him. But he was here. I clutched his shirt, keeping him there as he lowered his mouth to mine. "It doesn't scare me anymore," I whispered. "I won't lose myself again because you won't let me."

He brushed the tip of my nose with his. "And if you happen to, I will light your way back to ensure *you* always find yourself. And then you find me."

I found him, first his lips with mine, then his roughened cheeks with my hands. I lost myself in his kiss, and there, I found something I never expected—an enemy made to love me.

EPILOGUE

Balanced on a ladder in the kitchen of my mom's house, I tightened the screws of a brass ceiling canopy Georgina and I had found to match our latest purchase, a vintage lighting fixture. I set my tools on the top cap when the front door opened and closed. The familiar *click-clack* of paws and nails sounded on the hardwood floors as Opal and Bruno came bounding in, wagging their tails and zigzagging around the ladder.

Georgina entered the kitchen in a green Tartan button-down tied at the waist and jeans that made me want to take a bite out of her ass. "Wow," she said, surveying the ceiling. "That fixture turned out so well. Not only handy, but you have an eye for design too."

I arched an eyebrow at her. "You picked it out."

"Oh, that's right." She grinned.

"Will you test it?"

She flipped the light switch and the lamp lit up. "My work here is done," I said.

"Not quite," Georgina said. "But we're getting close."

Opal barked at the base of the ladder. Feeling a tinge

of nostalgia over what was to come, I brushed my hands off and descended.

"You'd think they hadn't seen you just this morning," Georgina said as the dogs jumped on me. She opened the back door for them to sprint into the yard.

"Mmm, speaking of this morning," I said, taking her hand and pulling her to me. I wrapped my arms around her waist. "I've been thinking about it since I left the apartment."

"Don't get used to it," she said. "It's not healthy."

"But it's so fucking good." I kissed her and could've sworn I still tasted the cinnamon bun frosting from our breakfast.

"We're not in our twenties anymore," she said. "We can't eat like that every day. I only got them to celebrate the fact that the house is finally done."

"Ah," I said. "I thought celebrating was the reason for the blow job."

She shimmied closer to me. "I don't need an excuse for one of those, do I?"

Remembering the real reason for my great morning—Georgina's smoking-hot smirk a moment before she'd ducked under the sheets—made my jeans tight. She squeaked as I lifted her by the waist onto the counter and made myself at home between her knees. "I think it's only fair we christen the house before we list it," I said, nuzzling her neck.

"We *have* christened it," she said. "Several times. Once on this very counter, not long after it was installed."

"I couldn't help myself," I murmured into her hair. "The way you haggled over the price per square foot got me so fucking excited."

She laughed softly, wrapping her legs around me to pull me in. "Then there was that time in the laundry room . . ."

"That's one thing we're missing in our apartment," I said with a sigh. "A large vibrating machine."

"Ohh." She moaned. "Imagine if we never had to go to another laundromat."

I fingered the plaid collar of her shirt. "Does this choice of outfit mean what I think it does?"

She smiled. "Flights are booked for the whole family. We're spending Christmas in Dublin."

"The Irish won't know what hit them," I said.

"The *Irish*? We'll be lucky if we come home in one piece. We're going to drink our weight in Guinness."

I chuckled, glancing out back when dog tags jingled. Bruno rolled onto his side as he and Opal sunbathed on the freshly lain concrete patio. "They feel pretty at home here, don't they?"

Georgina bit her bottom lip as she seemed to get lost in a thought. There was something she wasn't saying. Before I could pry, she put her hands on my chest. "Should we do what we came to do?" Sensing my hesitation, she added, "We don't *have* to do it today. There's no rush."

"But we had the cinnamon bun and blow job celebration already." I helped her off the counter, even though what I really wanted to do was drop to my knees and return this morning's favor. "It's been long enough."

She nodded quietly, then rummaged through her pocketbook until I sighed and said, "What you're looking for is in your zipper pocket."

"Oh. Right." Smiling, she got out a small spiral bound notepad and pen.

Holding her to my side, I kissed the top of her head as we made our way out front.

"Justin will be upset he's missing this," she said. "He's run all the comps in the area and has opinions."

"Why do you think I planned it for a day I knew he

couldn't make it?" I snickered. Moving hundreds of miles away still hadn't made the bastard any less nosy. Aside from his daily request for renovation photos, it seemed as if he was crashing on our couch every other weekend.

From behind, I put my hands on Georgina's shoulders and tried to assess the front of the house with a sense of detachment. When deciding where to list it, it wouldn't do to see it as a place with history—*my* history. As my sister's and my roots, as my mom's home. I had to see it as a potential buyer would in order to determine the right price, but after seven months of restoring it with Georgina, that was nearly impossible to do. We'd put a lot of ourselves into the property, and our relationship had deepened and strengthened on so many levels right here in this house. "A million," I said.

She laughed. "We can't sell it for a million, but we do need to figure out if we're starting at the high end or hoping to incite a bidding war."

"What if someone snatches it up right away?"

She looked up and back at me. "That would be great, wouldn't it?"

"But then what?" I asked. My sister's husband had e-mailed me a new listing a couple days earlier for a foreclosure a few streets over. It was a bargain, and Aaron kept reiterating what a great team Georgina and I made. He and my sister both thought we should be flipping houses for a living. Somehow, I couldn't seem to muster the same enthusiasm. Fixing up the house had been a project brought together by a perfect storm—I had the emotional attachment to painstakingly restore it while keeping its charm, *and* I had good reason to set it free. In the months since I'd sold my New York apartment and had made the leap to living full-time in Boston, I'd made great strides— with Georgina's help—working through my issues over the house and my mom. It was time to let another family have their turn.

"Did you have a different idea?" Georgina asked.

"No, not really." I squeezed her shoulders and turned my attention back to the job at hand. "One of the shutters on the right window is coming loose, and the landscaper still hasn't fixed the hedge."

She made notes. "We should sic our secret weapon on him."

"My sister," I said, nodding gravely. "She's a beast when it comes to getting contractors in line."

We walked up the front steps and into the living room. I shut the front door, inspecting the marks on the inside of it. "We have to fix these scratches before the first open house."

"Mark that under 'Opal and her separation anxiety,'" Georgina replied.

We'd recently left the dogs at the house alone for the first time while picking up pizza for a long night of cleaning ahead. Opal had done a bit of damage.

Georgina pointed her pen at one corner of the living room. "There are still some spots of blue paint on the hardwood."

"I tried," I said. "It won't come up. Mark that under 'my frisky girlfriend.'"

Her cheeks reddened, a sexy complement to her chestnut-colored hair and cinnamon-sprinkle freckles. "It wasn't all me," she said. "If you hadn't started the paint fight in the first place—"

"It wouldn't have ended with what probably looked like Smurf porn?"

She shoved my shoulder. "There you go defiling innocent things again."

I caught her in my arms. "Like you?"

She shrugged and said in explanation, "I don't stand a chance against bad boys."

"Good thing for me. I'm bad at lots of stuff."

She laughed, wrapped one arm around my neck and smoothed my hair from my face with her other hand. "Sebastian, my love?"

"Georgina, my love?"

She pursed her lips as a mix of pity and sympathy crossed her delicate features. "Are you going to be able to paint over the kids' height charts?"

My sister and her husband had helped with the house as much as they were able to. They'd brought the kids nearly every weekend, and I'd gotten in the habit of measuring Carmen and José in the laundry room. Although it had always been the plan to paint over the marks before we sold, for some reason I'd envisioned filling the wall with colorful charts, from Libby's kids to our dogs to our own children. "We have to," I said. "Can't exactly list this place as gut renovated minus some random kids' height charts."

"Can I say something you might not want to hear?"

I gave her a quizzical look. Something was definitely brewing in that head of hers—something that simultaneously turned down her mouth and made her eyes sparkle. "You could," I said. "Or we can skip a potential argument and try out those sex positions Justin needs us to test for the next issue."

"This won't cause a fight." She played with the neckline of my t-shirt and took a breath. "I know Aaron is eager to sell, but what if we bought your sister out?"

"For what reason?" I asked. "To keep all the profit on the flip for ourselves? I'm guessing they're not going to go for that."

"No, no," she said. "Come with me." She took my

hand and led me upstairs to the master bedroom we'd completely redone. At the window, we overlooked the backyard where Bruno and Opal had moved to sprawl out in the grass.

"After everything we've put into the house, the money would be nice to have," Georgina said. "But you know what else is nice to have?"

I rubbed my jaw, fairly certain I knew where the conversation was going. It wasn't as if it hadn't crossed my mind—I just didn't know Georgina had been thinking the same. "A yard?" I guessed with extra-Boston-accent since it always made her smile.

"And a laundry room." Out the window, she scanned the lawn and the addition we'd made to the side of the house to gain square footage and an extra bedroom. "And a place for Justin to sleep that doesn't fold up when he leaves."

"Now you're hurting your case," I teased. In truth, I was glad Justin visited as frequently as he did. "If we tell him he has his own bedroom, I'm not entirely sure he won't just move in."

"He'd be so excited."

She was excited—I heard it in her voice. I turned to her. "Are you serious about this?"

"I haven't wanted to bring up staying," she admitted. "I know how hellbent you are on selling, and maybe it's the right thing to do. This place holds a lot of bad memories for you."

I glanced across the room to the spot my mother's bed had been. Along with a priest, we'd surrounded her as she'd held my hand in one of hers and my sister's in the other and closed her eyes for the last time. We had since reconfigured the room so it looked nothing like it had then. Even the bathroom had been remodeled. I thought of how

Georgina and I had climbed into a tub on the salesfloor to make sure it was deep enough for two, then recreated the NC-17 version of that scene a few nights after it'd been installed. I remembered, standing there at the window, lifting Georgina onto my shoulders so she could inspect crown molding. And then the way I'd gone barbarian on her, toting her around the room beating my chest until she'd bumped her head on the ceiling light and fallen giggling into my arms.

"There are good memories in here too," I told her.

"I know, and for the record, I can live anywhere, Sebastian. As long as it's with you. The apartment is fine—I'm happy there. I just don't want you to regret that we didn't even consider keeping the house."

I half-sat on the windowsill, putting us at the same height. "You want to stay?"

"I love it here." She took a small plastic bag of gummy bears from her back pocket. It was unlikely she even realized she'd done it. She ate some, chewing as she paced. I couldn't keep the smile from my face. I had my answer— she was in brainstorming-mode, and she _was_ serious about this.

"I've learned so much about your childhood and your mom over the past several months," she said. "And we've put our blood, sweat, and tears into making it perfect. We have the money to buy out your sister, but would she be okay with that?"

I followed Georgina with my eyes. My life had done a one-eighty in the past year. Each day with her was a gift, an adventure, and a challenge. We bickered as much as we bantered, made love as often as we went head to head. She'd stitched up what I'd thought was a permanent hole in my heart from my mother's death. It was a wound that would never truly heal, but now it ached less with Georgina around.

"We can even add a sound booth for you," she said, scribbling something on her pad.

Not only did she have healing powers, but she'd encouraged me too. My final piece in *Modern Man*'s February issue had gotten me enough press to launch a successful men's lifestyle podcast. We covered everything from sports to health to politics. I was now receiving regular invitations to athletic and entertainment events as a guest star or commentator. I even doled out the occasional piece of advice—which I always ran by Georgina first.

I grabbed her hand, pulling her back in front of me. Running some of her soft, silky hair through my palm, my heart clenched. I loved her. I wanted to spend my life with her. I wanted to make her happy. "It's a big commitment," I said, cupping the side of her face and thumbing the corner of her mouth. "It's not like Opal and me moving into your little apartment, cramping your style. There, we have a landlord, and if things go south, I can just move my boxes out. But getting a house together . . ."

She took my wrist, shifting her face to kiss my palm. "You can't scare me away, Sebastian."

"I'm just pointing out—after owning a place together, there's really only one direction to go," I said. "If I propose the idea of a proposal, is that the same as asking you to be the future Mrs. Quinn?"

She wrinkled her nose playfully. "You don't have to worry about that, because my answer would be no."

I narrowed my eyes on her. She wasn't going to fight me on this, was she? Because I'd win, hands down. "We've talked about getting married. This can't be news to you."

"I don't want to be Mrs. Quinn," she clarified. "But

Georgina Quintanilla? Well, that has a nice ring to it, doesn't it?"

In the same instant, a sense of possessiveness and a surge of love overwhelmed me. I hoped my mom was looking down on us now, proud of the strong, kind woman I'd chosen to be by my side. A woman worthy of being a Quintanilla. I brought Georgina closer to me, lifting her chin with my knuckle to tilt her mouth up to mine. "I can definitely say I've never wanted anything more. Well, except maybe what comes after the wedding."

She smiled brilliantly. "Let's start with the house. Then we can fill it."

"Are you suggesting I knock you up?"

"At least twice," she requested. "One Yankee and one Red Sock."

I rolled my eyes. "We don't refer to our individual selves as a red sock."

"It's more complimentary than how *I* would refer to a Sox fan." She batted her lashes, trying to suppress a smile. Deep dimples formed in her cheeks. "Oh, and two kids means when we argue, we have one on each side."

"Two kids," I repeated. Despite our joking, my voice was thick, love and longing coursing through me. A house full of family, dogs, and memories that spanned two generations. Fuck me, I hadn't let myself dare to want more than I'd already found in Georgina. Hadn't let myself think I could stay here, much less desire it. I'd thought the right thing to do was to let the house go and move on. But as Georgina filled my head with ideas, the way she'd filled my heart with love, and would fill my walls with colored-pencil measurements, I realized something special had happened over the past seven months without me even noticing.

Georgina and I had come home.

ACKNOWLEDGMENTS

This book was a wonderful exploration outside my comfort zone. That's a flowery way of saying it was more stubborn than I anticipated—appropriate given its characters. But I never doubted the outcome because of the wonderful team behind me. Elizabeth London more or less introduced me to my own characters, that's what a talented editor she is. I thought I knew them, but we all grew together.

Thank you to Katie of Underline This Editing for her insight and guidance through phase two (or one-hundred, depending how you look at it) of this book and to Erik Gevers for his eagle eye. Pulling up the caboose, Serena McDonald lent me her ear to help finalize the details of *Right Where I Want You*. Lastly, I'm convinced Hang Le employed magic to design such a perfect cover. All in all, I like to think Georgina and Sebastian would be quite proud as this "special issue" goes to press.

And as always, my eternal gratitude goes to all the readers, bloggers, and fellow authors who helped shape or share my latest book baby.

ABOUT THE AUTHOR

Jessica Hawkins is a *USA Today* bestselling author known for her "emotionally gripping" and "off-the-charts hot" romance. Dubbed "queen of angst" by both peers and readers for her smart and provocative work, she's garnered a cult-like following of fans who love to be torn apart…and put back together.

She writes romance both at home in New York and around the world, a coffee shop traveler who bounces from café to café with just a laptop, headphones, and a coffee cup. She loves to keep in close touch with her readers, mostly via Facebook, Instagram, and her mailing list.

Stay updated:
www.jessicahawkins.net/mailing-list
www.amazon.com/author/jessicahawkins
www.facebook.com/jessicahawkinsauthor
twitter: @jess_hawk

CPSIA information can be obtained
at www.ICGtesting.com
Printed in the USA
LVHW090224031219
639245LV00001B/217/P

9 780998 815589